Brognola detached himself from the group filing out of the Oval Office and returned to his chair. He no longer wondered why he had been asked to the meeting.

"We have to do something about this Skylance situation," the President stated, "and it looks like any conventional solution just won't work. I want you to send in Phoenix Force and clean up things as soon as possible."

"Phoenix Force is primarily a counterterrorist group. This really isn't our type of mission."

"No? Stop and think for a minute. Letting another country get its hands on Skylance would be bad enough, but these Star Flash weapons would be a screaming disaster. Think what would happen if a terrorist group gets hold of that kind of technology. A few of those fired over our major cities could cripple the entire economy and set us back twenty years. Your people are the best we've got for a covert mission. The job has to be done, and I'm asking your people to do it."

It wasn't a request that Hal Brognola could refuse.

"All right, Mr. President," he said formally, "we'll take care of it. I'll get the ball rolling immediately."

DON PENDLETON'S
MACK BOLAN®

STONY MAN

SKYLANCE

A GOLD EAGLE BOOK FROM
W●RLDWIDE®

TORONTO • NEW YORK • LONDON
AMSTERDAM • PARIS • SYDNEY • HAMBURG
STOCKHOLM • ATHENS • TOKYO • MILAN
MADRID • WARSAW • BUDAPEST • AUCKLAND

First edition November 1996

ISBN 0-373-61909-X

Special thanks and acknowledgment to
Patrick Rogers for his contribution to this work.

SKYLANCE

Printed in U.S.A.

SKYLANCE

CHAPTER ONE

Skylance—Low Earth Orbit

Skylance was in orbit, a blunt-nosed, dark gray triangle weighing more than fifty tons. Two days earlier, it had roared up from Vandenberg Air Force Base in California on a pillar of white-hot fire. It was orbiting the earth once every ninety-two minutes. Now, two hundred miles above the earth's surface, it was silently approaching the west coast of Australia. Captain Mary Clark, the systems operations and weapons officer, was sitting behind Skylance's pilot, Major Peter Greene, in the two-person, teardrop-shaped cockpit. There was nothing for her to do until they reached the next target area. She could sit back and enjoy the view, which was spectacular.

Skylance was flying in the inverted mode with its cockpit pointing toward the earth. Clark saw an immense blue arc, mottled by beautiful, gleaming masses of white clouds and the arid brown-and-yellow wastelands of northwestern Australia. She thought the earth observed from space was the most beautiful sight she had ever seen. She had always wanted to fly in space, and the view made the grueling two years of training to qualify as a Skylance crew member completely worthwhile.

Two hundred miles below, Australian space-surveillance radars noted its passing and flashed its orbital parameters to their main tracking center at Woomera. The center's computer calculated briefly and confirmed that an unknown satellite was passing by. There was no reason for alarm and nothing the Australians could do about it, anyway. Skylance was far above the altitude at which even the most advanced surface-to-air missile was effective. In turn, Skylance's attack-warning sensors detected and classified the Australian radars. No need to take countermeasures; it was routine, nonhostile surveillance only.

Skylance was passing over the west coast of Australia now, beginning to arc up toward the south coast of the huge island of New Guinea, north of Australia, moving steadily at five miles per second. Skylance's flight-control computer confirmed that it was approaching the next target area, the small island of Workai. Someone in the United States government was extremely interested in what was going on there.

Clark activated Skylance's superb sensor systems. Cameras, infrared systems and electronic listening systems came on-line and prepared to sense and record their data. A row of lights turned green. Clark smiled. All sensors were working perfectly. If there was anything worth knowing about Workai, Skylance was about to find it out. Suddenly her smile changed to a frown. A red light had begun to flash on her instrument-panel displays, and she heard a soft electronic beeping in her headset. The radar attack-warning system—RAWS—was trying to attract her attention. She looked quickly at the RAWS display: "High-resolution radar locked on and tracking. Make and model unknown. Analysis—probable hostile precision-tracking or fire-control radar.''

Instantly Clark pushed the intercom button. ''I think we've got trouble, Pete,'' she said quickly. ''Somebody has locked on and is tracking us. The radar is ahead of us, on the surface close to Workai. It looks like a fire-control radar for some kind of weapon system. Electronic countermeasures now?''

It was up to Greene to make the decision. He thought quickly. When you were moving into danger at five miles per second, you didn't have time for long, deep thoughts.

''I don't want you to start jamming unless you're sure it's a threat, Mary. With the engines off, we look like just another satellite. If we start emitting electronic countermeasures, we may attract a lot of attention we don't want. Are you sure you can't identify the radar?''

Clark looked at her displays again. ''Negative. Probable hostile precision-tracking or fire-control radar is the best the RAWS can do.''

''All right, Mary. In that case, we should—''

Greene never finished his sentence. An immensely powerful, pale blue beam flashed upward from the earth's surface and struck Skylance at the speed of light. Millions of watts of energy were perfectly focused on a spot two feet in diameter. For one split second, the laser beam blazed at its target. Clark stared in horror as a white-hot, glowing spot suddenly appeared in the left wing and molten metal sputtered away into space. The beam flashed again. Skylance shuddered as the laser struck the rear of the fuselage. Alarms flashed, and a huge plume of white vapor shot out into the surrounding vacuum.

Clark's finger pushed the countermeasures button, and Skylance's electronic defenses flashed into life, but as they did, the beam struck again. Clark saw an incredibly bright, eye-searing flash directly in front of her as the beam struck the pilot's compartment. An alarm howled as the pilot's compartment lost pressure. Half the lights on Clark's instrument display turned red. Skylance was in orbit. It couldn't fall, but it was beginning to tumble end over end as the attitude-control system failed catastrophically. Clark hung on grimly as the world seemed to revolve around her. She waited for Pete Greene to take emergency action. Nothing happened. She looked desperately into the pilot's cockpit. The man was still strapped in his seat, but his head was lolling back and forth as Skylance rotated. He had to be dead or unconscious.

She had to do something. She was a trained fighter pilot. The temptation to grab the controls was tremendous, but she couldn't think or move fast enough to save Skylance now. The tumbling was getting worse. There was only one chance. Quickly she pushed the emergency and automatic-flight-control buttons on her console. There was nothing else she could do but hang on and pray. Now, if only the flight-control computer was still working . . .

Skylance seemed totally lost, but the flight-control computer was intact. The situation was desperate, but computers are fearless. Calmly and efficiently it began to execute its emergency routines. It activated the fire-extinguishing system, and high-pressure, inert gases shot into the forward equipment bay and the fire went out.

The craft's accelerometers told the computer that it was tumbling. That had to be fixed next. Destruction was absolutely certain if Skylance reentered the atmosphere while it was tumbling. Something seemed to be wrong with the attitude-control system, but the flight-control computer overrode it and assumed control. At either end of Skylance's fuselage, small auxiliary rocket thrusters began to fire in short, precisely timed bursts, and the rotation began to slow.

The computer made a few quick calculations. Rotational torque would be zeroed out in approximately forty seconds, plus or minus two seconds. While the thrusters continued to fire, the computer checked and rechecked Skylance's status and its options.

A message appeared on Clark's display: "Propellant is escaping from number-two booster-engine fuel tanks—in two minutes reentry will be impossible. Recommend immediate emergency reentry."

Clark smiled grimly. Decisions were easy when you had only one choice. They were going in. Her finger moved nimbly across her computer control board.

"Set emergency reentry mode. Report subsystem status," the display read.

Data poured in. The flight-control computer made a few quick calculations.

"Probability of successful reentry 78 percent plus or minus 10 percent."

Skylance had stopped the tumbling now. The programmed emergency routine called for sending a message to ground control. The computer activated Skylance's space-to-ground communications link.

"Vandenberg—Skylance. Emergency. Acknowledge."

There was no reply. The flight-control computer transmitted the same message again and again, but there was no reply. The flight-control computer calculated.

"Probability of severe communications-system damage 99.9 percent—communications with ground improbable."

Clark didn't need a computer to tell her that. No help from Vandenberg. Skylance and Clark were on their own. She made her decision. Some other systems might be damaged and about to fail. All right, do it now!

She tapped her keyboard. "Execute emergency reentry now."

The flight-control computer responded instantly.

"Executing emergency reentry. Starting initial deorbit burn now."

Skylance rotated smoothly, end over end, until the booster orbit-deorbit rocket engines pointed forward along the line of flight. The engines' propellant valves opened, and liquid oxygen and liquid hydrogen flowed into their combustion chambers. They burst into flame, and the engines roared into life. Two white-hot lances of flame shot out of the engines, and the craft's velocity began to slow rapidly.

The flight-control computer sounded the alarm.

"Engine firing—full thrust achieved. Fuel-system pressure fluctuations beyond tolerance. Catastrophic failure possible. Recommend immediate shutdown."

There was nothing Clark could do about that. She had no choice. She had to take her chances and continue to go down. She engaged the manual override.

For another half a minute, the booster engines continued to fire, blasting a steady stream of yellow-white fire. Second by second, Skylance's velocity dropped, and the big plane began to slant downward in a shallow dive toward the atmosphere below.

Clark heard an electric motor whine, and the reentry heat shields rose smoothly out of the fuselage and enclosed her canopy in their protective cover. She could no longer see outside her cockpit. She was forced to depend on her computer displays.

At four hundred thousand feet, Skylance began to encounter the upper fringes of the atmosphere. There were only a few molecules of air per cubic inch, but the craft was moving at twelve thousand miles per hour. It was like slamming into a steel wall. Skylance's airframe began to creak and groan as the reentry stresses increased. The soft sighing sound of the air passing over the outer skin rose to a sustained rumbling roar as the plane plunged deeper and deeper into the thicker lower air. Skylance's heat shields began to glow red, orange, yellow, hotter and hotter, as superheated air flowed over the wings and fuselage.

"100,000—90,000—80,000 . . ."

The force of the passing air smashed at Skylance like a giant hand. The holes in its skin generated standing shock waves. The unplanned loads threatened to tear the craft apart or send it tumbling through the air out of control to its destruction, but the Lockheed Skunk Works engineers had designed it well. The airframe held together, and doggedly, determinedly, the flight-control computer maintained control and fought Skylance down.

Now the plane was moving through the air at sixty thousand feet and Mach 4, crawling along at a mere three thousand miles per hour. The flight-control computer activated its radar and looked ahead. Water! A broad ocean area stretched ahead. Here and there, the radar return indicated a few scattered islands, but there was a major land mass ahead on the horizon, significantly larger than any of the others. The reentry heat shields retracted smoothly back into the fuselage, and Clark could see again.

"80,000 feet, 2200 miles per hour. Landing imminent. Select land or water landing site."

Clark's fingers moved rapidly over her keyboard. "Report structural-integrity status."

The flight-control computer responded instantly. "Holes in outer structure. Watertight integrity lost. Recommend land touchdown."

Clark agreed with that. The Pacific Ocean was wide and deep, and she was a poor swimmer. Her fingers danced on her keyboard again. "Water landing rejected. Prepare for land touchdown. Target large land mass ahead. Identify land mass if possible. Execute."

There was an ominous delay that lasted for five or six seconds. Clark didn't like that. The flight-control computer was doing some heavy computing, and she was afraid that she wasn't going to like the answers.

The vertical-situation display flickered and changed. The news was bad. Skylance's reentry trajectory ended in the water thirty miles short of the coast. They were going into the water.

"Unpowered flight insufficient to accomplish requested maneuver. Powered flight mandatory," the display read.

Clark swore bitterly. That wasn't the answer she wanted to see. Well, she could damned well fly an F-15 Eagle. If the engines would only start, she would fly this bucket of bolts to land or die trying! The orbit-deorbit rocket engines were useless now.

"Eject," she typed.

Skylance shook and shuddered as the ejection charges fired, blasting the two engine pods and their spent fuel tanks away.

She pushed another button, and the command flashed to the engines.

"Emergency start."

The protective covers over the engines' inlets slid open. Air howled into the inlets, driven by Skylance's tremendous forward velocity. Fuel flowed into the combustors, and the two engines whined into life. She grasped the joystick with her right hand, put her feet on the rudder pedals and began to activate the control commands in a precise, rapid sequence.

Carefully she pulled back on the stick, and the nose came up. The craft was no longer falling through the air like a giant missile; it was flying like an airplane. Red lights were flashing, and an alarm sounded. Something was wrong with the fuel system. The engines were developing only forty percent of rated thrust. The hole in the left wing was making Skylance difficult to control. No matter what she did, Clark couldn't maintain altitude. They were going in.

"20,000 feet, 900 miles per hour."

They were over land now. She could see lush green tropical rain forests below. She could eject when her speed dropped below six hundred miles per hour. It was probably her best chance to survive, but she wasn't sure her pilot was dead, and Skylance was her responsibility. She fought the controls as the plane shuddered and vibrated.

Skylance was slanting down rapidly, losing speed and altitude every second. She needed a place to land. She could see a large valley ahead between two high ridges of tree-covered hills. The center of the valley seemed flat and clear of trees, almost as if it was farmland. She thought she saw a group of people staring up at her as she flashed across the sky, but she had no time for a closer look.

"4,000 feet, 300 miles per hour."

This was it. She couldn't fly much farther. She pointed the nose down and touched her rudder to align Skylance with the center line of the valley, and the valley floor seemed to rush up at her. She pulled back on her controls and skimmed along the surface of the ground. Gear up, flaps down! Now!

Touchdown! Skylance skidded along flat ground for six hundred feet and ground to a stop. Clark had forgotten to tighten her harness. Her head slammed into the control console, and everything went black.

The flight-control computer waited sixty seconds for instructions. None came. It followed its emergency-landing program and issued one last order.

"Down and safe. Standing by for recovery. All systems to shutdown mode. Execute."

On Skylance's upper side, a small transmitter began to send a short coded message into space over and over again.

"Skylance here. Skylance here. Skylance here."

Six hundred miles up, a U.S. electronic-surveillance satellite picked up the message and relayed it to Vandenberg Air Force Base. The mission-control officer stared at the computer display. Instantly he reached for a secure phone. Washington had to know about this immediately.

CHAPTER TWO

The White House, Washington, D.C.

Hal Brognola sat outside the Oval Office and waited. The President's secretary had assured him that the Man would see him as soon as possible, but at the moment, he was tied up in a meeting with the Joint Chiefs of Staff. That wasn't surprising. The morning news had been full of crises and disasters, and U.S. military resources were stretched thin. The Commander in Chief was going to have to make some hard choices.

The big Fed wasn't sure why he was there, but the President had called and asked him to come; when you worked for the government, you didn't refuse an invitation from the President of the United States. He glanced around the waiting room at the other people. Perhaps they would provide a clue. He saw an Army major general wearing the dagger patch of the Special Operations Command—SOCOM—on his left shoulder. An Air Force brigadier general and two men in civilian dress sat nearby. The Army general looked familiar. Brognola had seen him on TV, but he didn't remember his name. He couldn't place the Air Force general, which wasn't surprising. Washington, D.C., had more generals and admirals per square mile than any other place on the face of the earth. There was no way of telling if their presence had anything to do with him.

The door to the Oval Office opened, and the Joint Chiefs came out, four admirals and generals and the commandant of the Marines, each with four stars gleaming on his shoulder. The Joint Chiefs didn't look happy.

The President's secretary smiled brightly. "General Stuart, General Miller, Dr. Kline, Mr. Curtis, Mr. Brognola, the President will see you now."

The President was sitting behind his big desk, staring at a stack of papers. He looked up and smiled as the group came in, but he had a haggard look. There was one other person in the Oval Office, sitting in one of the guest chairs, a tall, distinguished-looking man in an elegant gray suit.

"This is John Marlowe from the State Department," the President said after motioning everyone to be seated. Marlowe smiled and nodded as the introductions were made.

"Now then, General Miller, time is critical. Please proceed with the briefing."

"At once, sir," Miller said. "But before we begin, Mr. Curtis must say a few words."

Curtis got to his feet immediately, peering nervously through his steel-rimmed glasses. It was obvious that he wasn't used to being in meetings with the President of the United States.

"Mr. President, gentlemen," he said quickly. "I am the assistant security officer of the Defense Department's Advanced Research Projects Agency. This meeting is classified top secret, special access required, code word Skylance. If anyone present does not have this clearance or has not had the related briefings, he must leave this meeting immediately. I will also remind you that anyone who discloses any information they learn in this meeting in any manner whatsoever to an unauthorized person is subject to the full penalties of the Espionage Act.''

"General Stuart's clearance has been faxed to your agency, and I will vouch for Mr. Brognola," the President said. "I trust that that will be satisfactory. Please brief them immediately."

Curtis hesitated. No one in the civil service would like to question the President in a public meeting, but there was no way out.

"Yes, sir," he answered quickly. "I understand why General Stuart is here, but this list says that Mr. Brognola is from the Department of Justice. It confirms that he is cleared for top secret, but just what is his need to know? Could I ask what possible connection the Department of Justice has with Skylance?"

"Mr. Brognola is an expert on certain points of international law, which may be very significant in this situation," the President said smoothly.

This was certainly news to Brognola, but he wasn't about to contradict the Man. He looked at Curtis and smiled modestly.

Curtis shrugged. Decisions were being made at a level high above his pay grade. He slid a form across the conference table to Brognola and another to General Stuart. The big Fed read the form quickly. It acknowledged that he had been briefed, quoted several sections of the Espionage Act and reminded him of the dire penalties he faced if he violated Skylance security regulations. He sighed to himself and signed his life away. He was cleared for so many things that it was probably a serious security violation if he talked in his sleep.

Curtis nodded to the Air Force general, who immediately opened a plastic case and took out a slide projector.

"Dr. Kline will give you the basic technical briefing," he stated.

"Mr. President, gentlemen," Kline said formally, "I am the project engineer for the XSR-92 Skylance Program. Skylance may best be described as an orbit-on-demand, manned, reconnaissance-strike aerospace vehicle."

Brognola looked blank. He was relieved to see that General Stuart didn't look any wiser.

"I'm not sure I understand what you're saying, Doctor, except that it flies and has people in it. Could you explain in plain English just what all the rest of that means?" Stuart requested.

Kline looked appalled. It was difficult for him to believe that a high-ranking officer in the United States armed forces was technically illiterate.

"Well, in the simplest possible terms, General, Skylance is a manned vehicle carrying a two-person crew. It can fly in the earth's atmosphere like a jet aircraft or fly in space like the space shuttle. It can take off from a conventional airfield and go into orbit under its own power. It can reenter and carry out missions in the atmosphere and then return to orbit. It carries a state-of-the-art sensor system for reconnaissance missions. It can also carry advanced weapons in an internal bomb bay and can carry out either nuclear or conventional attacks while operating in the atmosphere. This slide shows the internal construction. You will see . . ."

Dr. Kline continued smoothly. It was a briefing he had to have given many times before. Brognola listened intently. He was no rocket scientist, but the basic points were clear. Skylance was a marvel of U.S. technology. It could fly in space or in the atmosphere. It could discover just about anything with its advanced sensors, and blow the hell out of anything that it found that it didn't like. That was all he really needed to know. It sounded wonderful, but Brognola knew that they weren't meeting to celebrate the Department of Defense's latest triumph. He was absolutely certain that something had gone wrong. He waited quietly for the other shoe to drop.

The briefing was finally over. Kline looked around the room, waiting for questions, and seemed disappointed that there were none. General Miller stood and put up another slide. Skylance's image disappeared and was replaced by a map. Brognola recognized the outline of Australia. They were looking at the southwest Pacific.

Miller wasted no time on preliminaries. "We have conducted three successful missions with the Skylance prototype. Two days ago, we began mission four. Everything was successful until the twenty-sixth orbit. Just after passing over Western Australia, Skylance was attacked by what appears to have been a directed-energy weapon fired from the surface of the earth. We lost communications with the aircraft at the instant of the attack, but we were monitoring it with a tracking and data-relay satellite. Skylance survived the attack and made an emergency reentry."

He pointed to a large island north of Australia.

"It made a crash landing here, in the Baliem Valley, in the central highlands of Western New Guinea. This area is controlled by the Republic of Indonesia. We know that the basic structure of the aircraft is intact and that at least one crew member must have been alive during reentry."

Stuart looked skeptical. "If you lost communications, how do you know that?" he asked.

"Because Skylance reentered, and it flew after it reentered. If it had been blasted to pieces, it would have burned up during reentry. It made it in, and that means the heat shield was basically intact. If the crew was dead, the flight-control computer could have made a ballistic reentry, but it can't fly the vehicle once it's back in the atmosphere. The tracking data clearly shows that Skylance flew under its own power and made an emergency crash landing. The odds favor the aircraft being down and probably in one piece. Unless the crew was killed during the landing, they are alive in the crash area.

"There is one other factor that makes the problem worse. As Dr. Kline told you, Skylance is a strike-reconnaissance vehicle. DARPA is working on a number of advanced nonlethal weapons. We have achieved a breakthrough. Skylance was carrying two prototype Starflash weapons. When fired, they generate an extremely powerful electromagnetic pulse, so strong that it will burn out most electrical or electronic equipment over a wide area. If one was detonated over Washington, all computers, radios, television, telephone systems and electrically operated machinery would be burned out. Only specially designed military equipment would survive. In the past, a strong electromagnetic pulse could only be created by firing a large nuclear weapon. Starflash achieves the same results using nonnuclear technology. We can't let those weapons fall into foreign hands.''

Miller paused and looked around the table.

"That's the situation, gentlemen. Ideally we would like to have Skylance back, but that appears to be impossible. What we have to do is recover the data and the weapons and blow everything else to hell. And if we're right that the crew survived, we've got to rescue them if that's humanly possible.'' Miller paused and looked at General Stuart. It was obvious that Miller was talking about a special-operations mission. Stuart might not be a high-tech genius, but he was the assistant commander of SOCOM. He should know everything there was to know about special ops.

Stuart rubbed his chin and thought for a few seconds. Brognola glanced at the four rows of ribbons on his chest. He didn't know them all, but he recognized the Distinguished Service Cross, the Silver Star and the Purple Heart. Whatever he was, Stuart was obviously not just a paper pusher. He had earned his rank the hard way.

"Well, I don't see that it's a major problem, gentlemen,'' Stuart said. "I think SOCOM can take care of it for you. You don't need a large force. I would recommend that we use a small team of Green Berets or Navy SEALs. They can get your data and weapons and destroy what's left of the aircraft. If the crew is in the crash area, they'll get them out. The problem is getting our team there. We can send them in by helicopter if the Australians will let us operate from bases in Papua New Guinea. If not, the Air Force can fly them to the area, and they can jump in. Our planes will have to refuel in Australia before the mission, but the Australian military will not be directly involved. If we do it that way, the only problem I see is how we get them out. We ought to withdraw them by helicopters from Papua New Guinea. If we can't do that, we need a helicopter-capable ship off the New Guinea coast. That may take some time to set up. With your permission, Mr. President, I'll get the basic planning started immediately."

John Marlowe had been sitting and listening quietly. His professional smile had faded as he listened to Stuart.

"Excuse me, General," he said quickly, "I don't think you understand the situation. What you are proposing could have the gravest consequences. You're suggesting that we send armed troops to carry out a combat mission on Indonesian territory and launch that operation from Papua New Guinea. I am sure Mr. Brognola will agree with me. From the point of view of international law, that is an act of war against Indonesia. There is already a crisis in that area. Indonesia and Australia are already quarreling over the future of Papua New Guinea. Both nations are very important to United States foreign policy. Indonesia is the fifth-most-populous nation in the world. Australia is one of our oldest allies. We must do everything possible to prevent a conflict between them, and your plan, General, could lead to war."

Stuart started to answer, but Marlowe cut him off. "Excuse me, General, but there is something else you don't seem to understand. Australia doesn't own Papua New Guinea. It is an independent nation. Australia provides some military support. If we want to conduct military operations from the territory of Papua New Guinea, its government must agree in advance. Even assuming that they might give their consent, it will take weeks to obtain it. General Stuart's plan is simply an invitation to disaster. I strongly recommend against it."

Stuart flushed angrily. He wasn't used to being lectured by civilians, but he controlled his temper. The President intensely disliked interagency wrangling. He stared at Marlowe and spoke coolly.

"I understand what Mr. Marlowe has said. I know that there are times when political considerations influence military decisions. Maybe this is one of them, but I have given you my professional opinion and I stand behind it. If you want the job done, and done fast, that's the way to do it. If it's politically impossible to operate from Australia or Papua New Guinea, we can use a Marine amphibious assault ship positioned off the coast of New Guinea. A Marine Corps recon unit can go in by helicopter and accomplish the mission. The problem with that solution is that the closest amphibious assault ship is operating off Okinawa. It will take four or five days to get it to New Guinea. If that delay is acceptable, I will contact the Navy immediately and get the operation under way."

"That's completely unacceptable," General Miller said instantly. "Anything can happen in four days! The Marines could find the crash site occupied by Indonesian troops when they get there, or the Indonesians may have found the site and removed Skylance.

With all respect, Mr. President, the technology we have incorporated in the aircraft simply cannot be allowed to fall into foreign hands. We must act immediately!"

Marlowe shook his head. "It doesn't matter whether General Stuart uses Green Berets, SEALs or Marines. You're still talking about sending U.S. combat troops into a friendly nation without permission. That's an act of war. What happens if some of our men are killed or taken prisoner? No, a military solution is completely unacceptable."

Miller started to speak, but the President stopped him with a gesture.

"Excuse me, General, but I'd like to ask Mr. Marlowe a question. If we don't take a military action, what will we do? I'd like your recommendation, John."

"That's very simple, sir, if we can just get out of this military mind-set. Force is not the only answer to all our problems. I recommend diplomacy. After all, Indonesia is not an ally of the United States, but we do have reasonably friendly relations. I recommend that we contact the Indonesian government immediately. Let's tell them most of the truth. We will simply say that an experimental U.S. aircraft has made an emergency landing in Western New Guinea and request their assistance in recovering the aircraft and its crew. I see no reason why they would refuse."

The President considered Marlowe's recommendation for a moment. It was certainly a tempting idea if it would work, but there was one thing that bothered him.

"I understand your recommendation, John," the President said quietly, "but it seems to me that there may be a serious problem. If we do what you suggest, the Indonesian military are going to be the first people to reach the crash site. That means they will have custody of Skylance and the weapons for days, perhaps weeks. That's what concerns me. Can we trust them?"

Marlowe frowned. "Of course, we can, sir. If the Indonesian government promises to return the aircraft to us, I'm sure they will do so."

The President smiled cynically. He lived in the real world; he wasn't always sure about the State Department.

"Oh, I'm sure they would give us something, but suppose they decide to remove the weapons and sensors from Skylance, blow up the rest of it and give us the pieces. They can say everything else was destroyed and the crew was killed in the crash. The sensors and the weapons would be worth a great deal of money to certain people. Russia, China, North Korea, Iran, even some of the major terrorist organizations would pay hundreds of millions of dollars for Skylance's technology. You're our expert. You lived in Indonesia for many years. You know the government and the people, John. I don't. So, tell me, can we trust them?"

Marlowe looked grim. He didn't like what he was going to have to say, but he was an honest man, and lying to the President wouldn't improve his chances for promotion.

"No, sir, if you put it that way, you cannot. Corruption is epidemic in Indonesia. It permeates every level of the government from the lowest clerk to the highest officials. The Indonesian government itself admits that fifty percent of their gross national product disappears into bribes and illegal payments. Nothing stops it. If you have enough money, you can buy anything. The security police have a big anticorruption drive every year, but it's easy enough to bribe them. If some Indonesian general got hold of Skylance and knew even vaguely what he had, he wouldn't hesitate to sell it."

The President nodded. "All right, gentlemen, thank you for attending the meeting. I have to think this over. I will make a decision in a few hours. In the meantime, I want to keep all our options open. General Stuart, divert that amphibious ship to New Guinea and find out what other naval assets we have in the area. General Miller, assist General Stuart by providing any technical information he may need. Mr. Marlowe, prepare a draft communication to the Indonesian government in case we decide to go that way. Thank you, that's all, gentlemen."

The group stood and began to file out of the Oval Office.

"Just a minute, Mr. Brognola," the President said. "If you will please stay for a minute, I have a few questions I would like to ask you."

Brognola sat down, smiling grimly to himself. He no longer wondered why he had been asked to attend the meeting. He knew.

The President looked at the clock on his desk and smiled. "Time passes fast when you're having fun. We have to make this quick, Hal. I have to welcome the Japanese trade delegation in twenty minutes. We have to do something about this Skylance situation, and it looks like any conventional solution just won't work. I would like you to take care of the problem. Send in Phoenix Force and clean things up as soon as possible."

Brognola thought for a minute. "Phoenix Force is primarily a counterterrorist organization. This really isn't our type of mission," he said quietly.

"No? Stop and think for a moment. Letting another country get their hands on Skylance would be bad enough, but these damned Starflash weapons would be a screaming disaster. Think what would happen if a terrorist group gets hold of that kind of technology. A few of those fired over our major cities could cripple the entire economy and set us back twenty years. National security demands that we recover or destroy those weapons as soon as possible. Your people are the best we have for a covert mission. The job has to be done, and I'm asking you and your people to do it."

It wasn't a request Hal Brognola could refuse.

"All right, Mr. President," he said formally, "we'll take care of it. I'll get the ball rolling immediately."

CHAPTER THREE

The Baliem Valley, Western New Guinea

Mary Clark woke up with a start. Her head was throbbing. She stared out through the cockpit canopy and saw rugged hills covered with tall green trees, and a gray, cloudy sky. Skylance was lying on its belly in a long, narrow valley between the hills. For a second, the woman was disoriented. Where the hell was she? Then it all came flooding back to her, and she felt a quick rush of pride. She had done it. Skylance was down, and she was alive. It hadn't been the prettiest landing in the world, but she remembered what her flight-school instructors had always told her. "Any landing you can walk away from is a good landing."

Time to stop patting herself on the back and get moving. How long had she been out? She glanced quickly at her instrument-panel clock. Good, only three minutes. Time to start the emergency-landing routine. She might not have much time before the local authorities showed up and started asking embarrassing questions. She was not sure where she was, only that she must be somewhere on the island of New Guinea. She knew almost nothing about New Guinea. She wasn't even sure who owned it. She seemed to remember vaguely that it was the Australians. If that was true, she ought to get a friendly reception. But her orders were clear. Skylance was not to be allowed to fall into foreign hands, and that obviously included Australians.

Time to get going, then. She glanced at her displays. Emergency power was on. She pushed a button, and her canopy unlocked and opened slowly, admitting a hot, humid breeze. She wanted to get out of her flight suit, but first things first. Clark unfastened her flight harness and climbed out of her cockpit and onto the left wing. She moved forward to the pilot's seat. The canopy was still closed, smeared with smoke, and there was a round, two-foot-diameter hole in one side. Things didn't look good. She could see Pete Greene still strapped in his seat, but his head was slumped forward, lolling on his chest.

She opened a small access panel and pulled the emergency canopy release. She could hear the electric motor whining and complaining as the canopy rose slowly to the open position. Clark winced as she smelled the acrid scents of burned plastic and seared human flesh. There was nothing in this world she could do for Pete Greene. He had a two-foot hole burned completely through his chest. He had to have died instantly.

She moved quickly back to her cockpit and looked at her displays. The control panels showed a dozen red lights, but nothing terrible seemed to be happening. The fuel system was intact, and there was no sign of fire. She tried to activate the primary communications system, but nothing happened. A green light was flickering steadily, indicating that the emergency landing beacon was pulsing steadily. The unit would keep sending until its battery ran down.

Clark had a hard decision to make. She was certain she had seen some people on the ground just before she touched down. People could be on their way to the crash site right now. She could wait by Skylance until they arrived or go into hiding and escape and evade until she saw who had come. The more she thought about it, the less she liked waiting by the aircraft. If she did that, she would be at the mercy of whoever arrived at the site. Better play Girl Scout and take to the trees. She could hide a few hundred yards away and take a careful look at anyone who showed up. If they looked friendly, she could come out and greet them. If not, she would already be hidden. All right, then, it was time to go. She picked up her survival kit and started for the trees.

Operations center
Stony Man Farm, Virginia

HAL BROGNOLA FINISHED briefing Barbara Price. He had called to alert her before he left the White House, but he hadn't discussed the mission. He'd rather do that in person.

"That's all we know," he concluded. "General Stuart has requested satellite-reconnaissance surveillance of the crash site, but there is thick cloud cover over central New Guinea at the moment. That blocks both optical and infrared sensors. We won't get any satellite data until it clears. Any questions?"

Barbara Price shook her head. "I did an immediate Stony Man status check as soon as you called. We have one piece of luck. Striker and McCarter are still in Australia, playing war games with the Australian

SAS. If you want to send just the two of them in, they could be in the target area in ten or twelve hours. That's assuming we can get transportation from the Aussies.''

Brognola thought for a moment. He didn't like sending Bolan and McCarter in by themselves, but unless the Indonesian army was camped on the crash site, they could do the job.

"All right, let's alert them as soon as we're through here. The President is going to talk to the Australians and call in a few debts. It's unlikely that they'll send any of their own people into Indonesian territory, but we can probably get a plane to fly our team in. Getting them out is going to be the problem. Where's the rest of the team?''

Price glanced at her computer display. "Rafael and Calvin are at Pearl Harbor getting checked out on some new underwater-operations equipment. Carl Lyons is off on a personal errand, and Katz is doing offsite research. Jack Grimaldi and Gadgets Schwarz are in Las Vegas at some kind of electronics show. Gadgets is checking out the latest miracles of modern science. If I know Grimaldi, he's checking out the show girls. T. J. Hawkins is on a survival-training course in the Arctic and isn't available. He's out of radio contact for three days.''

Brognola nodded.

"Where's Gary Manning?''

"Gary's up in Canada, out in the woods trying to shoot a record-size something or other. We can find him if we need him.''

The big Fed considered his options. He needed more time and more information, but they paid him to make hard decisions. Time to earn his pay.

"Alert Striker and David immediately. Brief them and tell them to get ready. They're going in."

Northern Command Headquarters
Darwin, Australia

MACK BOLAN LAY in the prone position and waited with his rifle in his hands. It wasn't a pretty weapon. Its dull black, nonreflective finish and matte black plastic stock gave it an almost cheap look. But the Remington 700-P sniper rifle had been an excellent rifle when it left the Remington Custom Gunshop. When John "Cowboy" Kissinger, the Stony Man armorer, had finished fine-tuning it, it was superb. It was loaded with .308 M-852 National Match ammunition from Lake City Arsenal, some of the most accurate military rifle ammunition in the world. When Bolan did his part, the combination would put five shots in a three-quarter-inch-diameter group at a range of one hundred yards. If he missed, it would be hard to blame his rifle or his ammo.

It was two hours before dawn. The dim moonlight was enough to let him see flat, marshy ground and some ramshackle wood buildings. He couldn't make out any details, but he knew that his targets would have to appear in that direction when they came. The Executioner flicked the switch and turned on his AN/PVS-10 night sight. It added four pounds to the weight of his rifle, but Bolan felt it was worth every ounce.

He set the sight for its full 8.5-power magnification, which let him see details clearly but reduced his field of view. He would have to live with that. He would need the scope's full power if he had to shoot at long range. McCarter was lying next to him with wide-angle, laser-ranging, night-vision binoculars. He would spot targets and direct Bolan to outside his rifle scope's field of view.

The Australian SAS captain in command of the mission spoke quietly in his nasal Australian twang. He seemed skeptical of the whole idea of long-range nighttime sniper fire.

"There are an unknown number of terrorists in the area. There are no friendly military personnel in the area. Any armed person you see is a terrorist and may be fired on without warning. Be careful, however. There are civilians in the area being held hostage. They must not be harmed. Any questions? Good. Sniper team ready?"

Bolan concentrated on his breathing, keeping it slow and steady.

"Team ready," McCarter said.

The Australian captain smiled. He had bet McCarter a hundred Australian dollars on the outcome. He didn't think he was going to lose.

"Very well, fire at will!"

Bolan felt the adrenaline start to flow. A few seconds crawled by.

"Motion at the left corner of the far building, range six hundred meters," McCarter said softly.

The Executioner swung his rifle until the vertical cross hair in his scope was aligned with the left edge of the building. For a second or two, he saw nothing, then spotted a flicker of motion. A man's head. Someone was peering around the corner. Instinctively Bolan put the light, first pressure on his trigger, but he didn't fire. Six hundred meters was too long for a head shot, and he couldn't be certain the target was hostile.

He took a deep breath, let half of it out and waited, his finger on the trigger.

Six hundred meters away, a man stepped out from behind the corner, followed a second later by another. Through his scope, Bolan could see that both men were carrying automatic rifles. The Remington was sighted in for four hundred meters. It would shoot two feet low at six hundred. There was no time to change his sights. He placed the cross hairs on the first man's head, and squeezed the trigger. The Remington roared, and he felt the push of the recoil against his shoulder.

Instantly Bolan's hand flashed to the bolt handle and drove it up, back, forward and down in one perfectly coordinated, blurring motion that reloaded and cocked his rifle.

"Hit!" McCarter snapped.

Bolan swung his scope smoothly and put his sights on the second man. He saw a series of bright muzzle-flashes as the man fired back. He was brave to stand there firing rapidly, but he wasn't smart. The Executioner squeezed the trigger and sent a 168-grain .30-caliber bullet through his chest. Instinctively, without thinking, he worked his rifle's bolt and chambered a fresh round.

"Hit!" McCarter said happily.

A third figure came around the corner of the building. It looked like a woman in a dress.

"Hold your fire. Hostage!" McCarter snapped.

"Right," Bolan said, but he kept his scope's cross hairs centered on the woman's body. McCarter was probably right, but the woman was holding a bundle in her arms, and the soldier had learned a long time ago that a woman could kill you just as dead as a man.

Two menacing figures broke cover about fifty yards away. One of them had an automatic weapon. Bolan saw the yellow flashes dancing around the muzzle of his weapon as he fired a series of fast, short bursts from the hip. The second man had what looked like a length of black pipe over his right shoulder. Rocket launcher! Bolan swung his cross hairs on the middle of the man's chest and pressed the trigger. The Remington roared, and the man went down.

The first man was still firing. The soldier worked his rifle's bolt as he swung his sights back to him and fired. The man stopped firing abruptly and fell. Bolan had been counting his shots as he fired. Four were gone, only one was left. One weakness of the Remington 700-P was that its built-in magazine held only five rounds. Bolan snapped the bolt open and pushed four fresh rounds into the magazine. He closed the bolt and was ready to fire again.

McCarter was scanning the area in front of them rapidly.

"Motion between those two buildings to our left front, range two hundred meters," McCarter said quickly.

Bolan swung his rifle smoothly until it pointed at the two buildings and stared through his scope.

"No targets," he said quietly.

"Someone just ran between the right-hand building and the left. Watch the area."

The big American placed his cross hairs on the inner corner of the building and waited patiently. Nothing happened for ten seconds. Then a man shot around the corner and dashed for the other building. He made the mistake of running at a constant speed. Bolan moved his rifle smoothly, maintaining a constant tracking speed, and squeezed the Remington's trigger. His rifle roared, and the man stopped and fell as if he had run into a solid wall.

The other man popped out from behind the left-hand building and ran back toward the fallen terrorist. Perhaps he was just going to help a wounded comrade, but that wasn't the way the game was played. Bolan got his sights on and fired. The man went down and lay still.

Everything was quiet. Perhaps thirty seconds went by.

"Very good work, men," the Australian captain said. "That was good shooting, Belasko, damned good."

Perhaps he was getting too suspicious, but Bolan noted that he hadn't said "Cease fire" or "Clear your weapons." Was the exercise really over?

Twenty yards in front of him, the ground abruptly erupted. Two menacing figures suddenly appeared from superbly camouflaged fox holes. Instantly Bolan's right hand flashed to his hip holster, and he drew his .44 Magnum Desert Eagle. The big weapon bucked and roared again and again as he shot each target twice just as fast as he could pull the trigger, hammering each target with two quick shots in that lethal technique serious pistol shooters call the double tap. Both men went down instantly.

"Bloody hell," the Australian SAS captain said. "Is that thing a pistol or a cannon? Cease fire and clear your weapons."

Bolan tried to relax, but the adrenaline was still flowing. The computer-controlled, three-dimensional plastic targets were too real for comfort.

The captain pulled a printout from his computer terminal and handed it to McCarter.

"Every terrorist engaged and hit, all shots in the kill zone, no shots fired at hostages. A perfect score. I'm afraid I owe you some money, Captain. Your friend really does know how to shoot, even in the dark."

Bolan smiled modestly. He was far from being perfect, but he had always been a superb shot.

Dawn was starting to break in the east. Bolan thought some breakfast would be a good idea. He only hoped the Australians weren't planning another of their surprise survival tests. He drew the line at fried crocodile steaks for breakfast.

A military-style jeep pulled up to a quick stop just behind the firing line. An Australian SAS sergeant got out quickly. He had the look of a man on urgent business and headed immediately for Bolan and McCarter.

"Captain? Mr. Belasko? Please come with me. Colonel Fraser says he must see you immediately."

Bolan had been in the Army long enough to know that a sudden summons from a colonel usually meant trouble.

"What's going on, Sergeant?" McCarter inquired as they bounced along a rutted dirt road.

"I'm not sure, Captain, but there is a message for the two of you from Washington. It's got every kind of bloody priority there is. Somebody important back in the States wants to talk to you, and they want to do it now!"

Kiunga, Papua New Guinea

THE RED-AND-BLACK FLAG of Papua New Guinea hung limply in the hot and humid air. It was eleven o'clock in the morning, but the temperature was already more than one hundred degrees. The jeep dropped Bolan and McCarter in front of a battered metal Quonset hut that had obviously seen better days. A stocky officer wearing Australian camouflage fatigues and the sand-colored beret of the SAS was waiting at the door.

"Good morning, gentlemen," he said cheerfully. "I am Major John Gates, Number Two Squadron, Australian SAS. Welcome to Papua New Guinea. I have a message from NORCOM directing me to give you all possible assistance in your mission, consistent with Australian government policy."

Bolan noticed that Gates didn't ask what their mission was. He had to be curious, but he was too old a hand to ask questions about a classified operation.

"Thank you, Major," McCarter said. "We appreciate your assistance."

"Step inside, and I'll fill you in on the local situation."

He led them into a small briefing room and pointed to a large map that covered one wall.

"This is the island of New Guinea. It's the second largest island in the world. It is divided roughly into halves by this north-south border. We're here, in the eastern half, in Papua New Guinea. The western half is controlled by the Republic of Indonesia.

"We're here to provide military training and technical assistance to the Papua New Guinea army, which consists of six thousand officers and men. Their combat units are limited to three infantry battalions. There is a four-hundred-mile border with Western New Guinea to cover. As you can see, they are stretched rather thin.

"We're also here to lend a hand, particularly when the Indonesian troops come across the border. Most of the people in Western New Guinea are not Indonesians, and they resent the Indonesian takeover in 1963. They aren't the same race or culture as the Indonesians. They are Papuans. The Indonesians consider them a bunch of bloody savages, and they treat them as such."

"You said when the Indonesians come across the border. Has there been fighting?" Bolan asked.

Gates nodded. "Small-scale, so far. We hope to keep it that way. There is an organized resistance movement operating in Western New Guinea, the Free Papua Movement. The FPM has some base camps along the Papua New Guinea side of the border. Indonesian special-operations forces make raids across the border to destroy the FPM camps. When they do that, we give the Papuans a hand and reason with them. It's all very hush-hush and unofficial. Both sides would deny it if you asked them, but it goes on. Our objective is to deter the Indonesians from making a full-scale attempt to take over Papua New Guinea. We won't allow that. If they try, it will mean war."

"Is Indonesia really a serious threat to Australia?" Bolan asked. That seemed hard to believe.

"Too right, they're a bloody threat. There's 185 million of them, and 15 million of us. And look at the map. Indonesia is seriously overpopulated on the main islands, and their population is growing rapidly. If you were running Indonesia, and you had to have more land and more natural resources for your people, where would you look?

"They got all of Western New Guinea in 1963. They wanted Papua New Guinea then, but we weren't about to let them have it. If they had it, they would be not much more than forty miles away from Australia and just a hop, skip, and a jump from Darwin. The Japanese tried to invade Australia that way in World War II. We fought them all the way across New Guinea and stopped them just short of the south coast. Most people have forgotten that, but we Australians haven't."

Bolan nodded. That was clear enough. He could see why Washington was nervous. If serious fighting developed between Australia and Indonesia, it would be hard for the United States to avoid getting involved.

Gates smiled. "Well, now you've had the two-dollar briefing, but I doubt you came here for a vacation tour of New Guinea. I'm not briefed on your mission, but you wouldn't be here if it didn't involve going into Western New Guinea. What can we do to help you?"

Bolan let McCarter take the lead. The Australian SAS officers knew him and would speak frankly.

McCarter had vouched for the big American, but to the Australian SAS, he was still an unknown quantity. There might be things they would hesitate to say to him.

"Here's the story," McCarter said smoothly. "We've received an urgent message from Washington. There's a very advanced, supersecret American reconnaissance satellite down in the Baliem Valley across the border in Western New Guinea. Washington very badly wants the data the satellite recorded, and they don't want any of its hardware to fall into Indonesian hands. They realize that the political situation here is a bit dicey. They want Mike and me to slip in quietly, get the data recorders, destroy the satellite and slip back out. No muss, no fuss, no bother. Piece of cake, really, but we are going to need to borrow some equipment, and we'll need a bit of help getting there."

"You may need more than a little bit of help," Gates said. "New Guinea is larger than it looks on a map. After Greenland, it's the biggest island in the world, fifteen hundred miles long and four hundred miles wide. From here to the Baliem Valley is over two hundred miles across some of the worst country you've ever seen. Believe me, you aren't going to just stroll in there. There are lots of Indonesian troops along the border. And getting out will be almost as bad. The Baliem Valley is in the center of Western New Guinea. Whether you try for the north coast or the south coast, it's one hundred fifty miles either way."

Bolan stared at the map. Gates was right. It wasn't going to be an easy mission. "We can't wait. We have to go in as soon as possible and get there fast," he said quietly.

"Too right, you do. Well, we can give you a hand. We've just received a priority message from NOR-COM headquarters. It seems you two blokes have friends in high places. Our government says that no Australians can be directly involved in the mission itself, but we'll see that you get there and arrange for people to meet you when you arrive and give you a hand. We'll fly you in tonight. I assume both you gentlemen are qualified parachutists."

BOLAN AND MCCARTER WALKED through the humid night air into the small briefing room. It was half an hour past midnight, but the heat was still brutal. They were already sweating in their dull black combat suits. The Australian SAS hadn't invested in air-conditioning. Major Gates was waiting for them.

"Right on time, gentlemen. That's good. Your plane will touch down in thirty minutes. We load your gear, and off you go. We'll have you there in half an hour. Piece of cake, really."

Bolan and McCarter sat at a battered wood table, and Gates pointed to the wall map.

"Here's where you're going, gentlemen. The Baliem Valley. The area you're interested in is here. We're going to drop you about twenty miles to the north, here, about ten miles south of the settlement of Wamena. It's the only town of any size in the valley. It basically consists of government offices and mission schools and offices. The good news is that we have excellent FPM contacts there. We've been in touch with them, and they've agreed to help you. The bad news is that Wamena is the Indonesian military and police headquarters for the highlands area. Stay away from the town if you possibly can."

"Why is the FPM willing to help us?" McCarter asked.

"Shameless bribery," Gates said with a grin. "The FPM is always short of arms and ammunition. We're dropping forty AK-47 rifles and ammunition in with you. The FPM is willing to be very nice to you for forty rifles."

"Very good, Major. You seem to have thought of everything," McCarter said with a smile. "Let's go drop in on our friends in the FPM."

Port Darwin
Northern Territory, Australia

RAFAEL ENCIZO DROVE the Australian navy jeep along the Port Darwin harbor. He passed a Royal Australian Navy Oberon-class attack submarine and drove up to the last berthing position in the naval area of the harbor. He stopped the vehicle and stared at the long, black shape moored to the pier. The four-hundred-foot-long hull had the characteristic elongated-egg shape of a U.S. Navy nuclear submarine. There was no nameplate on the flat black hull, but he saw the number 609 painted in white on the conning tower.

He was in the right place. The hull number of the USS *Sam Houston* was 609. A small gangway led from the pier out to the vessel. A sailor armed with an M-16 assault rifle stood guard on the dock. Encizo seldom argued with men carrying automatic rifles. He showed the sailor his ID and the first page of his orders. The sailor looked at the ID and immediately called the chief petty officer in charge of the watch, who took one look at the orders and led Encizo through a hatch in the deck and down into the multicompartmented labyrinth of the hull.

They walked down a narrow corridor and entered the attack center. The chief led him to a tall, thin, balding officer wearing the insignia of a U.S. Navy commander.

"This is Mr. Brown, sir," the chief said, introducing Encizo under his cover name. "He has priority orders from SUBPAC."

That attracted the commander's attention immediately. SUBPAC was Submarines Pacific, the headquarters that controlled all U.S. submarines operating in the Pacific Ocean. He looked at the orders and smiled.

"We've been expecting you, Mr. Brown. We had an alerting message from SUBPAC that you were on the way. I'm Frank Scott, the commander of the *Sam Houston.* These orders say I'm to support your mission in all possible ways, but they don't say what your mission is. What can I do for you?"

"My organization is about to carry out a mission in Western New Guinea. We'll insert a team into the Baliem Valley area in the next few hours. We anticipate that they'll have completed their mission and be ready for extraction in forty-eight hours. We think they'll be coming out by air. Our plan is for them to rendezvous with the *Sam Houston,* land in the water and be picked up, and be returned to Australia."

Scott nodded. He was experienced enough in covert operations to ask any questions about the mission, like who, where or why. If he needed that information, Encizo would have told him.

"I'm sure we can handle that, but why do you want the *Sam Houston?* She's an old boat, launched in 1961. She had a major overhaul last year, so she's in good shape, but we don't have all the latest bells and whistles. We can only do fifteen knots on the surface and twenty knots submerged. Are you sure you don't need something newer, like one of the Los Angeles class?"

"We asked for the *Sam Houston* for two reasons. One is location. You're here doing exercises with the Australians. You can be on station in forty-eight hours. The other is you're equipped for SEAL team operations. I saw two dry-deck shelters on your aft deck as I drove up. Do you have an operational Swimmer Delivery Vehicle in each one?"

Scott raised an eyebrow. This was beginning to get interesting. "We have two Mark VII MOD-6 SDVs on board, and both are fully operational."

Encizo smiled. They weren't the very latest model, but he and Calvin James had used them many times in the past. If they had to use the SDVs, they would have no problems operating them.

"When will you be ready to sail?" Scott asked.

"My associate, Mr. Green, will be here in twenty minutes with some special equipment. As soon as he's on board, we're ready. Our mission is urgent, Commander. I would like to sail as soon as possible."

"I'll tell the executive officer to be ready for sea in an hour. Welcome aboard, Mr. Brown."

CHAPTER FOUR

The Baliem Valley

The big Royal Australian Air Force Lockheed C-130H flew steadily on through the night. Mack Bolan sat in one of the cramped nylon web seats in the troop compartment. He was strapped snugly but uncomfortably into his web equipment and his parachute harness.

The C-130 was no ordinary Lockheed Hercules. It was one of the new C-130H models, specially designed and equipped to support Australian SAS missions. The plane and its crew were from the Royal Australian Air Force's Number Thirty-six Squadron. McCarter had worked with them before. He swore they were some of the best aircrews in the business. He said if anyone could get Bolan and McCarter to the right place at the right time, they could.

Bolan didn't have time to worry about that statement. Sergeant McDonald, the jump master, suddenly appeared, moving quietly through the dimly lit cargo compartment. He looked at Bolan for a second to be sure he had the right man. In the dark, Bolan and McCarter looked the same in their dull black, nonreflective uniforms, Kevlar helmets and combat gear. The Executioner wasn't wearing anything that was shiny or reflective. He wasn't going to make life easier for enemy snipers.

"Mr. Belasko?" the sergeant inquired. Bolan nodded. "Captain Lynch says to tell you we are on final approach for the drop zone. Course and location are confirmed by the inertial navigation system and satellite global positioning system."

"Get ready, men!" McDonald's voice rang through the troop compartment, loud and clear over the whine of the C-130H's engines.

He gestured upward with both hands. "Jump party! Stand...up!"

Bolan and McCarter heaved themselves to their feet, each man fighting the drag of 150 pounds of parachutes, weapons, combat equipment and survival gear.

"Check equipment. Prepare for troop compartment depressurization!" McDonald shouted.

Quickly Bolan checked McCarter's equipment, and the Briton checked his. Now for the critical step. Everyone in the troop compartment had to go on oxygen. The big C-130H had been climbing steadily since it left the Papua New Guinea air base. It was flying at thirty-five thousand feet. The C-130H's aft compartment had to be depressurized now. The high-altitude, low-opening parachute jump required opening the tail door. If the pressure inside the troop compartment didn't match that of the thin outside air, a hurricane would blast through the compartment the instant the door was opened. That meant Bolan and McCarter had to start to breathe oxygen from the two individual bailout bottles strapped to their harnesses before the door was opened. Each bottle could supply thirty minutes of oxygen. Their bailout bottles and their oxygen masks would keep them alive until they were below ten thousand feet.

The four-minute-warning light was on. Bolan and McCarter were breathing from their bailout bottles now. McDonald gave each man a final equipment check. He looked closely to see that both men's heads and faces were covered by their jump helmets and oxygen masks. Their boots, gloves and insulated jumpsuits protected the rest of their bodies. It was sixty-five degrees below zero outside, and the air would be howling past the C-130H's fuselage at 130 knots when they jumped. Any unprotected skin would suffer instant frostbite. Bolan and McCarter each gave the thumbs-up. McDonald nodded and pointed toward the tail door.

Slowly, careful not to tangle their equipment, they moved toward the C-130H's tail door. They would jump at five-second intervals. Bolan would go first. He would be the jump leader, the low man. McCarter would jump five seconds later.

Two-minute warning. Bolan and McCarter were standing at the end of the cargo compartment now, facing the C-130H's tail door. When the door opened, there would be nothing below them for thirty-five thousand feet but dark night air. The pilot was waiting until the last moment to open the door. McDonald signaled for the final oxygen check. Red warning lights came on, and Bolan heard the high-pitched whine of hydraulic motors as the big C-130H's tail door was lowered and locked open in the horizontal ready position. Icy outside air flooded the troop compartment. Bolan stared into the blackness outside.

One-minute warning! Bolan looked back and made a thumbs-up gesture to McCarter. He returned the gesture with his own thumbs-up signal. Neither one of them was having breathing problems or trouble with his other equipment. They were both ready to go.

The thirty-second warning light flashed. There was a sudden change in the roar of the four engines as the pilot throttled them back. He was holding the C-130H as close to its stalling speed as he dared in order to reduce the strength of the airflow around the big plane's fuselage. When he was satisfied, he would push the ten-second warning light. Unless Bolan or McDonald called an abort, the team would go. The big plane began to shake and vibrate as its speed dropped to within a few knots of stalling. Satisfied, the pilot pushed the button. The ten-second warning light came on.

"Stand by!" McDonald shouted. The stand-by order was the last warning before the jump. Bolan felt a quick surge of adrenaline. There was nothing left for him to do now but go out the door.

Suddenly the go light went on.

Bolan heard McDonald scream, "Go! . . . Go! . . . Go!"

The big American took two long strides along the ramp and dived out the open door into the icy blackness outside. Instantly he was in free-fall. The slipstream buffeted and spun his body, turning him over and over like a rag doll. Looking back, he could see the bright moonlight reflected from the big wings and fuselage of the aircraft. The whine of its engines faded as it pulled away and vanished into the dark. Bolan used his arms and legs to stop his spinning and turn his body to a facedown position.

He was falling faster and faster through the dark. The only sounds were the sighing of the air as it rushed past him and the harsh, rasping noise of his own breathing inside his oxygen mask. He looked down. All his night-vision goggles showed him were the tops of a thick layer of clouds below. The scene didn't seem to change. Bolan knew he was falling several hundred feet each second toward the ground below, but he seemed to be suspended in space.

He knew McCarter should have jumped and cleared the aircraft by now. He should be above and behind Bolan. "High man, give me the count," Bolan said. The sound of his voice activated the microphone on his throat, and the low-probability-of-intercept radio transmitted his message. In theory, his radio was almost impossible to intercept, and even if someone on the ground picked it up, the message was scrambled. Still, people on the ground would certainly be alerted if they detected mysterious, indecipherable messages coming from the sky overhead. He had to keep radio transmissions to a minimum.

"I see one, Leader," McCarter reported. Bolan found that reassuring. They were both falling through space toward the target now. Even if he or McCarter passed out from oxygen-mask failure, their parachutes would open automatically when they reached one thousand feet.

Bolan looked down again. He no longer seemed to be suspended motionless in space. He was getting close to the cloud tops now. It looked as if he were falling faster and faster toward the tops of a range of snow-covered mountains. He checked his altimeter—16,000 feet. The clouds seemed to be rushing at him at breakneck speed. Suddenly he was surrounded by thick gray mist. Moisture condensed on his goggles, obscuring his vision. Then he was through the clouds, bursting out into the clear air below them.

His goggles cleared. Bolan checked his altimeter again—12,000 feet. He began to scan the land below. He could see a modest V-shaped lake and a small stream, which looked like the target area. There wasn't much else to see but a jumble of rugged hills and broad, flat valleys. Now, where was the beacon? There it was! From the edge of a wide, flat patch of ground near the lake, the beacon began to blink, sending out pulses of infrared light. It would have been invisible to the naked eye, but Bolan's night-vision goggles showed him a steady series of bright, flashing pulses. The beacon's light was shrouded by a funnel-shaped shield. Even with night-vision equipment, it would be invisible to anyone on the ground.

The beacon was putting out a steady, rhythmic series of infrared pulses. That was the go code. If the operator thought the landing zone wasn't secure, he would have been pushing the warning button, and the beacon's output would be a series of faster, flickering pulses. It was a standard Australian special-operations clandestine beacon. Their FPM contact had to be at the landing zone. Now, to concentrate on his landing. He was a bit to the left of the LZ, but their rectangular MT1-XX ram-air canopy parachutes could be flown like hang gliders, allowing them to come down at angles as great as forty-five degrees. He and McCarter should come down close together near the blinking infrared beacon, which marked the center of the LZ.

He checked his altimeter—2,000 feet, and grasped the rip cord's D-ring. He was counting to himself without thinking as he glanced quickly to the left and right. All clear.

Three! Two! One!

Bolan pulled his rip cord. His pilot chute deployed, pulling the high-performance ram-air canopy out of its pack and into the air. The canopy blossomed, and Bolan felt a bone-jarring jolt as it filled with air and abruptly slowed his fall. Quickly he slipped his hands into his steering loops, ready to maneuver if he had to. A collision with McCarter could end the mission.

"High man, give me a check," Bolan said.

"Roger, Leader. Chute open. Have you in sight," McCarter responded quickly.

Bolan felt a surge of relief and looked around rapidly. He could see McCarter's chute above and behind his own. The Briton didn't seem to be having any trouble. Now it was time to concentrate on his own landing.

He pulled on his parachute's steering loops and began to move to the left, toward the steadily blinking beacon. He had to make a good parachute-landing fall now. Long ago, when he had trained as a Green Beret, his instructors had drilled it into him again and again, no operational jump was worth a damn without a good PLF. A broken knee or ankle deep inside New Guinea was likely to be just as fatal as a burst from a well-aimed AK-47.

The ground was getting closer and closer. He tensed and slightly bent his knees. He kept his hands in the steering loops with his elbows turned inward, close to his chest. Now he was almost on top of the beacon. He released his equipment rucksack. It dropped away and dangled fifteen feet below him on the end of its heavy nylon line.

He pulled on the steering loops and went to full brake. His forward motion stopped immediately, and he went straight down. He felt a heavy jar through the nylon line as his rucksack hit the ground. Bolan felt a jolt through every bone in his body as he struck the ground in the controlled crash landing of a heavily loaded military parachutist. He did a forward roll and came to a stop. Everything seemed to be in one piece. He was down and safe.

No time to celebrate. First things first. He had to be ready to fight before he worried about anything else. He reached for the nylon weapons case under his left arm, snapped it open and pulled out his dull-black M-4 Ranger carbine, the deadly, shorter and lighter version of the M-16 rifle. There was a round in the chamber, and a full 30-round magazine was inserted in the receiver. Bolan flicked the carbine's selector switch to automatic and slipped a 40 mm high-explosive grenade into the M-203 grenade launcher clipped under its barrel. Now he was ready to fight if he had to. He would worry about getting out of his parachute harness when he was sure the landing zone was secure.

He saw a flicker of motion through his night-vision goggles. A tall, strangely dressed young woman was crouching in a cluster of scrubby bushes fifty feet away. She held a pistol ready in one hand and a flashlight in the other. It certainly looked as if she had to be his contact, but he had better make sure. He dropped to a prone position and covered her with his M-4 carbine. He kept his finger in the trigger guard, but he was careful not touch his trigger. It would be a tragedy if he accidentally shot his Free Papua Movement contact. The only thing worse would be if she accidentally shot him.

Bolan heard a soft, sighing noise as McCarter glided in to a perfect stand-up landing. There was enough dim moonlight that the woman saw McCarter, too. She pivoted toward him, holding her pistol steady in both hands.

"Wombat!" Bolan whispered.

"Boomerang," the woman responded.

The Executioner felt the tension drain away. They had done it. They were down in one piece and in the right place.

CHAPTER FIVE

Mack Bolan stared at the woman. She was dressed in a thick cloth skirt worn remarkably low on her hips. She had something that looked like a woven cargo net over her head and shoulders. She wore nothing else. He couldn't tell what color her skin and hair were through his night-vision goggles, but she looked nothing at all like the photograph of the tall, blond Dutch woman he had been shown at the briefing. As he watched, she lifted one side of her strange skirt and slipped her pistol into a holster strapped to the inside of her right thigh.

She moved slowly toward the two men, keeping both hands in front of her, palms up to show that her hands were empty. She stared at Bolan and McCarter. Dressed in their dull black jumpsuits, wearing their night-vision goggles and festooned with weapons, they weren't a reassuring sight.

"Belasko?" she asked tentatively.

Bolan smiled. She had to be from the Free Papua Movement. No one else in Western New Guinea would know that name.

"I'm Belasko. You are Marie Van Heyn?"

"No, I am not Marie," the woman said quickly. "My name is Lahka. I am a Dani, and I am with the FPM. Marie has been captured. Listen to me, we are in great danger here. We must leave at once. Indonesian soldiers may come here at any minute. They are very bad men. They will kill you on sight if they find you here. Let us go quickly."

She spoke English with a strange accent, but Bolan had no trouble understanding her. He could hear the urgency in her voice. She obviously believed what she was saying, but the soldier wasn't going to be stampeded into sudden action until he understood the situation a little better.

He turned to McCarter. "Contact the plane. Tell them to drop the equipment canisters now. Then cover the way into this place. The lady says we may have company, Indonesian soldiers in a bad mood."

McCarter spoke quickly into his radio, slipped out of his parachute harness and pulled his silenced 9 mm Sterling submachine gun from its padded nylon scabbard.

Bolan turned back to Lahka. "We can't leave here for a few minutes. The plane is dropping some equipment we have to have. I want you to tell me exactly what happened to Marie Van Heyn."

Lahka took a deep breath. "Very well. Marie led a party of five men from my village. I work for Marie at her mission station. I am not a Christian, but it provides excellent cover for our work for the FPM. Marie is very clever. She always tries to take precautions. She asked me to follow two hundred meters behind the main party. If anything happened, I was to hide and then come here and meet you. Marie and her party were ambushed by Indonesian soldiers who opened fire without warning. They were all killed or captured."

"How do you know Marie is still alive?" Bolan asked.

"They did not want to kill her. They have suspected her of helping the FPM for a long time. They would want to take her alive. Besides, they had already started to beat her before I left. I could hear her screaming. That is why we must leave here. Marie will try to hold out as long as she can. She is not a coward, but they do awful things to women. She will tell them everything they want to know in the end."

"You're sure it was the army, not the police?"

"Of course I am sure," Lahka said curtly. "I do not make stupid mistakes. They were KOPASSUS, special elite troops, about a dozen of them. They used flashlights after the ambush. I saw their orange berets with the gold eagle badge."

Bolan nodded. Lahka sounded as if she knew what she was talking about.

Now for the important question.

"How were they armed?"

"No heavy weapons, but they all had automatic rifles, American M-16s, and some had pistols and grenades."

Lahka had just gone up in Bolan's estimation. Despite her strange costume, she seemed to understand what was important, who the enemy was, how many there were and how they were armed. He began to think rapidly. A rescue wouldn't be easy. Perhaps they could do it if they had the advantage of surprise, but a failure would jeopardize the entire mission. Could he justify taking that risk?

"What does Marie Van Heyn know?" he asked. That was the critical question. If the Indonesian commandos made her talk, what would they find out?

"She knows that two Americans are coming, and that you are looking for something very important to the United States here in the Baliem Valley. Of course, she also knows the location of the landing zone. She said you are bringing us forty automatic rifles in return for our help. I do not see them. Where are they?"

"Heads up, incoming!" McCarter said suddenly.

Bolan looked up. Two big, black parachutes were gliding down through the dark, homing in on the infrared pulses from the beacon.

"Here they are now," he said.

Lahka jumped as she heard two thuds behind her. The two heavy equipment canisters struck the ground a few feet from the beacon. Their black nylon parachutes collapsed with a soft sighing sound.

McCarter moved rapidly to the canister marked with a single narrow white band. He unfastened the cover and looked quickly inside. He grinned and gave Bolan a quick thumbs-up. The contents of their canister were intact. They could live and fight for days with the supplies in the canister, and most important of all, it held their satellite communications radios. Once they were set up, they would be in direct contact with Hal Brognola and Barbara Price at Stony Man.

Bolan led Lahka to the second canister. A dim, battery-operated light came on as he opened the lid.

"Here you are. Forty automatic rifles with spare magazines, ammunition and web equipment, as promised."

The rifles were AKS-47s, the version with a folding metal stock. They had seen some use, but they were all in excellent condition. Lahka's eyes sparkled as she pulled one of the rifles out of the canister and examined it carefully.

"Very good. You are a big man. You kept your promise. These are excellent rifles. My brother, Wejak, has a rifle like this. He says rifles are for warriors and pistols are for women, but he has let me shoot his a few times." She pulled back the AKS-47's bolt and chambered a round, smiled and set the selector lever on safe.

The woman was telling the truth. She had obviously handled an AK-47 before. Bolan reached inside the canister and pulled out a web belt with three spare magazine pouches attached and handed it to her.

"Here, take these and keep the rifle. It'll be a hell of a lot better than your pistol if the Indonesian commandos show up."

Lahka beamed. Bolan had made a friend for life.

"You are a big man," she said. Bolan could hear the admiration in her voice. "You give good gifts."

"What does a 'big man' mean?" he asked.

"It is the finest thing you can call a Dani man. A big man is a great warrior who kills many enemies and is a great hunter of wild boars. He is a leader in his tribe. He gives fine gifts and has many wives and many other women. Of course, it is better if he does all of these things."

Lahka strapped on the web belt and spare AKS-47 magazine pouches.

Bolan pointed toward McCarter. "His name is David," the Executioner said, omitting the surname for reasons of security. "Tell him that I want to see him. You keep watch on the trail. If anyone comes, don't shoot. Come and tell me."

Lahka nodded and was gone.

McCarter was there in half a minute. "That ferocious young lady says the big man wants to see me immediately. I presume that she means you, Mack. You may not have been wise to give her that rifle. She told me she can hardly wait to kill Indonesian commandos."

"I did the right thing. She says a dozen of them are a few miles away. They ambushed the FPM party that was coming to meet us. If we're going to take them on, we'll need all the firepower we can get."

McCarter listened quietly while Bolan told him everything Lahka had said.

"So, we have two choices, as I see it. Try to rescue the Van Heyn woman, or strike out on our own. I don't think Lahka would be willing to go with us if we do that. She seems determined to rescue the Dutch woman and get the rifles we brought to the FPM. What do you think?"

McCarter was silent for a moment.

"Lahka's right about one thing. The Indonesians torture military and political prisoners routinely. They'll torture the Van Heyn woman until she breaks. The fact that she is a woman won't make any difference. It'll probably make it worse. Once she talks, they'll be after us like a shot. They'll know about this place and about the rifles. She can't tell them what our mission is because she doesn't know, but she does knows two Americans are coming. And a patrol that size will have a radio. Once they tell their headquarters we're here, the whole Baliem Valley will be swarming with patrols, all looking for us.''

Bolan nodded somberly. He didn't like it, but as usual, McCarter made sense.

"One other thing. With Marie Van Heyn and Lahka with us, we can probably get help from the Dani. Without them, I don't think there is one chance in a million of that.''

"All right," Bolan said. "I'm convinced. What can you tell me about these Indonesian special commando troops?''

"KOPASSUS? I've fought them when I did an exchange tour with the Australians. The Indonesians have a lot of different special-forces troops. These are some of the best. They're well trained and tough fighters, but they aren't really special-operations troops as we know them. They're more like elite combat troops that the Indonesian government uses to put down dissension. We can probably surprise them if we're lucky, but we had better expect a serious fight when the shooting starts.''

Bolan nodded. Surprise was absolutely essential if they were going to stand a chance. Bolan made up his mind. He didn't know Marie Van Heyn, but she was being tortured and perhaps killed because she was a part of his mission. As he saw things, that made her part of his team. He had never left a man or woman on his team behind, and he wasn't about to start now. He signaled to Lahka, and she joined them with a look of eager anticipation.

"All right, Lahka, David and I are going to rescue Marie and her party. You stay here and guard things. If we're not back in four hours, you—''

"No!" Lahka said fiercely. "My father was a chief and a big man. I am a Dani! I will not sit here like an old woman while you go to kill my enemies and rescue my friends!"

McCarter shook his head. "She certainly is an obstinate young lady. Perhaps we should tie her up and leave her here."

The Briton heard the distinctive sound of a safety lever being pushed into the firing position.

"On the other hand, she knows the terrain and we don't," McCarter said smoothly. "We may need all the firepower we can get. Perhaps it would be best if we take her along."

"All right," Bolan said, "let's all go pay a call on KOPASSUS."

CHAPTER SIX

They had been moving steadily through the darkness for half an hour when Lahka raised her hand to signal Bolan and McCarter to halt. The Executioner admired her woodcraft. The Dani woman was as noiseless as a ghost as she moved through the valley. She crept silently to Bolan's side.

"We are almost there," she said softly. "Listen."

Bolan listened intently. At first he heard nothing except an occasional birdcall and the chirping of insects. Then a woman screamed, a long, hoarse, agonized shriek of pain that echoed in the dark. It was quiet for a few seconds, then the woman screamed again.

The soldier could hear the fury in Lahka's voice.

"That is Marie. She is a strong woman. They are doing something very bad to her to make her scream like that. Let us go quickly!"

"Take it easy. It won't do her any good if we rush in without a plan and get ourselves killed."

Lahka didn't like what Bolan said, but she didn't argue. He turned to McCarter, who was waiting quietly with his silenced 9 mm Sterling submachine gun in his hands.

"Go around to the right and get behind them. Stay in the woods until you find a good firing position.

When I open fire, you hit them from behind. How long will it take for you to get in position?"

"Give me five minutes."

Bolan watched as the Briton slipped into the trees, then he turned to Lahka. "Let's go. I want to get as close to their camp as I can and still stay in the trees. Remember, no shooting until I give the word."

"I understand," she said quietly.

Bolan looked at her closely. He didn't know if the woman had ever been in combat, but she seemed ready to fight. It wasn't her courage that worried him, but the thought that she might make some simple mistake and get them all killed. Well, it was up to him to see that she didn't.

Lahka moved silently ahead in the dark. She was a strange sight in her heavy cloth skirt and her AKS-47. He watched as she proceeded about thirty yards and dropped quietly to the ground. She stared ahead for a minute, then signaled him to move forward.

Slowly, carefully Bolan crawled to the edge of the trees and looked down the shallow slope into a small clearing. The camp fire was about forty yards away. He didn't need his night-vision goggles to see what was going on. The Indonesian commandos had built a good-sized fire, and its flickering light illuminated the area quite well. The large fire confirmed McCarter's estimation that they were tough men and hard fighters, but had grown overconfident from years of fighting people whose weapons and training were much worse than their own.

He scanned the area carefully, trying to locate every man. He had a minute or two to wait. McCarter would be moving silently through the trees to the far side of the clearing. Once he was in position, they could catch the Indonesian commandos in a cross fire. He counted carefully. Eleven Indonesians, seven by the fire, two watching the trail at the far side of the clearing and two more only thirty yards away, guarding the nearby trail. He could see their orange berets clearly. Bolan knew that special uniforms and insignia were important to military morale, but it wasn't a good decision to wear their bright orange berets out in the bush.

Lahka eased herself down beside Bolan. She held her AKS-47 ready for action, a 30-round magazine inserted, the metal stock unfolded and locked in place and the safety-selector lever set on safe. She touched Bolan's shoulder and pointed. He looked closely, past the flickering flames of the fire. Lahka was right. He could see five or six men lying on the ground. One of them was wearing a camouflaged uniform and military boots. Someone had thrown a poncho over him. The others were dark skinned. They seemed to be wearing almost nothing.

"Dani," Lahka whispered in his ear.

Bolan touched one finger to her lips. "Don't whisper," he said very softly. "The sound carries. Just speak very softly."

A tall soldier who seemed to be in command shouted an order. Two of his men dragged a naked blond woman and held her helpless in front of him. The officer slapped her hard across the face and spoke to her. His voice carried clearly, but Bolan couldn't understand what he was saying. Lahka had to understand Indonesian.

"What is he saying?" he asked very softly.

"He says she is a filthy, native-loving, Dutch whore. He says they have just been playing with her up till now. If she does not tell him everything he wants to know, he will really hurt her."

Marie Van Heyn didn't look as if they had just been playing with her. Her hands were tied behind her back, and her pale white skin was mottled with welts and bruises. She dropped to her knees, groveling and moaning softly.

"She says, 'Please! Please, do not hurt me any more! I am only a missionary. I am loyal to the government. I know nothing to tell you.'"

She stopped for a second and stared at Bolan. He could see the fury in her face.

"She cannot hold out much longer. They are heating a bayonet in the fire. Let us kill them now!"

Bolan felt the same way. "As soon as David is in position. Are you ready?"

Lahka nodded. The Executioner pointed to the two men guarding the trail.

"You take those two. Remember, semiautomatic fire only, and don't shoot until I give the signal."

The woman nodded again. She shifted position silently to get a better angle of fire at the two trail guards. Bolan hoped she really understood. This wasn't the time or the place for lectures.

He looked at his watch. Five minutes had gone by. McCarter should be in position by now. He stared at the trees at the far edge of the clearing through his night-vision binoculars. He saw three brief flashes of light, two long, one short. McCarter was using a small infrared flashlight. Its beam was invisible to the naked eye, but the night-vision binoculars showed it clearly. The Briton was in position and ready to fire.

Bolan put his binoculars away and aimed his M-4 carbine at the group by the fire. Damn it! Two Indonesian commandos had dragged Marie Van Heyn close to the fire, holding her by her arms in front of the tall officer. She cringed as he spoke to her in a cruel, gloating tone of voice. It didn't matter what he was saying. She was in the middle of the group, directly in Bolan's line of fire. As long as she was there, he didn't dare shoot.

Lahka understood. She touched Bolan's shoulder lightly in some sort of signal, but he wasn't sure what she meant. She took a deep breath and suddenly shouted a long, shrill, undulating cry. Bolan's blood froze, but the Indonesians paid no attention. It sounded just like another big bird, calling out in the night.

"That is the *jokoik,* the Dani war cry. Now Marie knows we are here," Lahka said quietly. "She is very smart. You will see, she will make an opening for us."

Bolan certainly hoped so. He scanned the group of men around the fire. He could pick off one or two men at the edge of the group, but he still couldn't fire at the officer or the two men holding the woman's arms without taking a serious chance of hitting her.

The tall officer took the bayonet from the fire. Its tip was glowing orange. Van Heyn screamed wildly as he touched it to the inside of her left thigh for two seconds and then sadistically did it again. He said something to her as he slowly brought the tip of the bayonet close to her face. The woman shrieked wildly. The men holding her arms had relaxed their grip a bit.

She jerked convulsively and threw herself down on her knees. The commando officer gasped a handful of her long blond hair and held her face motionless as he slowly brought the glowing tip of the bayonet closer and closer to her face.

He said something to her, and his men laughed.

Bolan did not care what he was saying. Van Heyn had given him a clear line of fire. He placed the front sight of his M-4 carbine on the commando officer's chest.

"Ready now, five, four—" Bolan said softly.

Clack! He heard a sound that froze his blood. Lahka had pushed the safety-selector lever of her AKS-47 to the firing position. She had forgotten the noise it made, and the sound rang out in the dark. No experienced soldier needed to be told what that sound meant. For a fraction of a second, the Indonesian commandos were frozen by surprise. Then they exploded into action.

As fast as they moved, Bolan and McCarter were faster. The commando officer had released the blond woman's hair and started to throw himself to one side. Instinctively, almost without conscious thought, Bolan squeezed the M-4's trigger. The deadly little carbine spit three high-velocity 5.56 mm bullets in a quarter of a second. They tore through the officer's chest, and he went down. The blond woman threw herself to the ground. The Indonesian commandos grouped around the camp fire dived desperately for cover. Bolan's thumb flicked his selector switch to full automatic, and he swept the clearing with four controlled bursts as fast as he could fire them.

A red dot seemed to flash toward the Indonesians. Bolan had used the old soldier's trick of making the last round in his magazine a tracer. He reached quickly for a fresh magazine. He could hear Lahka's AKS-47 firing rapidly. Someone fired from the clearing, an M-16 by the shape of the muzzle-flash. A deadly swarm of high-velocity, full-metal-jacketed bullets shrieked through the trees over Bolan's head. Bark and splinters flew. If the Executioner had been standing, he would have been a dead man.

He snapped in a fresh 30-round magazine, fired a quick burst and rolled to his right. A burst of M-16 bullets tore into his former position. They were firing at his muzzle-flash. Two could play at that game. Bolan placed his sights on the edge of the trees nearest the fire. He saw the dancing yellow flash of an M-16 as two long bursts raked the trees over his head. The big American didn't believe in the spray-and-pray theory of combat. He took half a second to align his sights and squeezed the carbine's trigger. The M-16 stopped firing abruptly.

Lahka was firing steadily. He could hear the lower-pitched blast of her AKS-47 as she dueled with the two commandos guarding the trail. The woman shrieked something Bolan couldn't understand. He hoped she wasn't hit, but he couldn't spare half a second to check. He saw sudden motion in front of him. The Indonesians were moving, coming up the slope straight for him. He could see four. Two were raking the trees with assault fire as they charged. The other two seemed to be empty-handed, but Bolan knew better. His blood froze. Grenades.

He swung his sights on one enemy and fired a quick burst. The man staggered, but he kept on coming. Bolan fired again, and his target went down. The two men with M-16s advanced, firing steadily as they charged. Yellow tracers streaked by Bolan's head. He fired back. Suddenly the two commandos with the assault rifles dropped to the ground. The third man's arm swung forward as he threw. Bolan saw a small black object hurtling through the air toward him.

The grenade's blast didn't kill. It was the steel shrapnel that was lethal, and Bolan had no cover. He plastered himself against the ground. The grenade exploded with a muffled boom, and Bolan heard the steel fragments shrieking through the air. He felt a blow as a fragment tore into his body armor, and a giant hand seemed to smash the M-4 carbine out of his hands. He heard Lahka scream, but he had no time to see what had happened to her. The Indonesian commandos leaped to their feet and charged as the grenade's blast faded away.

The Executioner reacted with the reflexes honed in a hundred gun battles. His right hand streaked to his side, and he drew his .44 Magnum Desert Eagle. There was no time to use his sights. He fired as soon as his arm was pointing at the closest commando, shooting twice, with his wrist and elbow locked, as fast as he could pull the weapon's trigger. The Indonesian seemed to slam into a stone wall as the two .44-caliber bullets struck with terrible force. He fell hard and lay still.

Bolan swung the big hand cannon toward the next commando. He was looking down the barrel of the Indonesian's M-16 as his sights came on. They fired together. The Executioner felt something smash repeatedly into his chest, like three incredibly fast jabs from a well-trained boxer. The Indonesian staggered and fell. He had taken two .44 Magnum hollowpoints through the chest, and was effectively taken out of the play.

The last Indonesian was racing forward. He didn't dare use grenades at point-blank range, but he had drawn a large black automatic pistol. Bolan tried to bring the Desert Eagle into target acquisition, but he knew he wasn't going to make it before the charging commando fired.

The Indonesian suddenly seemed to stumble and fall, his body jerking and twitching as he fell. McCarter was standing twenty feet behind the gunner, his Sterling up and searching for other targets. McCarter smiled grimly as he slipped a fresh magazine into his weapon.

"Sorry to have poached your last target, mate, but I thought your pistol just might be empty."

"That's all right," Bolan said. "I don't want to be greedy. What's the situation?"

"The Indonesians are all dead or seriously wounded. Our friends are all right. What about you? Are you hit?"

Bolan got slowly to his feet. A grenade fragment was protruding from his body armor, and he could see the bases of three 5.56 mm bullets in the middle of his chest, stopped by the Kevlar and the metal trauma plate of his body armor. He was hit but not hurt.

"I'm all right," he said as he snapped a fresh magazine into the Desert Eagle and slipped it back into his holster. He saw his M-4 carbine lying on the ground a few feet away. He picked it up and examined it closely. Grenade fragments had ripped into the barrel of the grenade launcher, which was clipped under the carbine's barrel. He would worry about that later. He reloaded the carbine and looked around. Where was Lahka?

He heard the dull crack of an AK-47 firing a single shot. He whirled in that direction, ready to fire. Lahka had been down on the trail below. Now she came back to Bolan and McCarter. Blood was trickling down her left side, but she was ecstatic. She had an M-16 rifle slung over each shoulder. McCarter unsnapped his first-aid kit and checked her wound.

"It's just a flesh wound in the arm. You'll be all right," he said as he reached for a bandage.

Lahka held out her arm, but she wasn't really paying any attention to McCarter.

"Dead birds," she said. Her eyes were shining.

"I beg your pardon?" McCarter said.

"Dead birds. I killed them both. These are their weapons. The Dani call the weapons of enemy warriors they have killed 'dead birds.' There is no finer trophy than that. My clan will be proud of me!"

McCarter smiled and patted her on the shoulder. "We're certainly proud of you, Lahka, and I'm sure Marie will be, too. You did your duty. No doubt of that."

Lahka smiled as the light of battle faded from her eyes. She suddenly looked concerned. "Marie! How is Marie?" Lahka went quickly to the fire.

Marie Van Heyn was still lying on the ground by the fire. Her hands were bound behind her back. Lahka lifted one side of her skirt and drew a wicked-looking, double-edged knife from a sheath strapped to her thigh. She cut the woman's hands free and helped her to her feet while McCarter freed the four Dani men.

Van Heyn threw her arms around Lahka.

"Thank God you came back, Lahka. I kept telling myself that if I just held on a little longer, you would come back."

"We killed them all!" Lahka said proudly. "Belasko and David and I killed them all, but are you all right?"

Van Heyn smiled. "I'm all right, and I'm glad to meet our friends."

Bolan admired her courage, but she certainly didn't look all right. Her body was patterned with welts and bruises, and he could see several angry red burns where the Indonesian officer had sadistically applied the red-hot bayonet.

The woman suddenly realized she was standing there naked talking to two strange men.

"Where are my clothes?" she asked quickly.

McCarter pointed to a pile of clothes and a backpack near the fire. "I believe those are yours," he said politely.

As the woman passed the commando officer, he suddenly groaned. Bolan's bullets had taken him low and in the right side of his chest. He had been bleeding heavily, but he wasn't dead yet. Van Heyn glared at him and walked stiff legged to her pile of clothes. She took something from her pack and walked back to the Indonesian officer. The firelight gleamed from a slender barreled 9 mm Luger automatic. She said something in Dutch, which Bolan didn't understand, but it sizzled. She pointed the pistol at the officer's head and pulled the trigger twice.

Bolan and McCarter stared at her.

"Perhaps I'm not a good Christian," she said calmly, "but I cannot forgive him for what he did to me."

McCarter nodded. "Well, I think all accounts are paid."

Bolan had no comment. If he had been in Marie Van Heyn's place, he would have done the same. "Let's get the hell out of here," he said.

THEY PUSHED ON STEADILY through the night. Bolan set a fast pace. He knew that daylight was certain to bring pursuit. He could feel it in his bones. No elite unit in the world would lose a dozen men without making an all-out effort to get the people who had killed them. If the Indonesians had aircraft or helicopters, Bolan and his team might not be able to move fast during the day. It was important that they get away from the battle zone as soon as possible.

Bolan knew that was the right thing to do, but it was hard going. He and McCarter were weighed down by their weapons, ammunition and survival gear, but they weren't about to leave any of it behind. The Dani seemed tireless. Two of them had left to secure the rifles, but Lahka and the other two men had stayed with the party. Marie Van Heyn was having a hard time keeping up. The sadistic beating she had received had taken a lot out of her. Although allowing one of the Dani men to carry her pack, she had kept struggling on. Bolan didn't think she was going to last much longer. She was beginning to stagger.

He was about to call a halt when one of the Dani men picked her up and carried her. Van Heyn protested, but he paid no attention. He carried her easily, and she didn't seem to slow him at all. The Dani all seemed to be incredibly strong and have unlimited endurance.

Bolan could feel fatigue burning in every muscle of his body. He and McCarter had had little rest and no sleep for twenty-four hours. It was beginning to take its toll. He glanced at the Briton. He was keeping up, marching along grimly, putting one foot in front of the other. McCarter believed in the old SAS rule of never being the first man to drop out on a forced march. He would keep going until he collapsed.

Lahka was leading the way. She stopped suddenly when someone ahead of her hissed a challenge in a language Bolan didn't know. Lahka answered and signaled them to move ahead. He followed her out into a clearing surrounded by trees. He looked around quickly. There were a dozen Dani sitting patiently by a small fire. He could see the equipment canisters and the parachutes lying nearby. They were back at the drop zone.

Van Heyn exchanged a few quick sentences with one of the Dani.

"Husuk is in command of this group. They came for the rifles. He has scouts out. We can rest here for a while, but not too long. That patrol had a radio. When they do not check in in a few hours, people will be looking for them."

Bolan nodded and slipped out of his pack straps with a sigh of relief and leaned back against a tree trunk. He loosened the web belt that carried his spare magazines and his canteen, but he didn't take it off.

Van Heyn slumped to the ground, moaning softly. She was obviously still feeling a lot of pain. Bolan opened his first-aid kit and started to redress the blood-soaked bandages.

"That's the best I can do," he said as he finished. "You really ought to see a doctor."

The woman grimaced. "I am a doctor. Don't worry, I will live."

Lahka came by and handed each of them something wrapped in palm leaves. It looked like some kind of meat cooked in a sauce. Bolan stared at it suspiciously.

"I don't feel hungry," he said.

Van Heyn looked at him and laughed. "Go ahead and eat it. It is roast pork. The Dani live on pork and sweet potatoes. When they give you roast pork, they are treating you as an honored guest. Eat it and smile. Lahka cooked it. She will be very insulted if she thinks you do not like it."

Bolan noticed that Lahka was looking at him and frowning. He took a bite of the pork and smiled. The smoked meat was surprisingly good.

Lahka smiled. "That is all the food I have with me, but if you can come to my village, we will cook you a big feast and celebrate killing our enemies."

She glanced at McCarter, who immediately took a bite of his portion and smiled.

"We need to talk," Bolan said to Van Heyn. "We need to make some plans and get moving."

She nodded. "You are right. I will get Wejak."

Bolan didn't want to be impolite, but he didn't want a committee meeting. "You're in command," he said quietly. "Let's settle it between us."

The woman looked startled. "I cannot do that," she said quickly. "I am not the commander here. A woman cannot lead warriors. Wejak is in command."

It was Bolan's turn to look startled. "The Australians said you were the contact. Are you telling me you're not a member of the FPM?"

"Of course I am a member of the FPM. My parents were Dutch, but I was born here. I have lived here all my life. This is my country, and I want the Indonesians out of it. I deal with the Australians because they can accept a white European woman far easier than a Dani. Many of them would say Wejak and Lahka are savages. So I am your contact, but Wejak is in command. He is a famous warrior. People are willing to follow him."

She turned to Lahka. "Go bring your brother. He and Belasko must talk."

Lahka was back in a flash, smiling proudly. "This is my brother. He is a big man and a great warrior. Wejak, this is Belasko. He, too, is a great warrior, and this is David. He fights at Belasko's side."

Wejak extended his hand and smiled. He was an imposing sight in the early-morning light. Like Lahka and the other Dani, he was tall and had curly black hair and brown skin. His face radiated strength and quiet authority. He had what an American soldier would have called command presence. Bolan had no trouble believing he was the FPM leader. Despite his great strength, he had an amazingly gentle handshake.

Bolan explained the mission carefully. Wejak, Lahka and Van Heyn listened quietly as he finished. "So we need to locate the plane, go there, destroy it and rescue the crew if they are still alive. We would appreciate all the help you can give us."

Wejak shook his head. "No, I cannot take my people there. If many people travel together, the Indonesians will see them. They have airplanes and helicopters with guns. We cannot fight them with rifles."

Lahka said something quickly in the Dani language.

"Lahka reminds me that you fought to save me and Marie from the Indonesians. She is right. That is a debt of honor. It must be paid. I will not take my men, but I will guide you there."

Lahka spoke again, and Van Heyn added something.

"They say that they, too, have a debt of honor. They wish to go also. Very well. Rest for an hour. We will go south toward the river then."

Bolan nodded and looked over his M-4 carbine. The basic weapon was intact, but the barrel of the M-203 grenade launcher was torn and dented with bullet holes. It would never fire again. It was a good thing he had brought a spare. He went over to the equipment canister and pulled out the spare carbine, checked it carefully and snapped in a 30-round magazine. The original carbine seemed to be in good shape. Perhaps he would give it to the FPM.

He went back to McCarter, who was slipping 9 mm cartridges into the spare magazines for his Sterling. Bolan leaned back against the tree trunk and closed his eyes, but there was no rest to be had. Someone coughed politely, and he opened his eyes.

"I am sorry to bother you," Van Heyn said quietly, "but there is a small problem. Wejak's men say that there are only thirty-nine rifles. We were promised forty. The Dani take such promises very literally. Do you have another rifle for them?"

"Yes, there are forty rifles, and you can have all the M-16s the Indonesians were carrying. Does that satisfy you?"

"You are a big man, Belasko. You give good gifts. I do not wish to seem greedy," Wejak said, "but I must have all the rifles that were promised. They must not think I am the kind of leader who does not see that promises are kept."

Bolan sighed. One AKS-47 didn't seem like a big deal to him, but he wasn't a guerrilla leader wondering where his next weapons were going to come from. Besides, he needed Wejak's cooperation. This was no time to quarrel over a small point.

"Lahka has the rifle. I loaned it to her. If that was wrong, I'm sorry. I don't know your ways."

Wejak sighed. He had the look of a man who was bracing himself for trouble.

He motioned to Van Heyn and pointed to Lahka, who was happily talking to McCarter.

The Dutch woman went to Lahka and said a few sentences in Dani. All the happiness went out of Lahka's voice. She and Van Heyn exchanged a few more words. Lahka's voice grew louder and louder. She stood and followed the woman back to Bolan and Wejak. Anger showed in every movement of her body. The big American hoped he hadn't violated some sacred Dani taboo. Lahka was a warlike sight. She had a black M-16 rifle slung over each shoulder, the AKS-47 in her hands and an automatic pistol on a belt around her waist.

Wejak spoke to her in Dani, and she replied angrily.

Her brother switched to English and spoke to Bolan. "Lahka says you gave her the AKS-47."

"He did!" Lahka snapped. "He said it would be much better against the Indonesians than the pistol Marie gave me."

Wejak shook his head. "I am sure that was so, but the rifle was not his to give. It belongs to the FPM. You cannot keep it."

Lahka glared at her brother. "Here. You are the leader. Take it!" she snarled, and thrust the rifle into his hands.

Wejak stared at the two M-16s slung over Lahka's shoulders. "What are these?" he asked softly.

"Dead birds, Wejak," Lahka said bitterly. "I killed two Indonesians. These are their weapons." She pointed to the bandage on her arm. "I shed my blood to get these rifles. Do you want to take them, too?"

Wejak smiled. "Truly, Lahka, you killed two? I am proud of you, sister, and our clan will be proud of you, but you cannot keep them. Rifles are for warriors, not for women. We have more men willing to fight than rifles. It cannot be said that I played favorites and gave my sister a rifle when there are warriors waiting for weapons. Still, you must have a trophy. You may keep the pistol."

"You are the leader, Wejak," Lahka said, and gave him the two M-16s. She was on the verge of crying, and that made her furious.

Bolan held up the M-4 carbine he had used against the Indonesians.

"This is my rifle," he said.

Wejak nodded. "It is yours, Belasko. No one questions that."

"Good. Then I want to give it to Lahka. She fought at my side. I give it to her to keep and remember the fight tonight. Do you object?"

"No, Belasko, it is your rifle. You may give it to anyone you please." He smiled at Bolan. "You are a big man. You give good gifts."

Lahka beamed as Bolan handed her the deadly little weapon. She took an oily cloth from her carrying net and began to wipe her carbine lovingly.

Wejak looked at her and sighed softly. "She is a good girl," he said, "but I am worried about her. She is almost twenty-four. That is very old for a girl not to be married. You can see that she is strong and smart, and she is fierce. Her sons will be great warriors, but she needs a strong husband. Now that our father is dead, I am the head of our family. It is up to me to find her one."

Wejak stopped and looked at Bolan speculatively. "Do you need another wife? Her bride price would be quite reasonable, say, twenty-five pigs."

Lahka looked demurely at her bare feet. A well-bred young woman didn't participate in a discussion of her bride-price.

Van Heyn smiled wickedly. "I do not think our friend owns any pigs, Wejak, but I will help him buy some. A good pig costs twenty thousand rupiahs, Belasko. If you don't have five hundred thousand rupiahs with you, I can loan you the money."

Bolan felt that he was tiptoeing through a mine field. He chose his words very carefully. "Lahka is a wonderful girl, Wejak, and twenty-five pigs is a fair bride-price. My work makes me travel all the time. I have no home, so I have no wives. I couldn't take proper care of them."

He glanced around quickly. Wejak didn't seem offended, and Lahka was still beaming as she polished her carbine. Bolan didn't think Lahka was in any great hurry to get married and settle down.

McCarter had been listening quietly with a nasty smile on his face. "Are you sure you won't change your mind, mate? It's about time you stopped all this running about and settled down. I'm sure you would make Lahka a good husband. I will be happy to be the best man and I—"

The Briton suddenly stopped and gestured for everyone to stay quiet.

Bolan listened intently. All he heard were birdcalls and the whine of insects, but he had learned long ago that McCarter had remarkably keen hearing. Then he heard it—the distant sound of helicopter rotors.

"Everybody under cover," Bolan snapped as the sound of the rotors grew steadily louder. Everyone faded into the edge of the trees. The soldier took a quick look around, thankful that the parachutes and equipment containers had been dragged back under the trees.

The sound of the helicopter grew louder. It was flying rapidly back along the trail, and the pilot didn't seem to be searching. Bolan felt the tension fade away as the helicopter passed by and continued back along the trail.

They hadn't been detected. People weren't searching for them yet, but he knew they soon would be. He turned to McCarter and Wejak.

"Time to go."

CHAPTER SEVEN

Captain Ahmed Thanrin watched the Indonesian army Bell 205 helicopter as it touched down carefully. Major Selim Hatta, the area military commander, was on board, and the major wasn't a man who tolerated failure. Thanrin wasn't looking forward to the next half hour. He hadn't personally led the lost patrol, but the men in it had been under his command, and this was his area of responsibility. Twelve valuable men and their weapons had been lost to the FPM. That wasn't going to be easy to explain.

He snapped to attention and saluted smartly as Hatta stalked up and glared around the scene of the disaster. The major was a formidable figure in his orange beret and camouflaged uniform. He was short and stocky, with a look of deadly menace about him. Rumor said he had killed three men with his bare hands. Thanrin believed it.

Hatta returned his salute with a cold stare. "Report," he demanded curtly.

Quickly Thanrin told the major everything he knew. "I believe Lieutenant Wiwoho's patrol made contact with a group of FPM guerrillas. They killed one, a Dani. His body is over there. He may have captured others. He camped here, probably to interrogate his prisoners. It looks as if he was then attacked by a large party of FPM guerrillas. It appears that he was heavily outnumbered. He and all his men were killed.''

Hatta glared. ''If there is a large, heavily armed FPM party in this area, there has been a total failure by our intelligence people.''

Thanrin agreed. He would be much happier if Hatta's anger was focused on the intelligence section rather than on him.

''Show me everything,'' he ordered. ''Sergeant Awang, follow me.''

A small, thin man seemed to appear from nowhere. Awang was the battalion tracker, a Dyak from the Indonesian part of Borneo. Once he had hunted deer, pigs and wild oxen in the jungles of East Borneo. Now he had traded his bow and spears for an M-16 rifle, and he hunted men for Major Hatta. Some of the men swore Awang was a headhunter and a cannibal, but none of the commandos could equal his skill as a scout or a tracker.

Thanrin led the way to the smoldering remains of the large fire. Wiwoho's body lay sprawled next to the ashes. Hatta rolled him over, his angry expression turning to one of cold fury.

''He was wounded here, in the side. Then someone shot him twice in the head at point-blank range. See the powder burns? He was not killed in battle. This was an execution. I will make the filthy savages pay for that.''

Awang had been looking at the soft, damp ground. He diffidently touched Hatta's sleeve and pointed at a group of tracks around the ashes of the fire.

''There were two, possibly three women here, sir. See, two sets of barefoot tracks, one larger than the other. Here are the prints of a woman wearing boots, but they may have been made by the woman with the smaller feet.''

"How do you know they were women?'' Thermion asked skeptically. He came from the teeming capital city of Djakarta. Awang's tracking skills were black magic as far as he was concerned. "Perhaps the tracks were made by men with small feet.''

Awang sighed. Captain Thanrin wasn't a bad officer, but like so many Indonesian soldiers, he was almost useless in the woods.

"Men do not walk the same way as women, Captain,'' he said tactfully. He stared at the ground. "Yes, two women. Look here, the woman with the smaller feet walked over here. I think she was the one who shot the lieutenant. Then she put on her boots and she walked away.''

He studied the ground carefully again, making a slow circle around the ashes of the fire.

He stopped and stared. "Look here, Major, men's tracks, men wearing boots.''

Hatta shook his head impatiently. "There are boot tracks everywhere, Awang. All our men were wearing boots.''

Awang smiled. The major was clever, but he didn't have Awang's skill when it came to tracking.

"You are right, Major,'' he said politely, "but look again. See the marks of the heels and soles? These are not our army's issue boots. These tracks were made by big men, bigger than any of our men, probably Europeans. And look how deep the tracks are, Major. They were carrying heavy loads. I would say that they were soldiers.''

Hatta stared at the tracks. He could see that his sergeant was right. This was bad. If the Australians had decided to give large-scale aid to the FPM and were sending their SAS into Western New Guinea, a real crisis was developing. He would have to tell the high command, and they wouldn't be pleased, but he would say nothing to them until he was sure.

"What else do you see?" he asked quickly.

"Nothing here, but look there," Awang said, pointing to a spot in the trees.

Hatta looked. He saw trees, nothing else.

"Look at the trees themselves. See, there are bullet marks on some of the trunks, and some small branches have been shot away. I think our men were fired on from there. Their bullets struck the trees when they shot back."

He led the way to a spot just inside the tree line. Hatta and Thanrin followed him. The major nodded. The ground was strewn with dozens of brass and steel cartridge cases. Someone had done a lot of shooting here. Awang was right again. The Dyak was worth a platoon in the forest. Thanrin picked up several cases and looked at them intently. He might be useless as a tracker, but he knew and loved guns. It was one of the reasons he had joined the army.

"Two different types of weapons, Major. These steel cases are from the short Russian cartridges. I would say one or more AK-47s or SKS rifles."

Hatta smiled. Thanrin's passion for firearms was sometimes boring, but there were times it was extremely useful.

"What of the others?" he asked.

Thanrin looked at the brass cartridge cases. "Nothing unusual here, Major, these are 5.56 mm rounds, like those we use in our own M-16s. They are—" He stopped suddenly and stared at the cases in his hand.

"Look at this, Major!"

Hatta took one of the cartridge cases and stared at the base. Around the fired primer he saw two letters and two numbers. They meant nothing to him.

"See, Major?" Thanrin said excitedly. "LC 92, made at Lake City Arsenal in 1992. This is American ammunition, recently made."

Hatta felt a cold knot in his stomach. Had the American CIA decided to help the FPM? He wasn't rich, and he had no political influence. This kind of trouble in his area could ruin his chances for promotion.

Thanrin picked up another cartridge case and stared at it. "This is strange, Major, very strange indeed."

Hatta stared at the gleaming brass cartridge case. It was too short to be a rifle case but much too big to be from a pistol.

"It is a .44 Magnum. I have heard about them, but I have never seen one. It is one of the most powerful pistol cartridges in the world. The Americans use them for shooting deer and bear. And look at the rim. See the marks of the extractor? This cartridge was fired from a semiautomatic pistol."

Hatta shook his head. He couldn't imagine anyone using such a large-caliber pistol, but he didn't doubt Captain Thanrin. When it came to guns and ammunition, he was never wrong.

"What do you conclude from this?" he asked.

"These are very dangerous men, sir. They are so skilled that they are allowed to select their own weapons. I do not think they are Australian SAS. I think they are highly trained paramilitary personnel, almost certainly Americans. They will be hard to catch and hard to kill."

Hatta nodded. Thanrin was probably right, but it made no difference. These men were operating in his area and had killed a dozen of his special commandos. He would track them down and kill them, no matter what it cost. He motioned to Thanrin and pointed to his map.

"I will take all the men here and Sergeant Awang and pursue these killers. You take the helicopter back to base. Send out a party to clean up things here, and I want three patrols to be placed here, here and here. That way, we will have them if they turn north or south. The third patrol will be ahead of them if they continue to go east. Brief the men carefully. We want no more disasters. I do not care who these people are, they are to be killed on sight. Do you understand your orders?"

Thanrin saluted smartly. "Yes, sir. I will carry out your orders immediately, but I have one request. These were my men who were killed here. I request your permission to join the pursuit as soon as I have placed the patrols. I would like a chance to kill the men who killed my soldiers."

Hatta smiled. That was the attitude he liked in his officers. Blood for blood.

"Very well, Captain. Use the helicopter to rejoin me. Bring the battalion sniper teams, and bring your fancy English rifle. It may well prove useful."

Thanrin turned and trotted over to the helicopter.

The major moved back toward the clearing. With Thanrin's men and the squad he had brought with him in the helicopter, he would have twenty men. That should be enough to get the job done. The men looked at him expectantly. Should he say a few words to them? No, they had seen the bodies of their dead comrades. That should be enough for special commandos.

"We move out in three minutes," he said curtly. "Sergeant Awang, find their trail for me."

Hatta looked up as he heard the helicopter taking off. It looked like rain, which would be bad. The damp, soft ground made for excellent tracks, but rain would quickly wash them away. It didn't matter. He would find the people who had destroyed his patrol and make them pay.

Awang noticed Hatta's look at the clouds and understood perfectly. He liked the major. They came from different backgrounds, but they saw things alike.

"Do not worry, Major, we will find them even if it rains," he said softly. He smiled, showing his yellow, pointed teeth. He touched the hilt of his Mandau, the spirit sword a Dyak uses to cut off his victims' heads. "And when we find them, we will take their heads."

EIGHTEEN MILES AWAY, Mary Clark lay on her stomach at the edge of a grove of trees. Every muscle in her legs ached and throbbed from the sustained effort of moving five miles as fast as she could walk, carrying fifty pounds of survival gear. The late-morning heat was brutal. Her blue flight suit was stylish and protected her from fire in a crash, but it was a bad choice for a forced march in hot weather.

She took out her binoculars and looked back toward the crash site. Nothing was going on. The site seemed deserted. Clark didn't want to go any farther. She had to be able to see a rescue party if one arrived, and she had to be able to signal them. Opening her survival kit, she began to check her equipment. She put her pistol and her Randall survival knife on her belt and slipped her signal mirror in one pocket of her flight suit.

The captain thought hard, concentrating on her survival training. She knew that when a pilot crashed in unfriendly territory, he or she experienced severe psychological shock. It was all too easy to give in to panic or despair. Clark had done well at the Air Force survival-training school. One of her instructors had said she was as tough as an old boot. He had meant that as a compliment. Successful survivors were those who used their equipment properly and thought about every move before they made it. She ran her hand through her short, black, curly hair. This time it wasn't a training course; it was for real.

She had enough food to last five or six days. In a pinch, she could stretch it to last a week or more, but she would need to find water before the two quarts in her canteen were gone. She checked her small emergency radio. It seemed all right. There was no way to be absolutely sure, and she didn't intend to transmit until she saw a rescue party. If people she didn't want to meet were looking for her, they were probably monitoring the international emergency frequencies.

She munched a chocolate bar and sipped some lukewarm water. It wasn't a gourmet lunch, but it would help to keep her going. She couldn't think of anything else to do that made sense. It would take a day or two for a rescue party to arrive if one was coming. She should try to get some rest. She was almost dozing in the heat when she heard a sound cutting through the whine of insects. It was the unmistakable sound of helicopter rotors. Company was coming.

The sound was coming from the north, which was behind her. She resisted the temptation to break cover and take a look. She was an optimist, but she knew it was very unlikely that an American rescue party could have gotten here this fast. As long as she stayed in the trees, she didn't think anyone could see her from the air. She focused her binoculars on the crash site. She was sure no search party would neglect looking at that.

She was right. Two helicopters came into her field of view and touched down near Skylance. Her small binoculars didn't provide enough magnification at that range to show her any details, but she could see people get out and swarm over the aircraft.

She turned on her emergency radio and quickly scanned the emergency frequencies, hoping against hope that this might be a friendly rescue party. She heard nothing but the faint hiss of static. She pondered her next move. Any intelligent person who looked at Skylance would deduce that it had carried a crew of two. They would know she had to be somewhere in the general area and would probably start looking for her. She could move deeper into the trees, but that would mean she would no longer be able to see the crash site. Better to wait where she was.

She saw a flicker of movement through her binoculars. One of the helicopters was lifting off. She watched as it turned and began to fly slowly along the trail to the west of the crash site, straight toward her. The chopper was flying in a strange pattern: moving slowly along, stopping to hover, touching down now and then while one of the crew jumped out, stared at the ground, then climbed back in. What were they doing?

The answer came to her suddenly, like a punch to the stomach. She stared at her muddy boots. Tracks! The ground was moist and soft, and the pattern left by the soles of her boots was distinctive. They were following her tracks, and the helicopter let them move far faster than men on foot. She looked down the slope that led from her hiding place to the trail and swore. She could see her tracks clearly, and so would they. She had only two choices: stay there and surrender, or escape and evade. She shook her head. The laser that had attacked Skylance had to belong to somebody. If the people who were looking for her belonged to the same group, their orders might be to make sure there were no surviving witnesses.

To hell with that! If someone wanted to kill her, she was damned well going to make them work to do it. She snatched up her gear and began to move deeper into the trees. She moved quickly, but she tried to step on rocks or logs, anything to break her trail. She ran on for ten minutes, then paused to catch her breath. The heat was brutal and she was sweating heavily under her flight suit, but she had nothing else to wear;

she wasn't about to charge through the trees in her bra and panties. The sound of helicopter rotors was louder now.

She looked up and saw the helicopter through a break in the trees. She had no trouble recognizing it. It was an American-made Bell Huey, but that meant nothing. Half the military forces in the world operated some version of the Huey. It wasn't a gunship, but it looked military, painted in mottled brown-and-green-camouflage patterns. She saw a red-and-white marking on the side of the fuselage that looked like some kind of national insignia, but she couldn't recognize it. That didn't make her feel any better.

Things were about to get serious. She took out her small pistol. It was a beautifully made and beautifully finished Walther PPK/S that her brother, a Green Beret, had given to her. It had one nonstandard feature. The armorer of her brother's unit had fitted a silencer to the end of the barrel. That made the deadly little pistol as silent as the grave. It might seem like a strange weapon for a U.S. Air Force officer, but Clark's brother had told her again and again that she wasn't going to win firefights with well-armed soldiers with any pistol in the world. She had to depend on avoiding a fight if she could and on utterly precise shooting if it came to that. There were ten high-velocity .22 cartridges in the magazine. Properly placed, any one of them could kill a person. Clark pulled back the slide and chambered the first round.

As she kept heading deeper into the trees, she could hear the sound of the helicopter's rotors and the whine of its engines. It seemed to be darting from place to place, circling around her. She fought to control the steadily rising panic. If she lost her head and ran like a hunted animal, she was through. Clark tried to think and plan. Maybe it made sense to stop running and hole up, if only she could find a place to hide. She paused for a second, crouched behind a tree trunk and looked ahead. She felt a cold knot in her stomach. The trees ahead were thinning out. Fifty feet in the distance, she could see the open fields.

As she looked, the helicopter appeared, hovering briefly while two men jumped from one of the side doors and ran toward the edge of the trees, crouching to avoid the whirling rotor blades. The men were clearly soldiers. They wore mottled green-and-brown-camouflage uniforms and bright orange berets. Worse than that, each man carried a deadly black M-16 automatic rifle. Clark had trained on the M-16 and knew what one could do. She had no chance at all if it came to a fight.

The captain heard a branch crack behind her. Desperately she turned. A soldier was standing twenty feet away with a look of triumph on his face, the M-16 in his hands pointing straight at her. He shouted something she couldn't understand and pulled the trigger. She could see yellow fire dancing in the M-16's flash hider as it spit a burst. Clark was showered with bark and splinters as the high-velocity, full-metal-jacketed bullets ripped into the tree a foot above her head.

She didn't think, but reacted instinctively. She swung up the little Walther until her front sight was pointing at the man's face and pulled its trigger again and again. She heard the hiss of the Walther's silencer and the metallic snick of the slide running back and forth as she emptied the 10-round magazine as fast as she could pull the trigger. The soldier swayed back and forth for a second, then slumped to the ground and lay still. Her brother had been right. A well-aimed .22 could kill anyone.

Clark shook with reaction. She had practiced shooting every year since she joined the Air Force, but she had never killed anyone before. She heard men shouting in front of her and behind. She started to re-load her pistol when two soldiers burst into view with their M-16s pointed straight at her. She didn't stand a chance. She was willing to fight but not to commit suicide. She dropped her Walther and slowly raised her hands. More soldiers were behind her. They grabbed her arms and twisted them cruelly high behind her back. Other hands tore open her flight suit and searched her trembling body brutally.

One of the soldiers examined the man Clark had shot. He stood and moved toward her, his face flushed with fury. He snarled something she couldn't under-stand and pointed his M-16 at her face. She watched helplessly as his finger began to tighten on the trigger. Another soldier shouted and knocked up the M-16's barrel. Half a dozen bullets tore into the branches above.

The soldier who had saved Clark's life stepped in front of her and slapped her across the face as hard as he could. He slapped her repeatedly as her head rocked back and forth on her shoulders.

"You filthy whore," he snarled in heavily accented English. "You killed Ahmed. I would like to kill you myself, but our orders are to take you alive. The helicopters have been called away. We will have to march back to our camp. It is ten kilometers, and I will see that you enjoy every step of the way."

CHAPTER EIGHT

Wejak made a swift gesture for everyone to be quiet. Bolan listened intently, but he heard nothing out of the ordinary. Wejak suddenly gave a perfect imitation of a forest birdcall. If Bolan hadn't been looking at him, he would have sworn it was just the call of another one of the birds flitting through the trees. Wejak looked grave as he spoke to Bolan. "They are still behind us. That was Nilik's message. He is in the trees about two thousand paces behind us. His message has been re- layed twice, but there is no mistake. Their scouts passed his position about two minutes ago. They are coming after us as fast as they can."

Bolan nodded. It wasn't good news, but he had been expecting it. It was what he would have done if he had been the Indonesian commander. He signaled to McCarter.

"They're gaining on us. They've probably dropped their packs and are just carrying their weapons and ammunition. At this rate, they'll catch us in half an hour. It's time to slow them a little."

McCarter nodded. "Right, I'll go with you. You'll need someone to spot for you."

Bolan shook his head. "No, you're the only one who knows how to work the satcom radio. Get in touch with Hal or Barbara at Stony Man. Tell them what's happened. The covert-mission plan is shot to hell. Find out what they want us to do.''

Bolan could tell by the look on McCarter's face that he didn't like it, but he also knew that the Executioner was right.

"All right. I'll get on it right away, but you shouldn't try to do it by yourself. You need someone to spot for you and watch your back while you're shooting.''

"I'll take Lahka. She likes to shoot Indonesians, and she'll love laser range-finder binoculars.''

BOLAN HAD PICKED his spot carefully. It gave him a clear field of fire and provided good concealment. The trail ran along the river, protecting his left flank. He cut several branches from the trees and placed them strategically to improve his cover. He took his prone position and checked his rifle and his telescopic sights. He was about six hundred yards from a sharp bend in the trail. He would let them come to him. The Indonesian commandos had been pushing the pursuit. Nothing had happened to them so far. There were many bends in the trail, and there was nothing particularly remarkable about this one. They just might be getting a little careless.

The firing position he had selected was excellent. He and Lahka were well concealed. Nobody, unless he was very lucky, was going to detect the ambush until Bolan opened fire. Even then, it wouldn't be easy. He handed Lahka his Leica Vector 1000 binoculars. He helped her to adjust the focusing rings to fit her eyes and showed her the ranging button.

"I need you to do two things. Use the binoculars to scan the area. Also pick out targets for me and look out for someone trying to flank us and attack us from the side. When you see a target, push the ranging button. Here, give it a try."

Lahka peered intently through the binoculars. She gave an exclamation of delight. "This is wonderful! I can see things as if I were standing next to them."

Bolan smiled. Lahka's education at the missionary college obviously hadn't included binoculars. The crystal-clear optics were remarkable. He had never used anything better.

"Now, put the small cross hairs on an object. Try those rocks. Then push the button. What do you see?"

"Small red numbers. They say 584. What does it mean?"

"When you pushed the button, you triggered a laser range finder. It sent an invisible beam of light to the rocks and measured the exact distance from here to there, 584 meters. That's the range. It helps me in my shooting. That's all there is to it. If I say 'range,' you just push the button and read it out. Got it?"

Lahka looked puzzled. "You are the leader. I will do what you say, but what does this have to do with shooting? When Marie taught me to shoot, she said to put the front sight on the target, put the front sight in the middle of the rear sight and squeeze the trigger. Wejak's AK-47 works the same way. Don't bullets go in straight lines? Why is this range so important to you?"

Bolan smiled. Lahka was a bright girl, but her education had obviously not included ballistics, either.

He picked up two small rocks and handed them to Lahka. He pointed to a tree about thirty feet away.

"Hit the center of the tree. Throw hard so that the rock goes in a straight line."

Lahka threw and hit the tree easily.

"Good shot," Bolan said, "but the rock didn't go in a straight line, Lahka. It curved in the air. Throw harder. Make the rock go straight."

Lahka threw the second rock as hard as she could. She hit the center of the tree trunk, but the rock's path was still curved.

"I do not think it can be done," she said. "I think the rock will curve no matter how fast I throw it."

"You're right. I can't do it, and neither can anybody else. Bullets go so fast that you can't see it, but they fly the same way. It doesn't make much difference at a hundred yards or less, but when you shoot at five hundred or a thousand yards, it makes the difference between a hit and a miss. My rifle's sighted in for four hundred yards. If I shoot at less than four hundred yards, the bullet will strike high. Beyond four hundred, it will hit low. If I know what the range is, I can correct my aim and still get a hit."

Lahka was fascinated. "It must be wonderful to be able to strike your enemies when they are so far away. Could you teach me to shoot like that?"

"Sure, no problem, except it takes a year or two to learn."

Lahka laughed. "I do not think we have that much time. I will range for you, and you do the shooting."

There was nothing else to do or say. They were ready. Bolan and Lahka settled down to wait. The minutes crawled by. Then he stiffened as he saw a man

come around the bend. He could see the orange beret
and camouflaged uniform clearly. Now it was time to
steady down and do it right.

The commando had a pair of binoculars slung
around his neck. As Bolan watched through his rifle's
scope, the commando raised them to his eyes and began to scan the trail ahead. The big American froze as
the binoculars swept over his position, but they didn't
pause. The Indonesian hadn't picked up Bolan's position.

"It is 590 meters," Lahka stated.

Bolan shook his head. He wanted more than one
target before he opened fire. He waited calmly.

A second commando came around the bend. He
held an M-16 rifle, ready to fire to cover the pointman when he moved forward. The large gray rock lay
about twenty feet beyond the bend in the trail. Bolan
watched as the two commandos quickly took cover
behind it. The 8.5-power magnification of the Executioner's telescopic sight showed every detail. The
rock provided perfect cover, even against high-
powered rifle fire. However, they couldn't stay there
very long, and when they moved, he should have a
perfect shot. Because of the range, the bullet would
strike below where Bolan placed the intersection of the
cross hairs. He placed the intersection of his cross
hairs higher on the man's chest to compensate. The
black line of the horizontal cross hair told Bolan that
the rifle was level, not canting to the right or left. One
of the commandos stood, then the other one. The first
soldier looked down the trail toward Bolan with his
binoculars.

The commando was six hundred yards away, and Bolan's sight picture was perfect. He pushed off the Remington's safety and began to apply a slow, steadily increasing pressure to the big rifle's trigger. The Remington bucked and roared. A giant, invisible hand seemed to slap the commando back toward the large gray rock. The commando died instantly. He never knew what hit him.

Bolan's right hand moved with blurring speed. His palm cupped the knob of the Remington's bolt handle and drove it up, backward, forward and down in one smooth, continuous motion as he chambered a fresh cartridge and fired again, driving another bullet through the commando's body. He wasn't vindictive, but he always liked to make sure that once his enemy was down, he stayed down.

He worked the bolt again as he swung his scope to the right. The second commando had reacted instantaneously, throwing himself down behind the large gray rock. The rock protected him against Bolan's bullets, but he couldn't stay there forever. The big American placed the cross hairs of his scope across the top of the rock and waited. The ball was in the Indonesian soldier's court.

Bolan didn't have to wait long. The commando leaped to his feet, snapping his M-16 rifle to his shoulder and firing a long burst. He had figured out where Bolan was positioned and was saturating the area with long bursts of full-auto fire.

Bolan kept his head down as 55-grain, full-metal-jacketed 5.56 mm bullets tore through the trees around him. Though the M-16 didn't have the range, there were such things as lucky hits. Quickly he peered through his scope again. The commando had stopped firing abruptly. His magazine was empty. He was drawing another clip from a pouch on his belt as the Executioner squeezed the Remington's trigger and sent a bullet through his chest. The commando staggered, then fell heavily and lay still.

Everything was still. Automatically Bolan opened the Remington's bolt and pressed four fresh cartridges into the magazine. He placed his scope's cross hairs on the edge of the bend in the trail. You never knew, someone just might be foolish enough to look around it. Someone was. A man's face appeared suddenly, peering up the trail. Bolan knew the man was not going to stand there to admire the view. He snapped off a quick shot, and the .308 bullet buried itself in the dirt six inches from the man's face. His head vanished instantly behind the cover of the bank.

It was time to go. They weren't stupid enough to try coming up the trail again. They knew approximately where he was. You didn't have to be a four-star general to see what would happen next. They would try to flank him, moving on the left side of the trail through the trees. At long range, his high-powered rifle gave him the edge. But if four or five of them could get in close with M-16s and grenades, he was probably finished. Bolan rolled to his feet and began to run steadily up the slope toward his next position.

MAJOR HATTA WAS in a cold rage as he wiped mud, flecks of blood and bits of gravel from his face. His look around the bend had been brief, but it was long enough for him to grasp the situation. His point team had been ambushed. He had lost two good men. He knew that he, himself, had been within fifteen centimeters of instant death. His men were looking at him, waiting for him to give them their orders. Very well, the situation was obvious. The American's rear guard had to be killed, and they had to catch the rest of them before dark. It was also completely clear that anyone who tried to move up the trail was going to face certain death. The major forced himself to speak calmly despite his anger.

"Our pointmen have been killed. Some of the Americans were in an ambush position. Not many, two or three. But one of them has a sniper's rifle. By now they have probably moved and have set up another ambush. We cannot go straight up the trail against the sniper. He would pick us off, one by one. So we will flank him. Sergeant Hasjim, take your section and move up the left side of the trail. Go as fast as you can, but stay under cover. The rest of us will stay here. We will keep the pressure on them and guard the trail. We must not let them slip behind us. Take no chances. When you find them, do not try to take them alive. Kill them. Take advantage of your M-16s. Pin them down, get him in a cross fire and kill them."

Hatta looked around him. His men were grim faced and angry as they checked their weapons, but he saw no signs of panic. Good!

"Are there any questions? No? Very well. Remember your training. Do not bunch up. Cover each other. Conserve your ammunition. Do not fire until you have a target. Use cover and concealment. Now, let us get a revenge for our brothers. Go with God."

Hatta heard a growl of agreement as the section faded into the bush. His men were in a mood to fight.

He took out his field glasses and prepared for the hardest thing of all a commander had to do—wait.

BOLAN WAS RUNNING steadily up the right side of the path, ten yards in from the edge of the trail. The ground was rough and overgrown with typical tropical-rain-forest vegetation. The going was hard. The temperature was over ninety-five degrees, and the humidity was close to one hundred percent. Already his dull black fatigues were soaked with sweat. Bolan was carrying a twelve-pound rifle, his two pistols and fifty pounds of gear. He could feel the strain before he had gone two hundred yards. Lack of sleep and the heat had taken their toll. If the commandos caught them moving without cover, they were dead. He might get two or three with his rifle, but the others would cut them to pieces with their M-16s.

He called to Lahka to stop. She wasn't carrying as heavy a load as he was and could move more rapidly.

"Go tell David he has got to move out. Tell him I'll hold them here for another ten minutes."

Lahka started to argue that she should stay with him, but she stopped when she saw the look on Bolan's face. She turned and ran up the trail.

The soldier took a few seconds to catch his breath. He was going to have to change his plans. He thought hard. What were the commandos looking for? What did they expect to see? A man with a rifle, a sniper waiting in ambush. All right, he would show them that.

A few yards ahead, he saw a small clearing. At the far edge was a tangled clump of bushes, a perfect place for a sniper's firing position. Quickly Bolan took off his bush hat and sniper's veil and pushed them into the bushes so that they hung a foot above the ground, just where his head would have been if he was hiding there in ambush. He slid the Remington into the bushes, bracing its stock against the branches until the big rifle's muzzle pointed menacingly down the trail. He hated to take a chance of losing the Remington, but that was what would make his trap convincing. The Indonesians simply wouldn't believe that a sniper would abandon his rifle.

Bolan moved to the right edge of the clearing and stood behind the trunk of a large banyan tree. He thought about using his 9 mm Beretta 93-R, but decided against it. He had seen men keep fighting after taking multiple hits from a 9 mm pistol. This was going to be kill-or-be-killed at point-blank range. He would need all the stopping power he could get. He drew his .44 Desert Eagle from its holster and checked the big pistol. A .44 Magnum round was in the chamber, eight more in the magazine and two spare magazines on his belt, ready for a fast reload. He held the Desert Eagle in both hands, palms vertical, his left hand cupping his right. He took a few deep breaths to steady himself and waited, listening intently. He didn't have long to wait. Bolan heard the sounds of people trying to move silently through the bush rapidly, but they were making too much noise in their eagerness to run him down.

The pointman entered the clearing. He looked disarmingly normal, except for his orange beret and the black M-16 rifle in his hands. He saw Bolan's rifle barrel pointing at him. He fired from the hip, three long, ripping bursts. Full-metal-jacketed rounds tore through the clump of bushes. An invisible hand seemed to snatch his bush hat away and throw it through the air. The commando yelled loudly, excitement and triumph in his voice.

Two more men in camouflaged uniforms dived into the clearing, coming low and fast, one to the left, and one to the right. They rolled into hasty prone positions and fired simultaneously. Several long bursts riddled Bolan's false firing position. A lethal cross fire of M-16 bullets tore through the bushes. Someone barked an order. The first man had reloaded his M-16. He covered the clump of bushes while the other two reached for fresh magazines. The Executioner stepped around the banyan tree, the big Desert Eagle steady in his hands.

Bolan could see his front sight clear and sharp against the first man's camouflaged shirt. He pulled the trigger, and the big Desert Eagle roared. He kept his wrists and elbows locked against the recoil and instantly pulled the trigger again. The two shots were so close together that they sounded like a single blast. The combined impact was terrible. The Indonesian dropped his M-16 and started to fall.

Bolan could see the right-hand man's face distorted by fear and surprise as he watched the Desert Eagle's muzzle swing toward him. His M-16 was reloaded and ready to fire, but he was facing forward, toward Bolan's ambush. He had to turn ninety degrees before he could fire at his enemy.

Too late. Bolan needed to turn only a few degrees. His upper body swung smoothly, like a tank's gun turret, his head, arms and the big Desert Eagle staying perfectly aligned. The instant the Desert Eagle's front sight was on target, the Executioner fired again and again. The man staggered and slowed, but he didn't go down. Two more .44 Magnum hollow-points smashed into the second man, and he went down hard.

The third man had turned toward Bolan, ready to fire. He had to hesitate for a second, because his teammate was in his line of fire. Now he had a clear shot. As Bolan swung his Desert Eagle toward him, the gunner fired a burst from the hip. He should have taken another half second and used his sights. Still, he missed only by inches. Bolan could see the yellow-white muzzle-flash dancing inside the M-16's flash hider, and splinters flew from the banyan tree behind him. The big American sighted on his enemy and fired rapidly, a double tap, as fast as he could pull the Desert Eagle's trigger.

The man was punched backward, dead before he hit the ground.

There was a sudden, deafening silence. Automatically, without thinking, Bolan pushed the button on the side of the Desert Eagle and dropped the empty magazine. He pulled a fresh clip from his belt pouch, snapped it into place, pushed the lever that released the slide and drove another round into the chamber. He swung the big pistol in a rapid arc around the clearing, but there was nothing left to shoot. He holstered the Desert Eagle, snatched up his Remington and faded back into the trees.

MCCARTER CAREFULLY unfolded the antenna of the AN/PCS-3 satcom radio. He checked his compass and slowly adjusted the antenna until it pointed at a spot in the sky. He pushed a button and waited until a green light came on. The radio was locked on a United States military-communications relay satellite 22,300 miles above the equator.

McCarter pushed the transmit button.

"Granite Home, this is Dagger. Acknowledge, Granite Home."

His voice flashed upward into space at the speed of light and was retransmitted to a second relay satellite over the continental United States and down to the satellite-communications antennae at Stony Man Farm. The operations center's satcom radio was monitored twenty-four hours a day when a mission was under way. McCarter waited for a few seconds and heard a familiar voice.

"Dagger, this is Granite Home. Over."

McCarter was always impressed by satellite communications. Barbara Price's voice was as clear as if she were standing a few feet away. He reminded himself to keep it short and sweet as he pushed the transmit button. The narrow beam of the AN/PCS-3 was focused on the relay satellite. In theory, it could be intercepted only by another satellite in a similar orbit, but McCarter was suspicious of theories when his life was at stake. He had learned years ago that if you wanted to live to collect your pension, you kept radio chitchat to a minimum.

"Team insertion accomplished at planned point. Contact made. Have had hostile contacts with local forces who are in pursuit. Striker says cannot accomplish mission covertly. Will probably involve combat with local forces. Request instructions immediately. Dagger out."

"Message understood, Dagger. Where is Striker?"

McCarter heard Bolan's Remington fire twice in rapid succession.

"Busy entertaining guests. Over."

"Stand by, Dagger," Price advised.

He heard Price's voice again, speaking precisely and coolly.

"Dagger, Granite Home. Your situation understood. Mission is critical. Reinforcements on the way. Should arrive your area next twenty-four hours. Instructions are, break contact, continue mission. I say again, break contact, continue mission. Granite Home out."

McCarter sighed. He didn't like the message, but that was the way the game was played. He only hoped they could stay alive until the bloody reinforcements got there.

"Message understood, Granite Home. Will comply. Dagger out."

Quickly he folded the satcom radio's antenna. The sounds of firing were getting closer. It was going to be a long, hard day.

MAJOR HATTA STOOD on the bank of the Baliem River and glared at the muddy water flowing by. He was still angry, but his fury was beginning to change to the cold certainty of failure. They had pursued the Americans for hours, but they hadn't caught them. It had been like fighting ghosts, not men. Whoever the American sniper was, his shooting was incredible. If you gave him a target for a second or two, he always seemed to hit it. Hatta had a dozen men killed or wounded and nothing to show for it. Now the trail had been lost.

He watched while Sergeant Awang moved slowly along the riverbank, studying the damp earth carefully. Hatta waited impatiently, but he knew there was no point in trying to hurry the Dyak when he was scouting.

At last Awang pointed to a spot on the ground. Hatta looked over the man's shoulder. He could see marks on the ground, but he wasn't sure what they meant. He waited for the Dyak to speak.

"I am sorry, Major, but it is not good," Awang said softly. "See these long, deep grooves? There were four Dani canoes here. And look there. That is the footprint of one of the Americans, and here are two of the woman who is wearing boots. They got into the canoes and left. There is nothing more I can do. They are gone, and there are no tracks on the river I can follow."

Hatta was tempted to swear, but Awang looked so downcast he patted him on the shoulder. "It was not your fault, Sergeant."

Awang nodded. That was true, and it was kind of Hatta to say so, but it didn't make him feel better. He had so looked forward to taking the Americans' heads.

"Major," his radioman suddenly called, "there is a message for you from Wamena. They have received a message from the high command at Djajapura. You are ordered back to Wamena immediately for a critical meeting. They will send out the helicopter to pick you up immediately."

SKYLANCE

"Acknowledge," Hatta said bitterly. As if things weren't bad enough already, he had to go back to Wamena to meet with some idiot from the high command.

CHAPTER NINE

Djajapura, Western New Guinea

Gary Manning woke up. The sound of the engines had changed. He had been dozing in his seat, recovering from the effects of ten thousand miles of high-speed travel across the Pacific Ocean. The Merpati Airlines Boeing 707 was losing altitude steadily, flying along the northern coast of New Guinea. The second officer was enthusiastically announcing in Indonesian and English that they would be landing at the Djajapura airport in five minutes. He glanced across the aisle. Jack Grimaldi was looking out the window. Gadgets Schwarz had his nose buried in a tourist's guide to Indonesia. He had been reading it since the plane took off from Java.

A charming flight attendant was smiling at Manning, offering him a refreshing hot towel. He smiled back. She was a very attractive young lady and very attentive. She leaned over him casually and pressed a firm breast against his arm as she pointed out the window.

"There is Djajapura. We will be touching down in a few minutes. If there is anything you would like, now or after we land, I will be very happy to see that you get it, Mr....?"

"Call me Gary," Manning said, and smiled at her. He would have liked to think that his charm and good looks had turned on the woman, but a small alarm was ringing in his mind. It was just a little too fast and a little too good to be true. You could call it paranoia, but Manning would have been dead a long time ago if he hadn't paid attention to subconscious warnings.

The woman was smiling expectantly. She was pretty, taller than most Indonesian women. She had pale skin, long, lustrous black hair and an excellent figure. Manning decided it was his duty to appear friendly and find out what she was up to.

He gave her his best smile. "Thank you, that's very nice of you. Do you fly back to Java tonight, or do you stay in Djajapura?"

Her smile grew broader. "I have a forty-eight-hour layover in Djajapura."

"Excellent," Manning said. "Why don't you have dinner with me tonight? What's the best restaurant in Djajapura?"

"The Hawaii, but it is very expensive. A dinner for two there can cost thirty thousand rupiahs."

Manning calculated quickly. That was about fifteen U.S. dollars. The Stony Man operational budget could certainly stand that.

"Don't worry about it. I'll just put it on my expense account."

The woman's smile was dazzling. It was obvious that she liked handsome, rich Canadians.

"My name is Meiko. I'll talk to you later this evening." She wrote a phone number on a card, passed it to him, then proceeded down the aisle.

Manning waited a few seconds and motioned to Schwarz. He nodded, stepped across the aisle and took the seat next to the Canadian.

"See that flight attendant down the aisle, the one with the long black hair?" Manning asked.

Schwarz took a quick look. "Long black hair isn't all she's got. That's one stone-cold fox. Has she fallen madly in love with me?"

"Well, as a matter of fact, she's been sending all sorts of signals that she's fallen madly in love with me. Sorry, but that's the way it is."

Schwarz made a face. "Damned if I understand these modern women. All you've got going for you is good looks and money. Well, what do you want me to do about it?"

"You're going to be tied up for a while getting all your gear through customs. Grimaldi ought to breeze through. Ask him to keep an eye on the charming young lady after we're on the ground."

Schwarz nodded and slipped back across the aisle.

Manning looked out the window. The plane was making a low turn over Djajapura. From the air, at least, it looked very nice, with white stone buildings and a brilliant blue harbor surrounded by dark green, forest-covered hills. Thirty years ago, when it was the capital of Dutch New Guinea, it had been called Hollandia. The Indonesians had renamed it Djajapura, the City of Victory, when they had "liberated" Western New Guinea in 1963. It was still the capital and the main point of legal entry for travelers coming to Western New Guinea, as well as the best place to get a flight to the interior.

The airport was south and west of the city. The pilot made a smooth landing and taxied to the ramp. Manning felt the heat as he went down the exit ladder. It was three o'clock in the afternoon, but the sun was still blazing down from a bright blue sky. The temperature was well over ninety degrees. He could feel himself starting to sweat. He walked into the terminal building, showed his passport to the immigration authorities and walked quickly to the customs desk. The terminal wasn't air-conditioned. The sooner he was out of there, the better.

He picked out the senior Indonesian customs official and showed him his Canadian passport. The official smiled when he saw the bright blue ten-thousand-rupiah bill that Manning had slipped inside his passport.

"Welcome to Djajapura. I hope your stay will be a pleasant one. Is there any way I can assist you?"

Manning smiled back. "I certainly wish to comply with all Indonesian customs regulations," he said smoothly, "but my business is rather urgent. I would like to reach the police station before the travel-permit section closes. I need a travel permit for the interior."

"Certainly," the customs official said. He spoke to two of his subordinates. They began to go through Manning's baggage with remarkable speed and efficiency.

"Is there anything else I can do to assist you?"

Manning pointed to three flat black plastic cases that were coming down the conveyor belt. "Those are my hunting rifles," he said casually. "Of course, you must inspect them, but I would appreciate it if they were handled very carefully. The telescopic sights are a bit delicate."

The customs official's smile faded. "You have firearms? Do you have a special firearms permit?"

Manning handed the documents to the official. "Of course."

The official's smile returned when he saw another ten-thousand-rupiah bill was folded neatly inside Manning's papers, but he still looked at the papers carefully. His eyebrows rose when he saw the date on the firearms permit.

"You obtained this permit yesterday?" he asked incredulously.

Manning nodded. "I explained to the customs and police officials that I was in quite a hurry. They were most cooperative."

The customs official stared at Manning, awestruck. If he had obtained a firearms permit in a few hours, it had to have cost him at least a hundred thousand rupiahs. He was very rich or very important, probably both.

"I will take care of it personally," he said quickly.

He opened the cases carefully and peered inside. He didn't touch the rifles, merely checked the serial numbers and nodded.

"Everything is in order. Those are beautiful weapons. Are you a big-game hunter?"

"I love to hunt. I do a lot of traveling around the world for North American Minerals. I try to get in some shooting wherever I go," he replied casually. "I hear that there is good wild-boar hunting in the interior. I intend to try my luck if my business allows me to take the time off. I trust everything is in order?"

"Of course. Enjoy your stay, sir, and good luck with your hunting."

Manning glanced over his shoulder. Jack Grimaldi was already through customs. There had been nothing in his nylon flight bag to attract attention, but Gadgets Schwarz was surrounded by an excited group of customs officers.

"Perhaps you could assist my colleague. He helps me in conducting mining surveys. He has quite a lot of technical equipment. I would appreciate it if it were handled very carefully and as quickly as possible."

He handed the official an envelope. "This will explain everything."

The official glanced at the two ten-thousand-rupiah bills inside and smiled broadly. "I will see to it at once, sir. If there is anything else I can do to assist you while you are here, do not hesitate to call on me. The police station is on Sam Ratulangi Street. You will want to take a cab into town. You may hire one outside."

Manning walked toward the terminal door, keeping an eye on the three porters who were handling his baggage. Jack Grimaldi joined him casually.

"Your girlfriend made two telephone calls as soon as she got off the plane, one local, one long-distance. No telling who she called."

Manning nodded. It proved nothing, one way or the other. Young women frequently made telephone calls.

"I've got to go by the police station and the bank. I'll meet you and Gadgets at the hotel."

Grimaldi nodded and went back inside the terminal. Manning hailed a cab and walked toward it, followed by his parade of three porters. He noticed

Meiko standing nearby. Was she waiting for someone or keeping an eye on him?

She walked to the cab quickly, flashing her lovely smile.

"Could you do me a favor, Gary? A girlfriend was going to pick me up, but I do not see her anywhere. Could you possibly give me a ride into town?"

What was that old SAS proverb that McCarter liked to quote? "The first time is happenstance, the second time is coincidence and the third time is enemy action." This was one damned coincidence too many. He took a quick look around. No one seemed to be paying the slightest attention. If the woman had accomplices, they were keeping out of sight. He kept a smile on his face.

"Certainly. Hop in, Meiko."

THE RIDE TO DOWNTOWN Djajapura had been uneventful. Two or three cars were behind Manning's cab all the way, but it was the only road from the airport into town. There was no way to know if anyone had been following them. The driver stopped at the police station, and Manning told the surly sergeant on the desk that he needed to speak to the officer in charge immediately. A five-thousand-rupiah note improved the sergeant's disposition immensely. He personally ushered Manning into the captain's small office.

Captain Dewanta looked at Manning's passport and smiled as he saw the two ten-thousand-rupiah notes folded inside. The big Canadian was obviously a man of the world, a man who knew how to conduct business, not one of these stupid foreigners who expected to receive many services for nothing. He looked at Manning's papers. He found one very interesting indeed. It was a letter of credit to the Djajapura Export-Import bank, establishing a line of credit in Manning's name for one hundred million rupiahs. The captain was impressed.

"Your papers seem to be in order. How else may I help you?"

"I need to go to the Baliem Valley, and I need to get there as soon as possible. My company and I will appreciate any assistance you can give me. You will find that we can be very grateful to those who help us."

"You will need a travel permit for the interior. I will see that one is issued immediately. There is a Merpati Airlines flight to Wamena once a day. You could take it tomorrow, but I would not advise it. Wamena is a frontier town. There are few facilities. You must walk from the airport to the town. There are no cars or trucks for civilians. Once you are there, you will be on foot."

He stopped and looked at Manning with a smile.

"I am sure a mining engineer needs to be able to move around freely. I would suggest you charter a light plane, or better yet, a helicopter. That will be expensive, but it will give you complete freedom of movement."

Manning smiled. "Money is no object, Captain. North American Minerals is a very large company. Can you recommend a helicopter charter company?"

"There is only one, sir. I will call them at once and tell them to reserve their best machine for you."

The police captain looked up as a clerk came in and handed him an official-looking piece of paper.

"Here is your travel permit for the interior. You can leave tomorrow morning."

He glanced at Manning's papers. "I see you are staying at the Matoa Hotel. It is expensive, but it is the best place."

He glanced out of his office, where Meiko was waiting patiently. "One word of advice, though. Djajapura is not the safest place in the world after dark. There are many undesirable people here. Enjoy yourself, but be careful."

Manning smiled. He intended to be very careful indeed.

He rejoined the smiling Meiko and went outside to his waiting cab. The driver smiled and opened the passenger door with a flourish, visions of five-thousand-rupiah tips filling his thoughts. Meiko snuggled close to Manning and pressed her thigh firmly against his. She certainly wanted something. The question was, what? He decided to give her an opening and see how she reacted.

"I am staying at the Matoa Hotel," Manning said. "Where can I drop you?"

"The Matoa is a fine hotel," Meiko said wistfully. "I wish I could stay there, but it is very expensive."

"Where are you staying?" Manning inquired.

"The airline rents economy rooms for us at the Hotel Triton. The rooms there are small and poorly furnished. They often smell bad, and some of the men who stay there frighten me. I would not stay there if I could pay for my own room somewhere else."

Manning smiled wickedly. "I wouldn't dream of letting a nice girl like you stay in a place like that. I have a first-class room at the Matoa. Why don't you spend the night with me?''

Meiko's smile widened. "That would be very nice."

They were driving through the downtown area now, along one of Djajapura's four main streets. The streets were full of an extraordinary people, Papuan tribesmen in colorful costumes, Chinese shopkeepers, Indonesian bureaucrats and policemen, and colorful people Manning couldn't begin to identify. He noticed that the darker-skinned Papuans seemed to perform the menial jobs. Positions of power or prestige were filled by the lighter-skinned Indonesians. It was easy to understand why the Papuans felt dispossessed in their own country.

They reached the hotel, and a swarm of porters carried Manning's baggage inside. A beaming bellboy ushered the big Canadian and Meiko to his room. Manning turned up the air-conditioning and looked around. It was a nice enough room, clean and well furnished. He turned to Meiko and smiled.

"How about a drink before dinner?" he asked.

"If you do not mind, I feel so hot and sweaty. I would like to take a shower first."

Manning nodded and watched appreciatively as Meiko took off her uniform and hung it in the closet. She was certainly a well-built young woman. He hoped she wasn't there to kill him. He waited until he could hear water running in the shower, then moved rapidly.

First things first. He opened a concealed compartment in one of his cases and took out his Colt Gold Cup National Match .45 automatic. He slipped the pistol and its holster on his belt and added a pouch that held two spare magazines. He cocked the hammer and set the safety, ready to draw and fire instantly if he had to. Manning wasn't an outstanding pistol shot. The rifle was his weapon. But if he had to fight at close quarters, the weight of the big Colt on his belt was extremely reassuring.

Manning carefully swept the room with one of Gadgets Schwarz's magic black boxes. This marvel of electronic technology swore that there were no bugs in the room. He was concerned about listening devices. If someone learned their plans, the whole mission would be in jeopardy. On a hunch, he brought the scanner close to Meiko's purse. A red light came on. Something inside the purse was using electric power.

He snapped open the purse and stared at the usual amazing collection of things women carried in their purses. He had no time to be subtle. He dumped the contents of the purse on the bed and scanned them. The red light stayed off. He carefully checked the purse itself. The red light came back on. Manning methodically felt the leather sides, encountering two hard, unyielding objects. He felt for and found a concealed catch. One side of the purse opened to reveal a flat compartment. Manning reached inside and pulled out a small flat box. It was a miniature, highly sophisticated tape recorder. He smiled. Perhaps Meiko added to her income with a little discreet blackmail.

There was another object in the compartment. He drew it out and stared at it. He was holding a small Beretta automatic, a .22 or a .25. That didn't surprise him. A pretty woman who traveled in a dangerous part of the world might feel she needed a little protection, but the small, neat silencer attached to the little automatic's barrel was another story. It made the little Beretta a professional's weapon. She could empty the magazine into someone, and a person in the next room wouldn't hear a sound.

He knocked softly on the connecting door to Jack Grimaldi's room and identified himself carefully. That was just as well. He noticed that Grimaldi was casually holstering a big .45 Colt automatic as Manning entered the room. The Stony Man pilot wasn't trigger-happy, but he was very high on the list of people whom Manning didn't want to startle.

"The room's not bugged, Jack," Manning said, "but our girlfriend is wired for sound, and she was carrying this."

Grimaldi looked at the Beretta. "You'd better be damned careful with that young lady. That's a serious piece."

"Where's Gadgets?"

"He's gone to his room to get his equipment. He should be here any minute."

Manning nodded. "Let's go back to my room. Meiko is likely to get out of the shower at any minute. We need to have a serious talk with that young lady."

"All right," Manning said. "I'm the good guy. You're the bad guy."

Grimaldi picked up his nylon flight bag and followed his friend back into his room.

Manning heard the shower stop. Meiko had taken a long one, and perhaps she simply loved taking long showers. On the other hand, she might have been stalling, waiting for someone to arrive. The bathroom door opened, and Meiko came out, wearing a large towel and a radiant smile. Her face suddenly froze as she saw Grimaldi sitting on the sofa aiming his .45 Colt automatic at the middle of her chest.

"Who are you?" she gasped. "What do you mean—?"

Manning smiled coldly and showed her the small Beretta in his hand. "Don't bother to put on an act," he said grimly. "Just start telling the truth, and start now!"

"Please, I don't know what you're talking about. Please don't hurt me," she gasped.

Grimaldi sneered. "Let's kill the lying bitch now, before her friends get here."

Meiko began to sob. "No, no, they made me do it! I didn't want to. They got me on drugs. They are blackmailing me. I have to do what they say! Please, don't kill me."

Manning thought quickly. It might even be true, but he had the grim feeling that if he had been a little careless, he wouldn't have lived through the evening. He pointed the silenced Beretta at Meiko's forehead and let her look down the cold black maw of the silencer. The soft click as he pulled back the hammer seemed to echo through the room.

"You're going to have to do better than that, Meiko. No more of this 'they' nonsense. Give me names if you want to live. Who are you working for? What are their plans?"

"They will kill me if I tell you," Meiko sobbed.

Manning took a step closer and prodded her with the Beretta's silencer. "I'll kill you if you don't."

He doubted that he could really shoot an unarmed woman in cold blood, but Meiko had no way of knowing that.

"I know nothing," she sobbed. "I get my instructions from an Oriental merchant in Djajapura. He calls himself Mr. Wu. He tells me what I must do and gives me money and drugs. That is all I know. Please, don't kill me. Please."

Manning thought for a second. She sounded convincing, but it still didn't explain the silenced Beretta.

There was a sudden knocking on the door to the hall. Someone knocked again, loudly and insistently. Manning frowned. Schwarz? No, the Able Team electronics wizard would have spoken up and identified himself. He didn't know anyone else in Djajapura. It could be someone from the hotel, but Manning hadn't lived this long by taking things for granted. He was careful not to stand in line with the door as he slipped the tiny Beretta into his pocket and drew his .45 Colt Gold Cup National Match pistol and thumbed off the safety.

He heard the hiss of a large zipper being opened behind him. Grimaldi was lying prone on the floor just to the left of the large sofa. He opened his nylon flight bag and pulled out something flat, black and deadly. Manning knew his weapons. Grimaldi had a .45-caliber Ingram M-10 submachine gun, with a MAC sound suppressor attached. It wasn't a standard U.S. military weapon, and it would never win a long-range shooting match, but it was incredibly deadly at close range. Manning heard a metallic click as the pilot unfolded the metal stock and snapped in a 30-round magazine.

Whoever was outside knocked again, louder and more insistently this time. Manning thought for a second. The lights were on, and they had been talking freely. No one was going to believe the room was empty. He gestured to Grimaldi with his left hand. It was obvious that whoever was at the door wasn't going to go away. Manning moved to stand alongside the door, but he was careful not to stand in front of it.

"Who is it?" he called. He tried to sound groggy, like a man who has had too much to drink and has been sound asleep.

No one spoke for a few seconds. Then a man began, "I am from the Directorate of Immigration. There is a serious problem with your passport. Open the door. I must speak to you immediately."

Manning felt the adrenaline start to flow. If there was anything wrong with his passport, he wouldn't have made it through the airport. Whoever was outside wasn't from the Indonesian Directorate of Immigration.

"All right, just a minute while I slip on some clothes," he said casually. That should buy them a few seconds. Manning stayed against the wall and stretched forward until the fingertips of his left hand touched the doorknob. He pushed lightly, and the knob started to turn. He jerked his hand back and flicked off the light switch.

The world seemed to explode. The hall was filled with the booming roar of semiautomatic shotguns firing rapidly. The middle of the door blew apart in gouts of splinters as dozens of hard lead buckshot tore through the wood and sprayed the room beyond. The mirror on the back wall shattered. The heavy leather sofa jerked and shuddered as dozens of buckshot smashed into it. The firing seemed to go on endlessly. If Manning had been standing in line with the door, he would have died instantly. He resisted the temptation to shoot back through the door. He couldn't see a target, and he had no ammunition to waste.

There was a momentary lull in the firing. Manning could hear Meiko moaning softly, but he had no time to worry about her. He dropped to the floor and rolled away from the wall, being sure to stay well clear of the door. He brought his pistol up in a hard two-handed grip and covered the door. There was a muffled roar, and metal shrieked and tore as someone shot out the lock.

The door smashed open and slammed against the wall. A man dived into the room and lay prone. He didn't shoot. Neither did Manning. He knew that trick. The attacker was waiting for a defender to fire, then would shoot at the muzzle-flash. Manning aimed at the man, the soft green glow of his night sights centered on the man's body.

Perhaps two seconds had gone by. The automatic shotguns roared into life again. Two men were firing. Manning could see them as they were illuminated by the flickering yellow light of their muzzle-flashes. One man was at each side of the door. They raked the back wall and blasted both corners of the room. They weren't wasting ammunition. The corners of a room were positions a defender would automatically take if he or she hadn't had close-quarters battle training. The room vibrated with the continuous booming blasts from the big shotguns. The firing seemed to go on forever.

Manning wasn't the only person who could see them. Grimaldi didn't know who the men were, but he had no doubt that they were hostile. He pulled the trigger of his MAC-10 and fired a burst at the man to the left of the door. It wasn't elegant shooting, but it was effective. Half a dozen heavy .45 caliber bullets tore into the attacker, and he went down instantly.

But now the man waiting on the floor had located Grimaldi. The muzzle-flash of his submachine gun had given his position away. He swung his weapon toward him, but Manning was ready. He pulled the trigger of his big Colt twice in a deadly double hammer. Two heavy .45-caliber bullets smashed into the man's side. He twitched and lay still.

Manning heard the hiss of Grimaldi's silenced MAC-10 as he fired a short burst through the open door. Someone outside fired back, raking the room with a series of booming shotgun blasts. Grimaldi gasped and swore. The big Canadian hoped he wasn't hit, but he had no time to look. He was tired of being outgunned. He rolled to the side of the man he had just shot and ripped his weapon from his hands.

It was a heavy, short-barreled shotgun with a black plastic stock and a long extension magazine protruding from the stock to the end of the barrel. Manning didn't recognize the make, but it didn't matter. Any cylinder-bored 12-gauge semiautomatic shotgun was an incredibly deadly weapon at point-blank range.

There were more men outside, and they were still determined to kill the people in the room. Only the threat of Grimaldi's MAC-10 was keeping them at bay. One of them began to fire around the right side of the door into the room, one blast of buckshot after another. They were trying to get Grimaldi to return fire so that they could pinpoint his position and cut him to pieces. The pilot took the bait and fired back, one burst, then two as he traded shots with the shot-gunner. But he had started with thirty rounds in the MAC-10's magazine. Manning heard a hollow clunk as the bolt of Grimaldi's submachine gun slammed home on an empty chamber.

Manning wasn't the only one who heard. A second man had been waiting just outside the door. With a snarl of triumph, he took a step forward and swung the lethal muzzle of his shotgun toward Grimaldi. The pilot reached desperately for a fresh magazine, but he wasn't going to make it.

The big Canadian could see the black bulk of the shotgun in the intruder's hands. Manning targeted quickly, his adversary silhouetted against the dim light in the hall. His shotgun roared and bucked in his hands, and buckshot ripped into the center of the man's body. His snarl of triumph changed abruptly into a shriek of agony. He staggered forward, his hands convulsing on his weapon. His shotgun erupted again. Manning could see the yellow ball of fire from the muzzle-flash as the weapon's gaping muzzle swung toward him.

The Phoenix Force commando saw puffs of dust and shreds of carpet flying as the striking buckshot moved toward him. To his left, he heard the hiss of Grimaldi's MAC-10 as he snapped a short burst into the man's side, but he still didn't go down. His weapon was still spitting flame and buckshot. He had to be dying on his feet, but that would be cold comfort if he managed to take Manning with him. The big Canadian pulled the trigger of his own weapon. The shotgun's buckshot was lethal, but it lacked the instant stopping power of a .45 round. Manning had to depend on the effects of multiple hits, and he had to get those hits fast. Pulling his trigger again and again, he fired blast after blast of buckshot into his attacker.

The heavy shotgun quivered, and its steel butt plate slammed repeatedly into Manning's shoulder. The recoil was brutal, and the deafening boom and the dazzling muzzle-flash seemed to go on endlessly as Manning emptied the shotgun's magazine in less than two seconds. The blasts of buckshot struck his target like an angry swarm of hornets. Flesh and blood could only stand so much. The attacker's weapon slipped from his nerveless fingers as he fell limply to the floor.

The big Canadian heard the connecting door to Grimaldi's room suddenly slam open. Gadgets Schwarz dived into the room and rolled into a prone firing position. He had his 9 mm Calico submachine gun ready to fire and sent a long burst through the doorway.

Grimaldi joined in, creating a cross fire from two automatic weapons that made the room's door a death trap for anyone who tried to come through it. But that worked both ways. They were still trapped inside the room. If the attackers had grenades, they were doomed. Manning caught a flicker of movement out of the corner of one eye. Meiko was dashing frantically for the connecting door to Grimaldi's room. She rushed through and vanished. He could hardly blame her. No matter whom she worked for, his room wasn't the safest place in the world just now.

Manning thought furiously, but he could suggest nothing they could do but stay in the room and shoot it out. Stalemate. For a long moment, there was silence, each side waiting for the other to make a move.

Then Manning heard shouting in the hall in a language he couldn't understand, followed by the echoing roar of sustained firing. Someone was blasting away with far more powerful weapons than shotguns or pistols. Someone screamed in pain, then everything was quiet. Manning listened intently. He was still a little deaf from the concentrated blasts of automatic weapons fired in a closed room. At first he couldn't be certain, but then he was sure. People were moving slowly and carefully down the hall in his direction. He kept his sights on the door, ready to fire, and waited tensely.

A man in the khaki uniform and black cap of the Indonesian national police force stepped into the room. Manning recognized the police captain he had dealt with earlier. The man looked around the room and shook his head.

"You cannot say I did not warn you. Djajapura is not the safest place in the world."

CHAPTER TEN

Mack Bolan crawled toward the top of the ridge line. He moved slowly and cautiously, staying close to the ground, being careful not to silhouette himself against the skyline. He tried to ignore the heat and the humidity and concentrate on business. He paused two feet from the top and checked his map again. These had to be the correct coordinates. He took out his Leica range-finding binoculars, worked his way forward and scanned the wide, flat valley below.

There it was, a blunt-nosed gray triangle, lying on its belly at the end of several hundred feet of skid marks scraped through the soft, moist dirt. It had to be Skylance. There could be nothing else in New Guinea that looked like that. The aircraft appeared to be in fairly good shape. The wings, twin tails and the fuselage seemed to be intact, although he could see what looked like burn marks in two or three places. Both the cockpit canopies were open, but he could see no signs of the crew.

He signaled to McCarter to move forward and handed him the binoculars. The Briton began a slow, careful scan of the area.

"It looks perfectly straightforward to me, Mack," McCarter said. "We go in after dark and set the charges. If the access panels are in good shape, we should have no trouble getting the data recorders out. Piece of cake, really.''

Bolan smiled. If he told McCarter the two of them were going to raid hell and kidnap the devil, the Briton would probably say that, too, was a piece of cake.

''The bloody thing is still in quite good shape. It's going to take all the explosives we've got to do the job. Even then, I doubt that we'll really destroy it.''

Bolan thought that over. McCarter was probably right. Still, Barbara Price's briefing had said that Skylance used a special high-energy fuel. If there was still fuel in the tanks, their charges would probably detonate it.

McCarter suddenly stiffened. ''Look just over the tail assembly, at that clump of trees about two hundred meters beyond the wreck. Use your rifle scope. I think we have company.''

Bolan unslung the Remington and flipped up the plastic caps that protected his scope's lenses. The scope was set for its full, 8.5-power magnification. He made sure he had a round in the rifle's chamber in case he had to shoot someone quickly. He aimed at the spot McCarter had described. For a second, all he saw were trees. Then he spotted it. A thin column of pale gray smoke was drifting slowly upward. Someone had built a fire in the clump of trees.

They continued to watch the trees and were rewarded by seeing a flicker of movement and a flash of color. Orange.

''KOPASSUS,'' McCarter said. ''More of our friends from the special commando force.''

McCarter was right. Bolan's scope showed him four Indonesian commandos walking casually toward

Skylance. As he watched, two more commandos stood up on the far side of the fuselage. They had to have been sitting down, leaning against Skylance, maintaining a casual guard. He could see their black M-16 rifles slung over their shoulders. Six altogether, and he was certain there were more in the trees. He watched as the four commandos unslung their rifles and began to move out along the trail to the west.

McCarter touched his arm. "Look to the east, along the trail."

Bolan looked through his scope. Four men were moving along the trail toward the crash site. They were too far away to make out details, but Bolan could see their orange berets.

"What do you make of it?" he asked McCarter softly. The Indonesians were too far away to hear them, but it was a basic instinct to be as quiet as possible in the presence of the enemy.

"At least a platoon, probably thirty or forty men, and they're sending out patrols. I would say they're looking for something or someone."

Bolan looked at Skylance again. "Take a good look at the cockpits. It seems that both seats are still there, though the pilot's seat looks damaged. I don't think the crew ejected. It looks like they rode it in. Chances are the Indonesians are searching for the crew—if they both survived."

McCarter nodded. "You're probably right. Well, we lost the race. The Indonesians got here first. So, what do we do now?"

"The original mission plan is down the tubes. We can't do anything until it gets dark, so we wait and check back with Stony Man to see what they want us to do.''

McCarter nodded. He was an experienced special-forces soldier. The odds were too long. To try anything during daylight would be committing suicide.

"All right. You go talk to Barbara and Hal. I'll just stay here and relax. Of course, I'll maintain surveillance if you like.''

Bolan smiled as he slipped back down the ridge line. McCarter was one of the few men he knew who would consider it relaxing to observe thirty or forty enemy soldiers who would try to kill him on sight.

He moved back fifty yards to where the rest of the party had halted. He carefully briefed them. They looked at him expectantly, waiting to hear his plan. Bolan wasn't ready to make a decision. He had to talk to Brognola and Price first. He could sense the tension they felt. They needed something to do, and it might as well be something useful.

"Go up, one at a time, to David's position and take a look," he said. "Try to fix everything in your minds. We may be going down there tonight. I'm going to check with my HQ and see what they want us to do. Any questions?''

Van Heyn shook her head and slipped up the slope toward McCarter. Bolan was glad to see that she had the sense to stay low and keep her head down.

Bolan took the AN/PCS-3 satcom radio out of its nylon carrying case. He carefully unfolded the antenna, checked his compass and slowly adjusted the antenna until it was pointing at the relay satellite 22,300 miles above in space. He pushed the transmit button and waited until the green light came on.

"Granite Home, this is Striker. Acknowledge, Granite Home."

Bolan waited while his voice was relayed to Stony Man Farm. In a few seconds, he heard the familiar voice of Barbara Price.

"Striker, this is Granite Home. Over."

Price's voice was as distinct as if she were standing next to him. As he pushed the transmit button again, he reminded himself that keeping radio messages short and sweet was the way to stay alive.

"Granite Home, object located, but no signs of people. Hostile forces estimated at forty men control the site. Original mission plan impossible. Request new instructions immediately. Striker out."

"Message understood. Stand by, Striker."

Bolan waited. He had handed Price a hot potato. He knew it wasn't a decision she could make. She would have to contact Hal Brognola.

He heard Brognola's voice this time, speaking coldly and precisely.

"Striker, Granite Home. Do you believe the crew is alive or dead?"

"Granite Home, no direct evidence one way or the other. Nature of damage to object suggests one dead. Hostile camp obscured by trees. Possible that second person is held prisoner there. Could investigate after dark. Advise."

"Message understood. Stand by, Striker."

Bolan waited. Brognola was calling the shots.

"Striker, Granite Home. We understand your situation, but the mission is still critical. Instructions are, do not search further for crew. Infiltrate target area after dark and destroy object. I say again, destroy ob-

ject, break contact and prepare to withdraw. Backup
team should be in area during the next twelve hours.
They will have evacuation plans. Granite Home out."

"Message understood, Granite Home. Will comply. Striker out."

He shut off the satcom radio and looked at his
watch. It was still four hours until darkness. There was
nothing to do until then but wait and check their
equipment. He opened the bottom compartment of his
pack and looked at his demolition gear. He had selected the explosives carefully, concentrating on the
types that had a high detonation velocity and great
shattering power against metal structures. Between
them, he and McCarter had about twenty pounds of
high explosives. They could only place their charges
with care and hope for the best. He ran battery checks
and confirmed that the remote-control detonating devices were functioning properly.

The equipment was ready. Bolan leaned back
against the trunk of a tree and began to plan. Stealth
and surprise were critical. They had two spare sets of
night-vision goggles. That limited the raiding party to
four. He and McCarter would go, of course. Wejak
was an obvious choice. He was amazingly strong. He
could carry the explosives, freeing Bolan and Mc-
Carter to use their weapons and take out the guards.

Did it make sense to take anyone else? Someone
would have to stay with the radio. If the raid was a total failure, someone would have to notify Stony Man
Farm. The satcom rig was as easy to use as any other
radio once it was set up and aligned on the satellite.
Should he take Lahka? Another pair of eyes was always useful. She could cover the withdrawal route.

He was about to make his decision when Van Heyn came rapidly down the slope. Her pale face was flushed from the heat and exertion.

"David says you should come at once. He says something important is going on," she gasped.

Bolan nodded, picked up his rifle and started up the slope. He worked his way quickly up to the ridge line and slipped down into a prone position by the Briton.

McCarter had taken the Bausch & Lomb spotting scope out of his pack and was staring through it intently. It wasn't a high-tech device, simply a high-quality spotting scope that could be used by a precision rifleman to spot his shots at long range. It provided twenty-four-power magnification that outclassed Bolan's rifle scope and binoculars completely. He was looking to the west, along the trail that ran on down the long valley.

"Take a look at this, Mack. I think you'll find it interesting."

The spotting scope was mounted on a miniature bipod. Bolan put his eye to the scope's eyepiece, being careful not to disturb its alignment. The scope's extreme magnification was good and bad. It brought distant objects incredibly close, but it also magnified every air tremor and puff of dust between the scope and its target.

Bolan looked carefully, waiting for a few seconds of distortion-free viewing. At first all he could see were distorted figures, five or six people coming slowly toward him, down the trail from the west. He could see the orange flash of Indonesian commando berets. It was probably another patrol returning to their camp near Skylance, but McCarter wouldn't have called him just for that.

He watched patiently. Then the air tremors subsided, and his view cleared. One of the figures wasn't wearing a camouflaged uniform and an orange beret. It looked like a woman, with black hair and brown skin. It might have been a Dani woman, but she was wearing a blue flight suit and black boots.

"It looks like we've found Captain Clark," Bolan said.

"Certainly looks that way. The Indonesians seem intent on interfering with our mission. I think we should do something about that."

"I agree. Let's go."

SOON, THEY WERE on the valley floor, pushing relentlessly along through the heat. Bolan knew that he was taking a chance moving along the trail, but he wanted the ambush to take place as far as possible from the crash site. McCarter's Sterling was the only silenced weapon they had unless he put a silencer on his Beretta. There was no way to be sure that they could take out the Indonesian commandos without firing other weapons. The farther away from the site they were, the less the chance that those shots would be heard.

The heat was brutal. Bolan took out his canteen and indulged in a few swallows of water. It tasted flat and tepid, but at least it was wet. He resisted the temptation to drain the canteen dry. There was no way to tell when he would have a chance to refill it.

He looked at McCarter. He was obviously feeling the heat, but he was maintaining the pace, despite the weight of the weapons and the equipment he was carrying. Lahka and Wejak were striding along. They didn't seem to feel the heat at all.

Bolan checked his watch; it was time to start thinking about picking an ambush site. It wouldn't do to stay on the trail too long and blunder into the Indonesian patrol. He and McCarter would have a very hard time explaining to the patrol commander that they were merely peaceful tourists interested in photographing the rugged beauty of the New Guinea highlands.

He looked to the left and right. Both sides of the trail were bordered by fields that looked as if they had once been used to grow crops. Where the fields had once been carefully cultivated, weeds and bushes now sprouted, lending an air of desolation to the whole area.

"What is this place?" he asked Lahka.

"It is a garden of war. No one lives here anymore."

"What did you say?" Bolan asked. He wasn't sure he had heard her correctly.

"A garden of war is a place where we fight big battles. When the Dani make war, we fight in two ways. One is a big battle with hundreds of warriors on each side. The other is small raids. This is a place where big battles are fought. It lies between two groups of tribes that are at war with each other. We fight with our spears and bows to kill enemy warriors. Their fresh blood appeases the ghosts of our tribe whom the enemy has killed. It is a wonderful sight. Hundreds of warriors on each side, fighting bravely to kill the enemy. When we win, we have a big victory ceremony called an *edai*. The women put on their finest feathers and furs and carry their spears. They sing and dance and taunt the enemy.''

She paused and looked at Bolan and McCarter. ''In the old days, we used to cook and eat the most famous enemy warrior we had killed. Naturally that shames the enemy and makes them vow revenge. Of course, we do not do that anymore. At least, not very often,'' she said shyly.

McCarter thought this over. It seemed to him that there was a problem.

''There's something I don't understand, Lahka,'' he said. ''If you kill warriors from another tribe, don't their ghosts demand fresh blood? It seems as if you'll be fighting forever.''

Lahka smiled. McCarter was clever. ''Of course. You understand perfectly. We are always at war. That is the way things are. The gods created men to fight their battles and kill their enemies. There is no word for 'peace' in our language. We had never heard of such a strange idea until the missionaries came.''

Bolan thought it made a certain amount of sense. He was beginning to see why the Dani were so intent on killing their enemies. It was time for him to think about his enemies. He had to achieve surprise, but that wasn't going to be easy. The fields on either side of the trail offered no real cover for an ambush, no groups of trees or thick clumps of bushes. There was something, though, when he looked closely. The fields weren't completely flat. Each had a central area surrounded by a shallow ditch two or three feet wide.

''What are those?'' he asked Lahka.

"The ditches? We grow sweet potatoes. The ditches carry the water away when there are heavy rains. If you do not do that, the roots of your plants will rot."

The fields and their ditches went on and on. There was nothing about them to attract attention or make the Indonesian commandos feel that they were in danger. This spot looked as good as any. He strode over to one of the ditches. It was about three feet deep and looked unpleasant. He could smell the wet, decaying leaves. The bottom was muddy, and there was still an inch or two of water here and there. It wasn't attractive, but it had one lovely feature. A man lying flat in the ditch would be invisible to anyone walking by on the trail.

He explained his plan to the others. Wejak had no questions. He hid his AK-47 in a clump of bushes and slipped quietly into the fields by the side of the trail. Armed only with his Dani spear, he moved quietly forward to scout out the Indonesians.

Lahka looked at Bolan steadily. "You need someone to make them stop right here, between you and David. I will do it," she said quietly. She took off her web belt and magazine pouches and placed them carefully behind a bush and removed her knife and pistol from under her skirt.

Lahka noticed the look on Bolan's face. Perhaps he was old-fashioned and didn't like sending a young woman into a situation where she might be killed.

"Don't worry," she said cheerfully. "If they do not see a gun, I do not think they will kill me. I can play the simple savage very well. They may beat me, but then we will kill them."

Bolan still didn't like it, but he couldn't see any alternative.

The Executioner sat down to do the hardest thing of all, wait for the enemy. Lahka sat quietly by his side. Bolan thought hard. No matter how he looked at it, there was a weakness in his plan. McCarter would have to be remarkably good and remarkably lucky to get five or six Indonesian commandos with his silenced Sterling before some of them could react.

If two or three of them could take cover and began to fire back, there would be a firefight, not a quick and lethal ambush. The main Indonesian force at the crash site might not be concerned if they heard a few shots, but they would react rapidly if they heard the sounds of sustained firing. What he needed was a way to add to the speed and force of his initial attack without making more noise.

There was a way, but it was risky. His 9 mm Beretta 93-R could be silenced, but that would be taking a chance. The 93-R was a remarkable weapon. The design engineers at Beretta had succeeded in getting the firepower of an eight-pound submachine gun from a specially modified, two-pound pistol. If the Beretta had operated like a conventional machine gun, it would have emptied its 20-round magazine in a single second, and its recoil would have made it uncontrollable.

The Beretta engineers had solved the problem in two ways. One was the burst limiter. When the safety selector was set for automatic fire, it limited a single burst to three rounds. The trigger had to be pulled again to fire a second burst. The 93-R was also fitted with a compact, efficient muzzle brake that directed high-pressure gas upward, pushing the muzzle down and keeping the weapon on target. The muzzle brake worked beautifully, but it magnified the sound of the firing, making the 93-R noticeably louder than a normal 9 mm pistol.

Bolan had a silencer for the Beretta in his pack, but it was totally incompatible with the muzzle brake. If he took off the muzzle brake and replaced it with the silencer, the 93-R would be as silent as McCarter's Sterling, but it would then be extremely difficult to control and fire accurately. He liked the Beretta much better in its normal configuration, but the silencer was the way to go this time. He took out the special tool, unscrewed the muzzle brake and installed the silencer.

Lahka was curious. "What are you doing?" she asked softly.

"Putting on a silencer."

Bolan finished the job and slipped a magazine loaded with heavy subsonic 9 mm ammunition into its butt. He didn't believe in taking unnecessary chances. He set the Beretta's selector for semiautomatic fire, aimed at a small rock about twenty yards away and squeezed the trigger. The Beretta hissed quietly, and the rock shattered into many pieces.

Lahka was impressed. "That is wonderful. I could hardly hear it. Why don't you do that to all our guns?"

Bolan didn't want to be rude, but it wasn't the time for a long discussion of ballistics, acoustics and subsonic versus supersonic bullets.

"It works better on some guns than on others."

Lahka was about to say something else when she suddenly stopped and listened intently. All Bolan heard were birdcalls, which wasn't surprising. Small groups of large white birds were busy foraging through the abandoned fields.

"That was Wejak," she said softly. "We must get ready. They are coming."

BOLAN LAY IN THE DITCH and watched as the Indonesian patrol came around the turn in the trail. He could see every detail of their camouflaged uniforms and their orange berets clearly through his binoculars. They didn't seem to be particularly alert, but they weren't being careless, either. The commandoes carried their M-16s in their hands, ready to fire. They were moving in pairs, one man on each side of the trail, with about ten yards between each pair. In the center, one commando walked alone, pulling along a woman in a torn blue flight suit by a rope around her neck. The woman's hands were tied behind her back. The man with the rope was amusing himself by jerking it and laughing as the pull of the rope forced the woman to almost choke as she stumbled and staggered along.

Bolan mentally checked her face against the pictures he had been shown in Australia. There was no doubt—it was Captain Clark. He looked around quickly. McCarter was waiting in the drainage ditch, keeping his head down and out of sight. Lahka was sitting by the side of the trail, holding her head in her hands and moaning softly.

The two pointmen saw Lahka. They immediately covered her with their M-16s and shouted an order.

Lahka simply sat there sobbing softly as they moved toward her. One of them reached down and grabbed her by her hair. Lahka shrieked as he pulled her brutally to her feet. They lifted her skirt with the barrels of their M-16s and seemed to relax when they saw that she couldn't possibly be armed.

They began to question her rapidly, slapping her across her face when she was slow to answer. Bolan couldn't understand what they were saying, but Lahka had told him her cover story before she took her position.

She was sobbing that she was an honest married woman. She had come to gather food in some fields where the plants were still bearing. She was alone and had no one to protect her. She had started home when two men had appeared. They had treated her very badly, taking her food without paying her, beating her when she tried to refuse. They were very bad men. Lahka hoped the soldiers would catch them and kill them.

Bolan could see the look on the men's faces change suddenly. He didn't need to understand Indonesian to follow the next question.

Men? What sort of men?

White men, Lahka sobbed. Cruel white men dressed in black, carrying many weapons. The two commandos motioned urgently to the man in the center of their patrol. He came forward, dragging Mary Clark behind him. There was a rapid buzz of conversation. Bolan watched tensely, hoping the two men in the rear would move forward also. No such luck. The last two men stopped where they were to provide cover for the rest of the patrol.

Lahka idly brought one hand up to brush her hair. Both Bolan and McCarter could see her clearly. That was the signal.

Now!

Bolan jumped to his feet, aiming his Beretta 93-R at the patrol leader. Behind the two men in the rear, McCarter rose silently like a grim, muddy apparition in his black combat suit.

McCarter's sudden movements disturbed one of the large white birds. It broke cover and flew away rapidly. The two Indonesians whirled at the sound of the big bird's wings and stared at McCarter in horror. The Briton was startled, but he kept his head. He swung his silenced 9 mm Sterling toward the closest man and pulled the trigger as his sights came on. Bolan heard the hiss of the Sterling's silencer as a 6-round burst tore into the commando's chest. Even as the man started to fall, McCarter swung his weapon toward the second man, who was bringing up his M-16. Bolan heard the hiss of the Sterling and the snarl of the M-16 as McCarter and the commando fired together.

Bolan had no time to see what happened. He had troubles of his own. The group in front of him was exploding into action. The man dragging Clark along had a big 9 mm automatic in his hand, and fired four fast shots in Bolan's direction. Clark threw herself back and down, jerking on the rope around her neck and spoiling her captor's aim. The Executioner put his sights on the man's belt buckle and pulled the trigger. The Beretta hissed and jumped like a scalded cat as it spit three 9 mm hollowpoints at the enemy gunner.

The bullets drilled into the commando's chest. Bolan knew the man was down and out, so he swung the

Beretta toward the other two men, keeping his hands locked on his weapon and pivoting from the waist. He took a fraction of a second to be sure his front sight was on target and pulled the Beretta's trigger. Three heavy subsonic 9 mm bullets smashed into the Indonesian, striking the middle of the man's forehead, killing him instantly.

But there was still the second man. Bolan pivoted toward him as fast as he could, but he knew he was going to be too late. No matter what he did, the commando was going to fire his M-16 before the Executioner could fire again. He saw a blur of motion as he turned. Lahka leaped up from her sitting position and smashed into the Indonesian with all her strength. Bolan heard the snarling crackle of the M-16 as it fired a burst, but Lahka had both her hands on the assault rifle's stock and barrel, trying to twist it away from the startled Indonesian. The bullets streaked harmlessly overhead.

The Stony Man warrior snapped the Beretta to his shoulder, trying for an aimed shot, but Lahka and the commando swayed back and forth, struggling frantically for control of the M-16. The Indonesian had the better grip, but the woman knew he would cut her to pieces instantly if he could pull the rifle away from her. She hung on frantically, gripping the deadly black rifle with every ounce of strength she possessed.

Bolan was about to lunge forward and finish the fight when he heard a woman's voice shrieking frantically. "Look out! Behind you! Behind you!"

He pivoted back to the right instantly. The first man Bolan had shot was on his feet. The big American could see spots of blood on his left side, but he still had the flat black automatic pistol in his hand. The two men fired together. Bolan saw yellow flashes as the pistol fired repeatedly. Something struck him on his body armor, two hard blows to the chest. The Beretta bucked and hissed as he fired two 3-round bursts as fast as he could pull the trigger. His last two rounds went high, but four 9 mm hollowpoints were enough. The Indonesian lost all interest in shooting. The big black automatic was suddenly too heavy for him to hold. It slipped from his fingers as he slumped to the ground.

Bolan heard Lahka scream behind him and pivoted toward her. The Indonesian commando had succeeded in hooking one of his legs behind one of hers, and had thrown her onto her back. He snarled in triumph and thrust the muzzle of his M-16 in Lahka's face. He said something taunting in Indonesian and started to pull the trigger. The woman frantically knocked the barrel aside, and a 6-round burst of high-velocity bullets tore into the ground inches from her head. Lahka grabbed the rifle's slender barrel and tried to push it away. The Indonesian laughed and began to force the muzzle back toward her face.

He had succumbed to target fixation, concentrating on Lahka and neglecting to watch what was happening around him. It was a fatal error. The sights of Bolan's Beretta 93-R were perfectly aligned on the man's web belt. He pulled the trigger, and three 9 mm hollowpoints struck almost simultaneously. He didn't go down but swayed on his feet, and the strength went out of his hands. Lahka tore the M-16 out of his grip with a shriek of triumph. Bolan pulled the Beretta down out of recoil and triggered another 3-round burst. He saw dust fly from the commando's uniform as the bullets smashed home. Lahka rolled to one side and fired a long burst from the M-16 as he fell. He was dead before he hit the ground.

Bolan wasn't sure how many times he had fired. He dropped the Beretta on the soft ground and drew his .44 Magnum Desert Eagle. He took a fast look back down the trail. McCarter and Wejak were standing over the bodies of two commandos. The Briton had shot one. The Dani warrior hadn't carried any firearms on his scouting expedition. He had come up behind the second Indonesian and driven his twelve-foot-long hardwood spear straight through him. It was a prehistoric way to kill someone, but it certainly worked. The man was dead.

Clark looked stunned and a little frightened. She had been as surprised as the Indonesians when the lethal, close-quarters combat had exploded around her. Bolan understood that perfectly. It had been close. That damned bird had nearly gotten them all killed.

Bolan moved toward the woman, smiling reassuringly as he drew his fighting knife and cut her hands free with a single slash. Bolan handed her his canteen, and she drank thirstily.

"Captain Clark?" he asked.

"Damned right, I'm Mary Clark. Oh, God, am I glad to see you! You're Air Force SAR? You've got a jolly green giant? Let's get out of here!"

Bolan wished he did have one of the huge green Air Force search-and-rescue helicopters. It would certainly have solved a lot of his problems.

"Sorry, we don't have a chopper," he said quietly.

Clark's smile faded. She stared at Bolan's blacksuit and the strange weapon in his hands.

"You're not an Air Force search-and-rescue team, are you? Just who the hell are you guys?"

"Call me Belasko," he said.

Clark was an intelligent woman. She noticed that Bolan hadn't answered her question and knew he wasn't going to.

"All right, Belasko. You are the good guys in black. I don't have to know who you work for, and I won't ask. But you are here to get me out, aren't you?"

"That's right," Bolan said. "You don't ask and I don't tell, but we are here to get you out and blow up Skylance."

CHAPTER ELEVEN

Meiko was still furious when she slipped into a small souvenir shop four blocks away from the hotel in Djajapura. The man behind the counter took one look at her face and ushered her quickly into the back room and left her alone. She picked up the phone and dialed a number quickly.

"Sunrise," she said as someone answered the phone.

"One moment," a man's voice replied. Meiko waited. She could still hear the man's voice, but he wasn't talking to her. "It is the *gaijin*," he said.

Meiko shook with fury. *Gaijin* was the Japanese word that meant "foreigner." It was never a compliment.

She heard a new voice. "Report, Meiko. Where are you? What is the situation?"

"Wu's shop. I am safe, Ohara."

"I am sure of that," Ohara said coldly. "But you are supposed to be at the hotel, using all your marvelous charms to seduce this rich Canadian. Why are you not there?"

"Someone ordered an assault on the hotel. I had no warning. I was almost killed."

"That would have been a great pity, Meiko. You know we would all have mourned for you."

"Let me speak to Tanaka. I must make a report," Meiko hissed furiously.

"Tanaka is not here. He has flown to Wamena. You will report to me. Is the Canadian dead?"

"No, as far as I know, he is alive and all our men are dead. Whoever made that stupid plan has much to answer for."

"I will take note of your criticism of my plan. So, the assault team was killed, but you escaped without a scratch on your pretty skin?"

"There was nothing I could do! I had been disarmed because of this stupid plan of yours. I could have killed Gary a dozen times if I had been given sensible orders instead of being told to play a simpering flight attendant. Listen to me, Ohara. I can locate the Canadian and his friends—"

"Be silent!" Ohara snarled. "You will do nothing more here. Take the next flight to Wamena and report to Tanaka there. You can explain your failure to Mr. Ito."

Wamena, the Baliem Valley

MAJOR HATTA STALKED into the headquarters building and glared at his battalion clerk. It wasn't the sergeant's fault. The orders directing Hatta to return to Wamena immediately for a critical meeting had come directly from the high command. It almost certainly meant that the idiots back at headquarters were going to interfere with his operations, perhaps put some HQ colonel in command who would take all the credit if they caught the Americans and see that Hatta took all the blame if they didn't. The major ground his teeth in rage. No matter how hard he tried, he couldn't overcome his one great weakness. He had no money or political influence.

The sergeant snapped to attention and saluted smartly. "Your visitor is waiting in your office, sir."

"And who is this mysterious visitor who is sitting in my office?" Hatta snarled.

"He did not say, sir, but he had a letter from General Hamzah directing that we give him all possible assistance. I thought it best to treat him as a very important visitor."

Hatta's temper cooled. His sergeant had done the right thing. The political maneuvering of the high command wasn't his fault.

"Very well, Sergeant, I will meet with this man. I do not wish to be disturbed unless there is a report from Captain Thanrin. In the meantime, be sure the helicopter is refueled and ready to take off. I expect to return to the field shortly."

Hatta stalked into his office. A man was standing staring intently at the large map of the Baliem Valley on the wall. The major was surprised to see that the man wore civilian clothes. Not army or air force, then. He had to be from military intelligence or the secret police. If that were so, he was a dangerous man.

"I am Major Hatta. You wish to see me?" he said politely.

The man turned to look at him and smiled. He wasn't an Indonesian. A Chinese? No, probably a Japanese or a Korean.

"Ah, yes, Major Selim Hatta, it is an honor to meet you. I have heard many good things about you. It is well-known that you are the finest soldier in New Guinea."

"I only wish it were well-known to the high command," Hatta said sourly. "May I ask who you are and why you are here?"

"Of course. Please forgive my bad manners. I am Raizo Tanaka. I am the chief security officer for the Kanabo Corporation. I wish to discuss certain matters of mutual interest with you."

Hatta thought quickly. He had heard of the Kanabo Corporation, of course. It was one of the four or five large Japanese corporations trying to exploit the natural resources of New Guinea. Its area of operation was to the southwest, toward the coast. The Japanese had never shown any interest in the Baliem Valley. Why was Tanaka here? Did it have something to do with the Americans? Perhaps, but in any case, the government in Djakarta was seriously interested in attracting foreign businesses to New Guinea. He had better appear helpful. Complaints to Djakarta would hinder his career advancement.

"How can I assist you, Mr. Tanaka?"

"The Kanabo Corporation is interested in developing mining operations and other types of industrial activities in New Guinea. We have been searching for large mineral and oil deposits. I will tell you in strictest confidence that we have been very successful. We have discovered very large deposits of copper and gold in the Agats area on the south coast. You have heard of the American Freeport Copper Mine at Tembagapura?"

Hatta nodded. The Freeport Mine was the largest industrial facility in Western New Guinea. The Indonesian government took in hundreds of millions of dollars per year in taxes on its exports. But what did it have to do with him or the Baliem Valley? The Agats area was 125 miles to the south.

"The Freeport Mine ships fifty thousand tons of high-grade copper ore a day. We estimate that our operation will be twice as large as theirs when it is fully developed. We should also mine six tons of gold per year. We also have many other interests. We may develop major operations here in the Baliem Valley."

Tanaka paused and pointed at the map on the wall. "Western New Guinea is a huge area, Major. Most of it is unexplored. We are certain that there are vast amounts of natural resources to be found and exploited, but there is a problem. It requires billions of yen to do this. Japanese investors are unwilling to put money into unstable areas. This so-called Free Papua Movement is a disturbing factor. It must be suppressed."

Hatta sighed. What Tanaka said had sounded very promising. Now it sounded like more complaints. That was the last thing he needed.

"I assure you that I do the best I can, Mr. Tanaka, but it is difficult. Very difficult. I have only one battalion to cover a wide area. They must carry out pacification and police operations. A central striking force of elite troops should be created with the authority to operate anywhere in Western New Guinea. There is no central direction. Authority is fragmented. There should be a single officer in overall command. And there are people in Djajapura who insist we coddle these damned savages. They do not seem to realize that cannibals and headhunters must be ruled with an iron hand."

Tanaka's polite smile broadened. "Precisely, Major. That is a brilliant analysis of the situation. I told my managers that they would not be disappointed in you, and I was right. Your plan will be implemented immediately."

Hatta smiled bitterly. "That is what should be done, but I cannot do it. I am only a major, stationed here in this wilderness because I have no money or influence. I have no authority to do what is needed. You must speak to the general staff."

Tanaka smiled again and handed Hatta an envelope. "We have, Major, or perhaps I should say Colonel. We are not without influence in Djakarta, as you will see. Here is a copy of your promotion and the order placing you in command of all counterterrorist activities in the central highlands. All military and police units in the area will report to you. A battalion of police mobile brigade troops will arrive in two days. They will assume all police functions and free your men for counterterrorist operations. Allow me to be the first to congratulate you on your promotion, Colonel."

Hatta looked at the copies of the orders closely. They seemed to be genuine.

"You may encounter unexpected expenses, Colonel," Tanaka said smoothly. "Here is a draft establishing a credit of fifty million rupiahs in your name at the Djajapura Export-Import Bank. If you should need additional funds, please do not hesitate to call on me."

Hatta smiled. "It is a pleasure to do business with you, Mr. Tanaka. What do you wish me to do? Would you like me to send soldiers to guard your facilities? That can be arranged."

Tanaka smiled coldly. "That will not be necessary, Colonel. Kanabo Corporation facilities are very well guarded indeed. There is one other thing that concerns us greatly. The two American spies who are operating in the Baliem Valley."

Hatta felt a cold knot in his stomach, but he kept a smile on his face. "There is some evidence that there are two Caucasians in the area. They are probably aiding the FPM."

"You may feel certain that there are American spies near here. We have detected satcom transmissions from this area. We have not been able to decode the messages because they were kept short. Even the best computers require a certain minimum amount of text before the code can be broken. Still, we know the Americans are here, and we believe we know their mission."

Tanaka paused and stared at Hatta for a few seconds. "What I am about to say is for your ears only. It must be kept secret. For some time, the Americans have been operating advanced reconnaissance satellites over New Guinea, spying on our operations."

Hatta was puzzled. "Why should the Americans do that?"

"Because America and Japan are at war. Not a war fought with missiles and hydrogen bombs, but an economic and scientific war. Since the Soviet Union collapsed, the Americans like to say there is only one superpower in the world, the United States, and they intend to rule the world. If you look only at military power, they are right. But they know our economic and technical power is growing rapidly, and they fear us. They have directed their CIA to discover our scientific secrets. Their satellites are their principal way of doing this. The Americans think their satellites are invulnerable, but they are wrong. Two days ago, we succeeded in throwing one of their spy satellites out of control. It came down here, in the Baliem Valley."

Hatta wasn't a scientist, but he grasped Tanaka's point instantly. "The American spies have been sent here to destroy the satellite."

"Precisely. We wish the Americans to be hunted down and killed. We want the satellite found, and we wish to examine it thoroughly. We wish you to concentrate your efforts to accomplish these objectives. No one can criticize you for this. It is clearly your duty to destroy foreign spies and protect honest businessmen."

Hatta nodded. The Japanese were paying him handsomely to do what he intended to do anyway. If they wanted the pieces of this American satellite, that was nothing to him. He smiled sincerely at Tanaka.

"I will concentrate all my resources on it immediately. The Americans will be found and killed. I will not fail. You may depend on it."

"I am sure we can, Colonel, but a word of advice. Our CEO, Mr. Ito, is a generous man and extremely loyal to those who serve him well, but he does not tolerate failure. Do not fail him."

TANAKA MADE SURE that no one was following him before he slipped into a shabby commercial building on the outskirts of Wamena. He spoke politely to the secretary who sat behind a battered desk. He smiled to himself while she announced him to Mr. Ito. It would be a clever man who realized that this was temporarily the New Guinea headquarters of one of the most powerful corporations in the world.

The secretary returned and bowed as she ushered the new arrival into Ito's office. Tanaka bowed with deep, unfeigned respect. Ito was in his sixties, but the Japanese revere age. He also had the keenest brain of any man Tanaka knew. There were few trappings of power in the small office. A sophisticated radio-telephone and fax machine sat on a low wooden desk.

There was only one decoration on the wall, a *shin-gunto,* a Japanese army officer's sword. Its plain brown metal scabbard showed signs of hard use. A collector of Japanese swords would have dismissed it as a common, modern blade, but Tanaka knew its story. Ito's father had carried it on Guadalcanal when he fought and died against the Americans in 1942. His father's first sergeant had brought it back to Japan as a last memento for a grieving widow and her proud young son. That was more than fifty years ago, but Ito hadn't forgotten. He didn't like Americans.

Ito motioned Tanaka to be seated. His secretary came in with a pot of hot green tea and delicate porcelain cups on a tray. She poured the tea with exquisite grace and left the room. The two men sipped the strong, bitter brew appreciatively. Tanaka relaxed. He wasn't in a hurry, and the old rituals were important to Ito.

''How did your meeting with Colonel Hatta go?'' the older man asked quietly.

"Very well, Ito-san. He is delighted with his promotion and his new authority. He has agreed to all our proposals."

"Good. Now, tell me, what are your impressions of this man? I am always a bit nervous about a man who will sell himself for money."

Tanaka nodded. "He is an excellent soldier. I am not concerned that he takes our money. He is an Indonesian, and most of their officials expect to be bribed. Besides, his interests and ours are the same. The Americans have already killed some of his men. He would try to track them down and kill them in any case. It is a matter of honor."

Ito smiled. He understood that perfectly. Any honorable man wanted revenge.

"You have done well. This man should be very useful. Now, I have another task for you." He opened a folder on his desk and handed his subordinate a slim stack of photographs. "Look at these, Tanaka-san. I believe we have found the American space vehicle."

Tanaka stared at the photographs. He had seen better pictures. The shots had been taken in a hurry and with a miniature camera, but he could make out a dull gray triangular shape lying on its belly. He looked at the other pictures and saw two cockpits, tail fins and two big jet-engine inlets. He could see no insignia or registration numbers, but he was sure Ito was right. It had to be the American vehicle. It could be nothing else.

"Where is it?" he asked quickly.

"Not more than thirty miles from here. The pictures were taken by an army helicopter pilot. He ferried reinforcements to the patrol who discovered it. You can see that the vehicle had a crew of two. The body of one was found in the forward cockpit, killed by our laser. The second crewman survived and escaped. The Indonesian commandos are searching for him now."

"Does Colonel Hatta know about this?" Tanaka asked.

"We cannot be sure, but if he does not know now, he soon will. I do not believe he will try to steal the vehicle and sell it on the international arms market. He lacks the money and contacts to do that. But he might be tempted to report it to his superiors. Who knows what they might do? We must gain control of the American space vehicle as soon as possible."

Ito paused for a moment and poured more steaming tea.

"This is what I wish you to do. I do not trust the Indonesians in this matter. Assemble a force of our best men. Take the heavy-lift helicopter. Secure the American vehicle and fly it to our main complex at once. I wish you to lead this operation personally. Inform Hatta of our intentions. Do you have any questions?"

"One, Ito-san. If I encounter the Americans, what shall I do?"

"Take the surviving crewman captive. He may have valuable information which we can persuade him to tell us, but the two spies are of no use. Kill them."

Tanaka bowed. "I understand, honored sir. I will carry out your orders immediately."

Ito took another sip of the bitter tea.

"This is an important mission. Remember what the samurai said. 'Death is lighter than a feather. Duty is heavier than a mountain.' Do not fail."

CHAPTER TWELVE

Mack Bolan waited patiently as the light faded and the moon began to rise. He and McCarter had taken turns keeping the Indonesians under observation. Their routine didn't seem to vary. A few men were posted as a guard near Skylance. They were relieved by fresh guards every two hours. Except for that, nothing happened. They didn't seem to be expecting an attack, but Bolan didn't like what he saw. It gave him the uneasy feeling that the Indonesians were waiting for something or someone. He wanted to get the job done and get out before the situation changed for the worse. He would go in as soon as it was really dark.

Mary Clark slipped up the slope and lay at Bolan's side. McCarter had been checking her out on the night-vision goggles. Now the soldier wanted her to look at Skylance and evaluate the situation. She knew far more about it than he and McCarter had been able to absorb in one quick briefing in Australia. He handed her the binoculars and waited while she slowly scanned the crash site.

"What do you want to know?" she asked quietly.

"Has anything changed since you left?"

Clark shook her head. "Negative. As far as I can tell from here, they haven't done anything but take my pilot's body out of the forward cockpit. The sensor-data recorders are probably still there. Do you want to try to take them out?''

Bolan nodded. "Washington wants them. They say the data will help them analyze the weapon that attacked you. We get the recorders, then our orders say to destroy Skylance."

"That's a shame. If she were on a runway, refueled and a few holes were patched up, I could fly her home."

Bolan frowned. That was the problem. Skylance was in too good a shape. If it wasn't destroyed, somebody else could repair it and fly it anywhere in the world.

"Sorry, Captain. My orders are to destroy it."

"I understand. Listen, you'd better take me with you when you go, and let me take the recorders out. I tried to set the destruct system to detonate before I bugged out. I couldn't make it work, but it may be armed. Anyone who opens any of the access panels had better know what they're doing and be damned careful."

That was the logical thing to do, but he couldn't order her to do it. He admired her attitude. She might not be a trained special-operations soldier, but she had guts.

"All right, you're on the team, Captain. You and I and David will go down as soon as it gets really dark."

Clark handed back the binoculars and frowned.

"I do see one problem. There are four or five of those special commandos on guard down there. They all have M-16s. What are they going to do when we come waltzing up to Skylance? Roll out the welcome mat?"

"Don't worry. They won't make any trouble. David and I will take them out."

Clark shuddered. She knew very well what "take them out" meant. It wasn't that she was fainthearted. She was a professional Air Force officer and a qualified combat pilot. But to her, combat was shrieking through the sky at Mach 2 in an F-15 Eagle, firing guided missiles. She knew enemy pilots died when their planes were hit, but somehow this was different. She wasn't used to knives and silenced weapons in the dark.

Bolan looked at the sky. The clouds overhead were getting thicker, and a breeze was springing up. It looked like rain. Light rain wouldn't matter, but if it really began to rain heavily, it would take away most of the effectiveness of their night-vision goggles and make fast movement difficult.

He left Mary Clark on watch and moved down the slope to the rest of the party. McCarter was giving Van Heyn one final checkout on the satcom. Wejak and Lahka were watching. The Dani woman wasn't happy. She wanted to go on the raid and hated the idea of being left behind in the covering party. Bolan admired her spirit, but his decisions were never based on sentiment. They had only one spare set of night-vision goggles left after stray rounds had destroyed one pair. Clark knew Skylance, so she was the logical one to go. Wejak and Lahka would wait on the ridge line. If things went wrong and the raiding party had to run for it, they could provide covering fire.

He listened while Van Heyn recited the directions McCarter had given her. She seemed to understand them perfectly. Bolan wasn't worried. Once the satcom was set up and locked on a satellite, it operated like any other shortwave radio.

"Remember, if we don't come back in an hour, send the message and tell them we failed and that I recommended an air strike to destroy Skylance. Got it?" Bolan said.

Van Heyn nodded. "I understand. I will do what you say, but I would much rather you come back and do it yourself."

Bolan smiled grimly.

"So would I."

BOLAN LED the raiding party slowly down the slope. McCarter followed him quietly, with Clark bringing up the rear.

The first scattered raindrops were beginning to fall. Bolan was determined to get the job done before the rain really started coming down. He looked ahead toward Skylance. He couldn't see any movement, but he knew the guards were still there. Bolan was leading his team along the valley floor now, moving slowly through one of the abandoned fields. It would have been quicker to move along the trail. Quicker, but not smart. He didn't think the Indonesian guards were expecting an attack, but they would be watching for movement along the trail.

Bolan stopped about a hundred yards from the aircraft and motioned for Clark to wait there, then pointed to his left, toward the tail. McCarter nodded and moved out like a silent black shadow. The Executioner headed to the right, toward Skylance's nose. He had his Beretta 93-R ready, with its silencer installed and set for semiautomatic fire. With any luck, they would take the Indonesians by surprise and catch them in a cross fire.

He worked his way to the nose and chanced a quick look around. He saw two commandos standing up, a few feet from the fuselage. Bolan scanned the site carefully. Where were the other two? All day long, there had been four men on guard. Why were things different now? Were the Indonesians changing the guard?

He had no time to worry. No one was going to answer his questions. If they were going to do the job, they had better do it now. Bolan took one long step and slid smoothly around the aircraft's nose. He aimed the Beretta at the nearer guard's head. The faint glow of his night sights looked like bright, glowing beacons through his night-vision goggles. The guard had to have seen a flicker of movement in the dim light. He whirled toward Bolan, bringing up his M-16 as he turned.

The Executioner fired twice, as fast as he could pull the trigger. The commando swayed for a second, then fell heavily. The second man swung his M-16 toward Bolan. McCarter was behind him, moving through the dark as silently as a ghost, and he cut the Indonesian down with a 6-round burst.

The Briton quickly checked the two commandos and confirmed that both were dead. Then he slipped into a prone position and covered the approach from Skylance to the main Indonesian camp. If he saw anyone coming, he would give the alarm.

Bolan slipped back around the nose of the aircraft and waved to Clark. She dashed forward.

"It's all yours," he said softly. "Get the recorders."

The captain didn't waste time on conversation. She moved along the fuselage, climbed up on the wing, reached into her cockpit and threw two switches. Bolan heard a soft metallic click. A small panel about as big as a man's hand had popped open behind the second cockpit.

"The batteries haven't run down. Emergency power's still on," Clark reported. "Now, I key in my personal identification number. That ought to open her up, but you want to stand back. There's a small destruct charge on each recorder. If something goes wrong, things may get very exciting."

Bolan nodded and moved back ten feet. Clark took a deep breath, and her fingers moved on the buttons. For a second or two, nothing happened. Then a larger access panel swung open. A dim light came on inside the fuselage. Clark reached inside gingerly and released two mounting fasteners. She slid out a flat black disk about a foot in diameter. Bolan could hear her sigh of relief.

"One down and one to go," she said. She handed Bolan the disk, which he slipped into his pack. Clark moved quickly to the other side of the aircraft to repeat the procedure. Bolan moved forward and touched McCarter lightly on the shoulder.

"Clark's in," he said as quietly as he could. "Let's set the charges."

The Briton nodded and followed him back to Skylance. They opened the bottom compartments of their packs and began to take out the small cubes of C-4 plastique and the detonators. Clark slipped back around the fuselage. She had the other recorder in her hands and a smile on her face as she handed it to Bolan. She had done her job. Now he and McCarter would finish theirs. Another five minutes, and the charges would be installed. Another ten minutes, and he would send the command to fire the charges. Then all he would have left to worry about would be getting out of New Guinea.

He picked up an M-16 rifle, handed it to Clark and pointed back toward the Indonesian camp.

"Go ten yards that way and take cover. If anyone comes this way, let me know."

The captain nodded and slipped into the dark.

McCarter was already starting to place the first charge.

"Bloody hell!" he said quietly. "This damned thing seems to be built entirely of nonmagnetic materials. We can't use magnets. We'll have to tape the charges on."

He started to reach into his pack and suddenly stopped.

"Listen!" he hissed.

Bolan listened intently. At first he only heard the sound of the wind and the soft patter of raindrops. Then his blood froze. He heard another sound, faint but unmistakable. Helicopters! Not just one or two, but several, flying together through the night. There were no friendly helicopters in New Guinea, and whoever was flying the choppers had to have night-vision equipment. There was no other way they could be flying in the dark. If the helicopters were armed, they would be caught out in the open on the valley floor and cut to pieces.

Bolan pointed to Skylance's triangular left wing. "Under there!" he snapped as he ducked and rolled under the gray metal wing.

McCarter was a second behind him. The sound of the rotors grew louder as the first helicopter soared past a hundred feet above them. The world seemed to explode into glaring, incredibly bright green light. Bolan flipped up his night-vision goggles. The helicopter was circling slowly overhead, playing a searchlight on Skylance.

The searchlight paused for a second. Clark stood frozen in the center of the beam. Bolan heard the snarling rattle of a machine-gun fire. Red tracers tore into the ground near the woman, and gouts of dirt shot into the air. It was a message that could be understood in any language. She threw down her M-16 and raised her hands in the air. The helicopter touched down, and eight men jumped from the side doors and ran toward Clark. Bolan could see half a dozen small red dots moving over her body—laser sights.

McCarter aimed his Sterling and looked inquiringly at Bolan. A second helicopter soared overhead, then a third. The Executioner shook his head. He could see the Indonesian commandos pouring out of their camp. A second helicopter touched down, and another group of men jumped out, short, deadly-looking automatic weapons in their hands. They were wearing strange blue-and-gray-mottled uniforms, a design Bolan had never seen before.

There was nothing they could do for Clark. Opening fire now would probably get her killed.

"Let's get the hell out of here," he snarled.

McCarter nodded. They slipped around the aircraft's nose. All clear. Bolan led the way back into the fields. Suddenly he heard the sound of rotors. A helicopter was flying straight toward them, fifty feet above the earth, probing the ground ahead of it with a searchlight mounted in the nose. The big American snapped his Beretta 93-R to his shoulder and fired a quick shot at the center of the glowing disk. The searchlight beam vanished in a blue-white flash.

The chopper turned abruptly, and the door gunner opened up with his machine gun, tracers streaking through the darkness. McCarter had a better target. He aimed at the helicopter's nose and emptied the Sterling's magazine in three long, ripping bursts. The helicopter seemed to stagger, then nosed down, trailing a stream of thick gray smoke. It smashed into the ground and vanished in a huge ball of orange fire.

Bolan stared at the flaming wreck for half a second. No one was going to get out of that alive. He signaled to McCarter, and they plunged into the night. Rain began to pour down harder as they ran. Bolan could hear shouting behind him, and he knew a pursuit had been mounted.

The voices behind them were getting louder. McCarter rammed a fresh clip into his subgun, whirled and fired a long burst. It was impossible to tell if he hit anything, but 9 mm bullets hissing overhead should slow the opposition. It was a good idea, but it might not be good enough. The two men were weighed down by their combat gear. Their pursuers seemed to be traveling light. A burst of bullets struck the ground five feet to Bolan's left. Someone behind him was trying his luck.

Bolan grabbed a flash-stun grenade from his web harness, pulled the pin and hurled the bomb over his shoulder. Three seconds crawled by, then the grenade detonated. It was designed not to kill but to disable. The sound of the blast wasn't nearly as loud outdoors as it would have been inside a room, but the incredibly bright flash was eye searing. Bolan heard screams and shrieks of pain behind him. He threw a second grenade down the slope and ran on as hard as he could. His lungs were on fire, and his leg muscles were burning from the all-out effort. He couldn't continue like this much longer. If they didn't reach the top of the ridge in another few seconds, they would have to turn and shoot it out.

Suddenly he heard a woman's voice as Lahka shouted a challenge.

"Belasko!" he shouted back with the last bit of breath in his lungs. The ground seemed to vanish from beneath his feet as he shot over the top of the ridge. He hit the ground and rolled. Bolan heard the snarling crackle of Lahka's M-4 carbine as she opened fire, then the duller boom of Wejak's AK-47 as he joined the fight. Someone stumbled over Bolan and fell heavily across him.

"Sorry," McCarter said apologetically as he rolled to his feet and fired two quick bursts down the slope. He ducked as red tracers streaked past him.

Bolan grabbed his last two flash-stun grenades from his web belt, pulled the pins and threw them down the slope. That ought to buy him a few seconds. He saw the black nylon case of his Remington 700-P in the flash of the first grenade. He lunged for it and pulled it out of the case, flicked the switch to the AN/PVS-10 sniper's night sight and dived for the ridge line as tracers streaked over his head. The rain was a heavy curtain. Even with the sight's magnification, he couldn't see beyond fifty yards, but that was enough.

Four blurred figures charged up the slope. Bolan snapped his cross hairs on the closest one and pulled the trigger. The Remington bucked and roared. The man spun and fell, his body rolling back down the slope. The Executioner worked the bolt and chambered a fresh round. A second man was firing at him, raking the ground in front of Bolan with one long, ripping burst after another. Particles of moist dirt spattered into the soldier's face, but he concentrated all his attention on his target and put a bullet through the man's chest. He cartwheeled spectacularly back down the slope. Bolan worked his bolt smoothly and snapped a shot at a third man. He couldn't tell whether it was a hit or a miss. The enemy was taking cover.

Bolan swept his scope over the slope below him. The rain was falling harder and harder. He couldn't see any clear targets to shoot at, but he could sense movement to the left and right. The enemy was taking advantage of the cover provided by the heavy rainfall and was moving to flank them. They weren't going to be able to hold them much longer.

"Too many of them. We've got to break contact," he yelled.

"Right you are, mate," McCarter said. "I may be able to do something about that. Hold them for thirty seconds."

Easier said than done, but Bolan had faith in the Briton. If he needed thirty seconds, Bolan would buy it for him whatever it cost. He thumbed fresh cartridges into the Remington's magazine and fired at muzzle-flashes and blurred movements. Lahka suddenly appeared by his side.

"Wejak has no more bullets left. I have only those in my pistol left. What shall we do?"

Bolan nodded grimly. He thought for a second of telling her to run for it, but he didn't think she would. "They'll be coming in a minute," he said quickly. "Cover my back when they do."

McCarter appeared, pulling something out of the bottom of his pack.

"They're getting ready to come on the left. I've lent Wejak my pistol. We'll try and stop them there. You hold them here."

"Take these," McCarter added with a wicked grin. "A little surprise for our friends. I got them from the Australians. I thought they might come in handy." He handed Bolan two round metal objects. Bolan felt the familiar shapes of antipersonnel fragmentation grenades.

"These are Australian L-2 A-2s. They are a bit lighter than your American M-61s, but I think you will find them quite effective. Four-second fuses. Don't dilly-dally once you've pulled the pin and let go of the safety lever."

Bolan heard Wejak shout.

"Duty calls," McCarter said, and slipped back toward Wejak.

The Executioner could hear shouting below them and to his right. They were getting ready. In a moment, they would be coming. He put down his Remington and fisted one of the grenades. The fingers of his right hand held the safety lever firmly. He slipped his left forefinger through the ring of the pin and waited tensely.

A whistle blew below, and the attackers came shouting up the slope, firing on the run. Bolan pulled the grenade's pin and released the safety lever. He heard a soft pop as the striker struck the primer and a reassuring sizzle as the fuse began to burn. He counted swiftly to himself.

"One thousand and one." His arm swept up and poised for the throw as he counted.

"One thousand and two." He threw it.

The grenade arched away into the dark, struck the ground and bounced down the slope. "One thousand and three." Bolan reached for his second grenade.

"One thousand and four!" The burning fuse reached the detonator, and the grenade exploded, hurling hundreds of preformed, high-velocity steel fragments outward in a spherical pattern. Anyone those lethal fragments struck would be killed or severely wounded. Bolan heard frantic yells and screams. He quickly pulled the pin and threw his second bomb.

He heard a dull boom from his left as McCarter's first grenade detonated, then the louder, closer blast as his own second grenade exploded. The attack dissolved in confusion and devastation. Bolan reached for his Remington. He would take a few more quick shots and convince their attackers that they never wanted to try to come up the slope again.

He heard Lahka suddenly scream and the flat bark of her 9 mm Browning automatic as she fired repeatedly. She was firing right past his head. He could feel

the hot breath of the muzzle-blast against his face as
he whirled to the right. Four men were rushing at
them. Lahka hit one. Bolan didn't have time to think
or even bring his rifle to his shoulder. He simply
pointed the Remington's long barrel at the closest
man's chest and pulled the trigger. The rifle roared,
and the high-velocity .308 bullet smashed into the
man's body. He spun and fell. The gunner just behind him almost tripped over his body, but kept coming on.

Bolan didn't have time to work the Remington's bolt
or draw a pistol. Guided by the combat instincts of an
ex-infantry man, he lunged at his attacker as if he were
in a bayonet fight. The heavy steel barrel of the Remington slammed into the attacker's middle with every
ounce of Bolan's weight behind it. The breath
whooshed out of the man's lungs, and he doubled
over, gasping in agony. But he was still clutching a
short black submachine gun. The big American instantly drove the steel butt plate of the Remington into
the man's jaw in a perfectly executed vertical butt-
stroke. He went down instantly.

Lahka was shrieking furiously. He whirled toward
her, dropping his rifle and drawing his .44 Magnum
pistol as he turned. Lahka and the fourth man were
struggling desperately for his submachine gun. The
attacker had the better grip, but Lahka knew she was
a dead woman if she lost the struggle. Bolan had his
Desert Eagle in his hands, but Lahka and the man
were swaying back and forth. If he pulled the trigger,
he could just as easily hit her as her attacker.

The man suddenly overpowered Lahka and threw
her down in a perfectly timed judo move, then pointed

his submachine gun at her face. The glowing green dots of Bolan's night sights were perfectly aligned on the center of the man's head. The big pistol roared as he pressed the trigger twice in a deadly double tap. Two .44-caliber hollowpoints struck like a sledge-hammer. Lahka's attacker instantly lost interest in shooting her or in anything else. He fell across the woman as his submachine gun dropped from his nerveless hands.

Lahka threw him off and rolled to her feet, making some remarks in Dani that sizzled with fury. Her body was spattered with blood, but none of it seemed to be hers. She snatched up her pistol, aimed at the body of the man on the ground and tried to pull the trigger. Nothing happened. The Browning's slide was locked open on an empty chamber.

Bolan's ears were ringing from the repeated close-range muzzle-blast. Without conscious thought, he slipped a fresh magazine into the Desert Eagle. He had only fired two shots, but a warrior never knew when he was going to need a full magazine. He holstered his pistol, picked up his rifle and began to carefully wipe off dirt from the stock and scope sight. Everything looked all right, but he couldn't be sure that his scope had not been knocked out of line until he got a chance to test fire it again.

McCarter appeared out of the dark, almost invisible in his black fatigues. He looked at bodies scattered around Bolan and Lahka and shook his head.

"We'd better go now," he said. "I'm starting to run low on ammunition, and I've got only two grenades left. I think they have a belly full just now, but give them a few minutes to reorganize, and they may attack again.''

Bolan nodded grimly. There was nothing they could do for Mary Clark, and they didn't stand a chance of getting close to Skylance now. He needed to talk to Stony Man and tell them about the change in the situation. It left a bitter taste in his mouth, but the only strategy that made sense was to withdraw and stay alive to fight another day.

McCarter led the way as they slipped off through the dark.

''By the way, mate, did you notice something interesting about our attackers?''

''Yeah,'' Bolan replied grimly. ''They were Japanese.''

CHAPTER THIRTEEN

Nothing was going right. The early morning was cold and gray, and the rain was continuing to fall. Half of it seemed to be running off Mack Bolan's sodden bush hat and down his neck. He could have pulled up the hood of his rain parka, but he wasn't about to cover his ears when a hostile patrol could be a few hundred yards away. The temperature was surprisingly low. It was easy to forget they were more than a mile high. He and McCarter had rigged their plastic ground sheets to make a small tent. There might have been room for one person inside it. However, they were trying to keep the satcom radio dry.

Lahka sat by Bolan looking utterly miserable. She had wrapped her arms around her breasts in the classic Dani method of resisting cold weather, but she couldn't stop shivering. Bolan took his blanket out of his pack and draped it over her. She smiled gratefully and didn't mention the Dani view that only weaklings wore clothes. Marie Van Heyn had taken a blanket out of her pack and wrapped herself in it. If she was lucky, she was asleep. Wejak was out scouting.

McCarter backed out of the little tent.

"Any luck with the radio?" Bolan asked.

The Briton shook his head. "No joy. I can't raise them. I'm afraid we're just going to have to wait until this bloody rain slacks off."

Bolan had been afraid of that. The satcom was a marvelous little radio, but its small size limited its power. Its high-frequency transmissions were partially absorbed by the rain. It simply couldn't put out enough power to contact the relay satellite through the heavy rain.

Wejak suddenly appeared, slipping through the rain like a ghost. Bolan was glad the man was on his side. The soldier noted that the Dani warrior had a compact black submachine gun slung over his shoulder. Bolan was curious. He had left armed only with his long spear and a knife.

"What's that?" he asked.

Wejak smiled and handed over the weapon. "It is a fine gun, Belasko, very quiet. It makes no noise."

Bolan looked at the weapon closely. He knew what it was instantly, a 9 mm Heckler & Koch MP-5 SD silenced submachine gun. Someone had added a wide-field-of-view telescopic sight and a laser aiming device. He thought it was actually a better weapon than McCarter's Sterling, more accurate and more reliable.

"A fine gun," he agreed. "Where did you get it?"

"It is a dead bird, Belasko. The man who carried it was clumsy and very noisy when he moved through the woods. He does not need it anymore. I will give it to Marie. Her old pistols do not always work very well. She needs a new gun."

Bolan smiled. "You are a big man, Wejak. You give good gifts."

Wejak and Lahka smiled. They liked Belasko. He was trying hard to learn good manners. It wasn't his fault he hadn't been born a Dani.

McCarter appeared. "Good news, mate. I think the rain is slacking off. I made intermittent contact with the satellite just now. I think you'll be able to get through to base in five or ten minutes."

The Briton returned to the little tent and began to fine-tune the satcom's antenna alignment.

"Were you able to get close?" Bolan asked Wejak.

The Dani warrior nodded. "Yes, I am sorry, but the news is very bad. Your special plane is gone. I saw a very large helicopter come and carry it away. All the other helicopters and all men in the strange uniforms are gone now, and I fear they took your friend, Mary Clark, with them."

"Any sign of where they were going?" he asked.

Wejak shook his head. "The helicopters flew away to the south. That is all I know."

"I think we're through to base," McCarter said as he joined the two men.

He handed Bolan the satcom microphone. The Executioner pushed the transmit button and began to send. "Granite Home, this is Striker. Acknowledge, Granite Home."

He waited for a few seconds and heard Aaron Kurtzman's familiar voice.

"Striker, this is Granite Home. Over."

Stony Man Farm, Virginia

HAL BROGNOLA WAS DOZING in his office when Kurtzman knocked on his door. He glanced at his desk clock. He had been asleep for three hours. It wasn't long enough, but Kurtzman wouldn't be bothering him for something unimportant.

"Striker's just made contact on satcom. He says the situation has changed and he has to talk to you as soon as possible."

That got the adrenaline flowing. Brognola followed Kurtzman down the hall.

"Did Striker say anything else?" he asked.

Kurtzman shook his head. "No, that was all, but to judge by the tone of his voice, it's not good news."

Brognola punched his personal identification number into the electronic lock on the operations-room door and waited for two seconds while the security system's computer decided that he was indeed Hal Brognola. Carmen Delahunt was monitoring the satcom. She smiled at Brognola as he took the microphone and pushed the transmit button.

"Hal here, Striker. What's your situation?"

Brognola listened carefully while Bolan told him what had happened.

"Message understood, Striker. You have the recorders, but Skylance and Captain Clark are in hostile hands, probably Japanese. Gary should be in your area within a few hours. He will contact you at your original insertion point. If you want to come out now, he has the extraction plan. Estimate you could withdraw in approximately fifteen hours from now. Do you want to come out then, Striker?"

"You heard all the briefings, Hal," Bolan replied after a few seconds. "Is this mission really as important as they told us in Australia?"

"Yeah, it is, Striker."

"All right, Hal. I won't withdraw the team. Find the damned thing, and we'll take it out. Striker out."

Brognola stared at the microphone. He might have just signed Bolan's death warrant. He could feel the stress start to build, but sitting there worrying would accomplish nothing. He had to get Bolan all the help he could.

"What do you think, Aaron?" he asked.

"Finding Skylance is the key to the puzzle, Hal. You need the National Reconnaissance Office and all their assets. That may not be easy. They're a hard group to deal with sometimes, and they don't like to work closely with people they don't know."

Brognola smiled grimly. "I think I can persuade them to cooperate, Aaron. Carmen, please get me the White House on the secure phone. Tell them I have to speak to the President. Say it's an urgent-star priority."

The National Reconnaissance Office, Washington

HAL BROGNOLA WAS SEETHING when he was finally ushered into General Benet's office. He didn't like to be kept waiting. His identity card and visitor's-facility clearance had been checked half a dozen times, but the National Reconnaissance Office security guards still seemed suspicious. He would have had far less trouble getting into the gold vaults at Fort Knox.

Benet was sitting behind his desk talking softly into a secure phone. He motioned to Brognola to be seated. The big Fed looked at Benet and smiled. Six feet tall, with iron gray hair, five rows of ribbons and wearing the silver wings of a command pilot, the man was the perfect model of a modern Air Force general. He hung up the phone and smiled thinly at Brognola.

"Good morning, Mr. Brognola. I seldom have visitors from the Department of Justice. What can I do for you?"

"General, I understand that you are responsible for coordinating and controlling all U.S. satellites with reconnaissance capability, military, intelligence, special agencies and black programs."

Benet smiled modestly. "That is essentially correct."

"General, I am coordinating a highly classified U.S. government project. I need satellite-reconnaissance support immediately."

"I'll be happy to see what can be done. Just what is the nature of your project?"

It was Brognola's turn to smile. "I'm sorry, General, that information can be given only on a need-to-know basis. Unfortunately you aren't cleared for that information."

Benet frowned. He wasn't used to being told that he wasn't cleared to know something the United States government was doing.

"Just what support are you requesting, then?" he asked coldly.

Brognola opened his briefcase and passed Benet a thin sheaf of photographs, carefully sanitized pictures of Skylance seen from above.

"This aircraft belongs to the United States government. It's currently somewhere in Western New Guinea. I am formally requesting that the NRO use every asset under its control to locate it as soon as possible."

Benet sighed softly. Everyone always thought that his program was more important than anything else.

"I'll do the best I can for you, Brognola. I'll put your request in the high-priority queue."

Benet punched a few keys on his keyboard and looked at the display. "I can get you optical scans in about sixteen hours, processed data in about twenty-four. I trust that is satisfactory?"

"No, it isn't, General. I need every kind of coverage you can get, and I need it now. I'm not exaggerating. Locating this aircraft is vital to protect the national security of the United States."

"You don't understand, Brognola. I'm sure your mission is important, but if I do what you ask, I'll be disrupting a number of extremely critical reconnaissance missions. Even if you work for God, I just can't do that!"

Brognola nodded and passed the general a small white card.

"I understand perfectly, General. Please call this number. Use the secure phone. Say that it's an urgent-star-priority call."

Benet looked skeptical, but he punched in the number.

"This is Lieutenant-General Charles Benet at the National Reconnaissance Office. This is an urgent-star-priority call. Who am I speaking to? Yes, sir, I understand. There is a Mr. Hal Brognola in my office who is requesting that— Yes, sir. I understand. I'll get on it immediately, sir." He hung up the phone.

Benet stared at Brognola for a few seconds. "All right, so you do work for God. Let's go down to the control center and get this show on the road."

He led Brognola through a bewildering series of narrow corridors and locked and guarded doors until they entered a large, dimly lit room. Two dozen men and women were sitting at computer workstations, peering at colored displays and talking into secure phones.

Benet guided Brognola into chairs facing a huge display screen. The big Fed stared at the display, recognizing the map of New Guinea, but the screen was covered with a dazzling array of colored circles, arcs, ellipses, and red, blue and white symbols.

"You did say everything, Mr. Brognola," Benet said with a smile.

"Is this a real picture coming from a satellite?" Brognola asked.

"No, the picture is being generated by a Cray-3 supercomputer, but the data is real. The computer is taking the near-real-time data from every satellite that can observe Western New Guinea."

Brognola stared at the display. There had to be thousands of lines and symbols on the large display screen.

"How in the hell can anyone work with that?" he asked.

"It's simple when you know how." Benet turned to an Army warrant officer sitting at a control console with his fingers poised over the keyboard.

"Geo and weather display only," Benet said. The warrant officer nodded and touched his controls.

The display changed. Almost instantly Brognola saw only the map of New Guinea with a large transparent green blob covering the huge island's center.

"The green area is rainfall heavy enough to register on radar. The rain is from a weather front moving from west to east. Fortunately for us, the weather's clearing. That's important, because we're going to have to be able to see your target to find it. Radar can see through the clouds, but to positively locate your target, we need visual images in visible light or infrared. Show the Baliem Valley, and let's have all optical and IR assets."

The display changed again. Colored arcs and ellipses appeared across the map of New Guinea, each identified by cryptic letters and numbers. A red dot appeared in the center of the map.

"That's the Baliem Valley," Benet said.

"What does the rest of it mean?"

Benet smiled again. "Let's just say they show the areas that can be observed ten minutes from now by a variety of assets coordinated by the NRO. Which satellites they are and which agencies own them is something you don't ask and we don't tell. Now, we have to get to work and tell each satellite-control center what we want them to do. We call that tasking. Then we wait."

The center seemed to spring to life as individual operators activated displays and spoke urgently into their secure phones. Tasking orders flashed to a dozen control centers scattered across the United States. Target descriptions were fed into computers. Communications antennae rotated smoothly and pointed precisely at relay satellites, and coded orders flashed into space. On the other side of the world, sensors on board a dozen satellites began to relentlessly scan the surface of New Guinea.

"All right, the show's on the road. Now we wait," Benet said.

Someone produced a carafe of coffee and some cups. Brognola took a cup and sipped it. He sat and stared at the screen. Minutes crawled by, but there was nothing to do but wait. If the satellite systems controlled from this room couldn't find Skylance, he was afraid it wasn't going to be found.

There was a sudden flurry of action at one of the control consoles.

"I think we've got it, General," a gray-haired woman called out.

Benet led Brognola to her console, and they stared intently over her shoulder. Brognola beamed. The picture was a little blurred, but there was no mistaking that triangular-winged shape. Nothing else in New Guinea would look like that. Skylance.

"Great work, Abby," Benet said. "What's the target's location?"

Abby glanced at her console. "It's at a private commercial airfield on the south coast, approximately ten miles west of the town of Agats, General."

"Is there any correlation with a known military or intelligence facility?"

"Negative. The CIA general data base lists it as a commercial mining facility belonging to a Japanese interest, the Kanabo Corporation."

Benet noticed Brognola stiffen as he heard Abby's words. He was a veteran of covert operations and the black world. He didn't waste time asking questions he knew Brognola wouldn't answer.

"Well, there it is, Mr. Brognola. Anything else we can do for you?"

Brognola was already getting to his feet, but he paused for a second.

"Yes, keep that area under continuous surveillance. Here's my number. Please notify me immediately if the target is moved. One other thing, General. You and your people have done an outstanding job, and have made a major contribution to a critical mission. Is there anything I can do to show my appreciation?"

Benet smiled. "Yes. The next time you talk to God, tell him we do good work. It just might help the next time he's thinking of cutting our budget."

CHAPTER FOURTEEN

Raizo Tanaka moved carefully down the muddy streets of Wamena. The helicopter flight back to the town hadn't been easy in the rain, and he had chosen to walk from the airport rather than take one of Wamena's handful of taxis. The fewer people who saw him the better. At least the rain seemed to be slackening, but he was still soaking wet when he reached the small commercial building that was Ito's temporary headquarters. He wasn't looking forward to his conversation with the man. Tanaka had been partially successful, but Ito might choose to concentrate on Tanaka's failures.

He smiled apologetically at the secretary while he dripped on her floor and asked to be announced.

Ito's secretary smiled. "He is speaking to the foreign woman, Tanaka-san, but I am sure he will wish to see you immediately."

She got to her feet with fluid grace and smiled as she moved toward Ito's door. "He has been talking to her for some time. I do not think the insolent bitch is enjoying herself."

Tanaka smiled. He didn't like the foreigner, either. Like many Japanese, he felt that anyone whose blood was only half-Japanese was an inferior being, not a real Japanese at all. The secretary returned and bowed, smiling as she ushered Tanaka into Ito's office. She respected Tanaka. His ancestors had been samurai.

Ito sat at his desk, carefully polishing the blade of his father's sword. Meiko stood rigidly in front of his desk. Her cheeks were flushed. The secretary was right; she wasn't enjoying herself.

He motioned Tanaka to be seated. His secretary came in with a pot of hot tea and small cups on a tray. She poured the tea for the two men with exquisite grace and left the room. Meiko hissed under her breath. She hadn't been offered any. It was a terrible insult. The two men ignored her humiliation and sipped the strong, bitter tea appreciatively. Tanaka relaxed a bit. He didn't seem to be out of favor.

"Excellent tea," Ito commented. "Now, tell me everything that has happened."

Tanaka spoke slowly and carefully. It wasn't wise to leave out information or appear to be evasive.

"So, I secured the area, and as soon as it was daylight, I used the heavy-lift helicopter to fly the American space plane to our Agats complex. I considered it unwise to use our men to pursue the Americans. I left that to the Indonesians and flew here immediately."

Ito looked at the light shining on the tempering pattern on the cutting edge of his father's sword. "You have done well, Tanaka-san. The space plane is the important thing, but I have a few small questions. First, how do you know you fought the Americans?"

Tanaka reached into his pocket and pulled out a small block of something that looked like a waxy gray plastic. "Our experts found this under one of the plane's wings. It is C-4, a powerful plastic explosive.

The markings show it is American made and recently manufactured. And there is the prisoner. She is obviously an American. I am certain she is the surviving crewman. All she will say so far is her name, her rank and her serial number. I will teach her better manners when I have the time."

Ito nodded. "I have one other question, Tanaka. Please speak frankly. You had more than fifty men, well trained and equipped. You say at the most there were four or five Americans. Yet more than half of our men were killed or wounded, and all but one of the Americans escaped. I do not understand. How could this have happened? Were our men lacking in courage?"

"Our men were well trained, and they fought bravely. They were not afraid to die, but bravery is not enough. We have a weakness that I do not know how to overcome. Japan has not fought since World War II ended. The men we fought were experienced warriors. Our men were not. It is as if in the old days fifty ordinary men attacked five samurai. The samurai would have won no matter how brave the fifty men were."

Ito nodded. He could understand that perfectly.

Tanaka knew that what he had said was true, but he still felt a burning sense of shame. It had been his responsibility, and he had failed.

"Let me pick twenty men, and I will find these Americans and kill them. I will not return if I fail."

Ito smiled. That was the proper attitude. He was glad not all modern Japanese were soft, but he shook his head. "No, Tanaka. You secured the space plane, so you did not fail. That is the important thing. These

Americans are not. I wish you to go to our Agats complex and take command there until I arrive. Ohara is flying in from Djajapura. Place him in command here. Before you leave, speak to Colonel Hatta. Encourage him to pursue the Americans. Tell him he will receive a large bonus when we see proof that they are dead.''

Tanaka stood and bowed. ''I will go at once,'' he said.

Ito glanced at Meiko, who was still standing rigidly in front of his desk.

''I am not satisfied with this unworthy person. She is intelligent and skillful, but she has no sense of honor or duty. She left her comrades to die. Assign her to Ohara. Perhaps he can find some use for her.''

Tanaka bowed again and left the room. Meiko followed him.

''It is not fair,'' she burst out as soon as the door was closed. ''I was given stupid orders, and now I am blamed because I did not throw my life away when they failed. I am being treated very badly!''

Tanaka stared at her coldly. ''Be thankful that Mr. Ito is a kind-hearted and generous man, *gaijin*. If I was in command, you would be dead.''

MACK BOLAN LOOKED at McCarter.

''You heard what I told Hal. We'd better get out of here while we can. The Indonesians may come after us once the rain stops. Strike the equipment and get everyone together. Let's leave in ten minutes.''

Bolan turned to brief the others quickly.

''We have to get back to our original landing zone. Another member of our team will meet us there with a helicopter in about fifteen hours. Our people back in the United States are going to try to locate Skylance. If they do, David and I will continue the mission and destroy it. The rest of you will be closer to home if you don't want to come with us."

Lahka and Van Heyn looked at Wejak.

He smiled. "I am a Dani. I do not leave my comrades in the middle of a raid. Let us go quickly, Belasko. As long as the rain is falling, it will wash away our tracks. Once it stops, we will be easy to follow."

Lahka nodded. She was going wherever Wejak went. The Dutch woman smiled and picked up her pack. "We are all in this together," she said softly.

"All right," Bolan stated. "It's not going to be easy. We've got to get back to the landing zone on time. You pick the route, Wejak. We want to avoid contact with Indonesian patrols if we can. If we can't, we've got to avoid any long fights. We break contact as soon as possible and move on. Understand?"

"Of course," Wejak said tolerantly. "I understand. It is like when you have made a good raid on an enemy tribe. It is time to go home as fast as you can with the pigs and women you have captured. You can fight them again some other day."

"You are a great warrior, Wejak. We can learn a lot from you."

The Dani smiled again. It was true, of course, but it would not be modest for him to say so. "You, too, are a great warrior, Belasko, and so is your friend. When this is over, you must come to my village. I will kill many pigs, and we will have a great feast. We will have a victory dance, get very drunk and tell many lies and impress the women.''

''I look forward to it.''

Wejak checked his AK-47, picked up his spear and seemed to vanish into the trees. Five minutes later, they were moving through the trees. It wasn't easy going. The ground was still wet and soft, and Bolan and McCarter were weighed down by their weapons and equipment. Wejak wasn't taking the easiest route. He was careful to avoid places where it would be easy for someone to lay an ambush, which was smart. They couldn't afford to relax and get careless. Indonesian patrols were undoubtedly in front of them, as well as behind them.

They walked on and on, through the endless forest. There was no clearly defined trail. Wejak simply picked a path, and they followed him, hour after hour, stopping only for a five-minute break at the end of each hour. Once, he found some tracks. It looked like an Indonesian patrol had passed by a few hours earlier.

The last thing in the world they needed was a firefight. Wejak picked up the pace, and they struggled on. Bolan heard a plane pass in the distance, but it was no real threat. He was beginning to realize how large the interior of New Guinea was and just how little of it was inhabited. Once you were away from one of the small towns, it was almost impossible for anyone to find you if you stayed off the major trails.

They pressed on. Bolan was beginning to think they would have to stop and rest for an hour or two when Wejak halted and held up one hand. He smiled and pointed at something. Bolan looked and recognized the area where they had landed. He felt a surge of relief. They had made it. Now, if only Gary Manning would come.

CHAPTER FIFTEEN

Jack Grimaldi pushed the throttle forward, and the whine of the turbine engine deepened as he lifted the Bell 205 helicopter into the air. Gary Manning looked back at the helicopter pad as the Stony Man pilot began to climb out over the hills that ringed Djajapura. If anyone had noticed their early-morning takeoff, they didn't seem to care. Perhaps the incident at the hotel last night had only been an attempt by a local gang to rip off a rich visitor, but Manning didn't like coincidences like that when he was on a mission. They made him cautious.

The chopper was climbing steadily to clear the range of dark green hills that circled the landward side of Djajapura, gaining altitude at a steady twelve hundred feet per minute. Manning looked at the map. He was beginning to understand just how big and wild New Guinea was. Except for a few small frontier towns, the interior was a vast expanse of mountains, hills and forests inhabited by people who were still living in the Stone Age. It wasn't the safest country in the world to fly over. If they had to make an emergency landing, they would be lucky if anyone ever found them.

He was glad that Grimaldi was flying. He was the best pilot Manning knew. He could fly anything that had an engine, and if you had to fly over dangerous country, Grimaldi was the man to have at the controls. The sound of the engine changed as the pilot leveled off and went to economical cruise speed. They were flying southwest now. The Baliem Valley and the airfield at Wamena were about 150 miles away.

"We should be on the ground at Wamena in about an hour and a half," Grimaldi said.

Manning nodded. There was nothing for him to do in the cockpit. He got up from the copilot's seat and went back to the passenger compartment. Gadgets Schwarz was there, setting up and carefully checking his equipment. Manning hoped all the electronic miracles were working well. He was beginning to see just how difficult it might be to locate Bolan and McCarter in the vast area of hills and forests below.

Schwarz looked up as Manning came in. "I got a satcom message off to Stony Man just before we lifted off. We won't be able to talk to them again until we're back on the ground. I can't keep the antenna aligned on the satellite while we're moving."

"Did Barbara have anything to report?"

Schwarz shook his head. "There's nothing new from Bolan and McCarter. Of course, she can't contact them unless they have their satcom set up and turned on. That's only going to be now and then if they have to keep moving."

Manning didn't like the sound of that. "So, how do we locate them?"

Schwarz shrugged. "We don't, Gary. They're not doing anything I can detect, even when they use their satcom. They're not going to use their tactical radios if someone's chasing them. The Baliem Valley's a big place. We could look for them forever and not find them. They have to tell Stony Man where they are. Barbara knows the score. She'll get their coordinates the next time they check in. Then we can pick them up."

Manning nodded. He didn't like it, but Schwarz was right. It was weird that he was within less than 150 miles of Bolan and McCarter and couldn't communicate with them, while Price, eight thousand miles away, could speak to them easily if only they would call.

There were too many unknowns. They were going to need a lot of luck to pull this mission off and get out alive. It made things worse for him that Grimaldi and Schwarz had things to keep them busy while he had nothing to do but worry. He sat down and began to carefully check his weapons and equipment. It might not be necessary, but it helped keep him occupied.

The helicopter droned on. Manning was almost dozing in his seat when he heard the sound of the engine change and felt the helicopter turn as Grimaldi reduced power and started down. He looked out the window. They were flying over a small town surrounded by cloud-shrouded mountains. He could see a hard-surfaced airstrip at one side of the town. It had to be Wamena. He moved forward to the cockpit. Grimaldi finished speaking into the radio and looked up as Manning slipped into the copilot's seat.

"Do you want to land and refuel or take a look around the area?" he asked. Manning was the team commander. It was up to him to call the shots.

"How much fuel have we got?" he asked.

"About sixty percent. I'd be a lot happier if we refueled. This would be bad country to run out of fuel over."

"Let's do it," Manning said. He remembered the old pilot's saying, "There are old pilots and there are bold pilots, but there are no old bold pilots." He preferred to fly with careful men. He watched as Grimaldi brought the Bell 205 to a smooth landing at one end of the airstrip. There were two big four-engine planes parked just off the runway. One was a Merpati Fokker 27 airliner. The other looked like a Lockheed C-130.

Manning didn't like that. If the Indonesian military were at the airstrip in force, they might have flown into a trap. He pointed at the big C-130.

"Indonesian military?" he asked quickly.

Grimaldi took a quick look and shook his head.

"That's a Lockheed L-100-30. It's a commercial version of the C-130. It's got Indonesian commercial-registration markings. It probably belongs to some mining company. I don't think we have to worry about it."

He shut the engine down and climbed out of the pilot's seat.

"I'll go take care of the paperwork, arrange for refueling and get our travel permits stamped at the local police station. You and Gadgets take care of things here. I'll try to stay out of trouble in this swinging town."

Manning walked around the small airport, trying to look like a tourist and turning down remarkable opportunities to buy souvenirs. He was walking slowly back toward the helicopter when Gadgets Schwarz stepped out of the passenger compartment and waved casually. Manning felt the adrenaline start to flow. Gadgets wouldn't have left the radio unattended unless he had heard from Stony Man. Bolan had to have made contact.

Schwarz looked up as the big Canadian stepped into the passenger compartment.

"I just talked to Barbara," Schwarz said quickly. "Bolan and McCarter have checked in. They're headed back to their original landing zone. I have the coordinates. Barbara wants us to meet them there. I told her we'd be on the way as soon as we refuel."

Manning heard the sounds of a vehicle rolling up and he looked out the window. Grimaldi was arriving, riding on a small refueling truck. The Phoenix Force Commando stuck his head out the door.

"Let's speed things up, Jack. The boss wants us to get going," he said. Grimaldi nodded and turned to speak to the refueling-crew foreman. The refueling was finished with speed and enthusiasm. A few five-thousand-rupiah notes passed to the foreman worked wonders for the crew's morale and devotion to duty. The Stony Man pilot made a quick check of the helicopter as the refueling truck drove away. His attention was concentrated on the rotor blades and the engine. He didn't notice that one of the refueling crew had attached a small black device to the inside of one of the helicopter's landing skids.

Ten minutes later, they were airborne, flying west along the Wamena River, passing over a patchwork of forests and fields. Manning was checking his map again when Schwarz stuck his head inside the cockpit.

"Have you got something special turned on, Jack? I'm getting a steady C-band interference that I didn't see before."

Grimaldi checked his instrument panel and shook his head. "Negative. Nothing's on that I haven't been using since we took off from Djajapura. Better check out your gear."

Schwarz vanished back into the cargo compartment.

Grimaldi looked at the global-positioning-system readout. Smoothly he brought the Bell 205 to the hover mode.

"We're here," he announced. "If the coordinates we got from Stony Man are correct, Bolan and McCarter should be right down there."

Manning looked out the window. He saw a small clearing, perhaps six hundred feet across, surrounded by thick clumps of green trees. He looked closely, but he saw no signs of life. Well, that wasn't surprising. Bolan and McCarter weren't going to stand out in the open and wave at every strange helicopter that came by. He took out his tactical radio and pushed the transmit button.

"Belasko, this is Granite. Come in, Belasko."

Manning waited for a few seconds. Then he felt a surge of relief as he heard Bolan's familiar voice.

"Granite, this is Belasko. Identify yourself."

"Belasko, this is Granite. We are overhead in a red-and-white Bell 205 helicopter. Can you see us?"

"Granite, I see two helicopters overhead. Which one are you?"

Manning's blood froze. He knew now that Schwarz had detected a tracking beacon, and someone was coming up behind them, staying in their blind spot.

"Heads up, Jack!" he shouted. "Someone's on our tail."

Grimaldi didn't waste time asking questions. He pulled the Bell 205 into a hard right turn. Manning saw a swarm of red dots streak by, passing through the space their helicopter had occupied just a few seconds before. Tracers! Whatever was shooting at them seemed to have an incredible rate of fire. He heard the sound of ripping, tearing metal as a swarm of bullets smashed into the Bell's upper fuselage.

The Stony Man pilot twisted hard left, trying to shake the helicopter behind them, but it was no use. The faster, more maneuverable helicopter stayed on their tail, firing burst after burst of machine-gun fire. The Bell 205 shuddered as it was hit. Manning heard a grinding howl as the engine began to vibrate. The helicopter's fuselage started to shake, and acrid gray smoke began to fill the cockpit.

Grimaldi fought his controls and dived for the ground. There was nothing Manning could do but hang on. Another burst streaked past the windscreen as the pilot dived desperately away. The red tracers seemed to miss the Bell by inches. The ground was rushing up with incredible speed. The fuselage began to fishtail from left to right. The engine's howl rose to a shriek of tortured metal. Grimaldi had no time to hover. The dying helicopter touched down and skidded forward toward the edge of the trees, its landing skids plowing furrows in the ground as it went.

"Hang on!" Grimaldi yelled as the Bell 205 slid into the trees. The rotors tore away with a loud ripping noise. The nose struck a tree trunk and crumpled as the smoking fuselage ground to a halt. Grimaldi's hands flashed to the control panel as he cut power and activated the fire-extinguishing system.

Manning staggered to his feet and threw open the copilot's exit door. Grimaldi was already going out the other side. The Phoenix Force commando hesitated for a split second. He didn't see any flames, and he was damned if he was going to leave his rifles. He lunged back into the cargo compartment. The gray smoke was thicker there. It seemed to be coming down from a hole in the ceiling. Schwarz lay sprawled on the floor, unmoving. The big Canadian grabbed the man under his arms and dragged him to a side door, which was stuck. Manning put every ounce of his weight into a flat-footed kick. The door groaned and shifted a bit, but it didn't open. He kicked again, and the door popped open with a screech of bending metal. Manning heaved with all his strength and dragged Schwarz outside.

Smoke was billowing from the helicopter's upper fuselage, which was peppered with dozens of bullet holes in the engine and transmission housings. The chopper wouldn't get airborne again. Manning remembered what the highlands of New Guinea looked like from above. He had to get their weapons and their survival kits. It might be a matter of life or death. He slipped back into the cargo compartment. The smoke was worse. His eyes began to water, and he started to cough and wheeze.

He groped for the plastic cases that held his rifles and slid them out the door, grabbed the packs and the black nylon case that held Schwarz's Calico submachine gun and lunged out the door. He dropped to his knees, gasping and coughing, trying desperately to clear his lungs. He looked quickly at Schwarz, who was still unconscious. Manning couldn't see any blood, but an ugly bruise was swelling on his forehead.

The big Canadian heard the sound of helicopter rotors and felt the rotor wash as the other chopper passed overhead. He caught a quick look through the tops of the trees as it flew by. It looked almost the same as their own shattered Bell 205, but Manning saw a streamlined pod attached to one side of its fuselage. Six black muzzles protruded ominously from the front of the pod. It was a .30-caliber Gatling gun, which could fire 125 rounds per second. They were lucky to be alive.

Grimaldi came around the fuselage, moving quickly with his MAC-10 in his hands. "We'd better get the hell out of here. I think they're going to land."

The pilot was right. He could hear the change in the sound of the other helicopter's rotors. It was hovering, coming in for a landing.

"Gadgets is hurt. I don't know how bad."

Grimaldi cursed. They wouldn't get very far trying to drag an unconscious man through the bush. The noise of the rotors changed. The helicopter was hovering a few feet above the ground. An amplified voice suddenly rang out through the trees.

"You do not have a chance. Come out of the trees at once with your hands up and surrender. If you give up immediately, your lives will be spared. Resist, and you will all be killed.''

The muzzles of the Gatling gun suddenly spouted fire. Swarms of full-metal-jacketed bullets tore into the trees above Manning's head. The Gatling fired so fast that he couldn't hear the sounds of individual shots, just a tremendous ripping noise as if a giant were tearing a huge sheet of canvas apart with his bare hands. Showers of splinters flew, and leaves and branches fell to the ground.

''This is your last chance! Come out now!''

Whoever was firing the Gatling had deliberately aimed high. That meant the people in the helicopter didn't want to kill them. They wanted to take them alive. He snapped open one of his rifle cases and took out his .308 Winchester Model 70. He checked the scope and worked the bolt to chamber a round. He might not be much use in air-to-air combat, but he was a deadly shot with a rifle. If they wanted to come into the trees after him, he would make it cost them dearly.

The helicopter settled down on its landing skids. Its rotors began to slow. The side doors flew open, and armed men began to rush out of the passenger compartment, at least eight or nine. Through his four-power scope, Manning could see their blue-and-gray-mottled camouflage uniforms and the deadly black automatic weapons in their hands.

Manning snapped his rifle to his shoulder and squeezed off a shot. One of the men spun and fell. He heard the hiss of Grimaldi's silenced MAC-10 and saw another man go down. The big Canadian worked the Winchester's bolt and chambered another round. He looked quickly for a target, but the enemy had dropped to the ground and was firing from prone positions. Manning heard bullets tear into the trees around him. This time they weren't firing high; they were shooting to kill.

The firing intensified. Two men suddenly jumped to their feet, raced forward ten yards and threw themselves down. Manning snarled. It was fire and movement. Some of the men attacking them would provide covering fire while others moved forward. It was an old trick, but it was still extremely effective. He and Grimaldi had no way to tell when the next rush would come and who would fire and who would move forward. They might get two or three, but they wouldn't get them all, and now the enemy force was within hand-grenade range.

There was another blast of covering fire, and three men rushed forward. Two of them were firing bursts of full-auto fire as they came. The third man had something in his right hand. Manning saw his arm come up, poised to throw.

He heard Grimaldi shout "Grenade!"

Manning snapped his scope's cross hairs on the man's chest. Before he could fire, the man suddenly slumped and fell. Manning heard a muffled explosion as the grenade detonated under the man's body, followed by the dull boom of a high-powered rifle and the snarling crackle of an M-4 carbine. The other two men went down simultaneously. Manning saw a flicker of movement along the helicopter's side. A man in mud-splattered black fatigues was slipping into the passenger compartment. He couldn't see his face, but Manning recognized the unmistakable outline of a silenced Sterling submachine gun. It had to be David McCarter.

The big Canadian heard rapid firing on the other side of the helicopter, then a sudden silence. He saw a flicker of motion behind the men who had been shot. Mack Bolan was walking across the clearing with a Remington rifle in his hands. A half-naked young woman walked beside him, waving a captured rifle ecstatically.

Manning got up slowly and shook his head. Perhaps he was suffering from combat fatigue. Bolan looked at him and smiled.

"Glad you could join the party, Gary," he said. "What took you so long?"

CHAPTER SIXTEEN

Bolan watched as Grimaldi slipped into the pilot's seat and began to check the captured helicopter's instrument panel. McCarter sat next to him in the copilot's seat, quietly checking the weapon controls.

"What do you think, Jack?" Bolan asked. "Can you fly it?"

"You know I can. It's an Augusta-Bell 212, an Italian-built, improved Huey. I can fly it standing on my head if your trigger-happy British friend hasn't blown away something important."

"Trigger-happy? I think you'll find I was bang-on, mate," he protested. "And I selected my line of fire very carefully. Two 6-round bursts, and they never knew what hit them. If you look, I think you will find that the only bullet holes are in the copilot's door."

"I'll take your word for it. I'm ready to go whenever you say so, Sarge."

That was good news, but Bolan wasn't sure where he wanted to go until he heard from Stony Man operations center.

"How far can we go without refueling, Jack?"

Grimaldi looked at his fuel gauges. "She's nearly full, and we've got auxiliary fuel tanks. We can fly about four hundred miles without refueling. I can get you to either coast or across the border into Papua

New Guinea from here. Just tell me where you want to go."

Bolan thought hard. He didn't have a place to go at the moment, but it was dangerous to stay here on the ground. Any plane or helicopter that flew by was certain to spot them. Flying around aimlessly would only burn up precious fuel that might be impossible to replace. Worst of all, their satcom wasn't designed to work from a moving vehicle. Unless Schwarz could come up with an electronic miracle, they couldn't send or receive while they were in flight. He had better check to see how Schwarz was doing.

He stepped out of the helicopter and looked around. Manning and Wejak had finished dragging the bodies of the men who had attacked them into the trees. They had done a good job. It wouldn't fool anyone who searched the area on the ground, but they probably wouldn't be seen from the air. Bolan signaled to Manning.

"We may be leaving here in a hurry. Get Gadgets's equipment and anything else you want out of your chopper and load it on this one. Then rig an incendiary charge on a delay fuse. I don't want anything left of it after we're gone."

Manning nodded and was on his way. Bolan didn't have to worry about him. He was one of the best demolition men the Executioner had ever seen.

Bolan moved back to the passenger compartment and looked in the side door. Schwarz was sitting in one of the passenger seats. Marie Van Heyn was peering in his eyes and holding up fingers for him to count. The man didn't look good. He seemed disoriented, and the bruise on his forehead was ugly.

Bolan motioned to the doctor, who nodded and stepped outside.

"How is he?" Bolan asked.

She shook her head. "It is hard to say. All I have is the helicopter's first-aid kit. I do not think his skull is fractured. I can tell you he has a concussion. Whether it is mild or severe, I cannot tell. If I could, I would take X rays and put him in a hospital for observation. There is no real hospital closer than Djajapura, and I do not think it would be wise to go there. I have given him something for pain, but that is all I can do for him here."

"Can he be moved?"

"Yes, but if you wish to leave here, we must fly. He is in no condition for a long march."

Bolan frowned. That was bad. If Schwarz was seriously injured, the only way to get him out was to fly him to Papua New Guinea, but that meant giving up the mission. Well, Van Heyn was the doctor, and she knew the territory. Perhaps she could come up with something. He laid out the situation for her carefully.

She nodded and thought for a minute.

"I understand. We need to leave here and hide somewhere until you talk to your people in the United States. I must do something more for Gadgets. Very well. Wejak's people live northwest of Wamena. Go there, and you can conceal the helicopter and wait for your message. I am a medical missionary. I have a small clinic in my house in Wamena. Touch down near the town, and I will take your friend there and examine him thoroughly. I will need Lahka and one other person to help me."

"All right, we'll do it." Bolan thought for a second. He would have liked to go with Schwarz, but he was the team leader and he had to talk to Stony Man.

"I'll send Gary with you. Believe me, he is a very competent man, and he's the only one here besides Jack who has civilian clothes."

Bolan called to McCarter, and they joined Manning and Wejak in transferring equipment from the crashed helicopter to their new acquisition. The sooner they were gone, the better.

MEIKO SAT at a small table in the Kanabo Corporation building in Wamena and seethed. Ito was gone, but his secretary was still there, relishing the woman's humiliation. She wasn't the only one. Ohara had been careful to see that everyone knew she was in disgrace. He had spoken to her loudly in the insulting manner a Japanese used when speaking to a person of inferior status. He had given her an assignment a child could carry out. When she dared to question him, he had slapped her four times, not lightly, but with the skilled hand of an accomplished martial artist.

She stared into the mirror on the office wall. Bruises were forming on her high cheekbones, and her lips were swelling. Ohara had gone too far. She would kill him for that if she got the chance. That wasn't just wishful thinking; Meiko had spent years training in some of the deadlier martial arts. She could kill Ohara in two seconds if she took him by surprise, but then what? She no longer felt any loyalty to the Kanabo Corporation, but they had a long arm. If she killed Ohara, she would have to run fast and far or they would hunt her down and kill her.

She heard a knock on the door. An Indonesian police sergeant handed the secretary a flat package and left, counting his five-thousand-rupiah fee. The secretary smiled maliciously and handed Meiko the package.

"Here are the files you requested, *gaijin*. Work hard, and perhaps your failures may be forgotten."

Meiko took the package. It contained duplicate police files of possible FPM supporters in the Wamena area. Ohara had ordered her to investigate and see if any of them might be helping the Americans. Meiko thought that if any of them were, they wouldn't be stupid enough to do it openly, but Ohara had refused to listen to her. She opened the file and began to leaf through the folders. Until she could find a way out, she had to appear to be humbly obeying Ohara's orders.

Five of the folders described Dani men. Meiko sneered. Even Ohara had to be smart enough to not expect her to wander into a Dani village and start asking questions. If she was stupid enough to do that, she would probably find out very quickly if the Dani still cooked and ate their enemies.

The sixth folder was more interesting. The picture showed a blond woman in her thirties, a Dr. Marie Van Heyn. The woman was described as a medical missionary to the Dani, probably an FPM sympathizer, but not to be arrested without positive evidence. It wouldn't do to let the missionaries scream religious persecution. Best of all, Dr. Van Heyn had a clinic in her house outside Wamena. Meiko looked at the bruises on her face. She had a good excuse for going to see a doctor. Very well, she would investigate this Van Heyn woman.

She went to the secretary's desk and handed her the folders. "I am going to investigate one of these suspects. I need a pistol and a radio."

The secretary opened her safe and handed Meiko a small, silenced .25-caliber Beretta automatic and a miniature radio.

"If I were you, *gaijin,*" she said sweetly, "I would take this pistol and put an honorable end to my miserable life."

Meiko bowed. "I thank you for concerning yourself with my worthless affairs." She turned and stormed out the door. Before she considered committing suicide, there were several people she would kill. She added Ito's secretary to the list.

Wamena was a small town. She didn't bother looking for a cab. She walked briskly down Trikora Street past the arts-and-crafts market toward the outskirts of town. She knew she had to control her temper. If this Van Heyn woman was a member of the FPM, she might be dangerous. Meiko began a martial-arts breathing exercise as she walked, calming her nerves and preparing her mind and body for danger.

She followed the dirt road through scattered clumps of trees until she came to Van Heyn's house. She knocked on the door, but no one answered. As she had nothing else to do, she concealed herself in a clump of trees across the road and settled down to wait. Meiko spent her time thinking about her future. She wanted out of Indonesia, but she didn't have much money. If she left the Kanabo Corporation, she would need a new identity and a new job. She was thinking hard when she heard voices.

One of the voices she heard seemed familiar, but she couldn't place it. She looked out carefully. Two Indonesian national police officers were talking to two men and two women. One of the women was wearing a woven reed skirt low on her hips and nothing else, obviously a Dani. But the other woman had long blond hair and wore dirty European clothes. She had to be Marie Van Heyn.

One of the men handed the senior police officer his passport. "My friend and I were walking to Akima to see the sights. He fell and hurt his head, as you can see. Dr. Van Heyn was in Akima. She was kind enough to treat him. We are going to her clinic for some more checks."

Meiko felt the same thrill a hunter felt when he faced a man-eating tiger. It was the Canadian she had met in Djajapura. She didn't know who the man really was, but she had seen him in action. He was no simple mining engineer but a CIA agent or perhaps from British Intelligence. She didn't know the name of the second man, but she recognized his face. He had been at the hotel in Djajapura. It would be a remarkable coincidence if they had just happened to meet Marie Van Heyn in Wamena.

The two policemen were satisfied and left. Manning had the proper papers, and their orders were to be nice to tourists. The Canadian's party went into the Van Heyn woman's house. She thought quickly. Perhaps her career with the Kanabo Corporation wasn't over after all, but she had to be careful. Ohara would steal all the credit if he got the chance.

She pushed the transmit button on her tiny radio and asked for Ohara. Ito's secretary answered. Ohara wasn't there, but he was expected back shortly. Meiko outlined the situation quickly. "Tell him the Americans are at Dr. Van Heyn's house. I cannot be sure how long they will stay there. Ask him to come at once with a strike team. These are dangerous men."

The secretary said she would give Ohara the message as soon as possible. Meiko believed her. She despised Meiko, but the Kanabo Corporation was her religion. She would do nothing that harmed its interests no matter how much she disliked Meiko.

It would be risky, but Meiko decided to see what she could learn before Ohara got there. She waited five minutes and then walked quickly across the street and knocked on the door. The Dani woman answered the door. She looked at the bruises on Meiko's face and gasped. Meiko remembered that the Dani regard someone being beaten as a terrible thing. Good, she would play on the savage's sympathies.

"A man beat me. I need to see the doctor," Meiko gasped softly.

The bruises on her face were completely convincing.

"I am Lahka, Dr. Van Heyn's assistant. She is with another patient, but she will be free in a few minutes. Please, come in." She opened the door and motioned for the woman to enter.

Meiko followed her, casually slipping her right hand into her purse and gripping her Beretta. The little automatic wasn't very powerful, but it held nine shots. It could be lethal at close quarters in the hands of a good shot, and she was very good.

Lahka led her into the waiting room. A man was sitting on an old sofa, glancing at a magazine. He looked up as the two women came in. Meiko felt a surge of elation. She hadn't made a mistake. It was Gary. She drew her small Beretta and pointed it at his chest.

"Do not move. Do not cry out. I will kill you if you do," Meiko said coldly.

Manning stared at the woman. This wasn't the playful flight attendant he had met in Djajapura. She held her pistol in a perfect two-handed grip and radiated the cold menace of a professional who was ready to shoot to kill. There was no chance at all that he could draw and fire his .45 Colt pistol before she shot him several times.

"What are you doing here, Meiko?" Manning asked.

It was a stupid question, and Manning wasn't stupid. He was trying to distract her. She had been focusing her attention on him, but he wasn't the only threat. She risked a quick glance at Lahka. She hadn't moved, but her right hand was sliding slowly up her bare right thigh.

"If you put your hand under your skirt, I will kill you," she said.

Lahka froze.

"Clasp your hands behind your head and sit down next to Gary," Meiko ordered. Lahka obeyed and moved slowly to sit by the Canadian. Meiko could see by the look on her face that she was angry, not frightened. She didn't think Lahka was stupid enough to charge into the muzzle of a cocked pistol, but if she thought she saw a chance to take Meiko off guard, she would take it.

Meiko began to sweat. Perhaps it had not been such a good idea to enter the doctor's house alone after all. She was confronting two dangerous people. She was certain the man she knew as Gary had a pistol under his coat, and Lahka was probably armed. If she tried to disarm one of them, she would be giving the other one a chance. She could hold them at gunpoint for a while, but not too long, and she didn't know where Marie Van Heyn and the other man were. Where was that idiot, Ohara?

She heard the door click open behind her, but she didn't dare look around. She had seen the Canadian shoot in the hotel room in Djajapura. She knew he would kill her in a second if she was foolish enough to turn her head.

"Well, *gaijin,* it looks as if you may be good for something besides spreading your legs after all," Ohara said as he stepped into the waiting room, a SIG-Sauer 9 mm automatic clasped in his right hand. He immediately covered Manning and Lahka.

"Are you sure this is the man you met in Djajapura?" he asked Meiko.

"I am absolutely certain."

"Good. It will add greatly to my reputation that I have captured such a dangerous man. If you are very good, I might mention that you assisted me when I write my report."

Meiko glared at him. Suddenly she froze. Ohara was standing there alone.

"Where is the strike team?" she gasped. Surely he hadn't been stupid enough to come without them.

"I do not need a strike team to deal with two Americans," Ohara boasted.

"But—" Ohara had fast reflexes. He slapped Meiko hard across the face with his left hand, and her head rocked on her shoulders. Pain flared through her bruised face.

"You do not question my decisions, *gaijin*," Ohara grated. "You obey." He slapped Meiko hard again.

"Do you understand, *gaijin?*"

Meiko bowed her head submissively. Humiliation and rage burned through her. To be struck in front of other people by this son of rice farmers was more than she could bear.

"Yes, Ohara-san, I will obey you. What shall I do?"

"Disarm him," he ordered, pointing to Manning. "Be careful to stay out of my line of fire."

Meiko dropped her Beretta into her purse and moved carefully to Gary Manning's side. She opened his jacket with her left hand and drew the .45 Colt from its holster. She moved away until she stood at Ohara's left side again. Manning's pistol was a beautiful weapon, one of the finest pistols Meiko had ever seen.

"Good. Now let us see about the woman. Take off her skirt."

Ohara smiled expectantly. He knew enough about the Dani to know that Lahka would be terribly humiliated to have her skirt taken off in front of a strange man. He was looking forward to that.

"What are you waiting for?" he snapped.

"This," Meiko said softly. Ohara froze as he heard the click of the big .45's safety being thumbed off. He started to turn and saw Meiko grinning savagely over the Colt's gaping black muzzle.

The booming roar was deafening in the small room as Meiko pulled the trigger twice. Two heavy .45 hollowpoints smashed into Ohara's chest with paralyzing force. His pistol dropped from his hand as he staggered backward.

"Goodbye, Ohara-san."

The man fell to the floor. Meiko didn't believe in taking chances. She shot him through the back of the head. "Peasant!" she hissed contemptuously.

Manning stared at her wide-eyed. Lahka was stunned.

"Who the hell are you, Meiko? Who do you work for?"

"I worked for the Kanabo Corporation, but I think I just became unemployed."

Manning looked at Ohara's body. Meiko had a remarkably effective way of turning in her resignation.

She set the safety on Manning's gun and handed it to him.

Meiko smiled. "You have a beautiful weapon. I am pleased to have had a chance to use it, but let us speak of business. Who do you work for, Gary—the CIA, British Intelligence or the Australians, perhaps?"

"Why does that matter to you?" Manning asked suspiciously.

"Because I need something very badly. A new employer who can get me out of New Guinea, give me a new identity and a fresh start in another country. Can the organization you work for do that?"

"I work for an organization that has excellent connections with the United States government. They could do that for you, Meiko, but why should they?"

"Because you need me. You are here on a mission. I believe you are here because of the American space plane. The Kanabo Corporation has it, and they will take it to Japan. You are fighting them, not the Indonesians. I know the location of all their facilities and how they are defended. I know their key people and how they will react. Give me what I ask, and I will help you accomplish your mission. Without me, you have little chance of success."

Manning stared at her. "You're offering to sell out the people you worked for. Why?"

Meiko flushed angrily. "I was loyal to them, but they treated me like a dog. I come from an old family, the Ashikaga. They were famous samurai. One of them was once the shogun. It is not my fault that my mother was a European, but no matter how hard I try, they will never let me forget it. They say I have polluted blood and am a filthy foreigner." She paused and glared at Ohara's body. "And this son of a rice farmer slapped me as if I were dirt. I owe them nothing."

Manning stared at her. It was tempting. They could certainly use someone who knew all their enemy's secrets, but could it be an elaborate trap?

"Make up your mind, Gary," Meiko said quietly. "We cannot stay here. Others from the Kanabo Corporation may be on the way here. If you do not want my services, I must try to escape on my own. You must decide now, yes or no."

Manning made up his mind.

"All right, you're on."

"You have made a wise decision. I know that you do not trust me, but you have your weapons. If I try to betray you, kill me."

Manning smiled coldly. "Don't worry, I will."

CHAPTER SEVENTEEN

Mack Bolan was sleeping the deep, dreamless sleep that exhaustion brings when someone touched his shoulder. He was awake instantly, his .44 Magnum in his hand.

"Easy, Sarge," Jack Grimaldi said. "I'm sorry to wake you up, but Stony Man is on the line. Barb says she has to talk to you."

No rest for the weary. Bolan got to his feet and stalked to the satcom radio. He took the microphone and pushed the transmit button.

"Granite Home, this is Striker. Over."

He waited for a second and then heard Price's familiar voice.

"Striker, this is Granite Home. Your target has been located. It's at a facility belonging to the Kanabo Corporation near the town of Agats on the south coast of New Guinea. This is approximately 170 miles southwest of your current location. I gave Jack the exact coordinates. Hal says to proceed to Agats and complete the mission. Any questions?"

Bolan had been burned by faulty data from intelligence agencies before.

"How certain is the target location, Granite Home?" he asked skeptically.

"Absolutely certain, Striker. We have optical imagery from NRO overhead assets showing your target less than an hour ago. I saw it myself. Hal requests you proceed as rapidly as possible. The pictures indicate that your target is being repaired and prepared for flight. Proceed with caution, however. Photographs indicate the Kanabo complex is heavily defended, but it is imperative that your target be destroyed as soon as possible. Over."

Bolan unfolded his map and scanned it quickly.

"Roger, Granite Home. Will comply. Has anyone figured out how we get out of here after the mission is complete? We won't have enough fuel left to reach the Papua New Guinea border after we fly to Agats."

"Roger, Striker. We have a nuclear submarine, the USS *Sam Houston,* operating off Agats. Rafael and Calvin are on board. Jack has the coordinates. After completing the mission, fly to the *Sam Houston.* She will be standing by to pick you up two hours after you contact me."

"Understood, Granite Home. There's a complication. Gadgets has a head injury suffered in a helicopter crash. Gary has taken him to receive medical aid from a friendly doctor in Wamena. We'll proceed as soon as they return. I'll notify you when we are about to take off. Over."

Price didn't answer for a few seconds. Bolan knew she hated the idea of one of her team being injured or wounded in the middle of a mission. She didn't like not being able to evacuate Schwarz immediately, but she was a professional. She knew that there was no way out.

"Understood, Striker. Continue mission. Granite Home out."

Grimaldi had been listening quietly. He had no questions.

"I can take off five minutes after you give the word. Here, drink this. You look like you could use it." He passed Bolan a steaming plastic cup. The Australians had thoughtfully provided them with U.S. Army Meals Ready to Eat. MRE coffee wasn't his favorite beverage, but at least it was hot and it would help keep him awake.

"Isn't that just what the doctor ordered? Wait till you see what I'm fixing for lunch. Trust me, you'll love it."

Bolan sighed. He had trusted Jack Grimaldi with his life a hundred times. He was a crack pilot. As a gourmet cook, he was a disaster.

Wejak suddenly appeared. "Marie is coming, Belasko. Lahka is with her, and your two friends, but a woman I do not know is with them."

"I do," Grimaldi said with a grin. "That's Gary's girlfriend from Djajapura."

Bolan was puzzled. Manning was usually all business on a mission. Well, he would find out what was going on. He studied the woman as Van Heyn's party approached. She was well built, looked Eurasian and moved with a subtle, catlike grace. He had seen that before. She was almost certainly a highly trained martial artist. It would be smart to keep that in mind.

Grimaldi passed around cups of coffee while Meiko studied Bolan casually. To the untrained eye, he might not have appeared impressive. His black combat suit was wrinkled and dirty, and he needed a shave. The woman wasn't deceived. His weapons were sparkling clean and ready for action, and he radiated what the military call command presence. He was clearly the leader.

"Who's your friend, Gary?" Bolan asked.

"Meiko Ashikaga. She used to work for the Kanabo Corporation. She says she's willing to work for us if we'll get her out of New Guinea and give her a new identity."

Meiko watched Bolan's face carefully as Manning spoke. His expression gave very little away, but she was sure she saw a flicker of interest when Manning mentioned the Kanabo Corporation. Good. It was obvious that he was the one she had to convince.

"That's interesting. Fill me in."

Manning went quickly over what had happened in Wamena. Bolan nodded and looked at Meiko.

"Do you agree that's what happened?" he asked.

"Yes, Gary is quite precise."

"One more question, Gary," Bolan said. "You said Meiko put on quite an act in Djajapura. Are you sure she's not doing it again? Could it be a setup?"

"I don't know. She certainly killed this man Ohara. She shot him with my pistol, twice through the chest and once through the head. I saw the body. There's no way that was faked."

Bolan nodded. "Do you know anything about the Kanabo complex at Agats, Meiko, particularly its defenses?"

"Yes, I was part of the Kanabo security organization. I have been at the Agats facility many times."

The soldier made up his mind. He couldn't be absolutely sure he could trust the woman, but he needed the information she could provide. Sometimes you had to take a chance.

"All right, Meiko, you're in. We're going to fly to Agats. After we accomplish our mission, we'll be leaving New Guinea. You can come along. I give you my word my organization will give you what you're asking for. Now, brief me on the Agats facility."

Meiko smiled. "I do not wish to appear ungrateful, but I would feel much better giving you this information once we are in the air. I would be very sad if there was some unfortunate mistake and I was left behind."

"You heard the lady, Jack. Fire her up. We take off in five minutes."

He and Grimaldi moved toward the helicopter.

"I wish to thank you," she said softly to Manning. "You kept your word. I am in your debt."

"We're all lovable when you get to know us."

"Yes, your Belasko is most impressive. Many Japanese have told me that all Americans are soft and weak. He does not seem so."

Manning smiled. "I'll tell you one more thing about him you ought to know, just in case it should cross your mind to double-cross us when we get to Agats. He never forgets anyone who betrays him. And his justice is swift."

JACK GRIMALDI LIFTED the Augusta-Bell chopper off and turned her south. He stayed low, following the valleys and skimming over the tops of the tree-covered hills. He didn't know whether there were any fighter aircraft or helicopter gunships in the area, but he wasn't one who took unnecessary chances. Bolan got up from the copilot's seat and stepped back into the passenger compartment. Schwarz was slumped in one of the passenger seats. He seemed to be asleep, but he still looked pale.

Bolan sat down next to Van Heyn. He hadn't had a chance to talk to her before they took off. He didn't think she would have brought Schwarz back if he was in serious condition, but he was still concerned.

"How is he?" he asked.

The woman looked tired and worn. The past three days had been hard on her.

"He has a mild concussion. He should probably be in a hospital for observation, but I knew you wouldn't want to leave him in Wamena. I have given him some medicine. With luck, he should be all right."

"I hope so. He's the best man I know when it comes to high-tech equipment. We'll probably need him when we get to Agats."

The doctor nodded and yawned.

"It'll be more than an hour until we get to Agats. Get some sleep," Bolan said.

He got up and took a seat next to Meiko. She was staring out the window, looking at the green landscape sliding by.

"We're on our way now. Brief me on the Kanabo Corporation and its Agats facility."

"Very well. You have kept your word. I will keep mine. What do you want to know?"

"Who are they? What are they trying to do?"

"They are trying to make Japan a great power again."

"I thought that Japan was doing well. What's the problem?"

"Japan is strong economically but weak militarily. Mr. Ito says America and Japan are at war. Not a war fought with missiles and hydrogen bombs, but an economic and scientific war. In the end, one of them will be the greatest power on earth. The other will be defeated. Your government knows Japan's economic and technical power is growing rapidly, and they fear us. The men who control the Kanabo Corporation believe the time will come when the United States will use its military power against Japan. When that time comes, they mean to be sure that Japan will win."

"Are they controlled by the Japanese government?"

Meiko thought for a moment. "It is hard to explain to someone who is not Japanese. They are not a government agency, but the men who control the corporation are very rich and powerful. They have many friends and supporters inside the government. If the Kanabo Corporation asks the Japanese government to do something, it will most probably be done. If they need weapons, technical experts or diplomatic support, they will get them. If one of their operations fails, the Japanese government will say it knew nothing about it."

Bolan had heard better news. It sounded like the odds were against him. It didn't matter a great deal. He was used to that.

"What are they doing in New Guinea?" he asked.

"Do you know why the war was fought in 1941?"

"I seem to remember Pearl Harbor."

Meiko shook her head impatiently. "That was merely a battle, fought after the decision had been made to go to war. Japan fought because its economy rests on a house of cards. It is a very poor country when it comes to natural resources. They have no oil and very little iron, copper or coal. Almost everything used by Japanese industry must be imported from other countries. If these imports are cut off, Japan will be ruined in months. In 1941, America and England tried to stop these critical imports. The war was fought over natural resources. Japan invaded Indonesia for its oil and metals, Malaya for its rubber, and Indochina for tungsten and brought them into the empire. Japan fought well, but in the end the strength of the United States was too great, and then there was the atomic bomb. Japan lost."

Bolan shook his head. "Are they going to be stupid enough to try that again?"

Meiko nodded. "Yes, they are already trying, but not in the same way. They take the long view. In ten or twenty years, they will control the economy of Indonesia and many other places in the Pacific area. And there is something else. Japan is very small and crowded. It is very hard to develop and test secret weapons there. Here in Indonesia, it is easy. If there is another war between the United States and Japan, the Kanabo Corporation will ensure that Japan's weapons are the most advanced."

Meiko smiled sweetly. "Of course, your government knows some of this, Belasko. That is why you and your team are here. To keep the Skylance technology out of Japanese hands. Well, be warned. It will not be easy."

BOLAN LAY QUIETLY at the edge of a group of trees, scanning the Kanabo Corporation complex with his binoculars. Price hadn't been exaggerating. The complex was heavily defended. It was surrounded by a heavy wire fence topped with razor wire. There were several guard towers, each manned by two guards. A thirty-foot-wide belt outside the fence had been completely cleared of all vegetation and bulldozed flat. There was absolutely no cover within a hundred yards of the fence. Inside the perimeter, he could see several small concrete bunkers. No weapons were visible, but Bolan knew a fire base when he saw one. Anyone attempting to fight his way in would be caught in a deadly cross fire.

The soldier passed the binoculars to Meiko. "See anything new or different?" he asked.

Meiko looked carefully and shook her head. "Nothing new, but they are on a high state of alert. There are four men on the main gate. Usually there would be only two, and look over there, to your left. That is the aircraft hangar. I see four guards. Usually there would be only one. I am sure your Skylance is there."

Bolan frowned. There was no way that the Japanese could know the Stony Man team was there, but they were obviously not taking any chances. Meiko was right. It wasn't going to be easy.

"There are some other things you should know," Meiko added. "They do not depend on guards alone. There are many intrusion-detection sensors, infrared, low-light-level television, lasers, and motion and metal detectors. At night there will be patrols along the fence, jeeps or trucks with machine guns. Their crews will have night-vision equipment. If they see anything, they will not hesitate to fire without warning."

"Could you get in the main gate?"

"Probably. My ID should still be good, but I could not get you and your people in. You do not look like Japanese."

He handed the binoculars to McCarter and waited patiently while he studied the complex. He knew it was time well spent. The Briton's advice on planning a raid could be invaluable. At last, McCarter handed the binoculars back and shook his head.

"It looks bad to me, mate. If they detect us once we break cover, the cross fire from those bunkers will cut us to pieces. I don't see how we get to the fence unless Gadgets knows some miraculous way to disable the intrusion sensors."

"What about flying in?" Bolan asked Meiko. "Suppose some of us stage a diversion, and the rest of us go in in the helicopter and land on the runway near the hangar. They may not be expecting that."

Meiko shook her head. "There are radars that are designed to detect low-flying aircraft, and the security forces have infrared homing missiles. You may get in, but you will never get back out."

Bolan noticed that Meiko had said "you," not "we." She obviously wasn't volunteering for a kamikaze air assault. He understood what she had said. The Kanabo complex sounded like a very tough nut to crack, but there might be a way that neither he nor Meiko could see. He had a good basic understanding of how intrusion detectors worked, but he was no expert. Schwarz was. It was time to talk to Gadgets.

SCHWARZ LISTENED QUIETLY while Meiko outlined the Kanabo complex's defenses. He still looked pale and shaken, but he seemed to be alert and to understand every word she said.

"Well, it's logical," he said when Meiko finished. "That's the way I would do it if I were setting up an antiintrusion system and I had all the latest technology."

"I'm not sure I understand this," Van Heyn remarked. "These lasers Meiko talks about, are they dangerous?"

"No, not the lasers themselves. They're small and low powered, just sophisticated invisible trip wires, really. If you break one of the beams, it will sound an alarm and tell the control center exactly where you are. They're really not the problem. Our night-vision goggles see into the near-infrared. We would see them as glowing lines of light and be able to just step over them."

Van Heyn looked relieved. "So with your equipment, we will be able to slip in at night undetected."

Schwarz frowned. "No. From what Meiko says, they're just the first line of defense. They have motion detectors. They use sound waves you can't hear to detect motion."

"Can you jam them, Gadgets?" Grimaldi asked.

"I could. But the minute I do, alarms are going to go off in the control center. But I don't have to jam them, Jack. I can fool them. What I can't take care of is the passive sensors."

"I do not understand. What is a passive sensor?" the doctor asked.

"There are two kinds of sensors you can use to detect intruders, active and passive. Lasers and motion

detectors are active. They're sending out beams and
signals all the time. They're actively looking for you.

"Passive systems are different. They don't do anything you can detect. They just sit there and wait for
you. They are like land mines. You never know one's
there until you step on it. That's what we really have
to worry about. Something out there just sitting patiently and listening, something we can trigger without ever knowing it was there."

"What kind of something, Gadgets?" Grimaldi
asked grimly.

"Probably seismic sensors buried in the ground,
Jack. They don't radiate anything I can detect. They
just pick up the vibrations in the ground when you
pass by one and tell the opposition you're there."

"So what do we do?"

"I don't know. I'm sorry. I can try, but the odds are
really against us. All that has to happen is for me to
miss just one sensor, and we'll be out in the open when
they commence fire. If we go, I'll do the best I can, but
I'd be lying if I told you I thought I could do it."

There was a long silence. Wejak, Lahka and Van
Heyn didn't really understand everything that Schwarz
had said. Grimaldi, Manning and Meiko were profes-
sionals. They did. The electronics expert was describing a death trap.

They looked at Bolan. He was the team leader. He
would have to call the shots. It was a hard choice. He
had never quit on a mission yet, but to try to infiltrate
the system Schwarz was describing wouldn't be bravery. It would be suicide. The team depended on him.
He wasn't going to lead them to certain death.

"All right. Trying to go in through the fence won't work. Has anyone got any other ideas?" he asked. No one seemed to have any.

"Perhaps we could go in through the main gate," Meiko said finally. "After dark they will send out vehicles to patrol the road from here to Agats. If we can ambush one and capture it, there is a chance we could get through the main gate. Then we make a dash for the hangar and try to destroy it before we are all killed."

"Before we are all killed?" Grimaldi asked.

"Yes, we will never get out alive. I am sorry. It is not a very good plan, but it is all I can think of."

"That's no good," Manning said. "What we've got to have is a diversion. If we can get a couple of people inside and plant some explosives at a few key points, we can disrupt the defenses and confuse them. Then we stand a chance."

"Great plan, Gary," Grimaldi said skeptically. "Just one little problem. How the hell do you get inside?"

"Damned if I know," Manning said, "but there's got to be a way."

Bolan stood. "Gary's right. We have to have a diversion. The meeting's over. I've got to send a message to Washington."

CHAPTER EIGHTEEN

Ito walked quickly into his office at the Kanabo Corporation complex. Raizo Tanaka waited patiently as the man placed his father's sword in a rack on the wall behind his desk. Ito seated himself behind his mahogany desk. He called his secretary and ordered tea, but he didn't wait for her to bring it. Tanaka was surprised. This was a breach of good manners, and his superior's manners were normally perfect. Tanaka kept his face impassive, but it was obvious that something was going on.

"How was your trip from Wamena?" he asked politely.

"Pleasant enough. However, I have just had a satellite-radio discussion with our headquarters in Tokyo. That was not so pleasant."

Tanaka was puzzled. "What troubles them? We have the American space plane. It is here now in a safe place. I have ordered a maximum security alert. Extra guards are stationed at all critical points. The repair team has arrived from Tokyo this morning. Dr. Hosokawa and his team are completing the repairs as rapidly as possible. The damage was minor. He says that the plane will be ready for flight in a few hours. It will be dark then, but he plans a test flight tomorrow. If all goes well, we will fly Skylance to Japan tomorrow. A flight of fighters will arrive tonight to provide an escort."

Ito smiled. "Skylance?"

"That is what the Americans call it. They love these boastful names."

"How did you learn this?"

"From the American woman, Clark. She is not co-operative, but I am teaching her to be humble and obedient. She does not like electric shocks on the most-sensitive parts of her body. Another day or two, and she will beg to tell us anything we want to know."

"What else have you discovered?" Ito asked.

"Skylance is a warplane. It is armed. There is a small weapons bay containing four American AIM-9 Sidewinder air-to-air missiles. These are obviously for self-defense when it is operating in the atmosphere. There is a second, larger weapons bay in the center of the fuselage. There are two unusual devices inside. They appear to be some strange kind of bomb, but Dr. Hosokawa is not certain what they are supposed to do."

Ito turned pale. "Nuclear bombs?" he asked quickly. Like most Japanese his age, he had a deep fear of nuclear weapons.

"No, they do not contain any nuclear materials. They do contain a number of charges of conventional high explosives and complex electrical and mechanical devices. Dr. Hosokawa was reluctant to investigate further. It is possible that there are antitampering devices that could cause these weapons to detonate. Hosokawa's team are not experts in disarming weapons. I thought it unwise to risk the destruction of Skylance and possible severe damage to the complex."

"That was wise. What does the Clark woman say they are?"

"She says that she does not know. I was quite persistent. She screamed a great deal, but she kept swearing that she is only the sensor-system operator, and they do not tell her about such things. It is possible she is telling the truth. If you wish, I will question her again immediately."

"No. Tokyo is concerned that the Americans will pressure the Indonesian government to investigate the disappearance of their precious Skylance. It is possible that the Indonesians will agree if the Americans threaten to cut off all aid if they refuse. It is possible the Indonesians may insist on coming here. I do not see how we can refuse if they insist. Skylance and the woman must not be found here under any circumstances."

Tanaka nodded. "I will dispose of the woman immediately. You may be certain that her body will not be found. We are proceeding with the repairs of Skylance as rapidly as possible. I do not think Hosokawa's team can work any faster without risking disaster."

"Very well. We shall have two strings to our bow like good samurai. The Noshiro is off Agats, ready to sail for Japan. Have Hosokawa remove one of the devices. Use a helicopter and transfer the weapon and the American woman to the Noshiro as soon as possible. That way, if we lose the airplane when we attempt to fly it home, we will not have lost everything. In the meantime, maintain your security alert. I have requested that Colonel Hatta deploy some of his commandos to the Agats area. I do not want them to be inside the complex. Coordinate with their commander, and have him patrol critical areas outside the complex."

Tanaka bowed. "I will see to these things immediately," he said respectfully.

"THE KANABO COMPLEX IS very heavily defended," Bolan said, concluding his report to Hal Brognola. "We have identified a dozen types of intrusion detectors, low-light-level television and infrared systems, lasers and mine fields, and a very large and well-equipped security force. Unless we have a major diversion, our chances of successfully penetrating the complex are less than one in a thousand."

"I understand," Brognola said quickly. "What do you need?"

"Something that will take out the key points in the defense. I recommend an air strike using precision guided weapons."

"There's a problem with that, Striker," Brognola said. "It'll take two or three days to get a carrier in position to launch an attack, and it won't be easy to get a strike approved. The State Department is already screaming bloody murder about the mission as it is. The idea of an air strike on Indonesian territory will put them in orbit."

"Hal," Bolan said, "listen carefully. If we try to go into the complex on our own, we will be committing suicide. I'm not going to do that. If Washington won't authorize a supporting strike, that's the end of the mission. I'm going to withdraw the team to Papua New Guinea. If Washington wants to hang me, all right, but I'm not going to lead people who trust me into a death trap."

Brognola thought for a minute. There was no point in arguing. Bolan's mind was made up. Besides, Brognola thought that he was right.

"All right, I understand. Stay where you are and stand by. I'll contact our friend in Washington immediately."

THE PRESIDENT'S SECRETARY ushered Hal Brognola into the Oval Office. The Man was sitting behind his big desk, staring at a stack of papers. He looked up and smiled as Brognola came in, but he had a haggard look. He motioned for the big Fed to be seated.

"You know General Stuart from SOCOM," the President said, "and this is Admiral Porter. He is assisting General Stuart. And you remember John Marlowe from the State Department."

Marlowe nodded coolly.

"Mr. Brognola has asked for this meeting," the President went on. "It seems that we have a crisis in the Skylance mission. I will let him explain the situation."

Brognola spoke slowly and carefully, maintaining security but explaining what had happened so far and finishing with what Mack Bolan had told him an hour ago.

General Stuart nodded. It was easier for him to understand than for the others. He had spent twenty-five years in special operations. He knew everything there was to know about them.

"So you have a paramilitary team inside New Guinea, they've located Skylance inside a heavily defended complex and your team leader says he won't go in and destroy it without some sort of strike to disable the defenses?"

Brognola nodded.

"You have confidence in your team leader's judgment?" Stuart inquired.

"Complete confidence," Brognola stated flatly.

Stuart rubbed his chin and thought for a few seconds. He didn't know who was leading Brognola's mysterious team, but the general had led dozens of hazardous missions in his career. He wasn't about to sit in Washington and second-guess the men in the field.

"I don't think we have any choice. Brognola's man is there. He understands the situation. I recommend we support him immediately. It sounds like a job for the Air Force. I recommend we use B-2 Stealth bombers and laser-guided bombs."

Marlowe frowned. His professional diplomat's smile had faded as he listened to Stuart.

"I hate to be the one who is always negative, gentlemen," he said quickly, "but what Mr. Brognola is proposing could have the gravest consequences. He is asking for an air strike against the facilities of a major Japanese corporation, and that facility is located on Indonesian territory. That is an act of war against Indonesia and, quite possibly, against Japan. General Stuart's plan could cause a major break in diplomatic relations. It could quite possibly lead to war."

Stuart stared at Marlowe coolly. "I understand what Mr. Marlowe has said, but we have to take some action or we are turning Skylance and all its technology over to the Japanese. Are you prepared to accept that, Mr. Marlowe?"

The diplomat shook his head. "I realize that that is a very undesirable outcome, but think it over, gentlemen. Do we really want to risk a war, not only with Indonesia but possibly with Japan?"

"I don't believe they have anything at this Japanese complex that can detect and shoot down stealth aircraft. I say send in the B-2s. They'll never know what hit them!''

"I've heard that kind of talk before, General. What happens if something goes wrong? What if just one plane goes down in New Guinea? Are you prepared to see one of our air crews on CNN as prisoners of war? If that happens, what do we do to get them out? No, General, your plan is completely unacceptable!''

Brognola's temper flared. "Goddamn it! We can't just sit here and do nothing. If we're not willing to act, let's say so and pull my team out now!''

Admiral Porter had been sitting quietly listening to the argument.

"Excuse me, gentlemen. I'm here because the *Sam Houston* is standing by to support Mr. Brognola's operation. I understand what General Stuart is saying and Mr. Marlowe's objections. I think there is a simple solution. We let the *Sam Houston* handle the job.''

There was a stunned silence. Everyone in the room stared at the admiral.

"Do I understand you correctly, Admiral?'' Marlowe asked. "You did say the *Sam Houston?*''

The admiral smiled. "Yes, gentlemen. The *Sam Houston*. I think you will find that she can handle the job.''

CHAPTER NINETEEN

Mack Bolan and Meiko lay quietly at the edge of a group of trees. The soldier scanned the Kanabo Corporation complex carefully. He didn't know how Brognola and Price intended to attack the complex, but they had never let him down yet. Price had said he could select four targets to be destroyed. All he had to do was tell her the most vital points, and she would take care of the rest.

He handed his binoculars to Meiko. "I need to pick four targets," he said. "I want the ones that will cause the maximum disruption and confusion just before we go in. What do you recommend?"

"The large, white, two-story building in the center is the complex headquarters. The building next to it is the security building. The complex defenses are controlled from there. Behind it is the generator building. All the power comes from there. To the right are the fuel tanks. They hold diesel fuel and aviation fuel. If you can destroy those, the complex will be severely crippled."

"If Captain Clark is there, where will they be keeping her?" he asked.

"In the security building. There are cells for prisoners there and an interrogation room. It is the most logical place."

"What part of the building?"

"The southwest corner. These must be some very precise weapons your friends are going to use."

"Trust me."

Meiko handed back the binoculars. Bolan took a final look. The woman's recommendations seemed good to him, but he took one last look at each of the targets. He would be betting all their lives when he made his decision. He noticed an odd flag flying from the headquarters building. It wasn't the Japanese rising sun. It showed a long dark object on a white field.

"What's that thing on the flag?"

"You do not know what *kanabo* means in Japanese?"

"No. Someone's name, I suppose."

"No, a *kanabo* is a weapon, the long iron war club of the samurai. It was a terrible weapon in the hands of a strong man. It shattered armor, crushed skulls and broke bones. It was the weapon that the samurai used to smash their enemies. The corporation chose it as a symbol of their determination to smash Japan's enemies. Do not underestimate them, Belasko. They are determined to win or die."

BOLAN BRIEFED McCarter carefully, going over every detail of his attack plan.

"Leave Marie to operate the satcom. She can notify Stony Man when the attack occurs. Bring everyone else. We are going to need all the firepower we can get. Any questions?" he concluded.

"I understand everything you said, but I don't understand why you said it. Perhaps you would care to explain?"

Bolan shrugged. "You're second in command. If anything happens to me, you have to lead the attack."

The Briton stared at him, a suspicious look in his green eyes. "The details you just went through indicate that you think you'll be absent during the attack, or else you believe you'll be killed as we go in. What are you up to?"

"There's something I've got to do. I lost Mary Clark, so I have to get her back. I'm going to take Meiko and go in before the attack. If she's there, I'll try to get her out."

"Your grammar shows your horrible American education, mate. I'm sure what you meant to say was, 'We lost Captain Clark. We have to get her back.' How soon do you want to leave?"

"I've read your personnel folder. Do you know it says, 'He has a long history of mild insubordination'?"

McCarter looked astounded, and cocked an eyebrow. "Mild insubordination? Too right."

Bolan smiled. "Get your gear together, then. We leave in five minutes. The plan is simple. There are a lot of Kanabo vehicles going back and forth from here to Agats. We pick a good spot on the road, hijack one and drive back to the complex. You and I hide, and Meiko drives up to the main gate and uses her ID to get us in. Then we'll visit the security building and see if we can find Captain Clark."

"Well, it's simple and straightforward. It just might work, but you're depending a great deal on Meiko. She has to make the plan work. Are you comfortable with that?"

"I guess I have to be. How do you feel about it. Do you think we can trust her?"

McCarter thought again. "Well, despite her European blood, she was brought up in Japan, and she thinks like a Japanese. They are a people who work best in groups, and they are very uncomfortable if they are forced out of theirs. I think Meiko has transferred her loyalties to you and to our team. And she wants revenge. The Japanese will go to great lengths to get revenge when they think they have been wronged. Yes, I would say that we can probably trust her. Of course, I could be completely wrong. I'll keep a close eye on Meiko. If she tries to betray us, I'll kill her."

HALF AN HOUR LATER, the ambush was set. Bolan had picked a place where there was a bend in the road and where trees grew close to the edge on each side. He and McCarter lay quietly at the edge of the trees. The Briton had his silenced Sterling, and the Executioner had borrowed Grimaldi's MAC-10. It lacked the range and accuracy of his M-4 carbine, but it was lethal at close range, and its Sionics suppressor made it even quieter than McCarter's Sterling.

Meiko finished tying Lahka up. Her wrists were tied to her elbows, and a rope was fastened around her neck and to her wrists. If she attempted to move her arms or struggle, she would choke herself. Bolan didn't like bringing Lahka, but Meiko had insisted that she needed someone to make her cover story convincing. She would claim that she was bringing in a native woman she had caught spying on the Kanabo complex.

Lahka had volunteered, but at the moment, she wasn't happy. Meiko was tying her arms to her body with another rope, pulling it tight until it bit into Lahka's body.

"That hurts," she gasped.

"It is supposed to," Meiko said casually. "It is the traditional Japanese way of binding women captives. The more uncomfortable you look, the more the guards will believe me."

McCarter whistled softly. Bolan listened for a few seconds and heard a car engine. Someone was about to drive into their trap. Meiko stepped out into the road. She pulled Lahka after her with one hand and covered her with her small, silenced Beretta with the other. A gray Land Rover came around the bend in the road. The Kanabo symbol was painted on its front doors. Bolan could see four men inside. Meiko held up her hand and signaled for them to stop.

The driver slammed on his brakes, and the doors flew open. One man stayed back, covered by the car. Bolan saw a silenced Heckler & Koch submachine gun in his hands. The other three drew their pistols and moved quickly toward Meiko and Lahka. The woman kept a smile on her face and pointed to the Kanabo Corporation ID badge clipped to her blouse. There was a short, hissing conversation in Japanese. Meiko was saying she was part of a security team that had surprised a band of natives lurking in the woods.

The three men relaxed when they saw Meiko's picture on her badge, but one of them was asking questions. She smiled and handed him her badge. He moved back toward the Land Rover's front door and started to reach inside for the radio's microphone. Bolan didn't hesitate. To allow a radio message to be sent would be fatal. He pulled the trigger, and the MAC-10 vibrated and hissed as it spit a 6-round, silenced burst. The heavy .45-caliber bullets tore into the man's chest and slammed him back against the vehicle's side.

Bolan swung the MAC-10 and cut down the other two guards with two short, hissing bursts. The burned-powder gas escaping from the muzzle of the MAC-10's silencer made the bushes in front of him dance and sway. The fourth man fired instantly at the motion. A burst of 9 mm bullets tore into the foliage over the Executioner's head. Leaves and twigs rained to the ground. Bolan tried to get off a shot, but the man was skillfully using the body of the Land Rover for cover.

There was a flash of movement, and Bolan started to tighten his finger on his trigger. The man staggered around the corner of the Land Rover, the Heckler & Koch submachine gun dropping from his hands. His body jerked and swayed as McCarter hit him with a second burst. He fell and lay still. The Briton came around the Land Rover with his Sterling poised and ready, but the fight was over. Automatically Bolan reloaded, slipping a fresh 30-round magazine into the MAC-10. The Phoenix Force commando picked up the Heckler & Koch and handed it to Meiko. They were probably going to need all the firepower they could get.

"We must go quickly," she said. Her voice was hoarse with excitement. "All vehicles outside the complex are supposed to check in on the radio at regular intervals. We must be through the gate before this vehicle is due to check in again."

Bolan knew she was right, but there were a few details to be attended to first. It would be foolish to leave the bodies of the security guards sprawled in the road. The next vehicle that came along would see them and sound the alarm. He and McCarter dragged the bodies a few feet into the trees. Anyone searching the road carefully would find them. Someone driving by wouldn't. It wasn't perfect, but it would have to do. There was no time for anything more elaborate.

Meiko helped Lahka into the passenger seat and slipped behind the wheel. There were some boxes in the back covered with a plastic tarpaulin. Bolan and McCarter tossed the boxes into the bushes and slipped under the tarp. They would be found if someone searched the Land Rover, but a casual observer wouldn't see them.

The woman started the engine, put the truck into gear and drove down the dirt road toward the Kanabo complex as fast as she dared. Bolan lay under the tarp. The plastic sheet made the heat and humidity feel twice as uncomfortable. He was sweating under his body armor. The seconds seem to crawl by. If a firefight erupted at the gate, he and McCarter weren't in a good position. It was very easy to shoot into a car but very difficult to fire accurately out of one. Their only option would be to bail out the tailgate and try to take out the guards before they could sound the alarm.

Meiko interrupted his thoughts. "Be ready, Belasko. I can see the gate. Lahka, remember you are a prisoner on her way to be interrogated. Try to look frightened, not so defiant."

"That will not be hard. I am frightened," Lahka snarled. She hadn't enjoyed being bound and helpless in the middle of a firefight.

Meiko pulled the Land Rover to a stop. Bolan heard a man's voice challenging her in Japanese. The driver's door opened and the woman stepped out. She moved to the opposite side, opened the passenger door and dragged Lahka out. Bolan heard her gasp for breath. Meiko said something in Japanese. Several men laughed cruelly. Lahka moaned.

"She does not speak Japanese," Meiko said, shifting to English, "but the filthy savage understands me now. These men say they would be happy to keep you here for an hour or two. I am sure you would enjoy it. You would beg to be allowed to obey me when they were finished with you. I would like that, but Mr. Tanaka is waiting for you at the security building. He will entertain you there. I will enjoy listening to you scream."

The guards laughed again. Meiko put the Land Rover in gear and drove smoothly through the gate. She sighed with relief.

"They did not seem to suspect anything. Stay hidden. We will be at the security building in five minutes."

It seemed to take forever, but Meiko was driving slowly and carefully. The last thing in the world she wanted to do was attract attention. At last, she stopped the Land Rover and cut off its engine.

"We are in the parking lot behind the security building," she said. "There are eight or nine vehicles here, but I see no one. If they are on maximum alert, most of the security people will be on guard at other buildings or outside the complex on patrol."

Bolan lifted one corner of the tarp and took a quick look around. It was starting to get dark. They had no time to waste.

"I can go in through the back door if my ID card still works," Meiko volunteered. Bolan thought it over. He didn't like letting Meiko go inside the security building alone. If she was going to betray them, she would never have a better opportunity, but he could see no alternative. There was no way he and McCarter could pose as Japanese security guards.

"All right, try it," he said, "and if you're not back out in five minutes, we're coming in after you."

Meiko smiled and was gone. Bolan watched as she went to the back door and put her ID into a computer-controlled card reader. She opened the door, waved and went inside. The Executioner took a length of flexible, linear-shaped explosive out of his pack. If he had to go in, it would be without knocking.

He waited as patiently as he could, staring at his watch. Meiko returned in three minutes, slipping back into the Land Rover.

"Clark is not there," she said quickly. "About four hours ago, Mr. Ito ordered her to be taken to the headquarters building. Why, no one knows. She has not been brought back. That is all any of the security people know."

Bolan nodded. Things weren't going their way, but he wasn't ready to quit. The light was fading fast. He looked at his watch. There was still time, not much, but enough if they hurried.

"All right, let's go."

"We had better take another vehicle," she suggested. "This one may be reported missing at any moment."

That made sense. There were a dozen cars and trucks parked behind the security building. Two of them were armed patrol vehicles, four-wheel-drive flatbed trucks with a heavy weapon mounted over the cab. Bolan went quickly to the closer one and pulled the cover off the weapon. He smiled grimly. Maybe some things were going his way after all. The dull gray weapon was an American .50-caliber Browning M-2 machine gun, armed with armor-piercing, incendiary ammunition. It was a superb weapon. Its .50-caliber bullets would destroy anything short of a full-fledged armored fighting vehicle.

The two women got into the cab, while McCarter joined Bolan in the back. The rear of the headquarters building was only a few hundred yards away. Meiko started the engine and drove slowly through the dusk, careful to avoid anything that might attract attention.

She pulled into the parking lot and stopped. Bolan looked at the two-story building. They got out of the patrol truck and slipped through the gloom to the entrance. No one was in sight. Meiko slipped her ID badge into a card reader. She waited tensely until she heard a soft click. The door was unlocked.

Bolan didn't like the idea of trying to search the building. They might encounter someone at any moment.

"Where would they be holding her?" Bolan asked.

"Mr. Ito's office or Tanaka's, or some nearby room. They are both on the second floor."

"Let's go."

Meiko nodded and led the way. She had her Heckler & Koch submachine gun slung over her right shoulder, but her hand was on the pistol grip ready to shoot. Whatever happened, she didn't intend to be taken alive. They followed her down a dimly lit corridor, up a narrow flight of stairs and out into a long, carpeted hall. Light was streaming out of one glass door.

"Mr. Ito's office," Meiko said softly. "Shall I go first?"

Bolan nodded, and Meiko went through the door, towing Lahka behind her. He risked a quick glance around the edge of the door as the pair entered. A woman was sitting at a desk, wearing a beautiful white-and-gold kimono. It contrasted strangely with the computer and the high-tech telephone on her desk.

The woman looked up and stared at Meiko as she came through the door. She seemed surprised to see her. She and Meiko exchanged several quickly spoken sentences. Bolan didn't need to speak Japanese to know that there was no love lost between the two of them. The woman snapped something that sounded like an order and reached for the telephone on her desk. Meiko didn't reply. She pulled the trigger on her subgun, and Bolan heard the soft hiss of the submachine gun's silencer as Meiko fired a burst from the hip. It wasn't pretty shooting, but it was effective. The 9 mm bullets slammed the woman back into her chair for a second, then she slumped forward over her desk.

Bolan raced through the open door. He swept the room with the muzzle of his Desert Eagle. No one moved. Meiko looked down at the woman she had just shot. There was a faint smile on her lips.

"Who's she?" he snapped.

"She was Mr. Ito's secretary," Meiko said. "I never liked her. She had a most unpleasant way of saying *gaijin*. I have cured her of that."

She pointed to a closed door in the room's far wall. "That is Mr. Ito's office. Do you want me to go in?"

Bolan looked at his watch and shook his head. They were running out of time for deception. It was time for direct action.

"Cover the hall and cut Lahka loose," he told McCarter. "I'm going to pay a call on Ito."

He opened the door with his left hand and stepped into the inner office. A gray-haired Japanese man sat behind a large desk. He was polishing the blade of a Japanese sword with a silk cloth. He looked up at Bolan, glanced at the gaping muzzle of his .44 Magnum pistol and smiled. He showed no fear or surprise. He acted as if Bolan were an expected guest.

"Freeze!" Bolan said quickly. "Don't try to touch anything on your desk. Drop the sword."

The gray-haired man's smile broadened. "This was my father's sword. It has been in my family for four hundred years. It would dishonor me to drop it, but I will put it down if it frightens you."

He placed the sword carefully on the desk and looked at the big man in black standing in front of him. "My name is Ito. I do not believe we have met. Who are you?"

"Call me Belasko."

"Very well, Belasko. You seem to have gone to a great deal of trouble to see me. I do not think you came just to kill me. If that was the case, I would already be dead. Do you wish to tell me of my evil deeds before you pull the trigger?"

"I don't care whether you live or die, Ito. You're holding an American Air Force officer, Captain Mary Clark, prisoner. Order her to be brought here at once. Do that, and I'll release you unharmed when I leave your complex."

Ito's smile deepened. "So, Belasko, you are the leader of these Americans who have caused us so much trouble. Tanaka is right. You are a warrior. I can tell by the way you stand and the way you hold your weapons."

"That's nice. I want Clark brought here now. Don't think I'm bluffing. I will kill you."

"I do not doubt you, Belasko. Many Japanese think Americans are soft and weak with no stomach for killing. I am not one of them. However, there is a small problem. Your Captain Clark is no longer here. She left four hours ago on her way to Japan."

He pointed to a piece of paper on his desk. "Here is the order for her transportation. You may examine it if you like. Of course, you may have some trouble reading Japanese."

"Not as much as you think. Meiko, I need you in here."

Ito's eyes widened as the woman entered his office.

"You are an American agent, Meiko? I cannot believe this."

Bolan wasn't interested in poignant reunions. "Read that," he said.

Meiko picked up the sheet of paper. "It is an order to put Mary Clark on one of the Kanabo Corporation cargo ships, the *Noshiro*. She is to be taken to Japan for further interrogation and to advise their experts after Skylance is flown to Japan."

She picked up another piece of paper. "This one says Skylance will be ready for flight testing tomorrow, Belasko. You must destroy it tonight."

Ito lost his smile. "How can you do this, Meiko? You are betraying your own people to the foreigners!"

Meiko smiled bitterly. "My own people? I am a foreigner, Ito-san. Tanaka, Ohara and your charming secretary have never let me forget that. No matter who my mother was, I am an Ashikaga. I will not be treated like a dog. I will have my revenge."

Ito nodded solemnly. He didn't like what Meiko said, but he understood. It was a matter of honor. The situation looked grim, but he still had one last card to play.

"You are here to destroy Skylance, Belasko? It is very important to Japan and my corporation. Are you a soldier in the American Army?"

Bolan shook his head.

"So. You are a contract employee, then. You work for someone, and they pay you for your services. I am prepared to do better. I offer you ten million dollars deposited wherever you wish to abandon your mission and leave here immediately. If you accept, you will not be harmed and we will not pursue you. Not even Meiko. You will have my word of honor. Ask Meiko. She will tell you. If I give you my word, I will not break it."

"That is true, Belasko," Meiko said. "Mr. Ito is a man of honor."

Bolan shook his head. "I have given my word. I won't sell out."

Ito smiled. "It pleases me that you are a man of honor. It would be disappointing if you were not."

"I'm glad you're happy. Stand up, we're leaving now."

Ito shook his head. "I am not afraid to die. I will not be your hostage."

"Be careful, Belasko. He is telling the truth. He is not afraid to die," Meiko said quickly.

"All right, but what about Tanaka and the others—will they attack us if we're holding Ito?"

Meiko thought for a second. "Probably not. They all revere Mr. Ito. If we—"

Bolan heard pistol shots crackling in the outer office. He pivoted instantly to cover the door.

Meiko screamed behind him. "Look out!"

The soldier wheeled. Ito was on his feet, moving toward him with fluid, catlike grace. He held his sword above his head, poised for the stroke Japanese swordsmen called the pear splitter because it cut a man's head in two, like a ripe fruit. Bolan pulled the trigger. The big .44 Magnum pistol roared and kicked. Mr. Ito seemed to run into a stone wall. His father's sword dropped from his hands, and he slumped to the floor.

"Why did he do that?" Bolan asked. "Didn't he think I'd shoot him?"

Meiko smiled. "He knew he could not win, but he would not be a hostage. He made you kill him, and he died fighting. It was an honorable death. Surely you see that?"

Lahka threw open the door to Mr. Ito's office.

"David says you must come quickly, Belasko. There was a silent-alarm button under the secretary's desk. We are being attacked. David killed two when they tried to break in, but there are many of them."

Bolan snarled. Now he knew why Mr. Ito had spun out the conversation. Even in death, the man had to be laughing. They were in a trap, and there was no way out.

USS Sam Houston, *off Agats, New Guinea*

THE NUCLEAR SUBMARINE was moving quietly at antenna depth. Only her periscopes and her satcom antennae were above the surface. Radio waves didn't penetrate water. There was no other way for the vessel to receive radio messages. Commander Scott knew that, but he didn't like it. Like most nuclear-submarine captains, he was much happier when he was running deep. Despite the fact that *Sam Houston*'s BQQ-5 sonar said there were no ships or submarines within thirty miles, Scott was prowling the attack center, looking over the sonar operators' shoulders and checking their displays. If anything happened, he intended to be ready. Rafael Encizo sipped a cup of coffee strong enough to float a torpedo and tried to stay out of the way.

Scott had been taking the *Sam Houston* up for ten minutes every hour for the past nine hours, but no messages had been received. Encizo looked at his watch. They had been at antenna depth for eight minutes. Waiting was beginning to make him nervous. Despite an occasional message relayed from Stony Man, he felt out of it. The rest of Phoenix Force was in the middle of a dangerous mission, while he and Calvin James were sitting here on the submarine doing nothing.

A chief petty officer entered the attack center and handed Scott a red-and-white folder stamped Top Secret.

"It's a priority message from the SUBPAC operations center, sir. They request immediate acknowledgment."

Encizo was instantly alert. SUBPAC was Submarines Pacific, the Navy command center at Pearl Harbor, which controlled all U.S. submarines operating in the Pacific Ocean. They weren't calling the *Sam Houston* to talk about the weather. Scott read the message carefully.

"Acknowledge. Send 'Message understood. Will comply.'"

He picked up a microphone, and his voice reverberated through every compartment in the vessel's long black hull. "Battle stations!"

Scott moved to the weapons-control console. "Stand by for guided-missile action. Unload all torpedo tubes. Load TLAM-Cs in one, two, three and four. Stand by to receive and record TLAM targeting data."

Encizo wanted desperately to know what was happening, but he knew you didn't ask a submarine commander questions while he was giving combat orders. He waited until Scott finished speaking and motioned for the Phoenix Force commando to join him at the weapons-control console.

"This is the attack order, Mr. Brown. We will hit the Agats area of Western New Guinea in two hours with TLAM-Cs."

Encizo looked puzzled. He was an expert in underwater operations and demolition work, but he wasn't familiar with some of the new, high-tech submarine weapons.

"TLAM-Cs?" he asked.

"Tomahawk Land Attack Missiles with conventional, high-explosive warhead. They don't let me play around with nuclear warheads. We carry only four, and my orders say we shoot the works and hit four targets west of Agats. I don't know why, of course. Maybe you do?"

Encizo shook his head. It had to have something to do with the Stony Man team's mission, but he didn't know what.

Scott's smile broadened. "It doesn't matter. Someone is going to get a big surprise."

Down below, in the center of the hull, inner doors swung open and the hydraulic handling equipment slid Mark 48 torpedoes out of the torpedo tubes and onto ready racks. Then four long blunt-nosed cylinders were slipped smoothly into the waiting tubes. In the communications compartment, long streams of ones and zeros were received and recorded. The digital targeting data was incomprehensible to a human being, but a Tomahawk missile guidance unit would understand it perfectly. The *Sam Houston* was going to war.

Scott glanced at the countdown clock as it ran down to zero. That was enough for him. For once, somebody in Washington had issued sensible rules of engagement. He had his orders. He didn't need permission to fire. He pushed the intercom button. "Torpedo room, ready one, two, three, and four for immediate firing."

The outer doors of the four torpedo tubes slid smoothly open. The four Tomahawk missiles waited silently in their protective capsules as the final checks were made. On the weapons-status display console in the attack center, four ready lights came on. Scott gave the order. "Fire one!"

"One fired!"

He waited twenty seconds. Tomahawk missiles were complex weapons. Scott wanted to be sure that number one was on the way before number two was fired.

"Fire two!"

"Two fired!"

"Fire three. Fire four."

The first Tomahawk shot smoothly forward from the number-one torpedo tube. A sensor calculated its forward motion. When it had cleared the long black hull, its solid-propellant rocket booster ignited, and the Tomahawk's guidance system steered the missile toward the surface. It reached the surface and broached, rising rapidly upward on a pillar of spray and fire. Twenty seconds later, number two emerged and followed number one at steadily increasing speed. Tail fins and wings unfolded. Squibs fired and blasted the protective coverings away. The booster motors burned out and fell away. The missiles nosed over and began shallow dives toward the ocean below. As the Tomahawks dropped toward the surface, their Williams turbofan jet engines started. The missiles' radar altimeters measured the exact distance to the surface of the ocean below. Number one pulled out of its shallow dive and leveled off at one hundred feet. At twenty-second intervals, numbers two, three, and four followed.

The missile-guidance units checked the missiles' positions and confirmed their targets' locations. The whine of their turbofan engines deepened as the four Tomahawks went to maximum cruise speed and headed toward Agats.

CHAPTER TWENTY

A burst of full-metal-jacketed 9 mm bullets tore through the walls of the outer office. Mack Bolan stayed low as splinters and chunks of plastic sprayed the room. By now the office was a shambles. Bullets had torn rips and gouges in the furniture, and the walls were riddled with bullet holes. The enemy wasn't particularly skillful in combat inside a building. However, what they lacked in skill, they made up in enthusiasm, and they seemed to have an inexhaustible supply of ammunition.

Bolan lay in a prone position to the right of the door. McCarter was to the left. Between the two of them, they could rake the hallway near the door on either side. If anyone made it to the door and tried to rush into the room, he would be caught in a lethal cross fire. Meiko and Lahka lay prone near the back wall of the office. If anyone should get through the door, they would cut them down.

It was a good defense. They had stopped three rushes so far, but they weren't winning. Bolan had fired half his spare magazines for the MAC-10. McCarter was no better off. Someone outside was shouting orders in Japanese.

"Be ready, Belasko. They are about to rush us again," Meiko called softly.

Bolan had two flash-stun grenades left. He unclipped them from his web harness, setting one on the floor just in front of him. He held the other in his right hand and slipped his left forefinger through the ring in the safety pin. More bullets tore through the walls and raked the room. He heard feet pounding down the hall.

"Flash!" he hissed to warn McCarter, pulled the pin and smoothly threw the grenade down the hall. One thousand one, one thousand two— He closed his eyes. The flash-stun grenade detonated. Even with his eyes closed, Bolan saw a bright red flash through his eyelids. To the men in the hall, the flash was blinding. The concussion blast rocked the hall. McCarter rolled to the door and fired a quick burst down the hall. Bolan heard screams and shouts of rage, then the sounds in the hall died away.

McCarter slipped the long, curved, 34-round magazine out of his Sterling and snapped a fresh one in place. He looked at Bolan and held up two fingers, which meant he had two spare magazines left. The Executioner checked his web magazine pouches by feel. He wasn't much better off. He had three 30-round magazines plus the one in the MAC-10. When they were gone, he would have to rely on his pistols.

He thought about moving Meiko to McCarter's position. She should have six spare magazines for her Heckler & Koch. He dismissed the idea. That would help a little, but not enough. It wasn't really a stalemate. The grim truth was that they could stop one more attack, maybe two, but then their attackers would overrun and kill them.

He had to get them out of there, but how? If they charged out into the hall, they would be caught in a cross fire. There had to be some way out. He remembered the layout of Ito's office. There were two large windows. Bolan motioned to Meiko, and she crawled to his side, staying low. No one was shooting just now, but that could change in a fraction of a second.

"We need to get out of here. Check the windows in Ito's office. See what's going on outside," he said quickly. Meiko nodded and wriggled off. Bolan waited.

The woman was back quickly. "There are four security guards outside. They have submachine guns. There is no way we can climb down the side of the building without them seeing us and opening fire."

"Can you think of any other way out?"

"No, there is none. There is something else I must tell you, Belasko. Two security vehicles arrived as I was looking out the window. Tanaka was in one of them. He is the chief of Kanabo Corporation security in New Guinea. Be warned. He is a terrible man. He will stop at nothing."

Bolan believed her. For the first time since he had met her, Meiko looked frightened.

"What do you suggest?" he asked.

"We must fight to the end and die with honor."

He was willing to do that if he had to, but not until he was absolutely sure there was no way out.

"Do they have any heavy weapons?"

Meiko shook her head. "No. There are machine guns for the patrol vehicles, but this is a security unit. They provide security against infiltrators and riot-control capability if the workers in the copper mines get out of hand."

Bolan nodded. It was still very quiet outside the office.

"What are they waiting for?" he asked.

"Tanaka is in charge now. He will be making a plan. When he is ready, they will come." She paused and stared at him somberly. "I do not want to be taken alive. Tanaka would do awful things to me when he learned that Mr. Ito was dead. I will kill myself when the time comes if I can. If I am wounded or unconscious, promise me that you will kill me. Give me your word."

Bolan stared at her for a second. She was deadly serious.

"All right," he said quietly.

The silence in the hall was broken. He heard a man shouting something, first in Indonesian, then the man switched to English. "You, in the office, the leader of the American team. Hold your fire. I wish to speak to you."

"Go ahead, I'm listening."

"I am Raizo Tanaka. I am the head of security of the Kanabo Corporation. I will give you one last chance. Surrender now, and I will spare your lives."

Bolan looked at Meiko. "Can I believe him?"

"No. When he learns that you have killed Mr. Ito, he will be mad with rage. Do not let him take you alive, Belasko."

"What is your answer?" Tanaka shouted.

"Come ahead. I have a dozen men waiting for you, and our reinforcements will be here any minute. If you have any sense, you will run for it as fast as you can."

"You are a clumsy liar, American. There was a surveillance camera in the secretary's office. There are four of you, two men and two women. One of them is that traitorous bitch, Meiko. This is your last chance. Surrender now!"

Bolan didn't believe in surrendering. "No way."

"Then die," Tanaka snarled.

Suddenly the lights in the building went out. Dim emergency lights blinked on. Bolan could hear men starting to move toward them down the hall. He picked up his last flash-stun grenade and prepared to pull the pin.

"Get ready," he said. "Here they come."

Something arched through the air and landed in the hall in front of the office door. It looked like a silver soft drink can. It was a chemical grenade. Bolan heard a dull pop and a soft hissing sound. Streams of gray white smoke began to flow out of the grenade. A second bomb landed near the first and began to spew smoke. Bolan and McCarter could no longer see down the hall. Precise shooting was impossible. The Briton fired a quick burst down the hall to keep the enemy honest.

Bolan heard two more grenades land outside the door and fire. That was strange; it seemed like overkill. The smoke was already filling the hall. Then he caught a scent as the smoke cloud began to flow into the office. Not the acrid scent of burning smoke grenades, but a sharp, pungent smell of pepper gas. Bolan and McCarter had gas masks in their packs, but Lahka and Meiko had no protection whatsoever.

"Get back in Ito's office," he shouted. They would make their last stand there.

TOMAHAWK NUMBER TWO FLEW smoothly through the darkness. Its radar altimeter constantly measured the distance to the surface of the water below and kept the missile flying steadily at a hundred feet, below the detection horizon of most early-warning radars. The guidance unit's sensitive gyroscopes and accelerometers sensed its speed and attitude. The guidance computer was as happy as a computer could be. All indications were that it was exactly on course.

A timer ran down. Number two should be approaching land. The guidance unit shifted to the update mode. The radar altimeter began to rapidly scan the area below the missile. Radar signals flowed to the computer. Number two was crossing the coastline. The computer began to match the radar-generated image with the satellite-generated image loaded into its memory before it left the submarine. The two scenes matched approximately. Number two had made landfall just west of the port of Agats. The two images were like the picture in a camera's viewfinder that was slightly out of focus. They didn't match perfectly. The computer calculated. The comparison told it that it was a bit to the left of its preplanned position. It corrected course and flew west toward the Kanabo complex.

Number two was flying at 560 miles per hour, closing in on the target at nine miles per minute. The computer calculated that the target should be in sight. The Digital Scene Matching Area Correlator—DSMAC—flicked on and began to look at the ground ahead, comparing what it saw with the pictures stored in the guidance computer. There! A group of buildings loomed up. The DSMAC made one last check. The target was the exact center of the two-story building in the center. The arming command flashed to the warhead's fuse. Number two's tail surfaces moved to make one last, tiny course correction. Number two went into a shallow dive. It was going to total destruction, but the guidance computer didn't care. Cruise missiles were fearless.

The blunt-nosed, torpedo-shaped fuselage struck the headquarters building at 560 miles per hour. The wings and tail surfaces were ripped off. The guidance unit in the nose was crushed, but the thousand-pound, steel-cased warhead was designed to penetrate targets, and it did. It drove forward into the building, spraying shattered steel and concrete in front of it. It wasn't a perfect hit. Number two was two feet high and a foot to the left when it struck, which made no difference whatsoever.

The fuse fired, and the thousand-pound warhead detonated in a shattering blast of orange fire. The flight to the target had been only sixty miles. The Tomahawk carried fuel enough to fly six hundred. Ninety percent of the high-energy fuel was still in the fuel tank. The tank split, and the fuel sprayed outward. The warhead's blast detonated the fuel in what ordnance engineers call a fuel-augmented explosion. The immense blast shook the building with incredible force. Not far behind, number three and number four roared toward their targets.

BOLAN HEARD GLASS shattering behind him. Meiko had picked up a chair and was smashing the windows in Ito's office to let in outside air. McCarter was pulling on a British S-10 gas mask. He swore that British gas masks were the best in the world. Bolan certainly hoped so. His eyes were already beginning to tear and sting from the effects of the CS pepper gas seeping in from the hall. He needed to put his on, but he didn't dare take the time before McCarter was ready to fight again. Bolan saw a man's figure suddenly looming through the smoke. The enemy had reached the outer office door. He pulled the MAC-10's trigger and fired a 6-round burst. The man staggered and fell.

Another grenade came around the edge of the door, struck the floor and rolled toward the inner office door. McCarter instantly snapped two short bursts, one to each side of the door. The full-metal-jacketed 9 mm bullets tore through the wall easily. Bolan heard someone in the hall shriek and fall.

Meiko was looking out a window and shouting. "Belasko, the generator building is on fire and—"

The headquarters building suddenly shook and shuddered as if it had been struck by a giant hand. Bolan hear a loud grinding, crashing noise and the booming roar of a large explosion. Then the world blew up. The building swayed as if it were in the middle of an earthquake. Dust and plaster cascaded from the ceiling. For one awful second, Bolan thought the whole building was collapsing, but the Japanese had built it well. The swaying and shuddering stopped, and Ito's office was still intact.

The big American looked quickly at the outer office. The hallway was blocked with rubble. At least for a few minutes, no one was coming at them that way. Time to get out of there if they could. He moved quickly to the windows and looked outside. They were in one corner of the building. He looked toward the front entrance. Two parked Land Rovers were half-buried in debris. Flames were beginning to lick out of a huge hole in the building. Two bodies lay still on the ground, killed by falling steel and concrete. Two other men were standing nearby. They seemed dazed and confused, but they had submachine guns in their hands.

Bolan motioned to Meiko and pointed to the two men below. Her Heckler & Koch MP-5 was one of the most accurate submachine guns in the world, as accurate as a rifle out to two hundred yards.

"Take them out," he said.

Meiko aimed carefully and squeezed her trigger. The subgun hissed as she fired two quick bursts. Both men dropped instantly. Bolan tore the window draperies off their hooks and tied the two of them together. It wasn't an expedition-quality climbing rope, but it would have to do. He shoved Ito's heavy desk over against the windows and tied one end of the improvised rope tightly around one of its legs.

Meiko was the lightest, and he motioned to her to go first. She slung her MP-5 across her back, took a deep breath, climbed out the window and started down. It was only twenty feet to the ground, and she was down in a few seconds. Lahka went next, shuddering as she went out the window. McCarter followed her. Then it was Bolan's turn. With his own weight and his weapons and equipment, he was putting a 275-pound load on the curtains. They stretched a bit, but Ito's decorator had bought the best. They held until he felt his boots touch the ground.

McCarter was already moving around the corner of the building, heading for the parking lot in back. Bolan ordered Meiko and Lahka to follow him. He took a quick look around. The attack on the Kanabo Corporation complex had been devastating. The security building was burning, and he could see two other big fires lighting up the night. It was a lovely sight, but he had no time to admire the view. He moved quickly after McCarter.

He came around the corner and felt a surge of elation. The collapse of the building had been confined to the front. The vehicles in the parking lot were intact. Meiko was slipping behind the wheel of the four-wheel-drive patrol vehicle. Lahka was climbing into the passenger seat beside her. McCarter was already in the back, with his hands on the grips of the big Browning .50-caliber machine gun. Bolan stopped for a second at the driver's door.

"Drive to the hangar. Don't stop for anything," he shouted.

Meiko started the engine as Bolan swung up into the back of the truck. He took a quick look around, seeing a scene of massive confusion. The loss of power and the attacks on their headquarters and security control center seemed to have completely disorganized the security forces. He could see other vehicles moving around aimlessly, but no one was trying to intercept them. They passed another truck headed the other way, back toward the headquarters building, but the people in it saw only another security vehicle and made no attempt to stop them.

They reached the hangar, but there was no sign of guards. Apparently they had left when the attack started. Meiko turned off the road and drove to the back of the structure. That was the meeting point. Manning, Grimaldi, Schwarz and Wejak should be there. Bolan saw a Land Rover sitting with its lights out. He covered it with the big .50-caliber Browning machine gun as Meiko pulled up. He hoped it was Gary Manning and the rest of the team, but he was taking no chances.

"Would you mind pointing that thing somewhere else?" Manning requested.

Bolan swung down from the back of the truck and walked quickly to the vehicle.

"Any trouble?" he asked.

"No, we borrowed this Land Rover from some people who didn't need it anymore, and here we are."

"You left Marie with the satcom?"

Manning nodded. "It was either her or Wejak, and I figured he'd be more valuable in a fight. I set the radio up for her. She was supposed to call Stony Man when she was sure the attack had started."

He looked around. "With all these fires, I don't think there could have been any doubt. I don't know how they did it, but that was a well-executed attack."

Manning looked at the patrol truck. "Where's Captain Clark?" he asked.

"She wasn't here. They put her on a ship before we got here. They're sending her to Japan. Skylance is still here, inside that hangar."

The big Canadian nodded. "Good. I've got my demolition gear. Let's do the job and get the hell out of here."

Bolan turned to Meiko and pointed to the small back door. "Can you open it?" he asked her.

She shook her head. "I am sorry. I cannot. The hangar is a secret experimental area. I was never cleared to enter it. The computer will recognize my ID card, but it will not open the door for me."

"That's all right. Gadgets is awfully persuasive."

Schwarz inserted a tiny plastic explosive charge into the door lock, checked his firing circuit and pushed the button. There was a sharp cracking noise, and the door swung partly open. The Stony Man team waited tensely for a few seconds, weapons ready, but no one inside the hangar seemed to have heard the noise, which wasn't surprising. The precisely organized Kanabo Corporation complex was dissolving into chaos. A tower of orange flame and smoke was rising above the burning fuel tanks. Security headquarters was burning and exploding. Sirens were blaring, and someone was sporadically firing a heavy machine gun into the night sky.

Bolan eased the door open and slipped inside. The interior was illuminated only by the dim glow of emergency lights. He swept the hangar with the muzzle of his Beretta 93-R, but nothing moved. The building was deserted. Tools and electronic checkout gear were scattered about. Whoever had been working here had left in a hurry when the complex alarms had sounded. But the important thing was the dull gray shape that sat in the center of the floor.

There it was, a blunt-nosed, twin-tailed triangle, sitting on its tricycle landing gear. Bolan felt a surge of elation. Brognola's information had been right. Skylance was here. Both the cockpit canopies and what had to be the weapons bay were open.

"Gadgets, you and Jack check it out. Find out if those two weapons are still on board," Bolan said as the rest of the team slipped quietly inside. Schwarz and Grimaldi moved quickly to the aircraft and began to examine it. Manning and McCarter covered the main door. Meiko stood by the Executioner and stared at Skylance. It was an impressive sight. As far as he could tell, the Japanese repair team had done an excellent job. All the damage caused by the laser attack and the emergency landing had been skillfully repaired. Skylance looked as if it had just rolled off the assembly line.

Schwarz peered up into the weapons bay. "There's good news, and there's bad news," he said. "One of the weapons is still here, but they must have taken the other one out."

That was bad news. Bolan looked quickly around the hanger. There was no sign of the second weapon.

"Where would they have taken it, Meiko?" he asked.

"I cannot say. Perhaps to one of the laboratories or to the security building. There is no way to be certain."

Bolan frowned. There was no way they could search the entire base. Washington wouldn't like it, but there was no other choice. They had to destroy Skylance and get out of there.

Grimaldi was standing on one of the wings, looking in the pilot's cockpit. He motioned to Bolan, who moved quickly to join him, and pointed excitedly at the pilot's displays.

"Look at this, Striker," he said.

Bolan looked, but all he saw was a group of panels covered by softly glowing green lights and yellow numbers. He was sure it meant something to Grimaldi. It meant nothing to him.

"What do you see, Jack?"

"She's ready to fly. Her fuel tanks are full, and it looks like all systems needed for flight in the atmosphere are ready to go."

"Looks like we got here just in time," Bolan said. "Meiko, go get Gary Manning. Tell him I want charges set on Skylance immediately."

"Wait a minute," Grimaldi said urgently. "She's ready to fly, and I can fly her. Just get the hangar doors open, and if I can start the engines, I'll be gone.

I'll have her on the ground in Australia in an hour or two."

Bolan thought quickly. He didn't doubt what Grimaldi said. He was the best pilot Bolan knew. It was tempting. Recovering Skylance intact would impress the politicians Hal Brognola had to battle.

"You're forgetting one thing, Jack. You're our pilot. If you take off in Skylance, who's going to fly the helicopter? I need to be free to return fire."

"Damn!"

"If you wish to do this, Belasko, that is not a problem. I can fly the helicopter. It was part of my Kanabo Corporation training," Meiko said quickly.

Bolan thought it over for a second. It would be putting their lives in Meiko's hands, but she seemed to be a very capable woman. He no longer doubted her loyalty, at least for the moment. After the havoc he had seen her wreak on the Kanabo Corporation complex, he had no trouble believing that she had a burning desire to get far away from New Guinea.

"All right, Jack, get ready to fire her up. I'll take care of the hangar doors."

Without another word, Grimaldi slipped into the pilot's seat.

"Time to take this baby home!"

CHAPTER TWENTY-ONE

Jack Grimaldi threw the auxiliary-power switch, then waited tensely for half a second. The cockpit was illuminated by the soft, glowing displays on the control panel. He breathed a sigh of relief as green lights marched across the panel. The Japanese repair team seemed to have done a good job. He ran his eyes quickly over the individual displays. Fuel check. All tanks were full. Flight-control system check. Sensor systems check. Weapons systems check. Skylance had no cannon, but there were four AIM-9P Sidewinder air-to-air missiles in the forward weapons bay, which might come in handy.

He touched the controls lightly. There were some specialized controls that clearly were intended for use only in space. He could ignore them. Aside from that, Skylance was basically a large jet fighter with stick and rudder controls. He had flown a dozen types of fighters like that. He could fly this one standing on his head. He smiled grimly to himself. He could fly it all right, if he could start the engines and if they could get the hangar doors open. Aside from those two trivial details, he had no problems.

Someone touched him on the shoulder. Mack Bolan was standing on the top side of the wing next to the pilot's cockpit.

"All set, Jack?" he asked.

Grimaldi could feel the adrenaline start to flow. He was about to fly a strange plane off a strange airfield in the dark with people shooting at him. There was no use worrying about it. He was as ready as he would ever be.

"All set, Striker. Just open those goddamned doors!"

"We're having trouble getting them open, Jack. Gadgets says there is some kind of remote-control system he can't override. Manning's going to blast them open. He's rigging the charges now. Gary says don't worry. He'll make sure they fall away from you."

Grimaldi smiled. If you had to sit on a plane load of high-energy fuel while someone set off explosions twenty feet away, Gary Manning was your man. He was the best.

"All right, Striker. Let's do it. Stand clear. I'm starting the engines."

Bolan nodded and was gone.

The Stony Man pilot pushed a button, and the canopy slid smoothly down and locked. He took a deep breath and pushed the engine-start button. Skylance was designed to operate from remote airfields. Its starters were self-contained. Grimaldi heard a soft whirring noise as first one and then both engines began to turn over. Fuel flowed into the engine combustors, and the engines whined into life.

Grimaldi looked at the doors. The Stony Man warriors were hugging the walls, staying as far away from the doors as possible. Manning had his left hand raised in a ready signal, the remote-detonator box in his other hand. Grimaldi snapped him a salute and waited tensely. There was a sudden series of blue-white flashes as the charges detonated. The big steel doors shuddered and fell outward into the dark.

The pilot pushed the throttles forward, and the whine of the engines deepened. Brakes off. Skylance began to roll out onto the taxiway toward the dark runways. He could see black shapes to the left and right as the Stony Man team moved with the aircraft, ready to cover his takeoff. Grimaldi noticed his running lights were on. There didn't seem to be any way to turn the damned things off. The complex was a scene of mass confusion. The missiles had done a first-class job. Fires were burning in several places, and the runway lights were out, but anyone who looked in his direction would see Skylance's wingtip and taillights.

He turned onto the main runway, put on the brakes and pushed his throttles forward. Skylance shuddered as its engines ran up toward full power. He heard a voice in his headset, someone speaking rapidly in what had to be Japanese. Grimaldi didn't speak the language and had nothing to say to the control tower even if he did. Time to get out of there! He released his brakes, and the aircraft began to roll down the runway, faster and faster. The world suddenly seemed to explode into brilliant white light. A searchlight was shining on Skylance from the control tower. Grimaldi cursed and tried to keep the aircraft on the runway, but the light was blinding. It suddenly vanished in a bright blue flash. Grimaldi smiled. It would be a cold day in hell when Mack Bolan missed a large searchlight at four hundred yards.

Skylance was moving faster now. Grimaldi eased back on the stick a little, and the aircraft shuddered. She wasn't quite ready to lift off. Red tracers streaked over his canopy. Someone was firing at him with an automatic weapon. The end of the runway seemed to be rushing toward him. He was running out of time. The pilot pushed his throttles forward and pulled back on the stick. Skylance rotated smoothly. The nose came up, and she was suddenly airborne. He pulled the lever and felt a thump as the landing gear came up and locked.

He felt a wild sense of elation. He was airborne, and like any good fighter pilot, he felt he was in control of the situation when he was in the air. A red light suddenly began to flash on his control panel, and he heard a soft electronic beeping. He stared at the display. RAWS warning! The Radar Attack-Warning System had detected something that made it nervous and a message appeared on the display.

"AN/APG-63 airborne radar in search mode. Range 40 miles and closing. Aircraft are F-15C Eagles. No IFF response."

Grimaldi scowled. He didn't need the Identification Friend or Foe system. He didn't think he had any friends flying over New Guinea. He thought fast. The Indonesian air force didn't have any F-15s. Who did? The United States, of course, Israel, Saudi Arabia, and Japan. Damn it, Japan!

The RAWS beeped again.

"AN/APG-63 airborne radar in missile-launch mode, and locked on. Range 30 miles and closing. Aircraft are F-15C Eagles. No IFF response."

Grimaldi pushed a button, and Skylance's electronic countermeasures system flashed into life. To the human eye, nothing seemed to happen, but in the electromagnetic spectrum, the sky seemed to explode as the aircraft's advanced ALQ-165 electromagnetic countermeasures system flashed into action.

"Sparrow radar-guided missiles launched. F-15s classified as hostile. Chaff and evasive action recommended."

Grimaldi swore and pushed a second button. The Expendable Countermeasures System flashed into life. Chaff cartridges shot out of the dispensers, and clouds of rapid-blooming chaff blossomed behind Skylance. Millions of tiny, aluminum-coated Mylar fibers reflected radar energy back at the F-15s. To the naked eye, they were almost invisible, but to the F-15s' radars and to the guidance units of the two deadly AIM-7 Sparrow missiles streaking toward Skylance at supersonic speeds, they were impenetrable clouds. The two Sparrows were baffled by the jammers and the confusing clouds of chaff. They lost lock and streaked by the aircraft, vanishing into the dark.

Grimaldi smiled, but he didn't like being shot at without shooting back. He reached for the panel that controlled the Sidewinders. He pressed the power button and watched as four green lights appeared on the control panel a few seconds later.

It was his turn now. He pressed the arming switch, and the heat-seeking guidance units of the AIM-9P Sidewinders began to search for hot targets. The F-15s were at full combat power with their afterburners shooting out huge plumes of hot exhaust gasses. Grimaldi heard a growling whine as the first Sidewinder's guidance unit locked on. He pushed the firing switch, and the slim white missile's rocket motor ignited, sending it streaking toward its target at Mach 2.5. The F-15 pilots had activated radar countermeasures, but the Sidewinder saw things in the infrared spectrum. It was unaffected by their radar countermeasures.

The leading F-15 pilot tried a desperate high-G climbing turn, trying to outfly the oncoming Sidewinder and make it miss, but the Sidewinder was one of the new P models, far more maneuverable than the earlier version. It matched the F-15 pilot's frantic turn and struck just behind the cockpit. The Sidewinder's 22.4-pound blast-fragmentation warhead detonated in a ball of orange fire. Lethal fragments tore through the F-15, and it began to burn and explode. The pilot died instantly, and the big fighter dropped out of the sky and struck the ground at a thousand miles per hour.

Grimaldi didn't waste time admiring his shooting. He pushed his firing switch and sent a second Sidewinder on its way. The second F-15 pilot had a few seconds' warning as the missile shot toward him. He pulled his plane into a hard, right-climbing turn and activated his infrared countermeasures system. Blinding flashes of infrared light appeared behind the F-15 as fast-burning flares flashed into life behind it.

The Sidewinder's guidance unit suddenly saw a dozen brightly glowing targets ahead. Its microcomputer quickly computed target ranges and bearings. Some of the targets were in impossible positions. The computer rejected them instantly. Three targets were still logical. One of them had to be the F-15. The Sidewinder streaked forward and passed through the group of flares. There! Almost straight ahead, its heat seeker saw the glowing, red-hot cores of the F-15's two high-thrust, afterburning jet engines. The pilot turned hard right, but the Sidewinder matched his maneuver easily. The deadly little missile struck the left engine's tail pipe, and its warhead detonated. High-velocity steel fragments tore through the engines and fuel tanks. The F-15 started to smoke and burn, and its pilot had had enough. He pulled the handle, and his ejector seat hurled him up and out of the burning plane.

"Two down and two to go!" Grimaldi yelled gleefully, but he wasn't out of the woods yet. The two remaining F-15 pilots had recovered from the shock of discovering that the supposedly unarmed plane was equipped with air-to-air missiles as good as their own. What should have been an easy kill had turned into deadly combat. They broke left and right to take Grimaldi between them as they flashed by Skylance and turned hard to get on its tail. They would close in and use their own short-range, infrared-homing missiles.

Grimaldi thought hard. He had to do something and do it fast. He checked his Mach meter. He was doing Mach 1.2, near maximum speed for a high-performance jet fighter at low altitude, but Skylance wasn't an ordinary jet fighter. He shoved the throttles all the way forward. The aircraft shuddered and began to accelerate steadily as her two huge engines roared toward full thrust. Grimaldi felt the G forces press him back against his seat. He stared incredulously as his Mach reading steadily increased, 1.6, 2.0, 3.0, 4.0! He pulled back on the stick, and Skylance shot upward like a homesick angel.

The Japanese F-15 pilots watched in amazement as their target began to shoot away from them as if they were standing still. They pushed their firing switches, and two slim, deadly Sidewinders flashed after Skylance.

Grimaldi threw a switch, and infrared flares shot out of the aircraft and began to burn behind it, generating intensely bright balls of infrared light. The

Sidewinders' guidance units were confused, and they fell behind as Skylance accelerated faster and faster.

The Stony Man pilot was going straight up now as the aircraft's incredibly powerful engines reached full thrust. He stared at his altitude display—70,000 feet, 80,000, 90,000. The Japanese fighters were left far behind. Grimaldi smiled. Skylance was one hell of an airplane. He leveled off smoothly and turned toward Australia.

CHAPTER TWENTY-TWO

Mack Bolan watched as Skylance roared down the
runway and the orange glow from its afterburners
vanished into the night sky. Grimaldi was on his way.
There was nothing more the soldier could do for him.
It was time to get his team out of the Kanabo complex before the Japanese security forces recovered and
began an organized search. He gave a hand signal, and
his teammates began to fall back toward the hangar.

Meiko had the engine of the patrol vehicle running,
while Gadgets Schwarz was waiting behind the wheel
of the Land Rover. Bolan climbed into the back of the
vehicle and got behind the big Browning. The Able
Team electronics expert blinked his headlights. He was
loaded and ready to go. McCarter swung up into the
truck bed and gave Bolan a thumbs-up. He was the
last man.

The Executioner leaned forward and shouted,
"Go!"

Meiko put the patrol truck in gear and pulled away.
Schwarz followed her, staying twenty yards behind.

Meiko headed for the main gate. It was taking a
chance, but it was the only way to reach the road, and
Bolan wanted to move as far and as fast as he could
before he abandoned the vehicles. He checked the
.50-caliber machine gun. A 105-round belt was loaded
in the ammunition box on the side of the weapon. He
pushed the bolt-latch release and pulled back the bolt-

retracting lever and let it go forward, feeding the first long cartridge into the chamber. The big machine gun was ready to fire. All he had to do was push down on the thumb trigger.

They were moving fast now, with Meiko driving as fast as she dared. A Land Rover carrying several men passed them going the other way, but it made no attempt to stop them. In the dim light, they looked like another security team responding to an alarm.

They were out of the center of the complex now. Bolan looked toward the main gate. He could see dim lights ahead, and he caught a flicker of movement. The gate was still guarded. Meiko saw it, too. She pulled to a stop and stuck her head out the driver's window.

"The gate is still guarded, Belasko," she said quickly. "What do you want me to do?"

Bolan thought for a second. Both their vehicles had four-wheel drive. Maybe they could surprise the guards by avoiding the gate itself, and crashing through the fence to one side.

"How about going through the fence?" he asked.

Meiko shook her head. "The fence is reinforced on either side. I doubt we could get through it."

"All right, through the gate. Let's go!"

Meiko put the patrol vehicle in gear and drove forward. She had been driving with only the blackout lights on. Now she turned on her headlights and illuminated the gate. Bolan didn't like what he saw. Four vehicles were parked just inside the gate, a pair on either side of the road. Two of them were Land Rovers, but the other two were obviously patrol vehicles. They weren't as large as his, but he could see an automatic weapon mounted on each. He swiveled the Browning to point at the left-hand vehicle.

They were close now. Some kind of wooden traffic-control arm dropped from one side of the gate, blocking the road. A man in uniform stepped in front of the barrier and signaled for Meiko to stop. They couldn't risk that. If the guard looked into their vehicles, they were finished. There was no possible way they could pass for Japanese security guards. Meiko kept going. The man in front of the barrier shouted something. The woman yelled something in Japanese, but Bolan saw the men in the two patrol vehicles start to swing their automatic weapons toward him.

He pushed the thumb trigger, and the Browning roared into life. A swarm of red tracers flashed at the enemy vehicle. Bolan saw bright yellow flashes as the .50-caliber bullets moving at nearly three thousand feet per second struck the truck. The rounds from the big Browning could penetrate more than an inch of solid armor plate at close range. They tore through the truck's light steel body as if it were made of tissue paper.

One of the huge, armor-piercing, incendiary bullets pierced the gas tank, and the truck exploded in a ball of orange fire. Bolan fired another burst at the Land Rover behind the burning vehicle. Its crew bailed out and ran for their lives as flaming debris rained to the ground.

Something struck the roof of the cab in front of Bolan and screamed away. The gunner on the other patrol truck had the range and was firing. Green tracers streaked past the big American's head as he swiveled the Browning toward the second truck. The

Japanese gunner was firing high, but that wouldn't last long. Meiko floored the accelerator, and their truck's engine roared as it shot forward. A swarm of green tracers streaked by as the enemy gunner fired into their former position. Bolan didn't make that mistake. He took a proper lead and pressed his trigger. He fired a long burst, saw his tracers strike the hood of the truck, corrected his aim and fired again.

He couldn't shoot with total precision as he fired from the back of the swaying patrol vehicle, but a truck at short range was a big target. Bolan saw bright yellow flashes again as a dozen armor-piercing, incendiary bullets shrieked into the truck. Its engine began to smolder and burn. The gunner stopped firing abruptly. One of the heavy .50-caliber bullets had struck him in the chest. He wouldn't need a second round.

Their patrol truck roared forward. The guard standing in the road stared at it as if he were hypnotized, while Meiko drove straight at him. He threw himself to one side at the last, desperate instant as the vehicle rammed the barricade. Bolan heard a splintering crash, and wood splinters flew through the dark as the truck shot through. He reversed the Browning on its mount, ready to fire behind if he had to, but he saw no targets. They were roaring down the road into the night. He could see the headlights of Schwarz's Land Rover behind them, but there were no signs of pursuit. McCarter was taking no chances. He put a fresh belt of cartridges in the Browning's ammunition box.

Meiko was driving steadily away from the Kanabo complex. Bolan pulled down his night-vision goggles and began to study the sides of the road. He was looking for the place where they had hijacked the Land Rover. He saw a bend in the road where the trees grew close to the edge on each side, signaled Meiko to stop and climbed down from the patrol vehicle. It looked like the right place, but he had to be sure. It would be easy to get lost and stumble around in the dark if they started from the wrong point.

Yes, this was it. He could see the tire tracks where the Land Rover had skidded to a stop, and here and there fired cartridge cases littered the ground. He signaled Schwarz to join him.

"This is as far as we go. Everybody out," Bolan announced.

The team piled out of the two vehicles. McCarter looked wistfully at the Browning. He hated to leave it behind. So did Bolan, but the big machine gun weighed eighty-four pounds, and its mount weighed forty-five more. It was impossible for them to carry it through the rain forest. They had to get rid of their vehicles, but he didn't want to leave them here. It wouldn't be smart to give any pursuers a clear indication of where they had left the road and entered the forest.

He spoke quickly to Schwarz and Meiko. "Drive a few hundred yards down the road and leave the vehicles there. Get back here as fast as you can."

They climbed back into their vehicles and were gone in a few seconds. Bolan pulled his team back into the edge of the trees. McCarter and Manning took up positions to cover the edge of the road. Bolan was about to join them when Wejak lightly touched his sleeve.

"I will go ahead, Belasko, and scout our trail. If the Indonesians found our tracks, they may have laid an ambush. I will send Lahka back to tell you if I find anything.''

"Go ahead," Bolan agreed. His respect for Wejak went up another notch. The man might not be an expert on high-tech weapons, but he had been leading raids for many years. He knew that one of the most dangerous times came when a raiding party had successfully completed its attack and was withdrawing back to its base. It was easy to think that the danger was past, only to walk in to an ambush. He would feel much better knowing that Wejak was scouting the way ahead.

Wejak and Lahka vanished into the dark. Bolan rejoined the others. They waited quietly for a while, then they heard the sound of an engine. Someone was driving rapidly down the road from the Kanabo complex. It sounded like a single vehicle, and it was tempting to ambush it. The concentrated fire of their automatic weapons would riddle a car or light truck in a few seconds. He decided against it. Inflicting a few more casualties on the Kanabo security forces wouldn't really accomplish anything, and if the vehicle was in radio contact with the complex, it might give their position away. Better to let it go on by.

"Hold your fire," he ordered.

He could see lights now. Whoever was in charge of the vehicle was in a hurry, driving dangerously fast through the dark. Brakes shrieked, and tires squealed as the driver saw the bend in the road ahead. The Stony Man team had a good view of the jeep for a few seconds. Then the driver stepped on the gas, and it was gone.

McCarter stared at Bolan. "Did you see what I saw?"

"Orange berets."

"Too right, mate. It's our friends from the special commando force again. I don't like it. It looks like they're coming from the Kanabo complex. They couldn't possibly have driven there from Agats since we hit the complex. That means they were close by when we attacked. I don't believe four of them are wandering around by themselves. There must be a larger force in the area. We can't know why they were in the area originally, but now they're sure to be after us."

Bolan knew McCarter was right. The sooner they were out of the area, the better. He would head back to the helicopter as soon as Meiko and Schwarz got back. He didn't like the risk of a night takeoff. Flying a helicopter that didn't have night-vision equipment at low altitude in the dark wasn't easy. He wasn't sure Meiko could do it, but they might not have a choice.

"Gadgets and Meiko are coming in," Manning called softly.

TWO HOURS LATER, Bolan called a halt. They needed a short rest. Traveling uphill in the dark hadn't been easy. He was navigating by the stars, using the Southern Cross as a guide. There was no real trail to follow, just the best path he could pick out through the trees and underbrush. Meiko was having a hard time. She had no night-vision goggles, and she had been raised in Japan. A tropical rain forest was a totally alien place to her. They established a quick defensive perimeter and slumped gratefully to the ground.

Bolan checked his watch. They weren't moving as fast as he would like, but there was no use driving the team until they were exhausted. As long as they avoided contact with the Indonesians and reached the helicopter before dawn, he would be satisfied. He drank a few swallows of warm water from his canteen and tried to rest.

He heard McCarter call a challenge and Lahka's voice reply.

"I must talk to Belasko at once," she gasped. McCarter pointed her toward Bolan. The woman looked tired. Bolan handed her his canteen, and she took a few quick swallows.

"Wejak has found tracks that cross our path ahead. Men in boots. He is sure it is an Indonesian patrol, perhaps fifteen or twenty of them."

"How long ago?"

"It is hard to say exactly. A few hours ago, perhaps."

They had to get to the helicopter. He checked his watch again. Ten minutes had gone by. It wasn't much rest, but it would have to be enough.

"Where's Wejak?" he asked.

"He says we are getting close to our camp. He went on to scout ahead. He said I should stay with you and show you the path he has picked out."

Bolan nodded and heaved himself up. He briefed the rest of the team quickly and asked McCarter to take the point. They pressed on through the dark, trying to be as quiet as they could. Bolan listened carefully as he moved, but he heard nothing except a few forest birds calling in the night.

After a few minutes, Lahka called a halt and showed Bolan the tracks Wejak had found. He took a small infrared flashlight out of his pack and examined them quickly. The tracks in the soft ground were deep, almost certainly made by Indonesian soldiers, two or three squads carrying heavy loads of weapons and equipment. It wasn't encouraging, but Bolan remembered what he had seen from the air. The tropical rain forest stretched on and on. Unless the Indonesians were lucky or had someone who was a really good tracker, they weren't likely to find the Stony Man team in the dark. If they could avoid contact with the Indonesians for a few more hours, they would be gone.

They pushed on. The hillside was getting steeper, but that was a good sign. They had to be getting close to the top of the ridge that overlooked the Kanabo complex. Lahka suddenly appeared out of the dark.

"Wejak is just ahead with David. He says for you to come at once and for everyone to be very quiet."

Bolan moved forward with his thumb on the safety selector switch of his M-4 carbine. He no longer felt tired. The adrenaline was flowing. Wejak and McCarter were waiting silently thirty yards ahead. He slipped down beside them.

"I do not like it, Belasko," Wejak said very softly. "Something is wrong. Someone has built up the fire where we camped. It is very bright. Why would Marie do that?"

"Did you take a look?"

"I was going to, but I found something I do not understand. Come very quietly, and I will show you."

Bolan and McCarter slipped quietly after Wejak. The soldier could recognize the terrain now. They were very close to their improvised camp. Wejak was right about the fire. The smoke and heated air rising from the fire looked like a glowing pillar of light through his night-vision goggles.

The Dani warrior pointed to the ground with the tip of his spear. Bolan saw what looked like a thin electrical extension cord that stretched off toward the camp fire. Wejak followed it until it divided and ran off to the left and the right. He moved like a ghost to the edge of the shallow cup in the ridge that held their camp and pointed at something sitting on the ground.

"There, that is one of them. There are others. I did not touch them because I did not know what they were."

Bolan stared at the odd object Wejak had discovered. It looked harmless, a two-inch-thick rectangle bent in a shallow curve. It was mounted on a small tripod, and the wires ran into it. He didn't need to read the markings. He had used them many times in Vietnam. It was a United States Army M-18 A-1 Claymore antipersonnel mine. There were several hundred steel balls embedded in one side. When it was detonated, an explosive charge of 1.5 pounds of C-4 plastique would drive the steel balls outward in one direction in a lethal, focused sixty-degree arc. If a number of them were aimed at their camp, it had become a death trap.

"Bloody hell!" McCarter said softly. He took a miniature infrared flashlight and looked at the mine closely. "There's an extra wire. I'm not sure what it does. I'd better get Gadgets."

McCarter was right. If they had to tinker with strange electric circuits attached to high explosives, Schwarz was the one to do it.

The Briton was back with the electronics wizard in a few seconds. The sight of the mine seemed to cheer him up. He loved a technical challenge, even those that were dangerous. He took a small black box out of his pack and started to investigate.

"All right, it's pretty simple. This Claymore is connected in a standard, multiple-Claymore-firing electrical circuit. Somebody pushes the button, and they all go off together. That's standard. This other circuit is something special. There's a low-level electric current running through it continuously. If you disconnect it or the firing circuit, or cut the wires, something is going to happen. I can't be sure what, but it will probably fire the Claymores or trigger an alarm. Something else we'd better think about—if there's a ring of these things around the camp and somebody sets them off, we can forget about the helicopter. They'll blast it to hell."

"Can you do anything about it?" Bolan asked.

Schwarz thought for a few seconds. "I can try, but it won't be an easy job. I'll have to try to patch into the circuits and disarm them one at a time. That will take me ten or fifteen minutes per mine. If you figure there are ten or twelve mines, you're looking at an hour or two. Have we got that much time?"

"No," he said flatly. "We haven't got the time, and we can't take the chance. The Indonesians didn't just set up the Claymores and go home. They're almost certainly somewhere a few hundred yards from here, and they've got to have someone watching the camp. As soon as they see us go in there, they'll move up, fire the Claymores and finish us off."

"Bastards!" McCarter said. "What can we do?"

"A lot. There's an old trick I learned from the Vietcong in Vietnam. Remember what it says on this side of a Claymore?"

"Too right, I do, mate. This Side Toward The Enemy."

"Right. Gadgets, can you patch into their firing circuit without them detecting it?"

"Give me five minutes," he replied, and reached for his tool kit.

Wejak looked puzzled. "I can tell you have a plan, Belasko, but I do not understand. What are you going to do?"

Bolan reached out and turned the Claymore 180 degrees on its small tripod mount. "These Claymores kill in one direction. These are aimed at our camp. We're going to turn them around so that when they are fired, they'll shoot outward."

Wejak smiled. He thought it was wise to use the enemy's weapons against them.

"You go with David, Wejak, and cover him while he turns the others around. Be careful, but get back as soon as you can."

Bolan watched as they slipped away into the dark. He waited while Schwarz worked carefully with the Claymore firing circuit.

"All right, I'm in. I've rigged a remote detonator. I can fire them whenever you want me to. There was no activity on their special circuit, so there's no way for them to know I did it."

Bolan smiled to himself. He didn't mind surprise parties as long as he was the one who delivered the surprise. He sent Schwarz back to get Manning, Lahka and Meiko while he waited for McCarter and Wejak to get back.

Time seemed to crawl by, but at last the two men slipped silently back out of the dark. McCarter smiled and gave Bolan a thumbs-up sign.

"Did you see any sign of someone watching the camp?" Bolan asked.

"Negative. Maybe he's hidden in the camp and will slip out into the trees when he hears us coming. I took a quick look at the camp on the way back. There are two bodies lying by the fire. They look like Indonesian commandos, but I didn't see any signs of Marie. Maybe they captured her and took her with them."

There was no way to tell. They would have to go look for themselves.

Bolan briefed his team quickly, being sure everyone understood the situation. "So, we're going in as if we don't know they're there. We'll spring their own trap on them. David, Wejak and I will go in first. The rest of you follow us at a twenty-yard interval. Gary, take up a firing position overlooking the camp. If anyone tries to leave the camp, take them out. If you hear the Indonesian commandos coming in, fire two quick shots and get out fast. If that happens, Gadgets, give Gary thirty seconds to get clear, and then fire the Claymores."

Manning checked his rifle and its scope and moved out silently.

McCarter, Wejak and Bolan got to their feet and led the way toward the camp. The Executioner tried to look as if he had no idea he was about to be ambushed. He thought that he understood the Indonesian commander's plan and how to counter it, but he felt the hair on his nape stand up as they got closer to the camp. There could be an Indonesian sniper looking at him through his scope, eager to take out one of the dangerous Americans.

They reached the edge of the shallow depression in the ridge line that held their camp. The fire was blazing. Wejak was right. Someone had built the fire up since they left, and there was no reason Marie Van Heyn would have done that. The light was so bright the glare made night-vision goggles almost useless. Bolan pushed his up and scanned the area. He saw the two bodies Wejak had reported. There were no sounds except the crackling of the fire, and nothing moved.

He saw no sign of Van Heyn, but if she was still here, she would be near the satcom. They had put the radio under the branches of a large banyan tree so that it couldn't be seen from the air. It wasn't visible from where he stood. He motioned to McCarter and Wejak, and they moved down the shallow slope toward the fire. The rest of the party followed them.

Bolan listened intently, but all he heard were the sounds of the fire burning and a large bird calling nearby. Wejak touched Bolan's arm and shook his head. It sounded like a bird to the Executioner, but the Dani warrior had lived in New Guinea all his life. He wasn't likely to be mistaken. The sound had seemed to come from the right near the tree where they had left the satcom.

The Executioner started to move casually in that direction, pushing the fire-selector lever of his M-4 carbine to full automatic. Suddenly he heard the roar of Manning's big .308 rifle as he fired two quick shots. Someone out in the trees blew a whistle in long, insistent blasts. Bolan heard men shouting and threw himself away from the firelight, dropping into a prone firing position.

The world around him seemed to explode as Schwarz pushed his remote-detonator button. The camp was surrounded by orange flashes as the Claymores detonated simultaneously and swarms of lethal steel balls raked the area just outside the camp. Bolan heard men screaming. The Claymores had gotten many of the attackers, but he knew they hadn't gotten them all.

Five or six men wearing orange berets raced toward the camp, but they seemed dazed and confused by the Claymores' blasts. One man was in the lead, shouting orders and firing his M-16 from the hip as he ran. Bolan reacted instinctively, following the old sniper's rule of kill the officers first. He aligned his sights and squeezed his M-4's trigger. Six high-velocity 5.56 mm bullets struck the officer's chest, and he fell instantly. The Executioner looked for another target, but there was no one left to shoot. The team had fired with cool precision. The rest of the Indonesian commandos were dead.

McCarter moved forward carefully and checked the bodies. He pointed to the officer Bolan had shot.

"This one was a colonel."

Wejak stared down at the dead man's face. "That is Hatta, the commander at Wamena. He hated the Dani. Good riddance."

Bolan wished they had taken a prisoner. They needed to find out what the Indonesians had done with Marie Van Heyn. He had to work out some kind of plan to find her, but first he would use the satcom if the Indonesians hadn't destroyed it. He needed to talk to Brognola and brief him on their raid on the Kanabo complex.

He told Manning and Schwarz to stay on guard and led the rest of the group toward the banyan tree. McCarter stopped and checked the two bodies that lay by the fire. He was taking no chances that one of them was still alive, playing dead and waiting for a chance to take some of the American team with him.

"They're both dead, mate, but look at this." McCarter picked up a pistol from the ground and handed it over. It was Van Heyn's old Dutch army Luger, and it had been fired. The mouth of a fired brass cartridge case protruded from the breech in a classic stovepipe jam. That was the trouble with Lugers. They were accurate and beautifully made, but they weren't reliable. The doctor's pistol had let her down.

Bolan moved on toward the banyan tree. He carried his carbine with the safety off, ready to fire. He hadn't forgotten the mock birdcalls before the attack. The Indonesian commando who had made them might still be hiding in the camp. The satcom was on the edge of the flickering light from the fire, riddled with bullet holes. He put down his M-4 to take a closer look. No good. It was never going to work again.

"God Almighty!" McCarter said suddenly. Lahka screamed and shouted something in Dani. Bolan whirled, ready to fire. He stared at what the woman pointed at, and his blood went cold. Marie Van Heyn's severed head was swaying gently back and forth, tied to a branch of the banyan tree with her long blond hair.

"Hatta's Dyak!" Wejak snarled. He looked at the ground for a few seconds, then he thrust his long spear up into the tree. Bolan heard the crack of a breaking tree limb, and a man dropped from the branches, a flat black automatic pistol in his hand. He landed on his feet like a cat. Meiko was the closest person to him. He leaped forward and clamped his arm around her neck.

The Executioner drew his Desert Eagle, instantly, but the woman was in the line of fire. Instinctively, she whirled and threw her attacker over her hip with a classic jujitsu throw.

The pistol flew out of his hand as he crashed into Lahka, stunning her for a second. The light flashed from polished metal as the man drew a two-foot-long blade. He grabbed Lahka, twisted behind her, gripped her hair with one hand and pressed the edge of the short sword against her throat. The small man hissed something in Indonesian. Meiko translated quickly.

"He says he is Sergeant Awang of the special commando force. He will kill Lahka if we do not drop our weapons and surrender immediately."

Bolan looked over the sights of his Desert Eagle. The big .44 Magnum pistol was extremely precise, but he didn't have a clear shot. He might be able to hit the Indonesian in the shoulder or graze the side of his head, but only a center-brain shot could be counted on to kill a man instantly. Awang would almost certainly cut Lahka's throat before he died.

"Tell him not to talk like a fool. There are many of us, and he's alone. Tell him to drop his weapon and step back. If he lets Lahka go, we'll let him live."

"He does not believe you. He thinks you will kill him as soon as he takes his sword from her throat. He says if you will let him go, he will take Lahka with him and let her go when he is a safe distance from here."

Bolan thought quickly. He didn't care if the Indonesian lived or died. He was willing to let him go to save Lahka's life, but there was one big question.

"Can I trust him?" he asked.

"No," Wejak said. "He is a Dyak. They think it is always right to lie to their enemies. If we let him leave with Lahka, he will kill her before he has gone a mile and laugh when he does it." Wejak put down his AK-47 and stepped forward, his long spear in his hands.

"Excuse me, Belasko, but Lahka is my sister and Marie was my friend. This is my affair." He began to speak in Indonesian. Meiko translated softly.

"'I thought Dyaks were brave men, not afraid to die. You are hiding behind a woman like a coward.'"

"'I am not a fool,'" Meiko continued, translating Awang's reply. "'If I let her go, your friend with the big pistol will shoot me. You heard my terms. Let me leave here now, or I will kill her.'"

He pushed the edge of his sword harder against Lahka's throat. She moaned softly. Drops of blood started to trickle down between her breasts.

Wejak smiled coldly. "You are wrong, Dyak," he said. "Belasko will not kill you." He pointed at Meiko. "She will. What will you tell the ghosts of your ancestors when you go to them? Will you say that you killed a woman, hid like a coward behind a woman and were killed by a woman? Let my sister go, and we will fight like men."

Awang thought hard. He wasn't afraid of Wejak. The long Dani spear would be an awkward weapon at close quarters. His spirit sword would be deadly once he got inside the big Dani's guard.

"What happens if I kill you, Dani? Will your friends let me go?"

Wejak laughed. "Do not talk like a fool. You are a dead man no matter what happens. The only question is how you will die. If you kill me, Belasko will kill you with his big pistol. Then you can go to your ancestors and tell them that you died with a warrior's blood on your sword and another great warrior killed you. They will welcome you as a true Dyak."

Awang nodded. If he had to die, it was important that he die well. "I have heard that the Dani keep their word."

He let Lahka go and crouched in a ready position with his spirit sword in his right hand. "Come on, then, Dani. Let us fight like men."

Wejak held his spear with both hands at waist level, its point at Awang's face.

"We have to stop this, Belasko," McCarter said. "Wejak doesn't stand a chance against that sword. One good slash will cut his spear in two, and then he's finished."

Meiko laughed softly. "You would not say that, David, if you were Japanese. A sword cannot cut through a hard wood spear staff. Its edge will stick in the wood or chip and shatter if you try. You must have an ax to cut a spear shaft in two. And see how Wejak handles his spear. It is a fair fight."

Wejak suddenly thrust at the Dyak's face. It was a light, quick blow like a boxer's jab. Awang slapped the point aside with the flat of his spirit sword. Wejak made a quick half circle with his wrists and thrust at Awang's chest. The Dyak parried again. The two men circled each other slowly, looking for an opening in the other's guard. They didn't waste their breath talking. All their attention was focused on the subtle motions of their weapons.

"Wejak has the advantage as long as he can keep the Dyak at a distance," Meiko said approvingly, "but see how the Dyak moves. He is very fast. He will rush in when he sees a chance."

Wejak thrust again, and again Awang parried. Bolan was fascinated. He had seen men fight with knives, but never two skilled men trying to kill each other with a sword and a spear. As he watched, he saw a subtle shift in the Dyak's stance. He gripped the handle of his sword and brought it to the center of his body, the point leveled at Wejak's throat. The Dani warrior thrust again, driving the point of his spear hard for Awang's chest. The Dyak slammed the flat of his sword against his adversary's spear, parrying with all his strength.

The force of Awang's blow knocked the point of Wejak's spear up and to his left. It was no longer in line with the Dyak's body. Awang charged instantly, rushing in past the point of Wejak's spear, his spirit sword poised for the beheading stroke. Wejak didn't try to bring his spear point back in line. He knew it was too late for that. Instead, he pivoted to his left and drove the butt of his spear in a hissing arc into Awang's side. It was a terrible blow, delivered with all of Wejak's incredible strength behind it. Bolan heard the dull sound of breaking bones as some of the Dyak's ribs snapped.

He staggered backward, dazed by the force of the blow. Wejak brought the point of his spear back and drove it six inches deep into his opponent's chest. A successful thrust to the diaphragm was paralyzing. Awang's sword slipped from his fingers as he fell to the ground. Wejak brought his spear up over his head and thrust downward into the Dyak's body, driving through his chest and pinning him to the ground. His eyes were glazed with shock. He said something quickly, then blood poured out of his mouth, and he was dead.

"He wanted Wejak to take his sword. He said it is a true spirit sword, and it can only belong to a great warrior," Meiko said.

Wejak nodded and picked up the Dyak's weapon. "He killed Marie, and I am glad that I killed him," he said somberly, "but he was not a coward. He fought well. I will keep his spirit sword and honor it."

The fight had been a glimpse into the past, before such things as guns and guided missiles, but Bolan had problems he had to deal with now. The Indonesians had been in control of the camp area. He didn't think they would have destroyed the helicopter. It was too valuable a piece of equipment to them, but they might have booby-trapped it just in case. He asked Schwarz and Meiko to check it out.

He walked back to the fire. Wejak and Lahka were smearing each other's faces with clay, making intricate patterns. Lahka looked up as Bolan approached. He could see she had been crying. Wejak's face looked as if it had been carved from stone, but his eyes were dry. Warriors didn't cry.

"We are mourning for Marie. She was not a Dani, but she was our friend. She got me the scholarship to go to college. She taught Wejak to speak English. We will miss her more than I can say."

Bolan felt he had to say something. Wejak and Lahka were the closest thing to family Marie had known.

"She died fighting for what she believed in," he said at last.

It was true, but it was cold comfort.

"What shall we do with Marie's body?" he asked. "Do you want to bury her before we leave?"

Wejak shook his head. "The Dani burn their dead. The fire is all we need."

Bolan left them there with their grief and went to check the helicopter.

CHAPTER TWENTY-THREE

The whine of the twin turbine engines deepened as Meiko lifted the helicopter off and turned south toward the sea. She was a good pilot, keeping the craft low, following the contours of the hills. Bolan sat in the copilot's seat and looked to his right. The chopper was flying too low for him to see the Kanabo complex, but columns of thick black smoke were still drifting upward from the burning fuel tanks. There was no sign of pursuit.

Meiko looked at the instrument panel, checking her fuel supply and compass heading. They had crossed the coastline and were flying straight out to sea.

"We are on the course you asked for, Belasko, but we have about twenty minutes of fuel left. I will not have enough fuel to make it back to land from the rendezvous point. Your friends had better be there."

Bolan checked his map again. "They're at the coordinates I gave you. They're navigating using the global-positioning-satellite system. They can locate themselves to within fifty yards."

"That is much better than I can do with these instruments, but I should get us within two or three miles."

Bolan shrugged his shoulders. There was no choice but to go on. The minutes crawled by. Finally Meiko throttled the engines back.

"We are here, but I see nothing."

He took out his night-vision binoculars and began to scan the area. At first he saw nothing but water. Then he saw something that looked like a post sticking a few feet above the surface. It wasn't easy to see. It was painted in a mottled pattern that tricked the eye. Bolan smiled. He had seen that sort of thing before. It was the tip of the antenna mast of a U.S. Navy submarine running submerged.

He unclipped the radio microphone, checked the radio frequency and began to transmit.

"Rafe, this is Belasko," he said again and again.

He kept at it until he heard a familiar voice crackling in his headset.

"Belasko, this is Rafe. What's your situation?"

"Fuel's running low, but I think I have you in sight."

"The electronic intercept operator says it sounds like you're right on top of us. Stand by."

Nothing seemed to happen for a minute. Then he saw a huge patch of frothing, white bubbles in the water below, and the *Sam Houston*'s long black hull began to rise slowly above the ocean's surface. Meiko gasped. A nuclear attack submarine surfacing was an impressive sight.

"Land in the water alongside her," Bolan said. They had made it safely out of New Guinea. Now it was time for the *Noshiro*.

COMMANDER FRANK SCOTT listened quietly as Mack Bolan finished speaking. He, McCarter and Encizo were crowded around a small, map-covered table in the submarine's small wardroom. Scott was used to mysterious people and covert operations. His vessel frequently carried Navy SEAL teams on classified missions, but what the man known only as Belasko was telling him was new and different.

Scott looked at the map and made a quick calculation.

"All right, gentlemen, I think I understand the situation. The first part of what you want is easy. The *Noshiro* is old and slow. We can intercept her in a few hours, but the problem is just what the hell we do then?"

Bolan stared at Scott. He wasn't sure what the captain was getting at. It seemed strange that he wanted advice on a straightforward naval mission. Perhaps Scott wanted him to take responsibility by recommending a plan.

"Force her to stop her engines and heave to, Commander. Then board her and search her, recover the weapon and rescue Captain Clark. After that, we don't give a damn about the *Noshiro*. You can let her go on her way."

Scott shook his head. "I wish it was that easy, but it's not. I can sink the *Noshiro* easily, but I'm not sure I can make her stop and be boarded."

Bolan was puzzled. The *Noshiro* was an old freighter. Surely there was nothing she could do to resist a U.S. Navy nuclear attack submarine.

"I don't understand, Commander. What's the problem?" he asked.

"International law and weapons capability," Scott said. "You tell me you think Captain Clark and this secret weapon are on board the ship. I think you're probably right, but you don't know that for certain. We have no evidence of any illegal activity. The freighter may not be carrying anything but a cargo of copper ore. She's a Japanese merchant ship proceeding on the high seas. Her captain can argue that we have no right to stop him, and legally he's right. Any captain who is approached by a strange submarine is likely to radio an emergency message immediately. If the message is received by the Japanese authorities, we're going to have an ugly international incident. There's another problem. We are neither armed nor equipped to stop and board a ship. My men have no training for that kind of operation."

"If you stop her, we'll board her," Bolan replied.

"I'm not sure we can stop her."

"I beg your pardon, Commander, but I don't understand," McCarter said politely. "Surely you can put a shot across her bow and stop her. If we find the weapon and Captain Clark, they won't dare protest. If we don't, we'll let the lawyers argue."

Scott smiled. "I can't put a shot across her bows. I wish I could, but U.S. Navy submarines haven't carried cannons for forty years. The biggest guns I have are M-16 rifles. *Sam Houston* is armed with four 21-inch torpedo tubes. We carry two kinds of anti-ship weapons, Harpoon missiles and Mark 48 torpedoes. I can blow the *Noshiro* out of the water from fifty miles away with Harpoons or sink her with Mark 48 torpedoes closer in, but I can't just damage her. If we intercept the freighter and I surface and order her to stop, her captain may say 'to hell with you' and keep on steaming. If that happens, we either sink her or let her go."

"You can't just damage her enough to make her stop?" Bolan asked.

Scott shook his head. "She's a cargo ship, and she's small, only about twelve thousand tons. I can't control the exact spot a Harpoon or a Mark 48 torpedo will hit her. Both are powerful antiship weapons. One hit with either one of them will probably sink her. I'm not willing to do that without positive evidence she's involved in hostile acts.''

Bolan frowned. The legal scruples didn't bother him. He saw no difference between killing the enemies of the United States with pistols or torpedoes, but sinking the *Noshiro* with missiles or torpedoes would almost certainly kill Mary Clark. There had to be some other solution.

Encizo had been listening quietly. ''I think there's a simple solution, Commander. You have two operational Swimmer Delivery Vehicles in your dry-deck shelters. The members of our team are all qualified combat divers. You just intercept the *Noshiro,* and we'll borrow your SDVs and pay her a call.''

Scott thought it over for a minute. ''All right, that ought to work. We'll do it. There is one problem with your plan. If your attack is a failure, I won't be able to rescue you.''

The little Cuban smiled grimly. ''Don't worry about that, Commander. If our attack is a failure, we'll all be dead. I'll attach limpet mines with delay fuses to the *Noshiro*'s hull before we board her. If our attack is a failure, they'll blow her to hell.''

FOUR HOURS LATER, Bolan and Encizo were in the submarine's attack center, watching quietly as Commander Scott completed his approach. The vessel's long black hull was slipping quietly through the water a hundred feet below the surface. Only her electronic intercept antennae and one of her periscopes were above the surface. Scott was taking no chances. The leadership of the Kanabo Corporation sounded like serious people. They might have installed some serious weapons and sensors on board the *Noshiro*. The submarine was running in total emission control. Her sonar wasn't pinging but was listening passively. None of her electronic systems was radiating. She was being extremely quiet, but her sonar operators and electronic systems were listening intently.

Scott pointed to a symbol on his attack display. "There she is. We have been tracking her on sonar for the past half hour. She hasn't sent any radio messages. If she has any combat systems on board, we can't detect them. She's doing nothing unusual except for one thing. Her captain seems to be staying close in, following the contours of the shore. Most merchant-ship captains try to follow a great circle course to their destination. Following the coastline costs him fuel. It could be that they intend to turn for the shore and run her aground if they see that they're going to be intercepted by a warship."

Scott looked at his watch. "When will you be ready to go?"

Encizo nodded. "We've checked out the SDVs and our equipment. We're ready to go when you give the word."

"All right, we'll start maneuvering into SDV launch position immediately. I estimate we'll be ready for you to go in approximately twenty minutes. Good luck, gentlemen."

Bolan stayed behind as the rest of the assault team filed out and headed for the dry-deck shelters.

Scott looked at him curiously. "Anything else I can do for you?" he asked.

"One more thing, Commander. We have a good plan, but something can always go wrong. We may not make it."

Scott nodded. He knew that all underwater special operations were dangerous.

Bolan handed him a small piece paper with some numbers and three words written on it.

"You know I work for the United States government?"

Scott grinned. "I guessed that."

"I can't give you the name of my organization, but if we don't signal you that we've captured the *No-shiro*, I don't want to depend on the limpet mines. We may be dead before we get a chance to attach them. If that happens, it's critical that you sink her. I know you need authorization to do that, so call on your satcom on this frequency. Tell the person who answers that Belasko told you to call. Say that it is an urgent-star-priority message and ask to speak to Hal. Tell him the situation, and he'll get you orders to attack."

Scott tucked the small piece of paper into his pocket. "All right, Belasko, you can count on me. I'll do it if it's necessary, but I hope it's not. Good luck."

Bolan smiled grimly as he walked back to the hatches that led to the dry-deck shelters. He had planned everything as best he could, but he could always use a little luck.

"One more thing, Commander. We have a good plan. Let's not bothering our plan go wrong. We may not make it."

Bolan nodded. Everyone went wrong when special operations were dangerous.

Bolan handed him a small piece paper with some numbers and letters scrawled on it.

CHAPTER TWENTY-FOUR

Bolan followed Encizo up the ladder, climbing up into the submarine's aft dry-deck shelter. He moved slowly, weighed down by his black Viking combat diver's suit and LAR-5 closed-circuit self-contained underwater breathing apparatus. He was particularly careful not to bang his scuba as he climbed. The LAR-5 was a wonderful piece of high-tech gear, but it was complicated and tricky to set up before a dive. The submarine was running submerged at a hundred feet. The SDV was a wet vehicle. It didn't have a closed hull. Once the shelter was flooded, only his LAR-5 would keep him alive.

He followed Encizo through the hatch into the shelter. The thirty-foot-long, watertight shelter was bolted to the *Sam Houston*'s deck. It wasn't a place for a man with claustrophobia. The sleek, dull black Mark VII MOD-6 SD Vehicle filled most of the space inside the shelter, leaving just enough room for men in underwater gear to check out and board the vehicle. Encizo had already checked the batteries that drove the propulsion system and supplied power to the sonar and navigation systems. He slipped into the operator's seat and began his final checkout. Bolan checked the weapons and explosives storage compartments.

Everything seemed to be in order. He moved back to the hatch and motioned to McCarter and Meiko to climb up into the shelter. He wasn't worried about the Briton. The man had done this many times before, but he kept a close eye on Meiko. She knew how to use a standard civilian scuba, but the LAR-5 and the SDV were new to her.

The SDV could carry a maximum of four people. Manning and Schwarz were in the forward shelter. They would ride in the other SDV with Calvin James. That left one empty seat in the black commando's vehicle. If they were lucky, they would have room to carry Mary Clark when they returned to the submarine.

Encizo signaled that he was ready to load. Bolan helped Meiko into her seat and watched while she strapped in. He took one last look at her equipment. He really didn't like the idea of taking her, and would have left her behind if he could. However, once they were on board the *Noshiro,* he would badly need someone who spoke Japanese, and only Meiko could fill the bill.

The soldier slipped into his seat and strapped in. He looked over his shoulder. McCarter was on board. There was nothing to do but wait.

Encizo completed his final checks. Bolan heard his oddly distorted voice through the communications gear inside his full face mask.

"Swimmers ready?"

Bolan and McCarter answered immediately. There was a short pause, then he heard Meiko's soft "ready." She sounded nervous, and Bolan didn't blame her. Combat dives weren't soothing to the nerves.

"Two ready," Encizo reported to the attack center.

"One ready," James said from inside the forward dry-deck shelter.

"Very well, commence flooding," Scott ordered from the attack center.

The little Cuban pushed a button, and seawater began to flow into the shelter. The water reached the top of the compartment, although it seemed to take forever. The submarine was running at a hundred feet, and Bolan suddenly felt forty pounds of pressure squeeze every square inch of his body. Combat divers called it the Squeeze, and it was extremely unpleasant.

The flexible oxygen bag on his chest was flattened by the pressure, leaving his lungs unsupplied. It was a nasty sensation, but Bolan compensated by opening his oxygen-supply valve wider. The bag expanded again. He felt more pressure on his body, and his feeling of discomfort increased, but at least he was breathing normally again.

Encizo looked around. Bolan, McCarter and Meiko gave him a thumbs-up signal. The little Cuban nodded. It was time to go. Bolan heard the faint whine of the electric propulsion system as Encizo released the SDV and opened the shelter's outer door. The nineteen-foot-long, sleek, black shape eased out into the ocean. Bolan could see the *Sam Houston*'s long shape slowly pulling away through the water. Something else was moving toward them, the black torpedo shape of James's SDV.

Encizo increased speed and angled toward the surface. They were breathing pure oxygen now, and it wasn't smart to stay below fifty feet any longer than they had to. Bolan glanced at the softly glowing numbers on his watch. The LAR-5's oxygen bottle was supposed to supply oxygen for a minimum of two hours, and a skilled diver could stretch it to three, but there was no way to recharge it during a mission. If he wasn't back on the submarine or on the surface when the bottle was empty, he would be dead. It wasn't a comforting thought.

The SDV leveled off at thirty feet while Encizo checked the attack board and his instruments. He changed his heading, increased his speed slightly and gave Bolan a thumbs-up signal. If the *Noshiro* didn't change course or speed, they would intercept her in approximately fifteen minutes.

The water was clearer nearer the surface, and Bolan could distinguish James's SDV to his left, maintaining the same course and speed that Encizo had set. Ten minutes crawled by. The Cuban activated the SDV's sonar, not pinging actively, but listening passively for the sounds generated by the freighter's engines and propeller as she moved through the water.

Encizo made a slight course change, then extended one hand toward Bolan and held up four fingers. Four minutes to intercept. The seconds crawled by. It was still dark on the surface, and all the soldier could see was black water, as well as the faint glow of the displays on the instrument panel. Bolan looked at his watch again. Ninety seconds to go. There was nothing he could do but sweat it out. He had complete faith in Encizo's skill and judgment, but he knew one mistake could abort the mission.

The little Cuban tapped the side of his head, and Bolan listened intently. At first all he heard was the rasping sound of his own breathing. Then he heard it, off to his right, the faint rumbling of the *Noshiro*'s engines and propeller as she moved toward them through the dark water. Encizo brought the SDV closer to the oncoming ship, angling upward until they were running ten feet below the surface. The sound of the engines grew to a dull, steady rumbling as the SDV closed in on her prey.

Encizo flicked on a low-powered, water-penetrating, blue-green laser and began to read the exact distance and bearing to the *Noshiro*. Bolan looked along the line of the laser beam. Now for the tricky part. Scott had called the *Noshiro* a small freighter, and in a way she was, but sitting in the SDV, she looked gigantic. If her twelve-thousand-ton hull smashed into the SDV or it was drawn into her huge bronze propeller, there would be no survivors.

The SDV was turning now, running parallel to the freighter, angling slightly inward toward the side of her hull. The vehicle bobbed and shuddered as they entered the steady flow of water around the hull caused by the ship's motion through the water. It was like steering upstream in a turbulent river. Encizo kept both hands on the controls, making fast, small adjustments as he inched closer and closer to *Noshiro*'s side.

Now! Bolan felt a sudden bump as the SDV touched and the little Cuban activated the electromagnets. The faint whining sound of the SDV's electric motor faded as Encizo cut off the propulsion system. Bolan waited tensely for some sign of alarm. The ship had no sonar, and her radar couldn't detect a submerged SDV, but they had made some noise when they made contact. Neither their closed-circuit scuba gear nor the SDV gave off bubbles. Even if someone thought that they heard something and looked over the side, they should see nothing. But if some suspicious soul thought he had heard something and dropped a few concussion grenades over the side, the results would be disastrous.

He waited two minutes, sitting in the dark, staring at the dull green numbers on his underwater watch. Nothing happened. Calvin James should have made contact and attached his SDV to the *Noshiro*'s other side, but there was no way to be sure. Bolan had to proceed as if his team alone had to accomplish the mission. He tapped Encizo on the shoulder and watched him release his seat belt and float free, towing two flat disks behind him. They were the limpet mines. Once they were magnetically attached to the hull and their delay fuses were activated, the ship was doomed. Even if the Stony Man team's attack failed and they were all killed, the *Noshiro* would be blown to hell two hours later.

Time to get going. He released his seat belt and stood up carefully. He kept his feet hooked into the upper edge of the SDV's passenger compartment and felt McCarter grab and firmly hold his ankles. It was a necessary precaution. It would be extremely embarrassing, to say the least, if he was swept away by the water flow around the hull and found himself pulled into her propeller or floundering helplessly in her wake.

He straightened until his head and shoulders were above the water. He took a quick look around, but there was nothing to see except the dark bulk of the freighter and the dim glow of her running lights. He tapped McCarter's hand, signaling for him to pass up the grapnel. As Bolan took it, he was careful of the plastic-covered hooks protruding from the black cylinder. He aimed upward and pushed the button. He heard a soft whoosh as the gas cartridge fired, then the grapnel shot out of the cylinder and arched upward over the side, trailing a knotted nylon rope behind it. There was a soft click as the grapnel fell on the *No-shiro*'s deck. He pulled hard on the rope and felt the grapnel slide across the deck and hook against the rail. He pulled hard to be sure it was set and would bear his weight.

Bolan didn't want to try to make the climb with a rifle in his hands or slung across his back. He would have to depend on his pistols. He slipped the protective plastic covers off their holsters. It was time to go. The fuses on the limpet mines would already be methodically counting down. He grabbed the rope and began to climb. It was hard going. He hadn't had the time to take off his diving equipment, and the side of the ship was wet and slippery. At least the sea was calm. The ship was as steady as a rock.

Muscles burning with the strain as he reached the top of the rope, Bolan paused for a second and looked quickly over the rail. He was in the middle of the main deck. The *Noshiro* had a superstructure forward that contained the bridge, as well as another aft. Between them was a flat main deck with hatches that led down to the cargo holds. The deck was dimly lit and quiet. There had to be a deck watch somewhere, but he didn't see anyone. He heaved himself up and over the rail and dropped prone on the deck, facing some large boxes of deck cargo about ten feet to his right. He tugged twice on the grapnel rope with his left hand and drew his Desert Eagle with his right.

Bolan felt a quick pull on the rope as McCarter answered the signal. He slipped through the dim light like a ghost in his dull black diving gear and took cover behind the big boxes of cargo. He slipped off the mask of his breathing gear, but he had no time to take off the rest of his equipment. It was up to him to cover the rest of the party as they climbed up the side. He took a firm two-handed grip on the Desert Eagle and scanned the deck. Nothing moved. He waited tensely. Time seemed to crawl by. Then he saw a black shape appear over the railing as McCarter slipped quietly down onto the deck and moved to join Bolan behind the boxes. The Briton pulled off his mask, then unslung his silenced Sterling and checked it carefully.

"Rafe is back. The mines are in place. Meiko's coming up next," he said softly.

Bolan nodded and took off his combat diver's gear while McCarter covered the deck. The Executioner checked his watch. Where the hell was Meiko? She should be on deck by now. He slipped quietly back to the rail and looked down. She was nearing the top of the rope, but climbing slowly. The wet and slippery side of the ship was giving her trouble. He reached out with his left hand, took her by the wrist and pulled her up and over the railing.

Someone suddenly shouted behind him in Japanese. Bolan whirled, bringing up the Desert Eagle as he turned. Across the deck, a man in a sailor's uniform was looking over the rail and yelling. Bolan could see the hook of the grapnel at his feet. The sailor's hand flashed to his side, and he drew a big knife. The Executioner had no time to be subtle. He put the big pistol's front sight against the man's side and pulled the trigger. The Desert Eagle bucked and roared as two shots blasted from its muzzle.

The man fell instantly. It was good shooting, but it wasn't quiet. The double roar echoed along the deck.

He heard men shouting, and an alarm began to sound. A black form rolled over the rail, but Bolan had no time to see anything else. A searchlight on the forward superstructure snapped on and began to search the deck. He heard the soft hiss of McCarter's Sterling as he raked the superstructure with two fast 6-round bursts, the 9 mm bullets striking the steel structure and screaming away into the dark. The Briton fired again, and the searchlight suddenly went out.

Bolan heard men yelling and feet pounding on the deck behind him. Meiko hadn't waited for orders. She had turned quickly to cover their backs, raking the aft deck with three quick bursts.

"Cover me," Encizo called from the rail.

Bolan holstered his Desert Eagle and drew his Beretta 93-R.

"Go!" he shouted.

Encizo rushed across the deck as Bolan hosed the forward superstructure with short bursts. Bullets struck the deck two feet behind the little Cuban and shrieked away from the steel surface. He threw himself down and rolled behind the cargo boxes, splinters flying into the air as another burst smashed into the big wooden boxes.

Bolan risked a quick glance behind him. Meiko was in a prone position. She had switched her Heckler & Koch to semiautomatic fire and was pinning down the people behind them with rapid aimed fire. Encizo tapped the Executioner's shoulder and pushed his M-4 Ranger carbine into his hands. He leathered the Beretta and took a split second to be sure the M-4's 30-round magazine was locked in place and the weapon was ready to fire.

More bullets tore into the cargo box. It sounded as if a high-powered weapon was being fired from the forward superstructure, probably a light machine gun. They couldn't stay there much longer. Encizo was rapidly stripping off his underwater breathing gear. Bolan pointed forward. It seemed logical to try to capture the bridge, but the little Cuban knew more about ships than he did.

"The bridge?" the soldier asked.

"Right. The officers' quarters will be up there. That's where they'll be keeping Clark."

Bolan heard more firing and feet pounding across the deck. Manning threw himself down behind the cargo boxes.

"They're lousy shots. Understand, I'm not complaining."

"We have to take the bridge," Bolan said quickly. "You ready to blast?"

Manning grinned and patted the waterproof haversack filled with explosives he had slung over one shoulder. "Any time."

"Stand by. Rafe and I will be the artillery."

Bolan opened the M-203 grenade launcher mounted under the M-4's barrel and slipped in a 40 mm high-explosive grenade. Encizo had heard what he had said. He had his own M-4 out and was opening its M-203.

"Load smoke, Rafe. As soon as I've fired three, let them have it."

Bolan heard a click as Encizo closed the action of his grenade launcher.

"Ready, Mack."

The Executioner rolled to his left and looked around the corner of the cargo box. The machine gun was still firing short bursts. They seemed to be aiming at the starboard rail. He could see no sign of James or Schwarz, so they had to be pinned down, still on the side of the ship. There was no use waiting. They had to win now, or they weren't going to. He aimed carefully through the grenade launcher's sight and pulled the trigger. He heard a dull *blup* and felt the recoil as his M-203 fired. The 40 mm grenade arched through the air and struck. He saw a bright orange flash as it detonated, and the machine gun stopped firing abruptly. He snapped in a fresh grenade and fired, then repeated the process. The shooting from the back of the bridge stopped. The enemy seemed to be stunned by the blasts from his grenades.

Encizo began to fire, pouring in smoke grenades as fast as he could load and fire his grenade launcher. Clouds of gray smoke billowed out from the bridge. Now or never. Bolan got to his feet and charged, followed by Manning and McCarter. Meiko brought up the rear. Someone was shooting from the bridge. Bullets struck the deck to Bolan's right and ricocheted off the hard steel into the night. He resisted the temptation to stop and fire back. Whoever was firing couldn't see through the smoke. They were simply spraying the deck at random, trying to keep the attackers pinned down.

They charged down the deck as the bullets whined, following them, groping for them through the smoke. Bolan told himself it would be pure luck if one of them was hit, but the deck seemed to stretch forever as they ran. He heard a sharper boom as Encizo switched to high-explosive grenades and put one into the upper structure of the bridge.

Suddenly they were there. Bolan flattened himself against the steel wall that loomed up in front of him and waited for a second until the rest of his team joined him. They were relatively safe for a moment. No one could fire down on them from above unless he was willing to take a chance and lean out over the rail. Someone was. A burst of bullets struck the deck between Bolan and Manning. McCarter had the best angle. He snapped his Sterling to his shoulder and squeezed off a burst. A man screamed and a body came tumbling down from above and smashed into the deck.

A solid steel door led into the bridge structure. Bolan tried the handle, but the door was locked. He signaled to Manning, who was already opening the watertight haversack that protected his explosives. He quickly taped lengths of linear-shaped charges to the door hinges, stepped back and pushed the button on his detonation box. Bolan saw two blue-white flashes. The precisely focused planes of energy cut through the hinges instantly. The door fell outward and struck the deck with a loud clang.

Bolan wasn't careless enough to rush through the gaping doorway. That was just as well. Someone inside was still full of fight. A burst from a submachine gun suddenly streaked through the opening. Manning didn't like unfinished business. He fused a two-and-a-half-pound block of plastique and hurled it through the door. There was a one-second delay, then the charge detonated with a sharp roar.

The Executioner slipped an M-576 multiple-projectile round into his M-203 grenade launcher and signaled to McCarter. He moved to the left edge of the door opening, the Briton to the right. The former SAS commando signaled that he was ready. Bolan nodded, and they fired short bursts together. The bullets glanced off the steel walls and shrieked down the passage in a lethal crisscross pattern.

There was no reply. Bolan risked a quick look around the edge of the door. The passage was blackened by explosions, and three men lay dead or unconscious at the far end. Steel doors lined both sides of the passageway. They were all closed.

"Cover me," he shouted to McCarter, and rushed down the passageway. He had almost reached the end when two men suddenly appeared in front of him, holding stubby submachine guns. Instantly Bolan pulled the trigger of his grenade launcher. The multiple-projectile round was like a huge shotgun shell. Bolan was too close for the shot pattern to spread completely. The man on the right was struck by dozens of steel buckshot and died in his tracks.

The second man was dazed by the blast. He pulled the trigger of his submachine gun, but he wasn't aiming. The burst missed Bolan's head by six inches. He pulled the trigger of his M-4 and cut the man down where he stood, moving past the corpses. He could see a steel companionway that led up toward the main bridge. The ship was controlled from there, and anyone taking the steps would be caught in a death trap if someone at the top opened fire when he was halfway up.

Bolan signaled for McCarter and Manning to move up. He pointed at the companionway. McCarter frowned and shook his head. There was no way they could provide adequate covering fire for anyone who tried to climb them. The Canadian grinned and reached inside his haversack, pulling out four round objects and passing one of them to Bolan. He looked at it and smiled. They were U.S. Army M-61 fragmentation grenades, far better than guns for fighting in a closed area.

He took one of the grenades in his right hand and hooked his left forefinger through the safety ring. Manning stood behind him, ready to pass him more. Bolan stepped out to the foot of the stairs, but before he could throw, someone above him fired an automatic weapon down at them. McCarter replied instantly, saturating the top of the companionway with quick 6-round bursts.

Bolan pulled the grenade's pin and threw the bomb. It landed at the top of the steps and rolled out of sight, detonating with a dull boom. Someone on the bridge shrieked in pain. Manning passed the Executioner another grenade. He armed the lethal egg and hurled it upward, grabbing a third grenade and rushing up the companionway as he heard his second one detonate. He paused just short of the top and threw the third bomb inside the bridge. There was a sudden silence following the explosion.

He took the last two steps in a bound and stepped on the bridge with his M-4 carbine poised in the fire position. He didn't need it. The lethal fragments from the three grenades had swept the bridge with a deadly swarm of steel. Two men in officers' uniforms lay dead or unconscious on the floor. A sailor was draped over the steering wheel. They had done it. The Stony Man team had seized control of the *Noshiro*.

CHAPTER TWENTY-FIVE

Bolan signaled for the rest of the team to come up to the bridge. He looked toward the bow. The dead man at the wheel had turned it to the right as he fell. The freighter was responding to her helm and was moving in a slow, wide circle. He checked the two men in officers' uniforms who were lying on the floor. One was dead. The other was still breathing, but he was badly wounded.

He called down the companionway.

"Send up David and Meiko, Gary. Then get Rafe up here as soon as you can."

"Right. I'm on my way."

McCarter and Meiko came up the steel steps quickly. Meiko paled as she stared at the bodies. She had never before seen the damage fragmentation grenades could inflict on human flesh. The Briton looked at the wheel and the instruments that told the bridge crew what was happening throughout the ship. Then he looked at Bolan.

"Do you really want to go in circles?" he inquired casually.

"No. Do you know how to steer this damned thing?"

"I'll give it a go."

He pulled the dead helmsman away from the wheel and turned it to the left. Slowly the *Noshiro* responded to the helm and began to move in a straight line again.

Bolan turned to Meiko and pointed to the two men who lay on the deck. "Do you know who they are?"

She shook her head. "I do not know them, but I can read their insignia. The dead man was the captain. This one is the second mate. She bent over and examined him quickly. "He is badly wounded, Belasko. He will be dead in a few minutes."

"See if you can get him to talk. I need to know where Mary Clark is."

Meiko knelt down by the dying man, put her face close to his and began to speak rapidly in Japanese. The dying officer looked up at her. His eyes were glazed. Bolan doubted that he knew where he was or what was happening. Meiko spoke to him again, louder and in a harsh and insistent tone. The man gasped a reply. Then his head lolled on his shoulders, and he was dead. She reached in his jacket pocket and pulled out a key, which she held out to Bolan.

"How did you do that?" he asked.

"Simple. He saw a Japanese face and heard a Japanese voice. I told him that the Americans had attacked the ship and were trying to rescue the American woman. I said my orders were to kill her, but I must know where she was. He gave me the key and told me to make sure the bitch was dead. She is in the captain's cabin, through that door behind you."

"Hang on till Rafe gets here," he told McCarter. "You come with me, Meiko."

Bolan eased the door open and moved down the passageway. There were two doors on either side, three of which were open. One was locked. There was a nameplate on the locked door, written in Japanese.

Meiko put a finger to her lips and knocked urgently on the steel door. A man's voice answered in Japanese from inside the cabin. She knocked again and spoke rapidly. Bolan aimed his M-4 carbine at the door and waited. He kept his finger ready on the trigger as he heard a key turning in the lock.

A stocky Japanese opened the door. He looked annoyed and glared at Meiko. His eyes widened in horror as the woman threw herself to one side and he saw the grim figure in black behind her. His hand flashed toward an automatic in a shoulder holster, but he was drawing on the wrong man. Bolan pulled the trigger, and a 6-round burst tore through the man's chest. He staggered backward, trying to draw his pistol with his last ounce of strength. The Executioner pulled the trigger again, and a second burst drilled into the man. His pistol dropped from his hand, and he fell hard to the deck.

"Cover the hall, Meiko," Bolan shouted. He took a quick step into the cabin and swept it with the muzzle of his M-4, but there was no one to shoot. He heard muffled gasps to his right. Mary Clark lay spread-eagled on the bed, her wrists and ankles tied to the four corners, a gag stuffed in her mouth. Someone had given her a bad time. Bolan could see ugly bruises on the face and arms. He took the gag out of her mouth and cut her loose with his combat knife.

"Belasko," she gasped. "Thank God you're here."

Bolan finished cutting her loose.

"How are you, Mary?" he asked.

"I've been better. That bastard Tanaka told them to teach me to be humble and obedient while they took me to Japan. They haven't gotten there yet, but they've been working on it. They told me the United

States government had abandoned me. Nobody cared whether I lived or died. I knew they were lying. I remembered that you came to get me out of New Guinea. I kept telling myself to hang on no matter what they did to me. I kept telling myself, 'Belasko will come and get you out of here,' and damned if you didn't.''

"I try never to leave anybody behind."

Meiko stuck her head in the door. Mary Clark glared at her.

"Belasko," Meiko said.

"Who the hell's she?"

Bolan realized that Clark had never seen Meiko.

"This is Meiko, Mary. She's on our side."

"It is a great honor to meet you, Captain Clark," Meiko said formally. "Please excuse my poor manners, but I must speak to Belasko now. Rafe says to come back to the bridge at once. There may be an emergency."

Bolan raced back to the bridge. Encizo had the wheel. McCarter had picked up a pair of Japanese binoculars and moved out to one edge of the bridge to look intently back toward the *Noshiro*'s stern.

"Did you get Scott's message?" Encizo asked quickly.

Bolan shook his head. There had been too much steel around him, but his tactical radio should work now that he was back out on the bridge. He pushed the transmit button.

"*Sam Houston*, this is Belasko. Over."

The reception wasn't perfect, but he heard Scott answer immediately. "I'm told you are in control of the bridge. Have you found Captain Clark?"

"Affirmative, *Sam Houston.* Rafael said there is a possible emergency. What is the situation?"

"A warship is headed your way. Sonar analysis indicates it's a Russian Krivak Type Two frigate. She's making thirty-two knots. She'll reach you in half an hour."

"Did you say Russian, *Sam Houston?*" Bolan was baffled. What were the Russians doing here?

"Russian-built, Belasko. The Russians have sold them to a number of countries in the last few years. I don't think this one is Russian. She may be Indonesian, but maybe not. My electronic-intercept people have detected her transmitting in Japanese."

"Do you think she knows you're there, *Sam Houston?*"

"I doubt it. At thirty-two knots, the noise her hull makes moving through the water will make her sonar ineffective. I can stay up at antenna depth until she gets closer and slows down."

"Understood, *Sam Houston.* Can you sink her?"

There was a long pause.

"I can sink her, but attacking a foreign warship on the high seas is an act of war. I have to have authorization to do that. You understand that."

"Roger, *Sam Houston.* You remember that piece of paper I gave you? Make that call now."

"Understood. I will comply. *Sam Houston* out."

Bolan had no doubt that Commander Scott would do what he said, but the problem was time. He would have to reach Brognola, and the big Fed would have to convince the right people in the Washington power structure to give the order. Somehow they had to hang on until that happened. He needed to know more about this frigate and what it could do. Encizo knew more about naval warfare than anyone else on the team.

"Fill me in on the frigate, Rafe. How's she armed and what can she do?"

He thought for a moment. "A frigate is a small, light destroyer, Striker. Krivak is the NATO code word for a large class of frigates the Russians built in the 1970s. They displace three thousand tons and can do thirty-two knots. They're plain vanilla ships, not really high-tech weapons. They carry 100 mm cannons, 21-inch torpedo tubes and antisubmarine weapons."

"What can she do to us?"

"We can't outrun her. She's three times faster than the *Noshiro*. She will be in gun range in five minutes. Her guns aren't all that powerful, and it will take a long time for them to sink us with just cannon fire. The torpedoes are much more dangerous. Once she closes in, a spread of torpedoes will sink this ship in a couple of minutes. But I don't think they want to sink us. They lost Skylance. They want to get Captain Clark and that secret weapon back. I think they will try to stop us with gunfire and then board us."

Bolan thought hard. They could abandon the *Noshiro* in their SDVs, but there was a fatal flaw in that. They had no underwater breathing gear for Mary Clark. The plan had been for James's SDV to stay on the surface. There was no way it could hope to escape the frigate.

"Stay on your present course, Rafe," Bolan said, and went back to join McCarter. The Briton passed him the binoculars and pointed aft.

"There she is, coming up fast."

Bolan focused the binoculars and looked at the frigate. The ten-power optics made the ship look as if it was only a mile or two away. She was considerably smaller than the *Noshiro*, but she had a long, sleek, dangerous look. He could see white water boiling around her bow as she came on toward them at full speed.

"Keep an eye on her. Let me know if anything changes."

McCarter nodded and took the binoculars. Bolan moved to the center of the bridge, to join Meiko and Mary Clark.

"There's a message coming in on the ship's radio. It's on a preset frequency. They're speaking Japanese," Encizo said.

Bolan looked at Meiko. "What are they saying?"

"They are calling the captain of the *Noshiro*. They are ordering him to stop his engines and stand by to be boarded."

"Answer them. Stall them as long as you can."

Meiko took the microphone and spoke rapidly in Japanese. A man's voice answered, and they exchanged fast, hissing sentences. Meiko cut off the microphone.

"It is the captain of the frigate. I told him I am the ship's nurse. I said that there was an accident with the American weapon and that the captain and many of the crew are injured. He says that does not matter. We must stop. I said the captain is in sick bay. I must go and talk to him."

Bolan nodded. "Good job. Keep stalling him as long as you can."

"I will do as you say, but he is becoming suspicious. He cannot understand why I am on the bridge answering the radio."

"Belasko," McCarter shouted suddenly, "she's changed course. She's moving away from us at a thirty-degree angle."

"What do you make of that, Rafe?" Bolan asked.

"It's not good. Krivak Twos mount their gun turrets aft. He can't fire them while he's headed straight for us. He's turned to unmask his 100 mm guns."

The radio crackled again. Bolan heard the frigate's captain speaking. He sounded as if he were getting annoyed. Meiko looked at Bolan.

"Answer it."

Meiko spoke quickly, then turned off her microphone.

"I told him the captain has orders directly from Mr. Ito. Under no circumstances is he to allow his ship to be boarded and searched. I asked him what is his authority. He will check with Agats. That will buy us a few minutes. But after that, I am afraid I cannot delay him."

"Belasko," McCarter called, "they're training their guns on us."

HAL BROGNOLA WAS SLEEPING fitfully on the couch in his office when he heard an insistent knocking on his door.

"What is it?" he called.

"Better come at once, Hal. We have an incoming message from the USS *Sam Houston*," Barbara Price answered.

Brognola was instantly wide awake.

"Striker?" he asked.

"No, the man speaking says he is Commander Frank Scott, the captain of the *Sam Houston*. He's calling us on satcom. He's on our frequencies, using our call sign. He asked for Hal, and he says Striker told him to say it's an urgent-star priority. I think it's authentic, Hal. Only Mack could have given him that information."

Brognola pulled on his shoes and dashed for the operations center. He was surprised that Bolan had given the captain the call signs and code words, but he had faith in the man's judgment. But if the commander was calling, Bolan couldn't be on board the submarine, and there had to be a real emergency.

The big Fed sat behind his control console and picked up his microphone. "*Sam Houston,* this is Granite Home, Hal speaking. What's the situation?"

Scott answered immediately, giving Brognola a rapid briefing.

"All right, Commander. I understand. My people have captured the *Noshiro* and rescued Captain Clark, but there's an unidentified warship approaching the *Noshiro.* Can you take my people off before the warship gets there?"

"Negative, Granite Home. The frigate is within gun range of the freighter. If I surface, I'm a sitting duck. One shell through the pressure hull, and we're through."

"Can you sink her without surfacing?"

"I can, but I would be sinking a foreign warship. That's an act of war. I must have proper authorization before I can do that."

"I don't suppose you'd accept an order from me?"

"With all due respect, no. I do not know who you are or who you represent. I need an order from the commander of SUBPAC."

"Very well, I understand. Continue to monitor this frequency. I will get you your orders as soon as possible. Do you understand?"

"Roger, Granite Home. I will comply and—"

Scott stopped speaking for a moment. Brognola could hear a man's voice speaking in the background.

"Granite Home, do it as fast as you can. My executive officer is monitoring the situation through the periscope. He reports that the frigate has opened fire on the freighter. *Sam Houston* out."

Brognola turned to Price.

"Get me the chief of naval operations. Don't take no for an answer. Tell him it's an urgent-star priority!"

THE FREIGHTER SHUDDERED as another pair of 35-pound, high-explosive shells smashed into her stern and detonated. The frigate was firing her two 100 mm guns together, another two-gun salvo every twenty seconds. Bolan supposed that Encizo was right. The frigate's guns weren't big and powerful as naval guns go, but it was hard to accept that when you were on the receiving end. They had locked the *Noshiro*'s steering wheel and were crouching behind the steel rail on the deck. So far, the frigate's shells had struck aft. Probably they were trying to disable the ship's engines or her steering.

Bolan slipped a small steel mirror out of a pocket and used it to take a quick look over the rail. What he saw wasn't reassuring. The frigate was a few hundred yards away. She had slowed down and was running almost parallel to the freighter, angling in slightly. He could see groups of armed men standing on her main deck.

The Executioner had given his orders. The Stony Man team was ready. They were some of the deadliest men in the world, but hand-held weapons against even a small warship seemed like long odds. One thing worked in their favor. The frigate was a much smaller ship than the *Noshiro,* and her main deck was substantially lower. The enemy would have to fight uphill to reach the freighter's deck.

The frigate was coming closer and closer. He could see her communications antennae above the edge of the *Noshiro*'s rail. The two ships had to be almost in contact.

"Now!" Bolan shouted, and stood up. He aimed his M-4 carbine at the frigate's bridge and pulled the trigger of its M-203 grenade launcher. A 40 mm, high-explosive grenade struck the bridge and detonated. The snarling rattle of automatic-weapons fire filled the air as the rest of the team opened fire, sweeping the frigate's decks. Only Manning wasn't firing. He stayed behind the railing, waiting for Bolan's signal.

For thirty seconds, they fired grenades and bullets at the frigate. Then the ship seemed to explode in yellow flashes as she opened fire with her lighter weapons. Bursts of 30 mm cannon fire raked the *Noshiro*'s railing, tearing holes in the thin shell and spraying the deck with fragments. Bolan ducked and hugged the deck as the storm of shells swept by. He knew the gunners couldn't see him. They were sweeping the rail to force the Stony Man fighters to keep their heads down.

The soldier heard a long, grinding roar, and the freighter's hull shuddered as the frigate scraped along its side. Bolan saw a flicker of motion as something flew over the rail. Grapnels. The two ships were locked together. He heard men shouting on the deck below.

"Gary, now!" he yelled.

Manning pulled a pin on a grenade he had taped to the side of his explosives haversack and tossed it over the rail. The haversack struck, then twenty pounds of plastique detonated in a bright yellow flash. Bolan threw his last fragmentation grenade over the rail and listened as it exploded, sending steel fragments shrieking across the frigate's deck.

There was a momentary lull in the action. Then the frigate's 30 mm automatic cannons opened fire again. Bolan heard a plaintive bleeping between blasts. Someone wanted to talk to him on his tactical radio.

"Belasko here," he said quickly.

"Belasko, this is Frank Scott. What is your situation?"

"They are alongside and have grappled. They've made one attempt to board. We stopped them, but I'm not sure we can do it again."

"Roger, Belasko. I have my attack order. Your man Hal must know some important people. I am preparing to fire Mark 48 guided torpedoes. They have heavy warheads, so it may be a bit rough. Get your people to the side of the *Noshiro* away from the frigate, and be ready to abandon ship."

Someone on board the *Sam Houston* spoke to Scott.

"Very well, fire three. Fire four. Good luck, Belasko."

Bolan moved along the railing, staying low, telling his people to run for the opposite rail. He loaded a smoke grenade in his grenade launcher, jumped to his feet and fired it at the frigate's bridge. He didn't wait to see the effects of his shot. He turned and dashed for the far rail.

He put his back against the rail and looked behind him. Across the deck, he saw a man's head appear above the railing. Bolan fired a quick shot, and the head disappeared. He snatched a quick look to the left and right. Encizo and Meiko had helped Clark down the rope to James's SDV and followed her down. Schwarz and James were already in the SDV.

Bolan, McCarter and Manning were the only ones still on the deck. The soldier looked at his watch. He had no idea how long it would take the torpedoes to reach the frigate. It had to be soon. This couldn't go on much longer. They were starting to run low on ammunition.

He motioned to Manning and shouted, "Go!"

The Canadian swung over the rail and started down.

Bolan turned to McCarter, but before he could speak, he heard a tremendous roar. A huge column of water shot up from the far side of the frigate and cascaded down on both ships' decks. The Noshiro's hull shuddered. There was another thunderous roar as the second Mark 48 struck the frigate and its big warhead detonated.

The frigate was crammed with weapons and ammunition. The blasts from the torpedo warheads triggered a series of secondary explosions that ripped through the hull like a string of giant firecrackers.

Bolan yelled for McCarter to move and watched him go over the side. Now it was time for him to go. He looked back for a second as he went over the rail. A huge pillar of smoke and orange fire was streaming up from the frigate's shattered hull.

"Come on, mate," the Briton yelled. "We have to get out of here. Don't forget the bloody mines."

He swung over the side and started down. James, Clark, Meiko and Encizo were in the SDV. Schwarz, Manning and McCarter were holding on to its outsides. Bolan scrambled down and grabbed a handhold.

"Go, Calvin!" he shouted.

James went to full power immediately, and the SDV accelerated away from the doomed ship's side. He didn't worry about battery life. He kept the SDV at full power. It was going to be bad if they were too close to the *Noshiro* when the limpet mines they had attached to her hull went off. Bolan looked back at the doomed ship as the SDV pulled away. Flames and smoke were still streaming up into the sky. It looked as if the freighter was burning now.

Suddenly the ship shook and shuddered as the limpet mines blasted gaping holes in her hull. Bolan felt the shock of the explosions through the water and hung on as the SDV rocked and swayed. The *Noshiro* rolled over and went down, taking the shattered frigate with her.

Encizo shouted and pointed to the right. It looked as though a strange, mottled, gray-and-white post was rising out of the water. The surrounding water began to froth and bubble, then the long black hull of the *Sam Houston* rose smoothly from the ocean. A hatch opened in her conning tower, and an officer appeared and waved to the SDV. Bolan heard Commander Scott's amplified voice ring out.

"It looks pretty wet out there, Belasko. You'd better come on board."

CHAPTER TWENTY-SIX

Darwin, Northern Australia

Mack Bolan stood on the taxiway and watched as the ground crew finished the final loading of the big U.S. Air Force C-141 Starlifter. It would be taking off for the United States in a few minutes. Grimaldi and Skylance had already left, after having landed safely in Darwin.

He checked his watch. Encizo, Manning, James, Schwarz and Clark were already on board. McCarter was cutting it a little fine. He should have been back from Northern Command Headquarters half an hour ago. Bolan hoped nothing had gone wrong with his negotiations with the Australian SAS.

An Air Force sergeant appeared at Bolan's side. He pointed to a sedan with U.S. diplomatic license plates parked at the edge of the loading area.

"Somebody wants to see you, Mr. Belasko."

Bolan looked at the car. Meiko had just gotten out and was smiling and waving. He had never seen her look so happy. As he walked toward the car, she reached in her purse, pulled out a small booklet and held it up for him to see.

"Look, a genuine United States passport!"

Bolan smiled. "Congratulations, Meiko."

"You kept your word, Belasko. I have an obligation to you. I am flying to Honolulu to brief U.S. Intelligence personnel on the Kanabo Corporation's activities. I will be coming to the United States after that. Here is a telephone number. If you call it, the people who answer it will know how to get in touch with me. If you or your team ever need the services of a person with my limited talents and small skills, call and I will come.

"Goodbye, Belasko. Perhaps we will meet again."

Bolan smiled at her. "Perhaps. Good luck, Meiko."

The woman got back in the sedan, and it drove away.

The soldier checked his watch again. Things were starting to get tight. He thought about calling the Australian army headquarters to see what was going on. Then he saw a green Australian army jeep driving rapidly toward the loading area. The vehicle pulled to a stop. McCarter, Lahka and Wejak got out and walked toward Bolan.

"Any problems?" he asked.

The Briton smiled and shook his head. "It's all taken care of, mate. The Australian SAS will fly Wejak and Lahka back to Papua New Guinea and put them in touch with the local FPM leaders, who will get them back to the Baliem Valley. I had to be firm with a few regulation-happy headquarters types, but it was a piece of cake, really."

Bolan looked at Lahka and Wejak. Lahka looked remarkably different in a skirt and blouse. Wejak was wearing a short-sleeved shirt and a pair of khaki pants. He looked distinctly uncomfortable. Bolan smiled, but he refrained from commenting on what kind of men wear clothes.

"It isn't too late to change your minds," he said. "If you don't want to go back, we can do the same thing for you we did for Meiko. You can have United States passports and asylum in the United States for as long as you want it."

Wejak smiled. "Thank you, Belasko. I like you. You are a great warrior and a good friend, but what would I do in America? All I know how to do is fight battles and raise pigs, and Lahka tells me Americans must wear clothes all the time, even when they do these things. That is not for me."

Bolan looked at Lahka, who smiled.

"I will stay here. Wejak needs me, and one of these days he must find me a husband. I do not think many Americans would pay twenty-five pigs for me."

She paused for a moment and stopped smiling.

"Besides, New Guinea is my country. It may take us many years, but we will keep fighting until we will drive the Indonesians out."

Bolan understood. He reached into his kit bag and took out his binoculars and his combat knife. He handed the binoculars to Lahka and the knife to Wejak.

"Here, take these. They might come in handy."

Lahka smiled. "Thank you, Belasko. You give good gifts. I will remember what you taught me about the range when I shoot."

Wejak smiled as he took the knife. "It is a fine knife, Belasko. I will think of you when I use it. I am sorry I have nothing to give to you, but when we have won our war, you and David must come and visit us. Even if it is a long time from now and we are old, I will kill many pigs and make a big feast. We will stuff ourselves and tell everyone what great warriors we were when we were young."

"I look forward to it," Bolan said.

"Last call, mate," McCarter said. "They want us on board now."

Bolan shook hands with Wejak and Lahka and went up the ramp into the C-141.

He slipped into one of the passenger seats and heard the whine of the four jet engines as the C-141's pilot powered them up. He relaxed as the big plane started to roll down the runway. The mission was over. It had been a rough one, but they had done the job and there was relief in Washington about the rescue of Skylance and Clark. Another success for Stony Man. And there was nothing wrong with him that a few days' rest wouldn't fix. He felt the tension drain away. He had nothing to worry about. Until the next time.

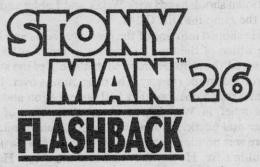